SHE

“There haven’t been

“What do you mean?” Jaci asked.

“Strange phone calls? Letters? E-mails?”

“Mike, we both know this isn’t about some neighbor who’s pissed off about me baking muffins or selling crafts in my garage. The locket has something to do with that body you found this morning.”

His lips flattened. “I don’t want to leap to conclusions.”

She flinched, disappointment slicing through her. How many times did she have to go through this?

First the fear. The knowledge some sicko was out there playing with her emotions. Then the pain at the realization that no one believed her.

“Right.”

She started to stand, only to be halted when Mike placed a restraining hand on her shoulder.

“Jaci, I’m trying to protect you,” he growled. “Something I can’t do if I don’t keep an open mind and investigate every potential threat.”

There was a sincerity etched on his face that made her heave a small sigh.

“I’m sorry.” She wrapped her arms around her waist. She felt chilled to the bone. “I just can’t believe this is starting again. . . .”

Books by Alexandra Ivy

Guardians of Eternity

WHEN DARKNESS COMES
EMBRACE THE DARKNESS
DARKNESS EVERLASTING
DARKNESS REVEALED
DARKNESS UNLEASHED
BEYOND THE DARKNESS
DEVOURED BY DARKNESS
BOUND BY DARKNESS
FEAR THE DARKNESS
DARKNESS AVENGED
HUNT THE DARKNESS
WHEN DARKNESS ENDS

The Immortal Rogues

MY LORD VAMPIRE
MY LORD ETERNITY
MY LORD IMMORTALITY

The Sentinels

BORN IN BLOOD
BLOOD ASSASSIN
BLOOD LUST

Ares Security

KILL WITHOUT MERCY
KILL WITHOUT SHAME

Romantic Suspense

PRETEND YOU'RE SAFE

Historical Romance

SOME LIKE IT WICKED
SOME LIKE IT SINFUL
SOME LIKE IT BRAZEN

And don't miss these Guardians of Eternity novellas

TAKEN BY DARKNESS in YOURS FOR ETERNITY
DARKNESS ETERNAL in SUPERNATURAL
WHERE DARKNESS LIVES in
THE REAL WEREWIVES OF VAMPIRE COUNTY
LEVET (eBook only)
A VERY LEVET CHRISTMAS (eBook only)

And don't miss these Sentinel novellas

OUT OF CONTROL
ON THE HUNT

Published by Kensington Publishing Corporation

PRETEND YOU'RE SAFE

ALEXANDRA IVY

ZEBRA BOOKS
KENSINGTON PUBLISHING CORP.
http://www.kensingtonbooks.com

ZEBRA BOOKS are published by

Kensington Publishing Corp.
119 West 40th Street
New York, NY 10018

First Printing: September 2017
ISBN-13: 978-1-4201-4377-5
ISBN-10: 1-4201-4377-8

eISBN-13: 978-1-4201-4378-2
eISBN-10: 1-4201-4378-6

10 9 8 7 6 5 4 3 2 1

Printed in the United States of America

Dedicated to Sheriff David Parrish
and the Lewis County Sheriff's Office
for their loyal dedication and their willingness
to go above and beyond the call of duty.
That includes their incredible patience
in allowing me to hang out at the office,
and answering my endless questions.
Any mistakes can be attributed directly to this author.

Prologue

Frank Johnson had endured his fair share of floods. He'd been born and raised on the small farm that butted against the bank of the Mississippi River. Which meant he'd spent the past sixty years watching the muddy waters rise and fall. Sometimes sweeping away crops, cattle, and during one memorable year, the barn that had been built by his great-grandfather.

The levee that'd been built by the Corps of Engineers over a decade ago had provided a measure of security. Not that he'd been happy when they'd come in and scooped up his fertile land to create the barrier. Frank was a typical midwestern farmer who didn't need the government poking their noses, or bulldozers, into his business. But eventually he'd had to admit it was nice not to have the waters lapping at the back door every time it rained.

But this was no typical rain.

On the first of February the heavens had opened up, and six weeks later the torrential rains continued to pound the small community. The river had become an angry, churning, destructive force as it swept toward the south. Frank watched in concern as the water had inched closer and closer to the top of the levee. He knew it was only a matter of time before it spilled over the ridge and into his back field.

But when he woke that morning, it wasn't to find the levee had been topped. Nope. It had been busted wide open. As if someone had set off an explosion during the night.

With the resignation of a man who'd lived his entire life dependent on the fickleness of nature, he'd pulled on his coveralls and boots before firing up his old tractor and heading down to see the damage.

Dawn had arrived, but the thick clouds and persistent drizzle shrouded the farm in a strange gloom. Frank pulled the collar of his coveralls up to protect his neck from the chilled breeze, starting to feel like Noah. Had he missed the memo from God that he was supposed to build an ark?

The inane thought had barely formed in his mind when he allowed the tractor to roll to a halt. As expected, his fields had become pools of brown, brackish water. In some places the nasty stuff was waist deep. There were also the usual leaves, branches, and pieces of flotsam that'd been caught in the swirling eddies.

What he hadn't expected was the long, dark object that he spotted floating in the middle of his pasture.

His first thought had been that it was a log. Maybe a piece of lumber torn from a building. But a piece of wood wouldn't make his stomach cramp with a sense of dread, would it?

Climbing off his tractor, he'd reached into his pocket for his cell phone. His unconscious mind had already warned him that whatever the floodwaters had washed onto his land was going to be bad.

And it was.

Really, really bad.

Chapter One

First came the floods. And then the bodies . . .

Jaci Patterson was running late.

It all started when she woke at her usual time of four a.m. Yes, she really and truly woke at that indecent hour, five days a week. On the weekends, she allowed herself to sleep in until six. But this morning, when she crawled out of bed, she discovered the electricity was out.

Again.

The lack of power had nothing to do with the sketchy electrical lines that ran to her remote farmhouse in the northeast corner of Missouri. At least not this time. Instead, it could be blamed on the rains that continued to hammer the entire Midwest day after day.

When the lights grudgingly flickered on an hour later, she had to rush through her routine, grateful that she'd baked two dozen peach tarts and several loaves of bread the night before.

As it was, she'd barely managed to finish her blueberry muffins and scones before she had to load them into the back of her Jeep. Then, locking her two black Labs, Riff and Raff, in the barn so they didn't destroy her house while she was gone, she headed toward Heron, the small town just ten miles away.

Predictably, she was barreling down the muddy lane that led to the small farm that'd once belonged to her grandparents, when she discovered the road was blocked before she could reach the intersection. *Crap.* Obviously the levee had broken during the night, releasing the swollen fury of the Mississippi River.

It was no wonder her electricity had gone out.

Grimacing at the knowledge that her bottom fields, along with most of her neighbors', were probably flooded, she put the Jeep in reverse. Then, careful to stay in the center of the muddy road, she reversed her way back to the lane. Once she managed to get turned around, she headed in the opposite direction.

The detour took an extra fifteen minutes, but at least she didn't have to worry about traffic. With fewer than three hundred people, Heron wasn't exactly a hub of activity. In fact, she ran into exactly zero cars as she swung along Main Street.

She splashed through the center of town, which was lined with a small post office, the county courthouse that was built in the eighteen hundreds, with a newer jail that had been added onto the back, a bank, and a beauty parlor. On the opposite side was the Baptist church and next to it a two-story brick building that the local celebrity, Nelson Bradley, had converted into a gallery for his photographs. Farther down the block was a newly constructed tin shed that housed the fire truck and the water department. On the corner was a small diner that had originally been christened the Cozy Kitchen, but had slowly become known as the Bird's Nest by the locals after it'd been taken over by Nancy Bird, or Birdie, as she was affectionately nicknamed.

Pulling into the narrow alley behind the diner, Jaci

hopped out of her vehicle to grab the top container of muffins, which were still warm from the oven. Instantly, she regretted not pulling on her jacket as the drizzling rain molded her short, honey-brown hair to her scalp and dampened her Mizzou sweatshirt and faded jeans to her generously curved body.

With a shiver she hurried through the back door, careful to wipe the mud from her rubber boots before entering the kitchen.

Heat smacked her in the face, the contrast from the chilled wind outside making the cramped space feel smothering.

Grimacing, she walked to set the muffins on a narrow, stainless-steel table that was next to the griddle filled with scrambled eggs, hash browns, sausage, and sizzling bacon.

The large woman with graying hair and a plump face efficiently flipped a row of pancakes before gesturing toward the woman who was standing at the sink washing dishes. Once the helper had hurried to her side, she handed off her spatula and made her way toward Jaci.

Nancy Bird, better known as Birdie, was fifteen years older than Jaci. When the woman was just seventeen she'd married her high school sweetheart and dropped out of school. The sweetheart turned out to be a horse patootie who'd fled town, leaving Birdie with four young girls to raise on her own.

With a determination that Jaci deeply admired, Birdie had bought the old diner and over the past ten years turned it into the best place to eat in the entire county.

At this early hour her clients usually consisted of farmers, hunters, and school bus drivers who were up before dawn.

"Morning, Birdie." Jaci stepped aside as the older woman efficiently began to place the muffins on a large glass tray that would be set on the counter next to the cash register. Many of the diners liked to have a cup of coffee and muffin once they were done with breakfast.

"Thank God you're here."

"I'm sorry I'm late. The electricity didn't come on until almost five."

Finishing, Birdie grabbed the tray and bustled across the kitchen to hand it to her assistant.

"Take this to the counter," Birdie commanded before turning back to Jaci with a roll of her eyes. "The natives have been threatening to revolt without their favorite muffins."

Jaci smiled, pleased by Birdie's words. She'd learned to bake at her grandmother's side, but it wasn't until she'd inherited her grandparents' farm that she'd considered using her skills to help her make ends meet.

Leaning to the side, she glanced through the large, open space where the food was passed through to the waitresses.

The place hadn't changed in the past ten years. The walls were covered with faded paneling that was decorated with old license plates and a mounted fish caught from the nearby river. The floor was linoleum and the drop ceiling was lit with fluorescent lights.

There were a half dozen tables arranged around the square room with one long table at the back where a group of farmers showed up daily to drink coffee and share the local gossip.

At the moment, every seat was filled with patrons wearing buff coveralls, camo jackets, and Cardinal baseball hats.

Jaci released a slow whistle. "Damn, woman. That's quite a crowd," she said, a rueful smile touching her lips. The rains meant that no one was able to get into the fields. "At least someone can benefit from this latest downpour."

"Benefit?" Birdie sucked in a sharp breath, her hands

landing on her generous hips. "I hope you're not suggesting that I'm the sort of person who enjoys benefiting from a tragedy, Jaci Patterson," she chastised. "People want to get together to discuss what's happened and I have the local spot for them to gather."

Jaci blinked, caught off guard by her friend's sharp reprimand. Then, absorbing the older woman's words, she stiffened in concern.

"Tragedy?" she breathed.

Birdie's features softened. "You haven't heard?"

Jaci felt a tremor of unease. She'd already lost her father to a drunk driver before she was even born, and then her grandmother when she was seventeen. Her grandfather had passed just two years ago. She was still raw from their deaths.

"No, I haven't heard anything. Like I said, the electricity went out last night and as soon as it came back on I started baking. Has someone died?"

"I'm afraid so."

"Who?"

"No one knows for sure yet," Birdie told her.

Jaci blinked in confusion. "How could they not know?"

"The levee broke in the middle of the night."

"Yeah, I figured that out when I discovered that the road was closed. . . . Oh hell." She tensed as her unease became sharp-edged fear. The levee had broken before and flooded fields, but the neighbor to her south had recently built a new house much closer to the river. "It didn't reach Frank's home, did it?"

Birdie shook her head. "Just the back pasture."

"Then what are you talking about?"

"When Frank went to check on the breach, he saw something floating in the middle of his field."

Jaci cringed. Poor Frank. He must have been shocked out of his mind.

"Oh my God. It was a dead person?"

"Yep. A woman."

"He didn't recognize her?"

Birdie leaned forward and lowered her voice, as if anyone could hear over the noise from the customers, not to mention the usual kitchen clatter.

"He said it was impossible to know if she was familiar or not."

"I don't suppose he wanted to look too close," Jaci said. If she'd spotted a body in her flooded field she would have jumped into her Jeep and driven away like a maniac.

"It wasn't that. He claimed the woman was too . . ." Birdie hesitated, as if she was searching for a more delicate way to express what Frank had said. "Decomposed to make out her features."

"Decomposed?" A strange chill inched down Jaci's spine.

"That's what he's saying."

Jaci absently glanced through the opening into the outer room where she could see Frank surrounded by a group of avid listeners.

When Birdie had said a body, she'd assumed it had been someone who'd been caught in the flood. Maybe she'd fallen in when she was walking along the bank. Or her car might have been swept away when she tried to cross a road with high water.

But she wouldn't be decomposed, would she?

"I've heard that water does strange things to a body," Jaci at last said.

Birdie tugged Jaci toward the back door as her assistant

moved to open the fridge. Clearly there was more to the story.

"The body wasn't all that Frank discovered."

Jaci stilled. "There was more?"

"Yep." Birdie whispered, as if it was a big secret. Which was ridiculous. There were no such things as secrets in a town the size of Heron. "Frank called the sheriff, and while he was waiting for Mike to arrive he swears he caught sight of a human skull stuck in the mud at the edge of the road." Birdie gave a horrified shudder. "Can you imagine? Two dead people virtually in his backyard? Gives me the creeps just thinking about it."

Jaci's mouth went dry. "Did Frank say anything else?"

Birdie shrugged. "Just that the sheriff told him to leave and not to talk about what he found." Birdie snorted. "Like anyone wouldn't feel the need to share the fact they found a dead body and a skull in their field."

A familiar dread curdled in the pit of Jaci's stomach.

She was being an idiot. Of course she was. This had nothing to do with her past. Or the mysterious stalker who had made her life hell.

Still . . .

She couldn't shake the sudden premonition that slithered down her spine.

"Is Mike still out at Frank's?" she abruptly demanded, referring to the sheriff, Mike O'Brien.

"Yeah." Birdie sent her a curious glance. "I think he was waiting for the Corps of Engineers to get out there so they could discuss how long it would take for the field to drain." She wrinkled her nose. "I suppose they need to make sure there aren't any other bodies."

More bodies.

A fierce urgency pounded through her. She might be

overreacting, but she wasn't going to be satisfied until she spoke to Mike.

"I need to go."

"You haven't had your coffee," Birdie protested.

"Not this morning, thanks, Birdie."

"Okay." The older woman stepped back. "I'll get your money and—"

"I'll stop by later to get it." Jaci turned to pull open the back door.

Instantly a chilled blast of air swept around them.

"What's your rush?" Birdie demanded.

"I have some questions that need answers," she said.

"With who?" Birdie demanded, making a sound of impatience as Jaci darted into the alley and jogged toward her waiting Jeep. "Jaci?"

Not bothering to answer, Jaci jumped into the vehicle and put it in gear. Water trickled down her neck from her wet hair, but when she'd gone into the diner she'd left the engine running with the heater blasting at full steam.

Which meant she was a damp mess, but she wasn't completely miserable.

Angling the vent in a futile effort to dry her soggy sweatshirt, Jaci stomped on the accelerator and headed back toward her house. This time, however, she swerved around the barrier that blocked the road, squishing her way through the muddy path that led along the edge of Frank's property.

It was less than ten miles, but by the time she was pulling her vehicle to a halt, her stomach had managed to clench into a tight ball of nerves.

It didn't matter how many times she told herself that this had nothing to do with the past, she couldn't dismiss her rising tide of fear.

Ignoring the avid crowd of onlookers who were

gathered at the edge of the field, Jaci skirted around the wooden barrier, her gaze taking in the sluggish brown water that had surged through the broken levee. Branches and debris swirled through the field. But no body.

Thank God.

"Jaci." A male voice intruded into her distracted thoughts as a skinny man dressed in a dark uniform stepped in front of her.

She forced a smile to her lips. "Morning, Sid."

The young deputy nodded his head toward the flooded field, trying to look suitably somber.

"I guess you heard the news?"

"Yep." Jaci's gaze moved over the deputy's shoulder, landing on the man who was pacing along the edge of the road with a cell phone pressed to his ear.

Sheriff Mike O'Brien.

Only a year older than Jaci's twenty-seven, he was wearing a crisp black uniform with a star on his sleeve that indicated his elected status. Beneath his shirt he was wearing body armor that emphasized his broad, muscular frame. He had light brown hair that he kept cut military-short beneath his black ball cap, and a square face with blunt features and eyes that were an astonishing shade of green. As bright as fresh mint.

He was the sort of solid, dependable man that Jaci had always told herself she should want. Which explained why she'd dated him for several months after returning to Heron.

Unfortunately, they just hadn't clicked. At least not for her. Mike continued to ask her out. She didn't know if he was truly smitten with her, or if she was a convenient date.

After all, Heron wasn't overrun with eligible women.

"I think half the town is here to gawk." Sid once again interrupted her thoughts, his chest puffed out. It was a rare treat to have so much excitement. Jaci, however, was intent on reaching Mike. She stepped around the barrier, neatly avoiding Sid's attempt to grab her arm. "Wait," he commanded.

She marched forward, the mud threatening to suck off her rubber boots.

"I need to speak with Mike," she said, battling her way toward her friend.

Sid made an effort to block her path. "The sheriff closed off this area. He said he didn't want no one here disturbing things until he finished up."

She darted around him. She was nothing if not determined. "I'll just be a minute."

"But—"

"Don't worry, Sid," she called over her shoulder. "I won't disturb anything."

Realizing he was going to have to physically wrestle her to the ground if he hoped to stop her, Sid returned to his post beside the barrier.

"He's going to put my balls in a vise," he groused.

Jaci concentrated on the increasingly marshy ground in front of her. Even before the breach in the levee the soil had been eroded by the pounding rains. One misstep and she could find her foot being caught in a hidden cavity. The last thing she wanted was to fall on her face.

Or worse, twist an ankle.

Thankfully Mike was distracted by his phone call. Which meant that he didn't have a chance to flee before she was standing directly beside him.

Belatedly realizing he was no longer alone, Mike abruptly turned to scowl at her with blatant annoyance.

"Shit." Shoving his phone into his pocket, he planted his hands on his hips. "I told Sid not to let anyone through," he growled. "I already ran off Nelson when I caught him creeping around, snapping pictures like this was a tourist sight, and Andrew drove his tractor down here to have a look before I could have the field blocked off."

Jaci pressed her lips together. Mike was referring to Nelson Bradley, the photographer who'd recently returned to Heron to open his own gallery. And Andrew Porter, a local farmer who cash-cropped Jaci's land.

"I'm not just anyone," she argued.

"No? And why is that?" he demanded. "Just because we dated doesn't give you special privileges."

She jerked at the unexpected attack. Was he being serious?

"I'm not here because we dated."

He paused, sucking in a deep breath. Clearly he'd had a stressful morning with a day stretching ahead that probably wasn't going to be any better.

And to top it off, the chilled drizzle was threatening to become yet another downpour.

"I'm sorry, Jaci. If you're worried about your land, I'll have Sid drive by and check it out," he at last managed, his temper still evident as he glanced toward the breach in the levee. "At least I will once the damned Corps of Engineers gets here."

Jaci gave an impatient wave of her hand. Did he really think she was interrupting him just to get someone to check a few muddy fields?

"I'm not worried about the land. I'm worried about the dead woman."

"Oh." His expression softened. "It's okay, Jaci. She was no one local."

"You're sure?"

He grimaced. "As sure as I can be, considering how degraded the body was." With a shake of his head, he pulled out his phone, which was buzzing. “I have a lot on my hands right now. You need to go home. I’ll stop by later.”

She clenched her teeth. A part of her wanted to turn and walk away. Why not accept that this was nothing more than a tragic accident that had nothing to do with Heron? Or her.

God knew she had enough to worry about.

But if she’d learned anything over the past eleven years, it was the fact that nothing, absolutely nothing, was worse than not knowing.

“How was she killed?” she demanded.

There was a short silence as Mike studied her with a searching gaze, clearly sensing her unease. Then he reached out to brush her bangs off her wet brow.

“What’s going on?” he asked, his voice gentle as he ignored his buzzing phone.

She bit her lower lip before she reluctantly revealed her worst fear.

“What if it’s starting again?”

“Starting again?” He wrinkled his brow, apparently baffled by her harsh question. Seconds later, realization hit and the green eyes narrowed with frustration. “Jesus Christ, Jaci. Don’t do this to yourself.”

She hunched her shoulder. “I can’t help it.”

He reached to cup her cheek in his palm as he towered over her. He wasn’t more than six feet, but she barely topped five foot two, which made it easy for him to play the overprotective lawman.

Something he enjoyed.

“Listen to me,” he ordered. “This has nothing to do with your crazy theories of the past.”

A familiar sense of aggravated fury pounded through Jaci. She was used to having her fears dismissed as being “crazy.” Hell, the previous sheriff told her that she was being a “hormonal” female.

No one wanted to listen to her fears.

Maybe not that surprising.

She'd just turned sixteen when she'd received the first golden locket. She'd found it on the porch swing when she'd come home from school. At first she assumed that it was a belated birthday gift from her grandparents. They enjoyed spoiling her with small, inexpensive surprises.

But when she opened it up, she'd quickly realized it wasn't a gift. Instead, tucked inside was a lock of red hair wrapped with a piece of ribbon that was smeared with blood.

It'd freaked her out enough to insist that her grandmother call the cops. They'd dismissed it as a Halloween prank. And Jaci had tried to do the same. There were plenty of bullies at the small school who would delight in terrorizing her. Including her half brother, Christopher.

But the second locket arrived only a few months later. This time the hair was dark, but it was once again wrapped in a bloody ribbon. Once again Jaci had taken it to the sheriff and once again she'd been dismissed.

For the next two years she'd continued to receive the lockets. Sometimes they would be up to six months apart, and sometimes it would be only weeks. But while she was growingly convinced that the hair in the lockets belonged to women who were being hurt, if not actually killed, no one would believe her.

In fact, it'd become a joke to everyone but her grandparents.

They were the only ones who'd offered her sympathy, even if they didn't entirely accept her belief that there was a maniac in Heron who was killing women and leaving bits of them in golden lockets on their porch.

The terror had finally stopped when she'd traveled to attend college at Mizzou, the University of Missouri. And thankfully, there'd been nothing since her return to Heron two years ago.

But now . . .

She shivered. "And how do you explain a dead woman and skull stuck in Frank's field?"

His jaw tightened, his expression guarded as he slid into cop mode.

"There's a thousand potential explanations, and none of them have anything to do with a killer."

"A thousand?" She arched a brow. "Really?"

"Most likely the body came from someone who fell overboard during a fishing trip. Or it could have been a victim who was dumped upstream and floated down here." He stepped back, waving a hand toward the muddy water. "Chicago is notorious for getting rid of problems by tossing them in the river."

He was right. Despite the danger, there were always people who took boats onto the water during a flood. Either because they had no sense, or because it was their job.

And it was also true that she'd been hearing stories about bodies floating down from Chicago her entire life. Not that one had actually been found, as far as she knew, but it was an urban myth that everyone was happy enough to believe.

She still wasn't satisfied.

"What about the skull?" she pressed.

Mike rolled his eyes. "Dammit. Is Frank telling everyone in town?"

"Yes."

Mike heaved a resigned sigh. "Look. The most reasonable answer is that both of them were accidental drownings. The recent floods would have churned up a lot of unpleasant things that were hidden at the bottom of the river." He shrugged. "Or it's even possible that the waters disturbed a cemetery and swept a few of the graves down here."

Okay. That actually made sense. A portion of her tension eased.

"When will you know?"

"The body and the skull have already been picked up by the coroner," he said. "He'll drive it down to the medical examiner in Columbia to do an autopsy. Until then, this place is off-limits to everyone. Including you, Jaci." He pointed a finger at her. "Got it?"

"Fine."

Turning, she stomped her way back through the mud.

"I mean it, Jaci," he called from behind her.

"Whatever," she said, cutting along the edge of the field.

She'd wasted enough time.

She still had deliveries to make. Not to mention doing her daily grocery shopping, stopping by the bank, the post office, and the vet to get cream for Riff's ear infection.

Later she could worry about dead bodies and strange skulls.

The breath was yanked from his body as he watched Jaci Patterson walk away.

Oh. It was glorious. The white-hot excitement that exploded through him made his heart pound and his cock jerk to attention.

It felt like he was standing in the center of a lightning storm.

How long had it been? Eight years? Maybe nine.

Too long.

He'd tried to replace her. After all, she'd abandoned him just when he was about to take their relationship to the next level.

But while he'd found a fleeting satisfaction with other players, no one had ever given him the same thrill as sweet, sweet Jaci.

He hid a smile, conscious that there were dozens of upright Heron citizens who could witness his every expression.

It was so ironic.

When he'd received the call that the floods had exposed his burial grounds, he'd panicked. The bodies had the potential to attract attention that could ruin everything.

Now he forgot his unease.

Okay, there might be a brief spark of interest, but it would quickly be forgotten. Especially if the majority of his victims had been swept downriver.

And any hassle at dealing with nosy neighbors, and even a potential investigation, was a mere nuisance when compared to the dazzling burst of pleasure as he watched the anticipation that was etched on Jaci's beautiful face.

She remembered their game.

And she was already eager for it to begin again.

Just as he was . . .

Chapter Two

Jaci's thoughts remained distracted as she drove the fifteen miles to Baldwin.

Larger than Heron, the city boasted a liberal arts college and several specialty shops, but it still managed to maintain the charm of a small river town.

Making a stop at the local B and B to deliver homemade loaves of bread, she headed to the quaint tea shop that was squeezed between a hardware store and a dentist office.

She whipped her Jeep into the closest parking space, and jumped out without paying much attention to who was pulling in beside her. Trina, the owner of Tea & Cakes, had already called twice to make sure she was bringing her tarts before the brunch crowd made their appearance.

Big mistake.

Jaci was just opening the back of her vehicle when the familiar scent of Dolce & Gabbana had her stiffening in dread. Oh . . . crap. Turning her head, she belatedly absorbed the sight of the silver Mercedes parked next to her.

Feeling like the deer caught in the headlights, Jaci

froze. If she was smart she would climb into the back of her Jeep and shut the door. With a little maneuvering she could wiggle her way into the driver's seat and take off before she had to endure the looming meeting.

Instead, she forced herself to slowly turn and meet the older woman's critical gaze.

"Hello, Mother." She pasted a smile to her lips.

Loreen Hamilton was a small, slender woman with golden-red hair that she kept swept into a smooth knot that emphasized her pale, oval face and finely carved features. In her midforties, she was a beautiful woman who managed to look polished and sophisticated despite the persistent drizzle. Of course she spent a fortune on her weekly facials, manicures, and hair tint. Plus her flared black coat and heeled leather boots probably cost more than Jaci's entire wardrobe.

Easy to look good when you had money.

The cold blue gaze skimmed over Jaci, taking in her hair, which was plastered to her skull, her soggy sweat-shirt, and the rubber boots caked in mud.

The older woman always made Jaci feel like a lumbering, awkward cow.

"Jaci." She arched a finely plucked brow. "Good Lord. What happened?"

"Nothing." Jaci glanced down in confusion. "Why?"

The woman thinned her lips. "You're a mess."

Jaci rolled her eyes. She would never comprehend how the lovely Loreen had ever allowed herself to get pregnant at the age of seventeen by a mere farm boy. Of course, old pictures revealed that her father, Samuel, had been ruggedly handsome with golden-brown hair and clean-cut features. Jaci had inherited his hair and light blue-gray eyes, as well as his love for the outdoors. Unfortunately, her own features weren't nearly so striking.

But Loreen was swift to make up for her mistake.

After Jaci's father was killed by a drunk driver, she'd handed her newborn daughter over to her in-laws and promptly married Blake Hamilton so she could move into his large brick home on a bluff overlooking the town.

She'd also produced a handsome son, Christopher, and an exquisite daughter, Payton.

The perfect Stepford family.

"I've been working," she said.

"And you couldn't clean up before coming into town?"

Jaci reached into the back of the Jeep to grab the last tray of peach tarts, making sure they were covered by the plastic wrap.

"I've been up for hours and I still have a thousand things to do," she said, the words clipped. "When I get back home I'll take a shower."

Loreen sniffed. "There's no need to be snippy."

Snippy? Did people still use that word?

"I—" She bit back her angry words. She'd tried every approach to forming a relationship with this woman. She'd played the dutiful daughter, the casual friend, the indifferent stranger. Nothing changed. Her mother was as cold and judgmental as she had been when Jaci was five and failed to win the crown as Little Princess at the Corn Festival. Thankfully for Loreen, her second daughter, Payton, had won it three years in a row. "Whatever," Jaci breathed. "I need to get these to Trina."

Expecting her mother to eagerly bring an end to yet another unwelcomed encounter with her daughter, Jaci was caught off guard when her mother pointed toward the tray in her hands.

"Wait," she commanded. "I'll take two of the tarts."

Jaci's eyes widened. "You?"

The woman looked uncomfortable. "I'll pay."

"It's not that," Jaci protested, reaching beneath the plastic to grab two of the tarts. "I've just never seen you eat dessert."

Her mother gave a lift of her shoulder, reaching to take the tarts.

"Blake is meeting clients at his office in St. Louis, but he promised to be home in time for dinner. And . . ." Her words trailed away before she was stretching her lips into a smile. "Christopher is home."

"Oh." Jaci managed not to grimace. She hated her half brother. He'd been born an arrogant ass, and as he grew older, he'd become a cocky bully who used his family's wealth as a "get out of trouble free" card. She doubted that the last three years he'd been away at Washington University in St. Louis had improved his slimy personality. "Is it spring break?"

"He's done with his classes."

Hmm. If the golden boy had actually completed his college education, there would have been trumpets blaring and a party fit for royalty.

Which meant he'd flunked out. Or more likely, he'd been kicked out.

"When did he get back?" she asked.

"A few days ago."

Well, that was vague.

"Does he plan to stay in the area?"

"For now."

More vagueness. Weird.

"I'm sure you're happy to have him back."

"Yes. Yes, I am." An unexpectedly fierce emotion

touched her mother's pale face before she was once again the cool, aloof matron. "How much do I owe you?"

"Consider it a gift for the prodigal son," she said.

Something that might have been fear flashed through the blue eyes.

"Why would you call him that?" she snapped.

Jaci frowned. What the hell?

Her mother was always brittle. As if she was spun from caramelized sugar. But at the moment she looked like she was about to shatter.

"He was gone and now he's come home," she clarified in wary tones. "That's all."

Loreen forced a small laugh. "Yes. Of course."

Jaci's brows pulled together as she studied her mother's face.

"Is something wrong?"

"Certainly not." The smile remained grimly pinned in place. "Everything is perfect."

"Right. Perfect." Bafflement was replaced by a sudden weariness that blanketed Jaci, as thick and dreary as the clouds above.

It'd been a hell of a morning. She didn't have the emotional strength to deal with this woman. With a resigned shake of her head, she turned toward the tea shop.

Whatever had her mother's panties in a twist had nothing to do with her. And the older woman wouldn't thank her for trying to interfere.

In fact, that would be the last thing her mother would want.

Pressing the door open with her shoulder, Jaci entered the pink-and-white shop that was decorated with overstuffed couches and low tables.

At her entrance, Trina rushed from behind the glass

counter at the back, her round face wreathed with a relieved smile.

"Thank God."

Handing over her tray of tarts, Jaci collected her money and hurried back to her Jeep before Trina could get her cornered. Everyone wanted to discuss the gruesome discovery.

Everyone but Jaci.

She just wanted to finish her errands and get home.

A hot shower was just what she needed.

It was past eleven o'clock before Jaci was at last leaving Baldwin and headed along the back roads to her grandparents' farm. The narrow road was isolated, and thick with mud. Which meant that the last thing she expected was to meet a large black SUV as she swerved around a corner.

Slamming on the brakes, she watched as the vehicle cruised past, missing her bumper by less than an inch. But even as she breathed a sigh of relief that they hadn't collided, she caught sight of the man behind the steering wheel.

A very familiar man.

Her stepfather, Blake Hamilton.

Absently, she turned her head to watch as the SUV disappeared around the corner.

The older man was the CEO of Hamilton Enterprises, a company he'd inherited from his father. She didn't really know what that meant beyond the fact that he made a buttload of money, and that he used the small airport north of Baldwin to daily commute between his home and his office in St. Louis. It was only a forty-minute flight, and he could enjoy the benefits of living in a small town.

After all, in the big city he was just another businessman. Around here he got to act like he was something special.

So what the heck was he doing out in the middle of nowhere?

And why did her mother think he was flying back tonight?

With a slow shake of her head, she pressed her foot on the gas pedal.

Weirdest. Day. Ever.

Chapter Three

Rylan Cooper climbed the narrow stairs.

He should feel triumphant.

After a week of caulking, sealing, and pumping water, he finally could proclaim victory.

A dry basement.

Entering the kitchen, he closed the door behind him. The narrow room had been built onto the old farmhouse nearly a hundred years ago, which might explain why it felt like it slanted downhill. The cabinets were worn, the linoleum floor was scraped to the studs near the back door, and the appliances should have been hauled to the junkyard in the sixties.

But there was a bank of windows that ran along the back wall that offered a priceless view of the Mississippi River, and the air was filled with the warm scent of pancakes and pipe tobacco.

The scents of home.

A warmth spread through Rylan, even as he tried to deny it. He didn't want to feel this constant sense of comfort even after two weeks of staying at his father's farm.

He was supposed to be eager to return to his California condo. It was a spectacular designer space with a stunning view of the beach. And, of course, there was his prosperous business with his friend and partner, Griff.

The two of them had met at the local college in Baldwin. Rylan had been finishing up his criminal justice degree with dreams of entering the FBI, while Griff had been a computer nerd. They'd met when they'd worked for the same security company installing alarm systems. Together they'd started tinkering with a new database that could track the burgeoning wave of cybercriminals.

He'd assumed that it would be a summer project that might bring in a few extra bucks. Something that would come in handy as he neared graduation and his student loans were looming over his head like the sword of Damocles.

Within a few months, however, they'd received an interest in their work that had stunned both of them. They leased the program to various law agencies. And then created several new security systems that had been licensed around the world.

Rylan was living the dream.

But he couldn't deny that more than once he'd felt a pang of restless dissatisfaction.

He assumed that at least a portion of his frustration was the fact that he missed his father. It'd just been the two of them after his mother's death when he was twelve. Of course he missed the old man when they were separated by a couple thousand miles.

Crossing the slanted floor, he joined his father, who was finishing up the last of the breakfast dishes.

Rylan leaned against the counter, folding his arms across his chest. He studied the face that looked remarkably like his own. Lean. Angular cheekbones. A narrow nose and wide brow. Both had the same unusual golden-brown eyes.

There were a few differences. Rylan's hair was bleached

to a light blond and his skin tanned from his hours in the sun, while his father had thick silver hair and a leathered face that was pale from a long winter and even longer spring.

Elmer had also been honed to the point he was little more than bones and sinew. Rylan, on the other hand, was slender, but he spent enough time in the gym to ensure he didn't embarrass himself on the beach.

"The patch is holding for now, but you'll need to call in a contractor," he informed his father. "Better yet, you can call in a mover and sell this damned place before it collapses on your head."

Elmer snorted, reaching for a worn towel to dry his gnarled hands. A lifetime of working the land had taken its toll on the older man.

"The only way I'm leaving this house is in a coffin." He repeated the words he'd been mouthing since Rylan had first suggested the move.

"Stubborn old coot," Rylan said.

Elmer tossed aside the towel. "Look at it this way, son. If the roof does fall, then my thick skull should protect me well enough."

"There is that," Rylan wryly agreed. Then, with a sigh, he glanced toward the torrential water that swept past the house less than a mile away. "Still, I wish you'd come and stay with me until the river goes down."

Elmer shrugged with the confidence of a man who'd seen about everything in his sixty years.

"It's supposed to crest the first of next week."

"As long as it stops raining." Rylan pointedly glanced toward the sullen clouds that hung so low they nearly brushed the tops of the trees. "And that doesn't seem likely."

"Don't fuss," Elmer said, moving to the narrow opening that led to the enclosed back porch. "I'll be fine."

Following behind his aggravating father, Rylan leaned a shoulder against the doorjamb. "Is there a reason you don't want to stay with me?"

Elmer reached for the muddy coveralls that were hung on a nail. The narrow space was built with a wooden plank floor. The slanting edge of the roof and framed screens that kept out the bugs and wildlife did nothing to block the icy breeze.

"LA has too much sunshine."

"Sunshine?" Rylan arched a brow that was several shades darker than his hair. "That's your reason?"

"Yep."

"You prefer endless days of rain?"

"I like to wake up and be surprised," Elmer corrected, stepping into the coveralls so he could pull them up and over his jeans and flannel shirt. "Here it might be hot or cold. Sunny or rainy. You might get a bit of snow or it might suddenly turn off with a blizzard." He pulled up the zipper before training his piercing gaze on Rylan. "What about you? When you open your eyes there's nothing but sun, sun, and more sun."

"It would only be for a month or two," Rylan insisted. It wasn't just that he would enjoy his father's company when he returned to California, but he wanted to have the entire house rewired and new plumbing installed. A home built over a hundred and fifty years ago was in constant need of repairs. "Just long enough for the river to go down and someone to make a few upgrades around the place."

Elmer grabbed his rubber boots and settled on the edge of a wooden chair.

"I have a better idea," he said, yanking a boot over his foot, which was covered by a thermal sock.

"What's that?"

"Why don't you move home where you belong and do the repairs yourself? Computers are fine and dandy, but a man needs to work with his hands on occasion."

Rylan's lips twisted. He'd walked right into that one.

"My business—"

"Can be done anywhere," Elmer interrupted, pulling on the second boot.

"Okay," Rylan conceded. It was true. Although he had to meet with the occasional client, most of his work was video chatting with his partner as they brainstormed their newest creation. He offered suggestions from a crime-fighting or security perspective, while his friend decided whether his vision was technically possible. "But unlike you, I prefer a view that includes beaches with beautiful, barely covered women to a muddy cow pasture."

Elmer shoved himself upright, sending his son a chiding glance.

"We have our fair share of pretty gals, although they're smart enough to cover up what God gave 'em."

Rylan snorted. "A sin."

Elmer shook his head, moving to open the screened door that led to the backyard.

"And speaking of pretty gals, I need to get going."

Rylan frowned. He'd assumed his father was headed out to finish his chores.

"Where?"

Elmer glanced over his shoulder. "I want to check on Jaci. She should be back from her deliveries by now."

Rylan frowned. "Why?"

The older man shrugged. "It's what neighbors do when we have bad weather."

"At least you admit it's bad," Rylan said.

Elmer stood in the open doorway, eyeing his son with a hint of impatience.

"Are you coming?"

Rylan grimaced, not overly excited at the thought of getting out in the chilled rain.

"Why don't you just call?"

His father gave a disappointed shake of his head. "Is that how you do it in LA? Talk to each other at a distance so you don't have to look each other in the eye?"

Rylan narrowed his gaze. The older man had been distracted all morning.

Something was up.

"Okay, old man," he said. "What's bothering you?"

Elmer grimaced. "Frank stopped by before you got up this morning."

Well, that explained the voices that'd woken him before the crack of dawn.

"I thought I heard someone here at some ungodly hour," he said. "What did he want?"

"He came to tell me that he'd got up early to check on his bottom fields. They were flooded after the levee broke during the night."

"And?"

His dad's eyes darkened with the worry he'd been trying to conceal.

"And, he caught sight of a dead woman floating in the water."

A shocking fear blasted through Rylan. Pressing his hand against the wall to keep himself upright, he swallowed the sudden lump in his throat.

"He didn't think it was Jaci, did he?"

"No." His father gave a shake of his head. "There

wasn't much light and the body was in pretty bad shape, but he was sure the woman had long hair."

Shit. Rylan forced himself to suck in a deep breath.

The intensity of his fear had been . . . cataclysmic.

Which should have been odd. He'd only seen Jaci on a handful of occasions since he'd left for California. And even when they were young, they hadn't been more than neighbors. He'd made very sure of that.

And, of course, there was the little fact that she'd never forgiven him for his refusal to believe her claims of a stalker when he worked part-time at the local sheriff's office.

Yeah. They weren't exactly BFFs, but there was a part of him that knew his world would be a darker place without her in it.

Grimly he hid his surge of relief. He'd never shared his confusing mix of emotions when it came to Jaci Patterson. And he didn't intend to start now.

"Then why are you worried?"

"Frank said he also saw a skull."

"Christ," Rylan breathed, his attention fully captured. "Did he call the sheriff?"

"'Course he did."

"I still don't understand what this has to do with your neighbor," he said, even as he moved to grab his old coat and boots that he left there for his visits.

God knew he didn't need them in California.

"Jaci has never accepted that those lockets she received were just someone's idea of a bad joke," Elmer explained as they headed down the back steps and across the soggy yard.

Rylan shivered as the icy rain pelted his face. Was the sun ever going to come out?

"Has she still been getting them?" he demanded.

"Not that I know of." Elmer stomped his way past a shed and the pole barn where he kept his lawn equipment. Then he angled his way toward the opening in the hedge that was a natural barrier between the Cooper and Patterson farms. There was no point in suggesting they take the old pickup parked a few feet away. His father was a firm believer that God gave him feet for a reason. "But a dead body floating in her neighbor's field is sure to bring it all back," he continued as they moved past the hedge and into the open pasture.

Struggling through the muck, the two of them managed to make their way to the two-story white farmhouse with a trellised porch and black shutters. It looked a lot like every other home in the area, except for the gorgeous stained glass in the upper windows that had been created by Jaci's grandfather.

"Looks like she's just getting home from her deliveries," Elmer said, nodding toward the black Jeep that had been backed toward the front porch.

"What deliveries?"

"She bakes all sorts of pastries and breads and sells them to various shops," Elmer explained. "She also makes crafts that she sells at art fairs."

Rylan nodded. That seemed a perfect choice for Jaci. He'd heard at one time that she was living in Columbia and working as a graphic artist. It never seemed to fit.

"Does she still rent out her land to Virgil Porter?"

"His son," Elmer said, heading across the front yard. "Andrew took over most of the farming last year. 'Course, if the rains don't stop, no one will be getting in any crops." Both men came to a halt as the woman rounded the back of the Jeep. "Hey, Jaci," his father called out.

The woman gave a sharp jerk, clearly caught off guard by their sudden appearance.

"Elmer." She pressed a hand to her chest, her gaze shifting toward Rylan. Her lips tightened, as if she'd just caught a bad smell. "And Rylan. I heard you were visiting."

Unable to resist, Rylan found his gaze skimming over the woman in front of him.

She'd always been cute in a fresh, farm-girl way. Her honey hair was kept in a pixie style that framed her face. She had large eyes that were more gray than blue today, and full lips.

But while she'd been chubby when she was very young, she'd developed the sort of curves in high school that made a hormonal boy think wicked, wicked thoughts. Which was only one of several reasons he'd kept a firm distance between them.

"Always a pleasure, Jaci," he said, trying to ignore the way the wet sweatshirt molded to her generous breasts, and the perfection of her ass beneath the tight jeans.

"I can tell," she said dryly, turning to yank open the back of the Jeep. Reaching inside, she grabbed a reusable cloth bag.

"Let Rylan help you with those groceries," Elmer ordered.

She reached for another bag. "There's no need."

Rylan rolled his eyes, stepping forward to tug the bags from her tight grip.

"I thought my dad was the most stubborn critter in these parts," he said.

"Critter?" she mocked.

He shrugged. "I was going to say Missouri mule."

"Nice." With a shake of her head, she turned to grab a stack of empty trays. "Is there something you need, Elmer?"

Elmer stepped forward to push shut the back of the Jeep, falling into step beside Jaci as she headed toward the front steps.

"Just wanted to make sure you haven't been flooded out."

"Not yet," she assured him, offering a sudden grin for the older man. As always, it was warm and sincere. Like the sun coming out. It had nothing in common with the too white, toothy smiles of the women he'd been dating the past five years. "The cellar has some water, but the sump pump is taking care of it."

His father nodded. "I suppose the back fields are flooded?"

"Probably." She grimaced as she glanced toward the drive, which continued past the side of her house to the outer buildings. Eventually it led to the land that had been farmed by the Porter family since Jaci's grandfather had a stroke ten years ago. "It looks like Andrew came out to check the water while I was gone."

Rylan scowled at the deep ruts caused by a heavy tractor. The tracks were ruining her drive.

"Why doesn't he use the county road to get to the fields?" he demanded.

She climbed the wooden steps. "The bridge has been closed for almost three weeks."

Rylan joined her on the porch, his gaze still taking in the deep furrows that were already filling with water.

"He's making a mess of your drive."

"I know." She gave a resigned shrug. "But there's not much to be done until the rains stop." She reached toward the handle of the old-fashioned screen door. "You can leave the bags on the swing. . . ."

Her words trailed away, her face losing color at an alarming rate.

"Jaci?" Rylan stepped forward. "What's going on?"

The trays dropped from her fingers, crashing to the

wooden porch as she stared at the door as if she'd seen a ghost.

It was only then that Rylan belatedly noticed that something was hanging from the handle. Leaning forward, he caught a glimpse of the golden locket that was threaded through a delicate chain.

A hiss was wrenched from his lips even as the woman next to him swayed and then abruptly collapsed in a dead faint. Muttering a curse, he dropped the bags and reached to catch her just inches from the hard, wooden planks of the porch.

Glancing down at her ashen face, he felt a tightness clench around his chest.

Someone had deliberately scared the hell out of this woman. And he intended to find out who it was.

Chapter Four

Mike O'Brien returned to Heron, pulling his patrol truck to a halt in the graveled lot. Once it had been the site of the jailhouse, but five years ago the building had been pulled down, and a new, modern facility had been attached to the back of the old courthouse.

The new jail had several sleek cells and a communal area for the prisoners during the day, along with a booking room that had all the bells and whistles. In the center was a deputy who kept an eye on the security monitors. And at the far end was a large interview room that had been intended to double as an office for the sheriff.

Mike, however, preferred the worn, quiet simplicity of his old office in the courthouse.

Built almost two hundred years ago, the two-story red-brick building had maintained the original paneling and wood floors, with plaster medallions in the center of the high ceilings. His office had a bank of windows that overlooked a small park where he could watch children play during the summer.

It emphasized the solemn traditions of his position, and at the same time, it offered him a reminder of the precious future that was his duty and honor to protect.

Even better, it had a door that led directly to the new addition.

The best of both worlds.

Halting at his private door at the side of the courthouse, he punched in the numbers on the electronic lock and stepped inside.

He stifled a yawn as he headed across the worn floorboards. It was just noon and he was already tired.

Glancing toward his desk, he grimaced at the stack of paperwork, which mysteriously appeared on it each morning. It was a part of the job he put off until his administrative assistant threatened to do bad things to him. Including handcuffing him to the desk until he was done.

With a shrug, he moved toward the table that was pushed into the corner. He poured himself a cold cup of coffee and grabbed a protein bar. He wasn't sure who the genius was who came up with the marketing idea of disguising a candy bar with the word "protein," but he fully approved. His mother would have a cow if he told her that he'd had gooey peanut butter drenched in chocolate for lunch. Now he could claim he had something healthy.

Polishing off the bar, he tossed away the wrapper and turned back to the desk. The files hadn't magically disappeared.

Damn.

Grudgingly accepting that he needed to get started, he was interrupted when the connecting door from the attached jail was pushed open and Sid stepped inside.

The young deputy had a nervous habit of shifting his weight from foot to foot. Today he was nearly dancing as he tried to control his excitement.

"Hal and Bobby are waiting in the interview room," he said. Mike had called him earlier to ask the deputies to come in for a meeting. "Did you want me to call Corey?"

Mike considered before giving a shake of his head. Corey was a deputy who served as a resource officer at the local high school.

"No. If we need extra manpower, we'll pull in the reserves."

Mike set aside his mug. No huge sacrifice. It tasted like sludge.

Following his young deputy through the door and into the reception area, he paused long enough to pour a fresh cup of coffee before heading past the dispatch room and into the interview room, which doubled as a conference space when necessary.

It was a long, narrow space dominated by a wooden table with six matching chairs. The floor was carpeted and the walls painted an institutional white. In one corner was a TV and camera set on a cabinet that was used to videotape any questioning of potential suspects. There was also a two-way mirror on the far wall that allowed him or the prosecutor to watch during the interview. On one wall was a framed map of the local county. On another wall were black-and-white pictures of the old jailhouse.

"Right. Let's get started," he said, walking to the head of the table as Sid took a seat next to Hal, a short, heavyset man with a fringe of gray hair. Hal had been an insurance salesman when he'd decided he wanted to work in law enforcement. He wasn't driven with ambition, but he was reliable and had an eye for detail. Two traits that Mike depended on.

Across the table was the third deputy, Bobby. He was younger than Hal, with chubby cheeks and blond curls. He was constantly boasting about moving to a bigger city where he could use the skills he was learning during his online classes. But they all knew he was just talking smack.

Bobby had a wife and three young kids. He could barely

make the payments on the double-wide that he'd installed on his parents' land, let alone find the funds to move to a city like Chicago.

Mike cleared his throat, feeling the buzz in the air. Finding a dead body floating in a field was big excitement in the rural community.

"What we know is . . ." His words trailed away as he gave a frustrated shake of his head. "Hell, we know jack squat beyond the fact that we have a woman's body and an unidentified skull. The remains were taken by the coroner down to the Boone County Medical Examiner Office. Hopefully we'll get an ID sooner rather than later, but when a body has been in the water any length of time it makes it more difficult to get a clean set of prints."

"Yep, floaters are always a pain in the ass," Sid said, acting as if he'd seen dozens of bodies instead of precisely three. Two of them drowning victims when a car went off a bridge three years ago, and the female found this morning. "The last ones we had took four days to dry out."

Mike scowled at his deputy. "Sid."

The young man flushed. "Sorry."

"Until we get the ID, we're going to treat this as we would any other drowning case," Mike continued. "Sid, I want you to start with calling the Water Patrol and Coast Guard in St. Louis. See if they have any reports of boats being overturned. Or anyone swept overboard."

Sid pulled out his notebook, scribbling down the instructions. "Yes, sir."

"Then I want you to call the Center for Missing Persons," he added. "Collect all the female names in the tristate area."

The deputy rose to his feet, the notebook still in his hand.

"I'm on it," he said, heading out the door and turning toward the office the deputies shared just down the hall.

Mike turned his attention to Hal and Bobby. "I want the two of you to walk both banks of the river heading north," he ordered. "Check for any abandoned cars along the bank, or small boats that might be tangled in the debris from the flood." He waited for both men to nod. "If you don't spot anything, then contact the authorities in the northern counties and ask them to continue the search. Tell them to contact me if they see anything unusual."

Bobby surged to his feet, eager to be out. He was the sort of guy who craved the action part of the job. Being stuck in the office was a misery.

"You got it."

Mike held up a hand, halting the impetuous young man from darting out of the office.

"And check with the barge companies," he continued, his gaze shifting to Hal, who was rising to his feet. The older man clearly didn't share Bobby's enthusiasm at the thought of spending the day slogging through the mud. "See if they're missing any workers."

"That all?" Hal asked.

Mike sipped his coffee, sorting through the tasks he intended to deal with personally and those he could hand off to his team.

"See if any cemeteries have been disturbed by the floods," he said. His day would be a lot easier if they could discover that the gruesome remains were nothing more than an unfortunate result of the river disturbing a few graves. "That's all for now."

The two deputies left the room and Mike took the opportunity to gulp down his coffee. God only knew when he would have time for another cup.

On cue there was the sound of footsteps echoing down the hall, and his assistant, Carol, poked her head around the door.

"You have a visitor."

With a small sigh, he set the empty cup on the table. "If it isn't an emergency, I really need for you to schedule them to come back later."

The middle-aged woman, with mid-length auburn hair, gave a shake of her head.

"I did try to tell her you were busy, but she insisted she had to see you. Immediately."

Mike frowned. "Is it Jaci?"

"Nope. It's the other one." A humorless smile touched her lips. "I think you'd better go talk to her. Election season is just around the corner, after all."

"Carol . . ." His words trailed away as she abruptly disappeared, scurrying back to her desk in the reception room.

Muttering a curse, he headed back to his office. He had a great staff, but sometimes he wasn't in the mood for their peculiar senses of humor.

Squaring his shoulders and wiping the irritation from his face, he yanked open the connecting door to discover a beautiful young woman standing in the center of his office.

Payton Hamilton.

Abruptly he understood his assistant's vague words, "the other one."

Damn. His lips tightened at the sight of her bleached blond hair that perfectly framed her oval face before brushing her shoulders. A discreet layer of makeup emphasized her high cheekbones and the full curve of her lips. Although it was sheer temper that darkened her blue eyes.

He allowed his gaze to lower to the designer coat that fell to her knees and was tightly belted to reveal her tiny waist. And farther down to take in the stiletto shoes that no doubt cost a fortune.

Who wore high heels in the middle of a flood?

Hearing the connecting door open, Payton glared at him with seething frustration.

"I need to speak with you."

His lips twisted. Three years ago he'd been idiotic enough to date this woman. For nearly nine months she'd dangled his heart on a string, blatantly allowing him to think they were developing a real relationship. He'd even started to plan a future together, including a diamond solitaire that was now hidden in his underwear drawer. Then, without warning, she'd dumped him and started dating a local lawyer.

He'd been treated like a piece of trash that'd been thrown in the gutter. At least until Jaci had returned to Heron and the two of them had spent an occasional evening out. Then suddenly Payton had started texting him again. She didn't want him, but she was selfish enough not to be willing to share him with her half sister.

"And what Payton Hamilton wants she gets?" he drawled.

Her chin tilted at his scornful tones. "Of course."

With a roll of his eyes, he closed the door to his office and moved to grab a chair. Arranging it next to his desk, he waved a mocking hand toward it.

"Please, make yourself comfortable, Payton."

Strolling forward, Payton ran her manicured fingers over his chest as she passed him.

"Do you remember how you used to make me comfortable, darling?"

Clenching his teeth, he ignored the sizzling memory of stripping her out of the tight dresses and too-high heels.

Instead, he folded his arms over his chest and leaned against the desk as he studied his unwelcomed visitor.

"I've had a shitty day that promises to get worse before it gets better, Payton," he said in grim tones. "I don't have the time or the energy for your games."

She gave a flip of her blond hair as she perched on the front edge of the chair. "Why do you always assume I'm playing games?"

"Aren't you?"

"Maybe." A hint of uncertainty touched her elegantly sculpted features. "I've done this for so long it's hard to know when it's a game and when it's real."

Mike's anger faltered before he was hardening his heart. He wasn't going to fall for her pretense of vulnerability.

Not again.

"I don't have the answer for you."

"Then who does?" she breathed.

He gave a shake of his head, pointing toward the door. "Get to the point or leave."

"Fine," she snapped. "I'm here to make a report."

"What kind of report?" Mike asked. "Someone parking too close to your big house on the hill?"

Her cheeks flushed at the reminder of her mother's shrill protests when a city worker parked his truck next to the ornate gates leading to the Hamilton estate.

"No," she said. "A missing person report."

He stilled. Okay. He hadn't been expecting that.

"What did you say?"

Her lips twisted. "Suddenly hard of hearing, Mike?"

"I hear just fine." With brisk steps, he moved to take his seat behind his desk and pulled out a report form. A subtle warning that in this office he was sheriff, not Mike O'Brien, the small-town boyfriend who couldn't measure up to the princess. "Who's missing?"

"Anne."

He glanced up in confusion. "Who?"

"Anne Dixon. Our housekeeper."

Mike had a vague memory of the woman with salt-and-pepper hair and an ample body squeezed into a black dress with an old-fashioned apron. She'd usually lurked in the background on the few occasions that he'd visited Payton's massive house. As if making sure he didn't steal the silver.

"You say she's missing?"

"Yes."

He grabbed his pen. "For how long?"

Payton leaned toward the desk, bringing with her the scent of warm orchids.

"I'm not sure."

"When was the last time you saw her?"

"Last night." She paused, as if shuffling through her memories. "Around eight or nine," she at last said. "I know it was right after dinner."

Disbelief jolted through him. "Are you kidding me?"

She frowned. "Why?"

He released a harsh breath. "A person isn't missing just because you haven't seen her for a few hours. I'm assuming she's allowed time off to sleep?"

She narrowed her gaze at his jeering tone. "Not even the Hamiltons are allowed to own slaves."

"Good to know." He once again pointed toward the door. "Now, if you'll excuse me, I have real police work to do."

Ignoring his dismissal, she rose to her feet and planted her hand on his desk.

"Don't try to blow me off."

"Dammit, Payton," he growled. "This isn't the time."

She'd always been stubborn, but she'd never interfered in his job. In fact, she'd been one of the few women he'd dated who'd never complained at his long hours and last-minute cancellations.

Of course, that could have been because she'd just been killing time with him until something better came along.

"Could you please just forget who I am and listen to me?" she demanded.

"It wouldn't matter who you are." He leaned back, pretending he didn't hear the protesting squeak from his chair. The dang thing was nearly as old as the office, but he could never remember to order a new one. "Fifteen or sixteen hours isn't long enough to report a missing person."

Surprisingly she refused to budge. Instead she folded her arms around her waist and glared at him.

"Give me five minutes." There was a tense pause before she said the word he never thought to hear from her lips. "Please."

He swallowed a curse. "You have four."

Her lips tightened, but realizing that he wanted any excuse to toss her out, she forced herself to bite back her angry words and concentrate on why she'd intruded into his office.

"Anne has been with us since before I was born. And in those twenty-five years she's never changed her schedule. Not once. She gets up early, takes a walk, and then cooks breakfast." She lifted her hand as his lips parted to make the obvious snarky comment. "Except for Sundays, which is her day off. Even then it's always the same routine. She drives to Quincy to go to church with her sister and spends the day, always returning at precisely seven. It's like clockwork."

Mike studied the perfect, oval face. She was really and truly worried.

"Maybe she's not feeling well," he slowly suggested.

She shook her head. "Anne refused to be taken to the hospital during a full-fledged appendicitis attack until she finished baking a casserole we could eat for dinner. Besides, I already checked her rooms. Her bed was made and the uniform she insists on wearing was lying on it, ready for her to pull it on." Her brows knit together. "It was like she went for a walk and just disappeared."

Mike considered. It did seem odd. Still, there had to be a logical answer.

"She might have had a family emergency," he suggested.

"She would never have left without telling us. Or at least leaving a note," she said with absolute certainty. "And her car is still in the garage. How could she have gone anywhere?"

"What about a cell phone?"

"She doesn't have one. She always uses the house phone if she needs to call anyone." Payton's lips tightened. "I tried to buy her a disposable cell for emergencies, but she hates new technology."

Hmm. He tried to put himself in the mind of a middle-aged woman who clearly had a thing for schedules.

"Did you call her sister?"

The blue eyes flared with impatience. "Of course. She hasn't heard from Anne since yesterday."

"Have you checked the gardens?"

"Yes. The first thing I did was to search the grounds and the house in case she'd fallen." She bit her lower lip. "I'm really worried, Mike."

He believed her. Payton could be shallow, and self-absorbed, but it was obvious she cared about the missing housekeeper.

And he couldn't deny he was increasingly concerned.

He pulled out a blank piece of paper and began jotting down notes.

"What time does Anne usually go for her walk?"

"She comes down around eight to start the coffee," Payton said. "Then she goes for an hour walk before showering and starting breakfast around nine thirty."

"Nine thirty?" His lips twisted even as he continued to write down the pertinent information.

"None of us are early risers," she said in defensive

tones. “Well, except Dad, who is out of the house before six. He never eats breakfast.”

“Does she walk alone?”

“Usually.”

Lifting his head, he met her anxious gaze. “Look, I can’t call this a missing person case.”

“But—”

“But I’ll send a deputy to the estate to do a more thorough search if she isn’t back by this evening.” He overrode her protest. “That’s all I can do.”

“Fine.”

Sending him a glare that assured him he’d once again proved to be a gigantic disappointment, she gave a toss of her head and turned to march toward the door.

A familiar sense of frustration raced through him and, before he could squash the impulse, he was calling out her name.

“Payton.”

She grudgingly halted, turning to face him. “Yes?”

Mike rose to his feet. “I heard Christopher is back.”

He watched the expression on her beautiful face become wary. Not surprising. Christopher had been a blight on the precious Hamilton name since he was caught stealing cigarettes when he was just ten years old.

He’d also been a source of contention between Mike and the powerful family since he became sheriff. They had the belief that he would follow in the footsteps of his predecessor and turn a blind eye to Christopher’s . . . what had they called them? Shenanigans?

He called them misdemeanors that were escalating to felonies. And worse, he suspected the young man had an addiction problem that none of them wanted to admit.

Not that they would listen to his warnings.

“He is.”

"He isn't working?"

"He's looking." She shrugged. "Jobs aren't that easy to find in the area."

"What about the family business?"

She arched a brow. "Could you work for your father?"

Mike shuddered. His father had been a local mechanic. Nothing wrong with that, except he'd been a mean drunk who'd beaten his three sons on a regular basis.

"Nope. But I never lived off his money either," he said in pointed tones. "I left the nest when I was eighteen."

She flinched as his jab slid home. Then she deliberately allowed her gaze to flick over him with an arrogance that set his teeth on edge.

"Aren't you special."

"Nothing special about me," he countered. "I'm just one of the commoners, remember?"

The blue eyes darkened before she was jerkily moving out of the office, slamming the door shut behind her.

Mike grimaced. What was wrong with him? Okay, he'd been dumped. It wasn't the first time. Heck, it wasn't even the last time. Jaci had stopped going out with him over the past few months.

It was unprofessional to let his wounded pride make him act like an ass.

Flopping back in his seat, he swiveled to glance out the window. The rain splattered from low-hanging clouds, the wind catching the nearby swings and making them sway as if being pushed by a ghostly form.

It was eerie as hell.

A chill inched down his spine and it was almost a relief when the intercom buzzed. Turning back toward the desk, he grabbed the phone and pressed it to his ear.

"What's up, Carol?"

"Ed called to say that he e-mailed the pictures you asked him to take."

Mike pressed his fingers against the headache forming at his temple. Ed Preston was a part-time deputy who had a skill with computers that was badly needed in the department. Mike had called him to take pictures of the body and skull before they'd been moved.

The rural area didn't have an official police photographer. Why would they? There hadn't been a murder in years. If they needed pictures of vandalism, or during the raid of a local meth house, Mike clicked a few pics with his phone.

But an unknown woman and a skull needed to be photographed by someone who could put them in a program where they could be enlarged and sent off to the federal authorities if it became necessary.

"Thanks, Carol," he said. "I'll take a look at them later."

After he'd completed the thousand other tasks on his to-do list.

Chapter Five

Rylan knelt on the damp porch, an unconscious Jaci gathered in his arms. He was acutely aware of just how fragile she felt as he snuggled her against his chest. Strange. When she was awake she was so lush and vivid and full of life that she seemed invincible.

Now . . .

A mixture of fear and fury thundered through him.

Who was depraved enough to leave the locket on the door? It had to be someone with enough balls to waltz up to her house in broad daylight. Or at least he assumed it hadn't been there when she'd left for her morning deliveries.

And what did it mean? There was no doubt it was some sort of a threat. But what? Was it just a way to terrorize the young woman?

Or was it something more evil?

And the million-dollar question: did the locket have any connection to the dead woman found floating in the field?

The questions whirled through his mind, and it wasn't until the porch creaked that he realized his father was moving toward the screen door.

"No," he said, his sharp tone bringing his father to an immediate stop. "Don't touch it."

Elmer pointed a gnarled finger toward the locket. "I don't want that filthy thing hanging here when Jaci wakes up."

"I know, but the sheriff needs to see it."

His father scowled, but he eventually gave a sharp nod. "I'll call once we get her inside. You carry her."

Rylan straightened, careful not to jostle Jaci. "We'll go around the back," he said.

He didn't know if the sheriff would actually treat the porch like a crime scene, considering no actual laws had been broken, but he didn't want to take the chance of ruining any evidence that might lead to the culprit.

Letting his father take the lead, he headed off the porch and circled to the back of the house. Holding Jaci tight in his arms, he carefully surveyed their soggy surroundings.

He assumed that whoever had left the locket had taken off, but there was no guarantee. He wasn't going to let himself be caught off guard.

He absently noticed that the garage had been expanded since his last visit. And that there was a new greenhouse at the back of the yard. The barn looked the same, although he could hear the sound of two very angry dogs barking from inside.

They were new.

Convinced there were no mystery lurkers in the shadows, he continued along the mossy pathway.

"Do you have a spare key?" he asked his father as they climbed the narrow stairs that groaned beneath their weight.

Elmer snorted as he glanced over his shoulder. "You've been gone too long."

"Why?"

"You've forgotten that no one around here locks their house."

Proving his point, his father reached to pull on the knob.

"Are you kidding?" Rylan snapped as the door easily swung open. When he'd lived in the area he'd never thought about whether or not people had sturdy locks. Now he felt a stab of annoyance at the knowledge that Jaci had allowed herself to be in such a vulnerable position. "She's a woman living on her own in the middle of nowhere."

"I doubt her grandparents ever locked the house," Elmer said, nodding toward the distant barn. "Besides, she has a couple of big dogs that are better than any fancy alarm system."

"Really? They're great help locked in the barn," Rylan said as they entered the narrow mudroom.

They both managed to kick off their splattered boots before moving into the kitchen, which smelled like heaven.

Loaves of bread and freshly baked muffins and golden tarts were sitting on the butcher-block counters. There were fresh herbs growing in pots on the windowsill over the old farm sink. And on the small table in the center of the linoleum floor were bowls filled with peaches and apples and lush blueberries.

Any other time Rylan would have melted at the tantalizing smells. Today, he wasn't in the mood.

Elmer pointed toward the doorway that led to a short hall.

"Let's take her to the living room."

Following his father into the front of the house, he entered a small space that had been made cozy with an overstuffed sofa and two armchairs that were arranged around the brick fireplace. There was a glass cabinet filled with the trinkets Jaci's grandmother had accumulated during their rare travels away from home.

A stuffed pig from the Iowa State Fair. A tiny replica of the Liberty Bell. A snow globe from Chicago. Hand-painted thimbles. And of course, the obligatory collection of Hummel figurines.

Exactly what a person would expect in a farmhouse.

The only thing that didn't fit were the large black-and-white photos on the walls that were framed with rough planks of wood. One was a rain-blurred picture of an abandoned warehouse overgrown with ivy. Another was a ghost town surrounded by a desolate, barren landscape.

"Just put her on the couch," Elmer commanded, hovering with concern as Rylan gently lowered her onto the deep cushions. "Poor thing."

Keeping his gaze trained on Jaci's too pale face, Rylan straightened and nodded toward the nearby telephone. In the more remote areas it was almost impossible to get a clear cell connection. Landlines were still a necessary household item.

"Call the sheriff," he ordered, reaching to tug off her boots. Then, too restless to wait for the authorities, he retraced his steps. "Stay in here with Jaci."

"Where are you going?" his father asked.

"To have a look around."

Moving back through the kitchen, he placed Jaci's boots in the mudroom and pulled on his own before he was out the back door.

He took time to glance in the windows of the barn. The dogs released furious growls as soon as he stepped out of the house, warning him to wait until Jaci could convince the animals he wasn't an enemy before he released them.

The angry response to his approach, however, proved that an unknown intruder couldn't be hiding inside.

He moved to the garage, surprised to find that it'd been converted into a large workroom with towering shelves loaded with various boxes of supplies that were clearly marked. In the center of the room she had a few small tools, including a circular saw and a sewing machine.

A woman of many talents.

Stepping out of the garage, he walked to study the driveway. At one time it'd been graveled, but the mud combined with the ruts from the tractor had turned it into a messy bog. Which meant he couldn't determine what sort of vehicle the intruder had been driving when he—or she—had delivered the locket.

He rounded the house, walking up to the front porch. There were muddy prints where the three of them had climbed the steps. But it was too much to hope that the rain hadn't washed away any earlier ones.

Crossing the wooden planks, he leaned forward, studying the small locket that dangled from the doorknob.

It had a dull sheen in the gray light, revealing it wasn't real gold. The locket itself was plain, with a tiny clasp on the side. There was nothing to distinguish it. In fact, he'd guess that it was one of those cheap necklaces you could mass order.

Which meant it would be almost impossible to trace who'd bought it.

Still, he pulled his cell phone out of his pocket and took several pictures, careful not to disturb the necklace. He had a few connections among the feds. Some of them high enough up the food chain to get him whatever information he needed.

Sending off the images to his contacts, he pocketed his phone and turned to leave the porch.

Ducking his head as the rain drizzled down his face, he hurried around the house and entered through the back door. He kicked off his boots before he was walking through the kitchen and back to the living room.

He found his father still standing at the edge of the sofa, keeping guard over the unconscious woman.

"Did you get ahold of the sheriff?" he asked.

Elmer nodded. "He's on his way."

There was a soft moan as Jaci began to stir.

"I'll make some hot coffee," the older man said. Clearly he had the same need as Rylan to feel as if he was doing something to help.

"Put in plenty of sugar," Rylan called after the older man, moving to perch on the edge of the sofa.

Jaci's lashes fluttered upward, revealing her blue-gray eyes that looked almost silver in the dim light. Her brows drew together as she caught sight of him looming over her.

"Rylan?"

"It's me," he assured her.

Some indefinable emotion rippled over her face before her expression hardened.

"I knew this was a nightmare," she said, shoving herself into a seated position.

With a grimace she swayed, nearly tumbling face-first off the couch before she managed to regain her equilibrium.

A wry smile twisted Rylan's lips. Over the years he'd become accustomed to women who were eager to please him. No doubt it was good for his ego to have it bashed on occasion.

"How do you feel?" he asked.

She wrinkled her nose. "Like an idiot."

"Why? You had a shock."

"Yeah." She shuddered, her gaze darting toward the front door. "Where's the locket?"

"We left it where it was," he said. "I'm hoping the sheriff will have it examined."

Her eyes widened, as if he'd just said he'd set the house on fire.

"The sheriff?"

"Dad already called."

"Why?"

He studied her pale face. "If they run it through the system, they might be able to get fingerprints or DNA off it," he said. "Something that will tell us who left the locket here."

Her jaw tightened. "I remember bringing you lockets before," she pointed out in dark tones. "You told me I was being silly."

Guilt sliced through Rylan. He'd started working in the sheriff's office when he was just sixteen. At first he was a glorified janitor, cleaning the jail and washing the vehicles. But when he'd started attending the nearby college to get his degree in criminal justice, he'd taken on more duties and eventually become a part-time deputy.

That was when Jaci had first started showing up at the office with the lockets. And when he'd turned her away with a lecture that she shouldn't be wasting his time.

"I was young and arrogant."

Her sharp, painful laugh only intensified his sense of regret. "You thought I bought the lockets and put the hair and bloody ribbon in them to get your attention."

He was instantly on the defense. "You did have a crush on me."

Her eyes flashed with anger. "I was a hormonal sixteen-year-old girl, Rylan. I had a crush on Justin Timberlake, Orlando Bloom, and my English teacher," she snapped. "I didn't send them any bloody lockets."

He released a heavy sigh. She was right to chastise him. He'd been an ass all those years ago. At the time he'd told himself he was doing what was best for her. After all, she'd been following him around for years, her big eyes begging for some hint of affection. He needed to make sure that she forgot him and found some nice farm boy.

Looking back, he realized that his reaction to Jaci Patterson was far more complicated than he'd ever suspected.

"I'm sorry, Jaci," he said, reaching out to touch her cheek with the tips of his fingers. "At the time it seemed impossible to believe there could be a crazed stalker in Heron."

"And now?" she demanded, knocking his hand away.

Rylan felt a strange twist in his gut at her rejection.

"Now I'm not nearly so young," he admitted.

"What about arrogant?"

"That's never going to change." He spoke the words they were both thinking. "But I've learned to think past my ego."

She rolled her eyes. "Shocking."

He leaned back in the cushions. The smell of brewing coffee filled the air, emphasizing the coziness of the room. It made the thought of someone creeping onto the porch to leave behind some sicko gift all the more awful.

"Jaci, I know you weren't lying about those lockets."

"Because a new one showed up?" she scoffed. "How can you be sure I didn't stage all this for your benefit?"

He shook his head. "You might be stubborn. And overly independent. And eager to speak your mind, even if it pisses people off. But you're honest to a fault."

"Thanks." She sent him a wary frown. "I think."

"If you wanted to capture my attention you might have shown up in my bedroom naked."

Her mouth fell open. "Hey."

"But you wouldn't have pretended to be in danger," he continued.

"No." She shivered. Whether from the memory of the

person who'd left her the lockets years ago, or the thought that the mystery stalker might be back, he didn't know.

Probably both.

Clearly she was in need of a distraction.

He deliberately allowed his gaze to drift down to the inviting curve of her lips.

"And just for the record, if you decide to show up in my bedroom naked now, I wouldn't say no," he assured her in throaty tones.

A charming blush stained her cheeks. "In your dreams."

"Probably," he agreed, his tone teasing. Inside, however, he acknowledged that she was most definitely going to play a starring role in his dreams.

Her lips parted, but before she could speak, the sound of a car door being slammed shut echoed through the air, quickly followed by the distant sound of barking. Her blush instantly faded.

"Someone's here."

Rylan was on his feet, swiftly crossing to glance out the front window.

"Those dogs aren't doing you any good locked in the barn," he said.

"They were muddy after I let them out this morning and I didn't have time to wash them before I had to take off for my deliveries."

"It's the sheriff," he said, watching as Mike O'Brien climbed out of a pickup he'd parked in the road, and headed across the yard toward the front porch. Rylan turned from the window. "I want to have a word with him."

Jaci started to rise to her feet. "I—"

"You sit back down, missy," Elmer commanded as he returned to the living room with a tray clutched in his hands. "You're not to get off that couch until you've had a hot cup of coffee and a muffin."

Rylan sent her a smirk. "You heard the boss."

"I need to speak to Mike."

"I'm sure he'll come in whenever he's had a chance to look around," he assured her, moving to lay a hand on her shoulder so he could gently press her back onto the sofa. "Just relax."

"Yeah, right," she said, but surprisingly she settled in the cushions and allowed Elmer to place the tray on her lap.

Was she still in shock?

The thought spurred Rylan to once again head out the back door so he could round the house. By the time he was climbing the steps onto the porch, the sheriff was carefully sliding the locket into a small evidence bag.

Mike swiveled his head to watch as Rylan moved to stand near the front door, his expression impossible to read.

The two had worked together at the sheriff's office, but they hadn't been particularly close. Mike was a year younger than Rylan and there'd been an unspoken competition that had extended beyond the sheriff's office to sports, girls, and even who had the fastest car.

Did that explain the sizzle of aggression he sensed in the air? Or was it new?

Rylan stiffened. Was it territorial? Did he have a thing for Jaci?

The thought was oddly annoying.

Mike gave a dip of his head. "Cooper."

Rylan returned the nod. "O'Brien."

Mike's gaze shifted to the front window, his expression tightening as he caught sight of Jaci perched on the couch with Rylan's father fussing around her.

"How is she?"

"Spooked," Rylan said in clipped tones, pointing

toward the evidence bag in Mike's hand that contained the locket. "Did you open it?"

"No." He tucked the bag inside his black Windbreaker, which had the sheriff patches sewn on the sleeves. "I'm sending it off to the forensics department in Jefferson City. I don't want to lose any potential evidence."

Rylan arched a brow. He'd expected a fight to get the man to spend money on having the locket inspected by experts.

"So you're taking this as a serious threat?"

Mike's square jaw tightened. "Today has been filled with nothing but trouble. I think it's best that I take everything as a serious threat."

"Good."

Mike finally turned away from the window, the aggression still thick in the air.

"Why are you here?"

Rylan met the fierce gaze with a bland smile. "Dad was worried about Jaci when he heard there was a body floating in the neighbor's field."

Without warning, Mike grimaced. "Yeah, I wish I'd been more worried."

"More worried about the body?"

"No. Jaci. She came to see me this morning. I was literally up to my ass in mud and I"—he gave a sharp shake of his head—"I told her not to bring up the past. I should have taken her concern more seriously."

"A lot of us can make that claim," Rylan said, regret clenching his heart.

It was bad enough to think that Jaci had truly been terrorized when she was young and vulnerable without adding in the knowledge he, and a lot of other people, had branded her a liar. It was a wonder she hadn't slapped his face the minute she'd caught sight of him.

His dark thoughts were interrupted as a car pulled up behind the pickup at the edge of the road.

"Who's that?" Rylan asked.

Mike nodded toward the two uniformed men who were crawling out of the car and heading in their direction.

"They're my deputies," he said, watching as the men approached. "I asked Ed out here to take pictures of any tracks, and Sid will check for DNA and prints on the doorknob."

"Not a bad thought," Rylan said as he glanced toward the drive. "But I'm not sure you'll have any luck with tracks. Most of them have been destroyed."

Moving to the edge of the porch, Mike glared at the ruts with a deep scowl. Clearly he hadn't noticed the destruction when he'd walked up to the house.

"Crap." Grabbing the railing, he leaned over to study the tracks that led past the house. "It looks like Andrew is out checking the fields. Probably destroyed any usable tire imprints."

"Convenient."

Mike turned to meet Rylan's suspicious expression. The lawman gave a slow nod.

They might never be friends, but they had an unspoken commitment to discover if Jaci was truly in danger. And to stop the bastard who was determined to frighten her.

"I'm going to have a word with Ed, then I'll come in to talk to Jaci," he said. "Don't use the front door until Sid is done."

Rylan nodded, heading toward the steps. He halted as he caught sight of a blue sedan creeping past the house. He assumed that he was a nosy neighbor who was trying to see what was happening. But as soon as the sheriff turned, whoever was driving the car gunned the engine to speed down the muddy road. Almost as if the driver was wary of being seen.

"Who was that?" Rylan demanded.

Mike frowned, his hand reaching to touch the handgun that was holstered at his side.

"It looked like Jaci's half brother, Christopher Hamilton."

Chapter Six

On some level Jaci knew that Elmer was keeping up a running conversation, but it was impossible to make out the words over the buzzing in her head. And thankfully the older man didn't seem to expect a response as he coaxed her to drink the overly sweet coffee and eat one of the muffins she'd baked earlier that morning.

God, it seemed a lifetime ago.

Since then, a dead body had been found floating in a field. And a skull. The sheriff had dismissed her fears as if she was a whackadoodle. She'd endured a meeting with her mother. And her mysterious stalker had made a return, leaving one of his creepy lockets for her to find.

She didn't know which was worse.

As she finished the muffin, however, the sugar kicked in and her shock began to ease. At least enough to be aware of the sound of the back door closing and Rylan moving to stand next to the sofa.

Tilting her head, she felt the familiar jolt of awareness.

The same awareness she'd felt when she'd returned home to see Rylan standing in her front yard. And again when she'd opened her eyes minutes ago to find him bending over her, his expression tight with concern.

Heck, she'd been aware of this man since she first understood the difference between boys and girls.

From a very young age, Rylan had been stunningly handsome. His features were finely chiseled, with a proud, aquiline nose and wide brow. His eyes had always been a fascinating shade of gold, but they were emphasized since his move to California, where his skin had been tanned to a rich bronze and his hair had been bleached to a light blond.

He also had the sort of body that made a woman itch to run her hands over every inch of his hard, perfectly sculpted muscles.

But it was his raw, male power that captured and held her attention. He had a potent energy that could fill a room and stir a woman's deepest fantasy.

It was really no surprise she'd been plagued by a desperate puppy love for her gorgeous neighbor. Even when he'd made it painfully clear that he wasn't, and never would be interested in her as more than a friend.

She was a young woman in a town where gorgeous men were few and far between. The only surprise would be if she hadn't been obsessed with Rylan Cooper.

Now she grimly squashed her predictable response to his presence as she glanced toward the window. She could hear people moving around her porch, but she couldn't see anyone.

"Where's Mike?" she demanded.

Rylan's gaze moved to the tray she'd set on the low coffee table, as if assessing whether or not he was satisfied with how much she'd managed to eat.

"He's doling out duties to his deputies," he at last said. "He'll be in once he's done."

She frowned in confusion. "What duties?"

"Dusting for prints and taking pictures."

"Pictures? Of what?"

"I asked Ed to photograph your driveway as well as the yard for any footprints," Mike explained as he entered the living room, clearly having used the back door. "It's a long shot, but it's better than nothing."

"Mike." She managed a shaky smile as she watched her friend move across the room, taking a seat on the sofa next to her.

"Hey, Jaci." He removed his hat, then reached to take her hand so he could give it a tight squeeze. "I'm so sorry. I should have listened to you earlier."

She wrinkled her nose. "It doesn't matter now."

"It does, but we'll discuss it later," he said. Mike was the sort of person who was always harder on himself than anyone else. He glanced toward the looming Rylan. "We'll need some privacy."

Rylan frowned, clearly not happy. "Why?"

Elmer moved to grab his son's arm. "Come on, Ry."

Rylan dug in his heels. "No."

Mike narrowed his gaze. "Is there a problem?"

"Yeah," Rylan said, his jaw tight. "Jaci just suffered a severe shock. I'm not leaving her here alone."

Mike scowled. "She's not alone."

With a firm tug, Elmer was urging his son out of the room. "We'll be in the kitchen."

Mike watched them leave before he turned his attention back to Jaci.

"Is there something I should know?"

She gave a slow shake of her head. Rylan had always been the sort of guy who stuck up for the underdog. He'd punched the local bully, Joey Burke, in the nose for picking on the younger boys. And risked his neck to save a baby duck that was trapped in an abandoned well.

Was he feeling some need to be her protector because she'd fainted?

Or was it a symptom of his guilt because he hadn't believed her when she'd asked for his help all those years ago?

"I think the world's gone insane," she said.

"Me too," Mike agreed. He sounded like his day had been almost as crappy as Jaci's. Quite a feat. "Now tell me about the locket."

Jaci gave an abbreviated version of her return home to find the necklace hanging on her doorknob.

She didn't need to share her breathless reaction when she'd first caught sight of Rylan. Or her awkward haste to get rid of him, which explained why she hadn't noticed the locket until she was just inches from the door.

Mike nodded, reaching beneath his jacket to pull out a small notebook and pencil that he'd no doubt bought at the local dollar store. In this area, cops had a limited budget. They had to trim costs whenever possible.

"Did you notice anyone when you were driving home?"

Assuming he meant after she'd turned onto the gravel road that ran in front of her house, she gave a shake of her head.

"No." She stiffened as she recalled the SUV. "Oh."

"What?"

"I thought I saw Blake, but I can't imagine what he'd be doing out here." She shrugged. "Besides, I spoke to Mother when I was in Baldwin and she mentioned he was flying back from St. Louis later tonight."

A strange expression settled on his blunt features. "What about Christopher?"

"What about him?"

"Did you see him today?"

She stared at him in confusion. "I haven't seen my half

brother for almost two years, although I heard he's back home," she said.

Mike didn't bother to write anything in his notebook. Instead he abruptly changed the direction of his questions.

"Is there anyone you can think of who would want to scare you?"

It was a question that had haunted her for years. "No."

"Any enemies?" He held up a hand as her lips parted. "Even if you don't think they would leave the locket?"

"No."

"You're sure?" he pressed. "You're a beautiful woman with a growing business. That can make people jealous. Especially if they think your success has come at their expense."

She forced herself to consider his words.

It was true that there had been a few local ladies who had their noses out of joint at the high demand for her pastries. And there had been at least two farmers who'd tried to pressure her into selling her grandfather's land after his death.

But they certainly weren't her enemies.

Well, not unless she counted her half sister, Payton. But she couldn't make herself believe the younger woman would sneak around to try and terrify her. She far preferred being a bitch in public.

"I really can't think of anyone," Jaci insisted.

Mike tapped his pencil on the notebook. "There haven't been any other threats?"

"What do you mean?"

"Strange phone calls? Letters? E-mails?"

She frowned with impatience. Why was he wasting time?

"Mike, we both know this isn't about some neighbor who's pissed off about me baking muffins or selling crafts in my garage. The locket has something to do with that body you found this morning."

His lips flattened. "I don't want to leap to conclusions."

She flinched, disappointment slicing through her. How many times did she have to go through this?

First the fear. The knowledge some sicko was out there playing with her emotions. Then the pain at the realization that no one believed her.

"Right."

She started to stand, only to be halted when Mike placed a restraining hand on her shoulder.

"Jaci, I'm trying to protect you," he growled. "Something I can't do if I don't keep an open mind and investigate every potential threat."

There was a sincerity etched on his face that made her heave a small sigh.

"I'm sorry." She wrapped her arms around her waist. She felt chilled to the bone. "I just can't believe this is starting again."

His hand lightly glided over her shoulder and down her arm. "You know you can stay with me until we figure this out."

It was tempting. Not only because she was a little itchy at the thought of remaining in such an isolated spot on her own. But because no lunatic would dare to try and get to her while she was in the protective custody of the sheriff.

Only the knowledge that she couldn't hide in Mike's house forever made her stiffen her backbone.

She had a life. And this was her home.

She wasn't going to let the mysterious jerk steal either of them from her.

"Thanks, but I need to stay here," she said.

He frowned. "Jaci."

"I have Riff and Raff." She overrode his protest. "I'll make sure they stay in the house with me."

Having dated Jaci, if only for a short time, Mike knew better than to argue.

"You have your grandfather's shotgun?" he instead asked.

She nodded toward the narrow door across the room. "It's in the coat closet."

She didn't like guns, but her grandfather had insisted she learn to shoot. If only to scare off stray animals.

"Keep it loaded," Mike ordered, tucking away his notebook before he reached for his hat.

"I will," she promised.

Mike stood, placing his hat on his head as he glanced toward the doorway leading to the back of the house.

"Do you want me to get rid of Cooper for you?"

She shook her head even as she wondered at the strange animosity between the two men.

Weird.

She would never understand the opposite sex.

"I can handle Rylan," she said.

Her confidence didn't come from any hope she could actually control her aggravating neighbor, but the knowledge he would soon walk out of her house. There was a good chance she wouldn't see him again for months. Maybe years.

She pretended she didn't notice the odd pang of disappointment.

Mike crossed the short distance to the front door. Jaci assumed that meant they were done collecting any evidence.

"You're sure he's not the one who left the locket?" he abruptly demanded.

"You mean Rylan?" she asked in surprise.

"Yeah." The sheriff shrugged. "They stopped showing up when he left town and now he's back."

"They stopped when *I* left town," she corrected, not believing for a second that Rylan had anything to do with the necklaces.

"Just keep your eyes open," he warned.

Jaci made a sound of annoyance. Seriously, what was going on between the two men?

"I will."

Mike was stepping out of the house when he paused to glance over his shoulder.

"One last question," he said.

"What?"

"You didn't happen to see Anne Dixon today, did you?"

It took Jaci a minute to place the name.

"My mother's housekeeper?"

"Yes."

She tried to think back. Most of the morning was a blur. She'd not only been rushed, but she had been distracted by the news of the dead body.

Still, she was fairly certain she hadn't seen the woman who'd been a steadfast fixture in her mother's house for years.

"No," she said. "Why?"

"Just wondering." His expression was unreadable. "Call me if you see or hear anything that bothers you. I'll have Sid do drive-bys as often as he can."

"Thanks, Mike."

Waiting until he'd stepped off the porch and headed for his pickup, Jaci impulsively rose from the couch and moved to lock the door. It ticked her off that she no longer felt safe in her own home, but she wasn't going to take foolish risks just to prove a point.

Until they found out who left the locket, she intended to take every precaution.

With a last glance out the window, she turned to walk into the kitchen. She found Rylan leaning against the counter, his phone in his hand as if he'd just finished a call.

A strange sensation swirled through the pit of her stomach. When they were young Rylan had occasionally stopped by to help her grandfather with changing the tire on a tractor, or repairing a fence. Just because that was the sort of boy he was. But she couldn't remember him ever lingering in the house for more than a few minutes.

Now she felt as if he'd sucked all the oxygen out of the kitchen.

Like a black hole.

Regarding her with a piercing gaze, he jerked his chin toward the doorway behind her.

"Is O'Brien gone?"

"Yes." She ignored the edge in his voice. Whatever beef he had with Mike was none of her business. She glanced around the small space. "Where's Elmer?"

Rylan pointed toward a window overlooking the backyard. "He's in the barn hosing off your two monsters. He claimed they knew him well enough not to take off a limb."

A portion of the tension eased as a smile touched her lips. She adored her goofy dogs. Even when they were turning over her trash, or digging up her garden, or chasing the neighbor's cows.

"They love your father," she said. "He sneaks them table scraps when he comes to visit."

"He misses Truman," Rylan said, referring to their old golden retriever who'd died the year before.

Without thinking, Jaci stepped toward him. Almost as if she intended to wrap him in her arms to comfort him for the loss of his family pet.

Yeesh. She really was rattled.

Coming to a halt, she forced a smile to her lips. "I appreciate you carrying me into the house and sticking around until Mike could get here, but I—"

"Where's your purse?" he rudely interrupted.

She frowned. "What?"

He straightened, shoving his phone in his front pocket. "I've discovered that women always feel the need to carry around half their belongings whenever they leave the house."

She grimaced. She really didn't need him to point out he was an expert on women.

"You do realize you're not making any sense?"

"We need to do some shopping," he said, as if that clarified everything.

She started to give a shake of her head, only to abruptly remember that she'd gone shopping just before she'd returned home.

"Oh, I forgot my groceries."

He held up a slender hand. "I got them off the porch while you were talking to O'Brien and put them away." A boyish smile curled his lips. "Although it's possible you might have to do a scavenger hunt to find them."

She refused to be charmed. "Thanks. I need them to get started on my baking."

"Nope." He folded his arms over his chest. "The baking will have to wait. We have things to do."

She made a sound of frustration. Couldn't the man take a hint?

"What things?"

"We'll start with buying an electronic surveillance system."

"I . . ." Her words trailed away. Her instinct was to argue, but thankfully she wasn't so stubborn she was willing to cut off her nose to spite her face. She'd just told herself that she was going to do everything possible to keep herself safe. And besides, she'd been planning on getting a security system since she'd started her small craft business. The only problem had been finding someone who was competent in setting it up for her. "Do you know how to install one?" she demanded.

His lips twitched. Had she said something funny?

"I can make this house as secure as the Pentagon," he assured her.

"I don't need anything that fancy, but it would be nice to know when a customer is waiting at the shop."

"Trust me, I can do better than that," he said dryly.

Hmm. A part of her wanted to say no. She'd spent a lot of time and emotional energy eleven years ago trying to convince this male she was being stalked by some pervert. Now she wanted to tell him that he could take his offer of help and shove it.

Then she gave a mental shrug. Her pride wasn't worth being in danger. Besides, Rylan would soon be headed back to California. Why not take advantage of his expertise?

"I need to shower and change my clothes."

"I'll go get my dad's truck and pick you up in half an hour," he said, already moving toward the mudroom.

Chapter Seven

Mike had intended to return to his office. He needed to log in the evidence they'd collected at Jaci's house and drive it down to the lab in Jefferson City.

Instead, he'd handed the duty over to his deputies, warning them to return as quickly as possible. Then, ignoring the turnoff that would take him to Heron, he instead drove toward the high bluff where a large mansion loomed like a monument to the excess of the ruling class.

Reaching the ornate gates, he rolled down his window to push a button on the intercom. Minutes passed before the barrier slid open and he could continue up the winding drive to pull to a halt in front of the plantation-style home.

Mike climbed out of his truck with a wry grimace.

He'd lived in the area most of his life, and even dated Payton, but he'd been invited to the mansion fewer than a dozen times.

Which would explain why he was still overwhelmed by the sight of the grand veranda that was framed by white, fluted columns and an upper balcony. The house itself was made of red brick with two long wings that ran along the ridge of the bluff. The high windows were designed to offer a view of the nearby river, as well as the manicured grounds.

It was stately and imposing and a tangible reminder that the Hamiltons lived in a different world. Wealth and privilege made sure that they didn't have to follow the same rules as others.

Locking his truck, he climbed the steps to the wide veranda, not surprised when one of the double doors was yanked open to reveal Payton.

She was the only one who would have buzzed him through the gates without demanding to know why he was there.

He strolled toward her, absently noting that she'd changed since he'd last seen her. Now she was wearing a pair of jeans and a soft cashmere sweater.

Unfortunately, the casual style did nothing to distract from her luminous beauty. In fact, it took every ounce of willpower not to let his gaze linger on the gentle swell of her breasts.

He clearly needed to find a woman.

A damned shame Jaci wasn't interested.

Watching his approach, Payton lifted a hand to her lips. "Oh my God. It was Anne, wasn't it?"

He blinked, caught off guard by her dramatic reaction. "Excuse me?"

"I just heard about the woman you found floating in the field," she breathed in a shaky voice. "You came here to tell me it was Anne."

He reached out to lightly touch her shoulder. She wasn't acting. She truly was distressed at the thought the housekeeper was dead.

"No, Payton, it wasn't Anne," he said.

She bit her bottom lip, her eyes damp with tears. "You're sure?"

"I'm sure."

Her hand lowered, but her troubled expression remained. "Then who was it?"

He'd spent the morning trying to scrub away the image of the poor female. She'd been ravaged, although he didn't have the expertise to know if it was from natural decomposition, from being in the water, or from the fish.

Still, there'd been enough of her left to come to a few conclusions.

"She hasn't been identified, but she was much younger than Anne and I'm guessing she wasn't local," he said, not adding the sight was going to give him more than one nightmare.

His hope now was that the unknown woman had drowned during the flood, and that she had no connection to the locket that'd been left on Jaci's door.

Or the missing housekeeper.

"Oh." She released a small sigh before her brows drew together. "Then why are you here?"

"I wanted to see if Anne was still missing." He grimaced. "Obviously she is."

Payton nodded. "Yes."

"I'll take a look around."

"Wait," she commanded as he started to turn around. "I want to go with you."

His lips parted to tell her to stay inside. Not just because a chilled drizzle continued to fall from the clouds, but because he intended to look for more than a missing housekeeper.

But he swallowed his protest, waiting for her to grab her coat and join him on the porch. If he was on his own, one of the Hamilton family might see him and demand he leave the property. It wasn't like he had a search warrant.

And besides, Payton would be able to answer any questions he might have.

With brisk steps, Payton led him down the stairs and toward the high hedge that ran along one wing of the house.

"She usually walks through the gardens," she said, her shoes crunching against the graveled drive.

At least she'd changed out of her ridiculously high heels.

"Do you have any other servants?" he asked, his gaze sweeping over the house. He counted three side doors, a set of French doors, and a dozen windows. It would be a simple matter to enter or leave the house without being noticed.

"None that live on the property since our gardener retired a couple years ago."

They entered the sunken garden between a break in the hedge. Walking down the pathway, Mike gave a cursory glance around the flower beds that were covered with layers of mulch and the fountains that had been drained to endure the harsh winter months. There was nowhere a person could be hidden. Instead he studied the hedge that surrounded them. It was high enough that only someone from the second floor of the house could see into the garden.

"Who takes care of your grounds?" he asked.

"Jarrod Walker, who comes three days a week," she said. "He's in charge of the gardens and the pool, as well as doing any handiwork in the house."

Mike felt a stab of surprise. Jarrod Walker was the uncle of his deputy, Sid. He hadn't realized the older man had started working for the Hamiltons.

"Is it his day to work?"

"No." They passed a trellised grotto before entering the

formal rose garden. "He comes on Monday, Wednesday, and Friday."

Mike studied the ground, searching for any hint of a struggle.

"What about a security system?"

Payton slowed her pace as they reached the back of the garden. "There are cameras at the front gate and in my father's office where he keeps most of the valuables."

He sent her a puzzled glance. "That's it?"

She shrugged. "My father hates the thought of the family being constantly monitored."

Hmm. Mike didn't believe for a minute there were only two cameras guarding an estate this size. What insurance company would write a policy without insisting they have a thorough security system?

So either Blake kept the other cameras hidden from his family, or Payton was lying to him.

Something he'd deal with if he concluded Anne's disappearance had anything to do with the dead woman in the field.

For now, he concentrated on the tall fence that surrounded the back of the gardens. It wasn't as ornate as the front of the house, but it was sturdy. It would take an effort to climb over it. And there was no way someone could get over the top with a body.

Anne didn't leave from the gardens.

So where was she?

"Let's check the outbuildings," he said.

She nodded, moving to lead him out a side gate that opened directly to the large pool that was still covered for the winter. A quick glance into the pool house proved it was empty, as was the outdoor kitchen area.

Together they moved to enter the long garage that had been converted from what had once been the stables.

Mike resisted the urge to roll his eyes as he caught sight of the cars that were parked in a perfect line. There was room for at least eight vehicles, although there were only seven currently inside the building.

He moved to the first car, peering inside before checking the trunk. Once assured that Anne wasn't hidden inside, he moved to the next car and did the same.

His brows rose as he moved to the third car. A blue sedan.

And not just any blue sedan. It was the same one he'd seen driving past Jaci's house less than two hours ago. He'd bet money on it.

"Who drives this?" he demanded, covertly moving to lay his hand on the hood.

Still warm.

"It's my father's, but anyone in the house can use it," Payton said.

Mike opened the car door, noting the mud on the floor mat on the driver's side. Not that it told him anything. There weren't many places in the Midwest that weren't coated in mud.

"Christopher?" he asked, reaching next to the steering wheel to press the button that opened the trunk.

Payton looked confused as he strolled to the back of the car and peered into the empty compartment.

"He could, but he has his own car," she said, nodding toward the black Jaguar.

Mike glanced toward the automobile. Sleek. Fast. And outrageously noticeable in this area of pickups and SUVs.

"What's your interest in my brother?" Payton demanded, her expression suddenly wary.

He slammed the hood down, ignoring her question as he took a step back.

"Which one is Anne's?"

"The white compact."

Doing a quick check of the remaining automobiles, he moved to do a more thorough inspection of Anne's car. He looked under the seats and rifled through the glove compartment. Then he checked the trunk.

Nothing suspicious.

He stepped back, his gaze scanning the open area of the garage. There was a workbench that looked as if it'd never been used. Tall, metal shelves. And a rack with two carbon fiber road bikes that Mike suspected belonged to Payton. It was her preferred method of exercise.

His attention was captured by a narrow door. "Where does that lead?"

Payton moved forward to pull it open. "The wine cellars."

Mike followed her down the spiral staircase, making a choked sound as he stepped into the wood-lined room that ran the entire length of the garage.

"This is bigger than my house," he said, strolling past the long shelves filled with countless bottles of wine.

He didn't add that it was probably worth more as well.

They both knew the Hamiltons were way out of his financial league.

Quickly able to determine that Anne wasn't in the cellar, they climbed the stairs and headed out of the garage.

"Are there any other places in the house you haven't looked?" he asked. "A basement or safe room?"

Payton gave a shake of her head, shivering as the raindrops ran down her pale face.

"I looked everywhere. The pantry, all the bathrooms." She gave a helpless lift of her hands. "Even the gym."

Mike nodded. He didn't doubt that Payton had done a thorough search. But he had an important task to accomplish before he was ready to leave.

"I'd like to see her rooms."

For the first time since his arrival Payton hesitated, glancing toward the house with an unreadable expression. Then, she visibly squared her shoulders.

"Okay, we'll use the servant's entrance," she told him, heading toward the door next to the back veranda.

He released a harsh laugh. "Ashamed to be seen with me, darling?"

She said something beneath her breath. It contained the word "ass," but he didn't think it was a compliment on his very fine backside.

"Mother didn't want me to contact the authorities," she said loud enough for him to hear.

"Why not?"

Payton pulled open the door and entered the small foyer. To the left was the old-fashioned butler's pantry and to the right was a narrow flight of stairs.

"She doesn't want any gossip until we're sure Anne is missing."

"Predictable," Mike growled as he climbed the steps.

He made no pretense that he was fond of Loreen Hamilton. In fact, he'd called her a cold, selfish bitch more than once.

What sort of mother allowed her oldest daughter to be raised by her former in-laws just so she could marry a rich businessman and start a new family?

And Mike didn't doubt for a minute that Loreen had put pressure on Payton to dump Mike so she could find a more suitable partner.

Reaching the second-floor landing, Payton pushed open the closest door and Mike stepped into a small sitting room.

He walked past the brocade love seat and the matching chair that were set near the window that had a view of the pool. The only other furniture was a wooden bookshelf filled with worn paperbacks.

There was an austerity to the room that he sensed came from the woman who lived there rather than any rules or regulations from her employers. He would guess that Anne Dixon was a woman who disliked clutter.

He moved into the bedroom, taking note of the black dress lying on the handmade quilt and the shoes set neatly near the door. He glanced into the small closet. There were two more black uniforms and a half-dozen velour jogging suits. He grimaced. He didn't know women still wore those things.

Turning away, he walked toward the small chair in the corner. A purse. It was possible, of course, that Anne had more than one, but she was too tidy to leave the spare one sitting around. It would be neatly tucked in the closet with her other belongings.

He continued into the attached bathroom, once again struck by the lack of clutter. The woman lived like a nun. After he pulled open the medicine cabinet above the sink, his lips tightened. There was a long, narrow, plastic container with the days of the week marked on top. A medicine organizer. And today's dose hadn't been taken.

The woman might have left without a note. And maybe even without her purse.

But she wouldn't take off without her medicine.

Reaching beneath his jacket, he pulled out a clear bag so he could collect Anne's brush, which had several strands of hair caught in the bristles.

"What are you doing?" Payton asked, watching as he tucked the bag in his pocket.

"I want her DNA."

She wrapped her arms around her waist. "You think something's happened to her," she said. "Something bad."

He held her gaze. "Don't you?"

There was a brief hesitation before she gave a slow nod. "Yes."

Mike barely resisted the urge to pull her into his arms. It wasn't his duty to comfort this woman. She'd made that painfully clear.

Abruptly pivoting on his heel, he walked quickly out of Anne's rooms. He didn't have time to be distracted.

Once Payton joined him in the hallway, he nodded toward the door she was pulling shut.

"I want the rooms kept locked," he said. "Can you do that?"

"Yeah." Her expression was grim. "There's a spare key in the kitchen."

About to head down the stairs, he glanced back at his companion.

"Is your father home?"

She looked predictably confused. "No, he's in St. Louis today. He'll fly home tonight."

"The six o'clock flight?"

"Yes. Why?"

He shrugged. He wasn't about to share the fact that Jaci had seen him on the isolated road to her house.

"I might have a few questions for him," he said, making a mental note to drive to the small airport north of Baldwin that provided commuter flights to St. Louis.

He intended to see for himself if Blake Hamilton got off the plane.

"I can have him give you a call when he gets home," Payton said, remaining close behind him as they climbed down the stairs.

"I can wait," he assured her. "At least for now."

He moved across the foyer. He needed to get back to his office and start calling in a few favors.

"You'll let me know if you find Anne?" Payton asked, halting at the door as he stepped onto the veranda.

"Of course," he promised. "Call me if you see or hear anything unusual."

"I will."

He paused to send her a warning glance. "And, Payton."

"Yes?"

"Be careful."

Eagerness blasted through him as he made his way to his hidden cabin deep in the woods. Not a normal eagerness. He'd understood from a very early age that his excitement was different from others'. It wasn't just a sense of anticipation. But a living, breathing force that curled through him and consumed his every thought.

He'd barely been able to contain his impatience as he'd gone about his business throughout the afternoon. Unfortunately, as much as he wanted to be in this private hideout, he couldn't just drop everything. Especially not when his every movement was under constant scrutiny.

Small towns could be a pain in the ass. Everyone had to shove their noses into everyone else's business.

Then again, they did have their advantages.

Most citizens of Heron were blessedly gullible.

Not one of them could imagine that an upstanding citizen in their community might be a cold-blooded killer. It made it far easier to hide in plain sight.

Simpleminded yokels.

Pausing to enter the code into the keypad, he shoved open the door and stepped into the pathologically clean room.

At a glance it looked like a small hunting lodge. Paneled walls, a flagstone floor, and open-beam ceiling. There was a small kitchenette in one corner and a leather couch and chair set near a stone fireplace in the opposite corner. Nothing to make anyone look twice. Which was, of course, the point.

Ensuring the door was locked, he did a thorough sweep, including the tiny bedroom. He went to his knees to look under the bed despite the knowledge no one could fit beneath the narrow cot. And then behind the door of the bathroom, which was nothing more than a toilet and sink.

Even then he wasn't satisfied. He made several circles through the cabin, checking the tiny pieces of tape that were attached to the windows. If someone had entered, they would be broken.

Meticulous care. Attention to detail. Self-discipline.

Those were the keys to every success.

At last convinced that no one had been snooping around, he pulled a small remote from his pocket and aimed it at what looked like a blank wall. With smooth efficiency a section of the paneling parted, revealing three flat-screen monitors.

Anticipation licked through him. Still he forced himself to wait until he was settled on the couch before he once again lifted his remote. With a faint click the monitors powered on.

Chapter Eight

It was late afternoon before Rylan returned Jaci to her farm.

They'd driven thirty miles to Quincy, Illinois, a town across the river that was large enough to provide stores that carried the equipment he needed to set up a security system. Not that he could find the sort of sophisticated electronics that he was used to working with, but he could at least get the cameras up and running until his partner in California could send the upgrades he'd requested while Jaci had been showering.

He'd also insisted they stop to eat lunch. She'd chosen a chain establishment, insisting that she couldn't waste time at one of the fancier restaurants. Rylan wasn't convinced that was the reason.

He had a feeling that she was trying to keep him at a firm distance.

He understood why. He'd hurt her in the past. But he didn't like it.

Once they'd returned to her home, Rylan shoved aside his annoyance and concentrated on setting up the small wireless cameras. He placed the first one to monitor the front porch. No one would be able to climb the steps without being caught on camera. The second he placed at the back door. And the third he attached to the side of the house to capture anyone who pulled into the driveway.

He was currently installing the fourth camera inside the garage Jaci used as a workroom.

Finished adjusting the bracket, he climbed down the ladder and stood back. From his angle it was impossible to see the camera. Which was precisely what he wanted.

Jaci moved to stand at his side, giving a shake of her head.

"When you said security system, I thought you meant a camera, not an entire production studio."

His lips twitched, but he didn't mention the fact that he had a box of cameras coming from his partner. The local stores didn't carry wireless equipment that was capable of monitoring from more than a few hundred feet. Once he had the long-range cameras he intended to install them around the entire farm.

"Trust me."

"You keep saying that."

He turned his head, his gaze sweeping over her pale face.

In the gathering dusk he could make out the tension in her delicate features and the shadows beneath her eyes. She'd endured a severe shock, but she was facing her fears squarely. Just as she'd done all those years ago, although he'd been too selfish at the time to realize her courage.

Now he felt a near overwhelming urge to wrap her in his arms and assure her that everything was going to be okay.

"You create art with pastry," he forced himself to say in light tones. She was clearly wary of him. He wasn't going to risk pushing her away when she needed him the most.

He nodded his head toward the hidden camera. "This is my area of expertise."

She arched a brow. "You install security systems?"

"I did when I was in college. My job at the sheriff's office was only part-time, so I made some extra bucks by doing local installations for a security firm out of Kansas City. That's how Griff and I met," he said, not ashamed of their humble beginnings. After college he'd expected to work for the FBI. That had been his plan from the time he was very young. But instead, he'd met Griffin Archer, who'd convinced him to take a chance and start their own business. "I would install the system while Griff took care of all the technical aspects."

She moved to straighten a shelf filled with bolts of fabric that didn't need to be straightened.

"What do you do now?" she asked in overly casual tones.

He studied her very fine backside, a small smile playing about his lips. She didn't want him to think she was actually curious about him.

"We've created new software that helps DHS and the FBI anticipate cyber-attacks before they happen."

"Wow," she breathed, although she continued her unnecessary work.

"That's nothing," Rylan continued, unable to resist the urge to brag. Weird, considering that he never, ever discussed his business outside the office. "We've just become consultants with a company that's designing a method to use DNA to create a facial composite that the police can use to identify the perp."

She slowly turned, her expression difficult to read. "Elmer said you had a successful career, although he never shared any details. He said it was top secret."

"Did he make me sound mysterious and dashing like James Bond?" he asked.

"I've never been a James Bond fan." She wrinkled her nose. "Give me Mr. Darcy any day."

Rylan pressed a hand to his heart in mock horror. "Sacrilege."

They shared a brief moment of humor before she was abruptly moving to the long, wooden table in the center of the garage.

"He's very proud of you," she said.

Rylan had never doubted for a second that his father was proud of him. The older man had been Rylan's most loyal supporter, never once trying to make him feel guilty for choosing a different path than becoming a farmer.

In fact, Elmer had only had one complaint over the years.

"All he does is whine that I'm never home," he said in teasing tones.

"He misses you," she said.

"I miss him too," he admitted. He hadn't realized how much until he'd returned home for more than a weekend visit. His gaze rested on her profile. "I miss a lot of things."

She sent him an incredulous gaze. "Really?"

"You don't believe me?"

"I remember you telling me you couldn't wait to shake the dirt of Heron from your feet."

He grimaced as she threw his words back in his face. Christ. Did she remember every stupid thing he'd said?

"I was young."

"And arrogant," she helpfully added.

"We've already established that."

There was a short pause before she at last asked the question that he'd suspected was trembling on her lips.

"So why were you so anxious to leave?"

He leaned his hip against the table, watching as she aimlessly stroked a finger over a frame made from weathered wood.

"A part of me was afraid that I would be trapped into taking over the farm," he slowly admitted.

She sent him a puzzled glance. "Trapped?"

He shrugged. Looking back, it was easy to see that his own sense of guilt had made him act like a jerk. It hadn't been easy to break a family tradition that'd lasted four generations.

"It was expected from the day I was born. My great-great-grandfather bought the land here over a hundred years ago. It's been passed down through the family ever since." He gave a short laugh. "A part of me wasn't sure it was possible for a Cooper to actually walk away."

She rolled her eyes. "I doubt your father would have locked you in the barn."

"No, but he was subtly putting pressure on me to start taking more of an interest in the family business."

She frowned. Was she surprised by his honesty?

"You said that was part of the reason," she at last reminded him. "What was the other part?"

"Like any young man, I wanted to see the world," he said, feeling a pang of wistfulness as he recalled the hours he spent glancing through travel brochures at the local library. "Meet new people."

"Ah yes." Her lips twisted. "I've seen the people you've met."

He didn't miss the hint of mockery in her voice. "What's that mean?"

"Your father showed me pictures of you in your fancy condo with a pretty bauble hanging on your arm."

His brows arched. He knew what picture his father had been showing around town. It'd been taken for a life and style magazine. The photographer had insisted that Rylan's current girlfriend be included in the photo shoot. He hadn't blamed the man. Jillian was a stunning woman who added a gloss of glamour that he was lacking.

"Bauble?" he teased. "Are you referring to a woman?"

Her eyes widened, a blush touching her cheeks. "I'm sorry. That wasn't nice. I'm sure she's a lovely person," she said, her voice sincere. "And your condo is gorgeous. I can't imagine how wonderful it must be to own a home with such a fabulous view of the beach. You've created a remarkable life for yourself."

Her words weren't profound. Except they were.

When he'd been young, he hadn't entirely known why he kept Jaci at a distance. He told himself it was because he didn't want to hurt her.

Now he knew why.

This was the sort of woman who urged a man to put down roots. She was warmth and kindness and solid earthiness that spoke of home.

Jaci was a woman whom a man wanted as a wife and a mother of his children.

So he'd pushed her away and fled to what he thought he wanted.

"As my father recently told me, paradise can sometimes be tedious," he said.

"Hmm."

He didn't try to press the point. He was still trying to figure out why the need to return to California wasn't nearly as pressing as it should be.

"What about you?" He deliberately turned the attention away from himself.

"Me?"

"You left for, what?" He did a quick calculation. "Six or seven years?"

She wrinkled her nose. "My grandfather insisted. He was afraid I would stay to help with the farm because I felt obligated to take care of him."

Lloyd Patterson had been a wise man.

And he'd known his granddaughter's sense of loyalty all too well.

"Isn't that exactly what you would have done?" he asked.

She hunched a shoulder. "Of course. They didn't have to take me in. I would have done anything to make life easier for them, especially when it was obvious my grandfather could no longer continue to keep up this place."

"They took you in because they loved you," he reminded her. "And they always wanted what was best for you."

"I know." An unexpected smile curved her lips. "And I'll admit that I enjoyed college. Sometimes more than I should have."

"Naughty Jaci?" Heat raced through him. He had a new, glorious fantasy. "That's a side of you I'd like to see."

"My college days are long behind me."

"Not so long," he said, his gaze taking in her pixie hairstyle and the blush that touched her cheeks. She looked as young and innocent as the day he'd left Heron. "Why didn't you find a nice boy and get married?"

She tilted her chin. "I like my independence."

Those were the precise words he used when people pestered him about choosing a wife. Somehow, however, he was annoyed as they fell from her lips.

Disturbed by his strange reaction, he turned his attention to various projects that she had spread over the table. There was a stack of round pillows that looked like dog beds, and glass jars filled with fake grass and jelly beans that were clearly intended to be used as an Easter decoration, and wooden frames that were set next to a stack of black-and-white photos that were already placed on thick matting.

He frowned, reminded of the large pictures he'd seen in her house.

"Did you take these?"

"No. Nelson did," she told him. "He's preparing a new collection and asked me to create frames for them."

Rylan leaned forward, his nose wrinkling as he shuffled through the pictures of barbed-wire fences tangled with weeds and old barns that were obviously abandoned.

"I like the frames better than the pictures," he said.

"You sound like Andrew," she said, nodding toward a pile of old boards in one corner of the garage. "Of course, he was the one who found the reclaimed wood for me, so he might be a little prejudiced."

Rylan straightened, his brows pulling together. "Do both men have regular access to this property?"

She took a step back, her wariness returning at his sharp tone.

"Andrew cash-crops the land, so of course he has access."

"And the photographer?"

She shrugged. "He travels a lot, but when he's in town he stops by to show me photos from his latest shoot."

"Is there anyone else?"

"During the summer Sid and his uncle mow the lawn."

"Deputy Sid?"

"Yes."

"Is that all?"

"No. I have deliverymen and the occasional customer who doesn't want to wait until an art fair to buy one of my crafts."

His scowl deepened. How was he supposed to protect her when she had a revolving door of visitors?

"You shouldn't stay here alone," he abruptly decided. "Not until we find out who left that locket."

She made a sound of impatience. "Mike already offered to let me stay with him and I told him no. I won't let some psycho terrorize me into leaving my own home."

He bit back a curse. O'Brien had wasted no time in trying to get Jaci beneath his roof.

The knowledge made him consider punching something. Or somebody.

"Do you have a relationship with the sheriff?"

She sucked in a breath at his abrupt intrusion into her privacy. "That's none of your business."

"It's a simplc question," he pressed.

"And none of your business," she repeated, firmly heading toward the door of the garage. "I assume we're done."

Rylan swallowed a curse as he quickly moved to walk at her side. Hard to fathom why some people believed he was actually skilled in charming women.

"I need to download the software on your computer," he told her. "I'll also connect your cell phone to the system. You can start your baking while I work."

Her lips flattened. "Will it take long?"

"Trying to get rid of me?"

Too polite to admit the truth, she sent him a meaningless smile.

"I don't want to interrupt your visit with your father. I know you'll have to return to California soon."

He waved aside her concern. "Dad is planning to go to bingo at the Masonic Lodge tonight."

"Your dad plays bingo?"

He chuckled at her surprise. He'd been baffled as well. Until he'd realized what was going on.

"He'll never admit it, but he only goes so he can flirt with Rose Arlington. I don't want to intrude on his fun."

His gaze skimmed over her pale profile. "Plus, if I stay long enough I can steal some of whatever you intend to bake."

A portion of her tension seemed to ease at his light teasing.

"Shameless," she chided, stepping out of the garage and into the deepening shadows.

"I try," he admitted, pulling the door shut behind him. She started to walk away, but he reached out to lightly touch her arm. "Lock it."

She rolled her eyes, but readily reached into the front pocket of her jeans to pull out the key he'd insisted she find before they'd come to the garage.

"Yes, sir," she said, locking the door before continuing her path to the house.

The security light was flickering to life, battling against the encroaching darkness. Rylan was struck by the sheer isolation of the house. Anyone could drive here without being noticed.

The realization sparked a sudden memory.

"Does your family drop by for a visit?"

She sent him a puzzled glance. "My family is all gone. . . ." Her impulsive words dried on her lips as a blush stained her cheeks. "You mean my mother?"

"Your mother, or sister or brother?"

Her sharp laugh echoed through the damp air. "My mother and precious sister wouldn't dare soil their thousand-dollar shoes by stepping foot out here."

"And Christopher?" he pressed.

She shook her head. "He's been at Wash U for the past couple of years. And even before then was always calling me his hillbilly sister. He didn't come down from his big house to rub elbows with the hicks."

Rylan arched a brow, but he didn't mention he'd seen

her half brother driving by just hours ago. Talking about the Hamiltons was clearly painful.

Rylan and Jaci had almost reached the front porch when he once again reached out to tug her to a halt.

"Wait."

She glared at him with open impatience. "What is it now?"

"I hear a motor running."

She paused, her head tilting as she listened. The peaceful silence that lay like a comforting blanket around the farm was disturbed by a distant buzz.

"It's probably Andrew," she suggested.

"No." He pointed toward the thick linc of trees that ran along thc border of her land. "It's coming from the south."

She brushed aside his concern. "That must be the people who rented the old Johnson place. Frank built a new house last year."

"Who rented it?"

"I'm not sure." She turned to climb onto the porch. "I don't think they're from around here."

Grimly Rylan followed behind her.

He intended to find out exactly who was living next to Jaci. Right after he had Griff do some searching on Andrew Porter, Nelson Bradley, Christopher Hamilton, Sid, Sid's uncle, and the local deliverymen.

And, of course, Sheriff Mike O'Brien.

Right now Rylan didn't trust any of them.

Chapter Nine

Jaci didn't need to worry about her alarm the next morning. She'd spent the majority of the night tossing and turning, her thoughts whirling and her stomach tied in a tight knot of dread.

It was relief when her clock hit four a.m. and she could crawl out of bed to start her baking.

With Riff and Raff underfoot and the kitchen filled with the warm scent of baking bread, a portion of her tension eased. There was a sense of comfort in the small space that no one could steal from her. As if her grandmother's love was too resilient to be banished.

Doing her best to concentrate on her busy schedule, Jaci arranged her trays with the various baked goods. Then, sucking in a deep breath, she carried them through the lingering gloom to load them into the back of her Jeep.

She wasn't going to be terrorized. And she certainly wasn't going to become a prisoner in her own home.

Keeping the dogs at her side, she placed the last of the trays in her Jeep before she returned the animals to the house. No one would get in while they were standing guard.

She was headed back to the Jeep, which she'd kept running to warm up, when a familiar pickup pulled into the drive beside her.

Rylan.

With a roll of her eyes she watched as he climbed out of his father's old truck, his hard body outlined by the zipped gray hoodie and worn jeans that clung to his long legs. He looked ridiculously handsome as he stepped into the beam from her headlights.

"Morning, Jaci," he said.

"What are you doing here?" she demanded, even as she knew exactly why he was there.

In fact, a part of her had been waiting for him to show up.

After all, he'd made no secret of the fact that he was not only connecting her new security system to her phone and computer, but he was going to have full access to the cameras. Which meant he would have known the second she'd opened her front door to check for a locket.

The knowledge should have annoyed her. Instead a part of her was deeply grateful to know she wasn't completely alone.

Not that her gratitude extended to having him walk around the hood of her Jeep to open the passenger-side door.

"I'm going to tag along on your deliveries," he informed her.

"Why?"

He glanced toward the door where the sound of furious barking echoed through the soggy morning air.

"I assume Riff and Raff are staying here?"

She grimaced at the chaos the dogs would create if she'd let them in the Jeep.

"They're good dogs, but they don't appreciate the fact that I need to sell my pastries to keep a roof over our head," she said. "They just smell food and think it should be eaten. Usually in one gulp."

"I don't blame them," he said, flashing a smile as he climbed into the Jeep and shut the door.

With a sigh, Jaci yanked open her door and climbed into the driver's seat, glaring at the man who was buckling his seat belt.

"I don't need a bodyguard," she informed him.

He shrugged. "I don't agree."

She made a sound of impatience. "Whoever is doing this just likes to scare me."

"How can you be so sure?"

She couldn't be sure, of course. But, as crazy as it might be, she wouldn't let herself think that the psycho intended to do more than leave creepy lockets. Otherwise she would be stuck cowering in her house, too afraid to step out the door.

"If they wanted to hurt me they could have already done it," she pointed out. "If not yesterday, then when I was younger."

He folded his arms across his chest. It was his "I'm not budging" gesture.

"First of all, we don't know if it's the same person who left the lockets when you were in high school."

His words caught her off guard. She'd never considered the idea it might not be the same person who'd stalked her in the past.

"Who else could it be?"

"You might not have told a lot of people, but it wasn't

exactly a secret you were being harassed during high school."

Her lips twisted at the reminder of exactly whom she'd turned to when the lockets started arriving.

"Or being an attention-seeking diva," she reminded him.

In the soft glow of the security light, she watched as his face tightened with unmistakable regret.

"Jaci, I've told you I'm sorry," he rasped. "Believe me, I'll never forgive myself for ignoring your fears. If something happens to you—"

"Do you really think it's a different person?" she interrupted, not sure why she was being such a bitch.

Maybe because a part of her suspected he was only there because he felt guilty for the past, not because he truly cared about her. Or maybe it was because she was wary of allowing herself to depend on his support. It wasn't like he was going to be around for long.

Then, like everyone else in her life, he would be gone and she would be alone again.

"It's a possibility." He thankfully intruded into her dark thoughts. "My point is that we know nothing about your stalker, and until he's caught I don't intend to give him the opportunity to hurt you."

She put the engine into gear and slowly headed down the muddy drive.

"You can't protect me all the time."

"I could if you would come and stay at my father's house."

Her heart missed a beat. There'd been a time when she would have given anything to be closer to Rylan Cooper.

Now . . .

Now she understood that it had been a foolish, teenage fantasy.

"And what happens when you leave for California?" she demanded.

"I don't plan on going anywhere for a while."

She sent him a confused glance. "What about your job?"

"I can work from here as easily as California," he told her. "Most of our business is done online."

She slowed the Jeep as she reached the end of the drive. There was a low spot that had become a hidden bog at the edge of the gravel road. It had trapped more than one unwary driver over the past weeks.

"Don't you have to schmooze your customers?"

"In the beginning I did a lot of traveling to meet with potential clients. It was the only way to fully understand the market and what was needed." His gaze scanned the darkness as if expecting something or someone to leap out of the shadows. "Now our product speaks for itself."

"I hope you're not delaying your return home because of me."

"And if I am?"

Her heart missed another beat. "I'd say that there's no need."

"I disagree."

"Rylan—"

"Stop."

His command came without warning and she instinctively slammed her foot on the brake.

"What's wrong?"

He leaned forward, gazing at the opposite side of the road that was visible in her headlights. The slow-rising bluff was covered in trees and underbrush. The land was owned by a developer from St. Louis who'd recently built a cabin that he intended to rent to hunters.

"I thought I saw someone in the trees," he said.

Jaci studied the darkness. Dawn was creeping in, but heavy clouds shrouded the landscape in a dismal gray.

Was someone lurking in the shadows? It was possible,

of course. But it was far more likely the movement he caught was a deer. The place was thick with them lately.

"Do you want to go check?" she asked.

He narrowed his gaze. "Will you take off without me?"

She shrugged. "Probably."

"Fine." He shook his head, no doubt concluding, like she had, the movement had been caused by some sort of wildlife. "Let's go."

Without warning, Jaci felt a pang of guilt.

Rylan might be bossy, and intrusive, and arrogant, but he was just trying to help her. Did she really want to drive him away just because he rubbed against her already raw nerves?

Turning in her seat, she reached into the back to grab a muffin off the top tray.

"Here," she said, apologizing with pastry.

What better way?

"Thank God," he said, eating half the muffin in one bite. "Hmm. I'm going to have to double the length of my run tonight."

"All good things come with a price."

"Unfortunately true," he agreed, polishing off the muffin as she drove down the muddy road. Then without warning, he reached out to lightly brush his fingers through the short strands of her hair. "And speaking of good things that come with a price." She forgot to breathe, nearly driving off the road. But even as his hand cupped her bare nape the sound of his phone buzzing provided a sharp interruption. With a low curse he reached into his pocket to pull out the cell. "I have to take this."

Jaci released a soft breath as she picked up speed. There was no point in pretending that his casual touch hadn't sent jolts of pleasure through her. Or that she wasn't going to spend the rest of the day fantasizing about the feel of those fingers touching something far more intimate than her hair.

Blocking out the soft sound of Rylan's voice as he spoke into the phone, Jaci bypassed the road she usually took into town. She didn't know if it was still closed from the flood, but she wasn't going to find out. Not this morning. The mere thought of driving past the field where the woman was found floating in the water was enough to send a shiver of horror down her spine.

Ten minutes later her detour ended at a paved road that led directly into Heron.

"Thanks, Griff," Rylan at last said, shoving the phone in his pocket.

"Work?" she asked.

"Nope." His gaze turned toward her as she pressed her foot on the gas pedal, a portion of his tension visibly easing as they neared civilization. "I had my partner do some investigating for me."

"Investigating what?"

"Everything and everyone."

Her brows lifted. "Everyone?"

"I started with those who had access to your property."

"That's a long list," she said. She might live in the middle of nowhere, but her home business meant she had numerous people coming and going.

"Yeah, that's what Griff said," he told her in dry tones. "It's going to take some time to run them all through our system."

Her brows drew together. It was weird to think of the people in her life being churned through various search engines that were designed to reveal their darkest secrets. It didn't matter if they had anything to hide or not. It was a violation of their privacy.

"I'm not sure if I'm comfortable with the thought of my friends being investigated," she said.

"That's why I didn't tell you."

"Is it even legal?"

"We have specialized connections in the world of law enforcement," he smoothly answered.

She slowed as they reached the edge of town. "You didn't answer my question."

"Plausible deniability."

Jaci gave a resigned shake of her head. She was wasting her breath. Rylan Cooper was determined to make up for not believing her years ago. Now he was willing to go to any lengths he deemed necessary to protect her.

"What did he find out?" she asked, giving in to the inevitable.

"Griff discovered who is renting the old Johnson house," he said.

"Who?"

"A Vera Richardson."

Jaci searched her memory. She'd had a fourth-grade teacher named Mrs. Robinson. The older woman had carried a ruler that she used to smack students on the back of the head when they misbehaved during class. But she couldn't remember a Richardson.

"I don't recognize the name."

"Probably because she's dead."

Jaci sent her companion a puzzled glance. Was he joking?

"A dead woman is renting the house?"

A smile flickered around his lips, although his expression remained somber.

"More than likely someone stole her identity after she died."

Jaci grimaced. There was nothing unusual about identity

theft, but actually renting a home and pretending to be a dead woman? Yikes.

"Why would someone use a fake name to rent a run-down house in the middle of nowhere?"

"Where better to hide?"

She couldn't argue. It was difficult to imagine anyone searching for a missing person in this remote area.

"A criminal?" she suggested.

"I intend to find out."

She pulled the Jeep to a halt and put it in park before she was swiveling in her seat to confront him with a deep scowl.

"No."

He arched a brow. "No?"

She ignored the hardening of his jaw. The mere thought of him going out to confront some stranger who might be a desperate felon was enough to give her a rash.

"It could be dangerous," she said. "I'll call Mike and have him check it out."

His eyes narrowed. "Was that a deliberate kick below the belt, or a lucky hit?"

Jaci sensed she'd struck a nerve. Male pride? The strange competition with Mike?

She didn't really care. All that mattered was keeping Rylan safe.

"It's the sheriff's job, not yours." She pounced on the most reasonable excuse to keep Rylan away from the house. "If Mike finds the person living there is hiding from the law he can arrest them. If they see you, they might take off." She deliberately paused. "Or shoot."

"Hmm." He didn't look impressed with her logic.

"Promise me you won't go over there," she urged.

He unbuckled his seat belt. "I promise I'll share the information with O'Brien."

She shook her head. This man took stubborn to a whole new level.

"Anything else?" she asked.

There was a short pause. Almost as if he was considering whether or not to share what his partner had learned.

"I don't know where Christopher has been the past couple of years, but it wasn't attending Washington University," he at last said.

Jaci jerked in surprise. First at the knowledge that he'd included her half brother in his investigation. She'd told him that Christopher never visited her house. Then, at the fact that her half brother hadn't been attending Wash U.

"I don't understand."

He gave a lift of his shoulder, his expression impossible to read.

"The school doesn't have any record of Christopher ever taking classes there."

"You're sure?"

Genuine amusement flared through his golden eyes. "Griff doesn't make mistakes."

She believed him, but it still didn't make any sense.

"I'm sure Mother told me that he was at Wash U, but maybe she said St. Louis University."

He was shaking his head before she ever finished her sentence.

"He hasn't attended any college in the state of Missouri."

"I—" She cut off her protest. Her feelings toward Rylan might be a jumbled mess, but she trusted his skill in snooping into other people's business. "Why would Mother tell everyone he was going to school?"

He shrugged. "Maybe we should ask her."

A disbelieving laugh was wrenched from Jaci's lips. He clearly hadn't dealt with Loreen Hamilton. Or if he had, he'd forgotten that she was a daunting, ice-cold woman who considered herself above most mere mortals.

"Good luck with that," she said.

He studied her with a curious gaze. "What do you mean?"

"My mother has a talent for deflecting questions she doesn't want to answer," she told him. Questions like why the older woman had walked away from her own daughter. And if she'd ever loved Jaci's father. And if she intended to spend the rest of her life pretending Jaci didn't exist. "I've learned not to even bother."

Easily sensing her reluctance to approach her mother, Rylan reached out to run a finger along the line of her jaw.

"There's other ways to search for the truth," he assured her.

Her mouth went dry as his finger continued down the curve of her neck, his touch branding a path of electric excitement. Holy cow. How long had it been since she'd felt a man's hands on her body?

Clearly *too* long.

"Your friend Griff?" she managed to ask.

His lips twitched, his gaze lowering to linger on the swell of her breasts beneath her Mizzou Tigers sweatshirt. "I have a few skills of my own."

Her heart fluttered, an aching need pooling in the pit of her stomach.

"So you keep telling me," she breathed.

His eyes darkened with a sensual promise. "I'm happy to demonstrate."

Heated awareness spiced the air, making Jaci's palms sweat. For a crazed second she actually swayed toward him, as if she intended to kiss him.

Then, with awkward movements, she was unbuckling

her belt and jumping out of the Jeep. On cue, the sullen clouds opened up to drench her in a chilled rain.

It was better than a cold shower.

Dammit. It wasn't fair.

He had risen early. So early that it'd been pitch black when he'd left his home and driven to the wooded area just across the road from Jaci's house.

He told himself that he wanted to check on the camera that he'd hidden inside a fake trail cam. No one would give it a second glance. Not when the area was used by hunters. Still, he'd been in a rush to get it up yesterday, and he wanted to make sure it wasn't visible from the road.

But the truth was that he wanted an up close and personal view of Jaci this morning.

Was she still rattled?

Would she creep onto the porch to see if there was another locket?

Or would she stay locked in her house, waiting for another gift from him?

Hidden in the bushes, he'd watched as she had at last peeked out the door, clearly looking for a locket. Then she'd started her routine of carrying out the trays of food, her head swiveling from side to side as she searched for a hidden intruder.

He'd become instantly hard.

Despite her best efforts, her fear was a tangible force in the air.

It was exquisite.

Even better than it'd been watching in the secrecy of his cabin.

This was so much more . . . real.

And then everything had gone to hell.

His hand had barely wrapped around his aching erection when the truck had pulled into the driveway and Rylan Cooper had stepped out.

Talk about ruining a mood.

This was why he hated doing things in a hurry.

He hadn't planned on creating a locket. At least not for a few more months. He had, after all, just sated his lust six weeks before. The woman he'd chosen had lived miles and miles away. Far enough not to arouse suspicion. But while she'd offered the usual smorgasbord of emotions—confusion followed by horror followed by a wide-eyed terror—it'd been less than fulfilling. Just like all of them. Only Jaci could inspire the joy that filled his body until he thought it might burst.

But having indulged so recently meant that he hadn't been prepared.

It had all been too hurried. Too lacking in the dignity he tried to offer the women who performed such a vital necessity in his life.

Granted, the video of Jaci discovering the locket had provided him hours of pleasure. Over and over he'd watched as her face had whitened with terror before she'd fallen into a dead faint.

She was so much better than any of his other obsessions.

But his haste had meant he'd screwed up his meticulous schedule.

He'd been forced to snatch a new sacrifice without the pleasure of hunting for the perfect martyr. He wanted a sacrifice that was perfectly selected after weeks of research. This one had merely been convenient. Then he'd hurriedly prepared the locket without giving it the care it deserved before rushing to Jaci's house to place it on her door. And finally, he'd arranged the camera to catch every precious moment, but that was never the same as watching in person.

To make matters worse, his inability to use his usual, meticulous care had aroused the interest of both the sheriff and Rylan Cooper.

The sheriff he was confident he could mislead. His experience with lawmen had proven they weren't very smart. Not to mention the fact they were always eager to take the easy way out.

Drop a few bread crumbs in the wrong direction and O'Brien would be chasing shadows for the next decade.

Rylan Cooper, on the other hand . . .

He might prove to be a problem.

Which meant he had to go. One way or another.

Chapter Ten

Jaci hurried into the kitchen of the Bird's Nest with Rylan a few steps behind, carrying the tray of muffins. As soon as she caught sight of Birdie's raised brows she realized she'd made a serious error.

If Jaci hadn't been so rattled, she would have told Rylan to wait for her in the Jeep.

Now it was too late.

Hastily unloading the muffins, she swallowed a curse as Rylan strolled through the kitchen. He nodded toward a stunned Birdie and her helper before he was moving through the door that led into the outer dining room.

Great. Just great.

"Morning, Jaci," Birdie said, moving to stand at Jaci's side.

"Hey, Birdie." Jaci could feel the older woman's gaze burning a hole in the back of her bent head. "I added a few extra muffins. I assumed you would have a full house today."

"You assumed right," Birdie said. "They were lined up before I even unlocked the door."

Jaci lifted her head to glance through the opening into the dining room, not at all surprised to see it packed despite the early hour. It was rare that anything exciting happened in the small town. The discovery of a body was going to have people buzzing for days.

Not that they were currently buzzing. Instead a silence had filled the room as the tables of men sent speculative glances toward Rylan before craning their necks to see into the kitchen.

Rolling her eyes, she forced herself to meet Birdie's broad smile.

"Is there any news?" she asked.

Birdie shrugged, wiping her hands on her apron. "Nothing more than gossip."

Right now gossip was preferable to the intrusive questions that were hovering on the older woman's lips.

"What are they saying?"

The older woman hesitated, clearly aware Jaci was trying to divert her attention.

"Most believe the floods disturbed a graveyard and carried the bodies down the river," she at last revealed. "There are a few who are saying that Heron is a dumping ground for the mob." She gave a soft chuckle. "They've all watched *The Godfather* movies too many times. Of course, that's not as ridiculous as those who are convinced that we have a serial killer. Might as well say that it was aliens."

Jaci flinched at her teasing words. Why was it so hard for the locals to believe they might have a murderer walking among them?

It wasn't like they were living in some sort of paradise that was without sin.

Still, she knew better than to say anything.

Until they discovered exactly what was going on it was probably best to keep her fears to herself.

"What about Mike?" she cautiously probed. "Has he said anything?"

Birdie moved to unlock a drawer next to the fridge, pulling out an envelope before she turned to hand it to Jaci. "I haven't seen anything of the sheriff or Sid this morning."

Folding the envelope in half, Jaci shoved it into her back pocket.

"Thanks, Birdie," she said, pivoting to head out of the diner to her Jeep.

"Wait," the older woman commanded.

Jaci glanced over her shoulder. "Did I forget something?"

Birdie snorted. "You're not leaving this kitchen without telling me what's going on with the gorgeous Rylan."

Jaci tensed, her gaze flicking toward the tall, golden-haired man who was ending his conversation with two high school friends so he could turn back toward the kitchen.

"Nothing's going on," she lied, her gaze locked on Rylan as he headed directly toward her.

Her heart skittered. Birdie was right. He was gorgeous. And sexy.

Indecently sexy.

"Do I look like I was born yesterday?" Birdie demanded.

"I don't know what you mean," Jaci said.

Birdie glanced toward the approaching Rylan before returning her attention to Jaci.

"When I see a man and woman together at this hour I figure they spent the night together."

"You figure wrong." Jaci was able to answer with full honesty.

Birdie tilted her head to the side. "Then why are you blushing?"

Was she blushing? She resisted the urge to reach up and touch her cheeks.

"Elmer was worried about the muddy roads and he guilted Rylan into helping me with my deliveries. You know, in case I got stuck," she said in a rush.

Birdie lifted her brows. "Stuck, huh?"

Belatedly realizing she was only making it worse, she pinned a stiff smile to her lips as she whirled toward the back door.

"I gotta go. See you tomorrow."

Birdie said something, but Jaci plowed out of the kitchen and climbed into her Jeep, slamming shut the door as she reached to crank up the heat.

A second later Rylan was in the seat beside her, his eyes narrowed.

"Now what has your panties in a twist?"

She put the motor in gear, pulling out of the alley. "Everyone in that restaurant is speculating whether or not you spent the night with me."

He reached over, pulling the seat belt she'd forgotten across her body and snapping it into the lock.

"Does it matter?" he asked, his lips brushing her ear.

Heat streaked through her. Oh Lord. Maybe it didn't matter. Maybe . . .

No, no, no.

She wasn't going to be sucked into making a fool of herself. Not again.

"Of course it matters," she said, turning onto Main Street, heading toward the nearby highway. "You might be able to fly off to California, but I live here."

He chuckled at her prim reprimand. "This isn't the seventeenth century, Jaci."

"Sometimes it feels like it," she breathed. In truth, a small town could make a young woman fear that she was being slowly smothered.

Still, there was nowhere else she wanted to be.

"Jaci, you're an adult, unattached woman, and I'm an unattached man," he said, his voice edged with impatience. "Why shouldn't we enjoy spending time together?"

She shot a covert glance toward him as she halted at the stop sign. Was he really unattached? What about the pretty blonde clinging to his arm in the glossy magazine article?

Then she gave a sharp shake of her head. *Argh.* What was wrong with her?

"You've clearly forgotten what it's like to live in a small town," she said, turning onto the highway and pressing her foot on the gas pedal.

Perhaps sensing she wasn't in the mood to be convinced that they should indulge in some raw, meaningless sex before he hurried back to his expensive condo on the beach, Rylan settled back in his seat.

Neither spoke as she drove to Baldwin, both lost in their thoughts. But he was first out of the Jeep when she arrived at the tea shop, carrying in the tray of tarts despite her protests. And then again at the corner restaurant where she delivered several loaves of bread to tide them over the weekend.

He even insisted on following her to pick out the fresh veggies and herbs that she bought at a local farmer's market.

They were loading the produce in the back of her Jeep when a flash of platinum-blond hair caught Jaci's eye.

Straightening, she turned to watch as her half sister pushed a cart from the nearby grocery store across the parking lot.

"What the heck?" she breathed in shock.

Rylan swiftly moved to stand at her side. "What's wrong?"

She nodded toward the pretty woman who was wearing a Burberry raincoat and carrying a Michael Kors handbag as she struggled to steer the cart.

She looked as out of place as an exotic bird in a cornfield.

"Payton," she said.

A portion of Rylan's tension eased. "You didn't know she was in town?"

Jaci released a sharp laugh. "It's not that. I assume she spends a lot of time in town."

"Then why the surprise?"

"I didn't realize she knew what a grocery store was, let alone how to find it." She abruptly frowned as a memory teased at the edge of her mind. "Oh."

Rylan sent her a questioning glance. "Jaci?"

"Mike asked me if I'd seen Anne yesterday."

"Anne?"

"Anne Dixon. My mother's housekeeper," she clarified, her gaze latched onto Payton as the woman halted, glancing around as if she'd forgotten where she'd parked. Or more likely she was waiting for fairies to magically show up and unload her groceries. "I wonder if she quit."

"Actually, I'm more interested in what Payton knows about her brother," he said. "Why don't we ask her?"

Jaci shook her head. "No way. I've already endured an encounter with my mother. That's my family limit for the week."

"It will only take a minute." He reached up to wipe a stray drop of rain from her nose. "And I promise to protect you."

"No."

Predictably, Rylan ignored her protest, angling across the parking lot to head straight toward Payton.

"Crap," Jaci growled, trying to keep up with his long strides. "You're a pain, you know that?"

"Yep," he acknowledged, his swift pace never slowing until he came to a smooth halt in front of Jaci's beautiful sister. "Hello, Payton," he said with a charming smile.

The younger woman flinched, clearly caught off guard to be recognized. Which was ridiculous considering everyone knew everyone in the area.

Then realizing who was standing in front of her, Payton's embarrassment was swiftly forgotten.

"Rylan Cooper," the woman drawled, her expression melting from annoyance to pure female invitation as her gaze drifted down Rylan's hard body. "This is an unexpected pleasure."

"I agree." He deliberately glanced toward her loaded cart and a flush darkened Payton's perfect ivory skin. "Very unexpected."

"Our housekeeper is taking a few days off," she hastily explained. "Unfortunately that means we all have to pitch in and cover her duties."

"A necessary evil?" Rylan teased.

"Yes." Her expression unexpectedly tightened, then with an obvious effort, she was shaking off her dark thought to reach out and lay her manicured fingers on Rylan's arm. "I heard you were in town. We should . . ." Her words trailed away as she suddenly realized Rylan wasn't there alone. "Oh. Jaci."

Jaci resisted the urge to roll her eyes. Payton always managed to make her feel as if she'd just crawled out of a pigpen.

"Hello, Payton," she managed in civil tones.

The blue eyes shifted from Jaci back to Rylan, then back to Jaci.

"Are you here together?"

It was the sheer disbelief in her voice that prompted Jaci to press herself against Rylan's side.

"Rylan insisted on helping me with my deliveries this morning."

The disbelief remained. "Really?"

Ignoring Rylan's bemused smile, Jaci pressed even closer. Okay, it was juvenile. But the Hamilton clan brought out the worst in her.

"Why are you so surprised?" she demanded.

"I thought you and Mike had a thing going," Payton accused with a deliberate attempt to cause trouble.

In response Rylan wrapped his arm possessively around Jaci's shoulders.

"That's in the past," he said, casually brushing his lips over her cheek. "Isn't it, Jaci?"

She swallowed a low moan. The warmth of his body chased away the chill that had plagued her since she'd found the locket on her door, his warm scent teasing at her senses.

The game was getting out of hand. Time for a distraction.

"I've never seen you at the grocery store before," she said, focusing her attention squarely on Payton.

Her sister shrugged. "As I said, our housekeeper is on vacation."

Jaci parted her lips to ask why the sheriff was interested in Anne when Rylan gave her shoulder a sudden squeeze. A silent reminder that they were supposed to be finding out about her half brother.

"I saw Mother yesterday," she instead said, her voice overly nonchalant. She sucked at playing spy. And it didn't help that Rylan still had his arm wrapped around her. How the heck was she supposed to think straight? "She said Christopher was home from college."

Payton shrugged. "He returned a few days ago."

"I haven't seen him around," Jaci pressed. "What's he doing?"

A blond brow flicked upward. "Doing?"

"He just graduated from college. I assume he's busy looking for a job."

Another shrug. "He's gone today, so he might be setting up some interviews."

Okay. This was getting them nowhere.

Time to be blunt.

"I never heard what his degree was in," she said. "I'm assuming he's going into business like his father?"

Payton stiffened, a sudden anger darkening her eyes. "What do you care?"

"He's a part of my family," Jaci forced herself to say, even managing a fake smile.

Payton's nose flared, as if she'd just caught a foul scent. "We might be related, Jaci Patterson, but you've never been a part of our family."

Ouch.

Jaci flinched as the poisonous arrow found its target. It was stupid. She'd endured rejection after rejection over the years from her supposed relatives. She should be used to their verbal blows.

Instead she instantly gave in to the childish need to hit back.

"If you think that's an insult, you're wrong," she assured the younger woman, barely resisting the urge to topple her off her absurd high heels. Seriously, who went grocery shopping in Louboutins? "My grandparents were the only family I needed."

Sensing the brewing fight, Rylan tugged her a step back as he spoke.

"I haven't seen Christopher in years." He intruded into the conversation. "I should stop by and catch up with him. When will he be home?"

Payton paused, no doubt struggling to regain her composure as she turned her attention to Rylan.

"I'm not sure," she told him.

"Ah." Rylan pretended to be disappointed. "Maybe I'll just stop by later today to see if he's made it home."

Payton glanced toward her groceries before giving a sharp shake of her head.

"I'm sorry, but this really isn't a good time. I'll have him give you a call."

With a meaningless smile she pushed her cart and hurried along the line of parked cars to the expensive silver SUV at the end of the lot.

Keeping his arm wrapped around her shoulders, Rylan steered her back to the Jeep.

"Interesting," he said.

"What's interesting?" she asked, pulling away from his distracting touch.

"She didn't want me visiting her brother. I wonder why."

Jaci snorted, yanking open the door of her Jeep. "I wonder a lot of things about Payton," she said, climbing into her seat and switching on the engine. "Mainly why she always has to be such a bitch to me."

"Because she's jealous of you," Rylan said as he joined her in the Jeep and shut his door.

Jaci jerked her head around to study his profile, waiting for the punch line.

"Is that a joke?" she at last demanded.

"Not at all." He swiveled in his seat to meet her accusing gaze. "Payton has always envied you."

"That's insane." As if to prove her point, Payton zipped past in her vehicle that was worth more than Jaci's house. "She has everything."

"No one has everything," Rylan assured her.

Jaci should have let it go. After all, she'd been trained her entire life to grin and bear it. She'd been told over and over that there was no need to air her family's dirty laundry. Not even if that dirty laundry was public knowledge in the area.

Today, however, her nerves were too raw to be so easily pacified. She had to vent before she exploded.

"Payton was raised with a mother and father, plus a brother." She grimaced. "Although I wouldn't wish Christopher on anyone," she conceded, before continuing to list Payton's numerous blessings. "She has money, she's beautiful. And she gets treated like a princess wherever she goes." Her lips twisted with . . . not envy—she would never change places with her pampered sister—but a bitterness she'd never been able to fully purge. "I was the one whose father died when I was a baby, whose mother abandoned me, and who had to work for every penny I have."

Rylan held her gaze, seemingly indifferent to her grievances.

"Think about it, Jaci," he insisted. "She has a father who's gone ninety percent of the time and a mother who I doubt is capable of loving anyone. And as you said, Christopher is a self-centered dick." He reached to grab her hand, threading their fingers together. "You, on the other hand, had grandparents who openly adored you." He gave her fingers a light squeeze. "They never missed one activity you were involved in. It didn't matter if it was a basketball game or if you were playing flute in a music concert. It was a running joke that they always got to every event an hour early so they could have front row seats."

Her gaze lowered to their clasped hands, an intoxicating warmth surging through her. She tried to tell herself it was the memory of her grandparents, but that didn't explain the fluttery excitement in the pit of her stomach.

"That's true," she conceded.

Rylan wasn't done. "And what has her money ever gotten Payton?" he continued. "A bunch of fake friends who she could never be sure really liked her or just pretended to like her so they could go to her big house and ride in her expensive car."

Jaci slowly shook her head. Payton had always been swarmed with friends. It couldn't just be because she had a flashy car. Could it?

"She was homecoming queen," she insisted. "More than once."

He shrugged. "Because she promised everyone who voted for her an invitation to her yearly pool party."

Someone had once told Jaci that Payton was buying votes, but Jaci assumed she was just being catty.

"I didn't know that."

"Listen, Jaci." He tugged her hand to his lips, pressing a kiss to her knuckles. "I'm not saying Payton had a rough childhood. She was clearly spoiled and her last name is Hamilton, which gives her special privileges in this area. But she was never truly admired by her classmates." He turned her hand over, kissing her open palm. She shuddered, desire sizzling through her. "Not like you."

She was once again stunned by his words. He clearly had a much different memory of high school than she did.

What was that saying . . . truth is in the eye of the beholder?

"I was never popular," she protested.

"Of course you were." He leaned toward her, his gaze lowering to her lips. "Everyone liked you. They might not have fussed over you like they did Payton, but they genuinely wanted to spend time in your company. Not because of what you could give them, but because they enjoyed being with you. And I'd bet that most of them are still your friends, aren't they?"

It was increasingly difficult to concentrate on the conversation.

"Yes," she managed to agree, less concerned with her large circle of friends than the hope he was about to kiss her.

"You're a welcomed member of this community," he continued, leaning another inch closer. "Can you say the same for Payton?"

"I don't know," she said, although she did.

Her half sister had always considered herself too good to associate with the yokels of Heron, or even the larger town of Baldwin.

She belonged in her big house on the hill.

"I'm not trying to make you feel sorry for Payton, but she had to live with the stigma of your mother's selfishness."

His soft words abruptly jerked her out of her sensual haze.

Did he just say that it was Payton who had to suffer because of their mother?

"I was the one abandoned," she reminded him in sharp tones.

"Which meant you got all the sympathy."

"That's . . ." With a frustrated sigh she yanked her hand free and grabbed the steering wheel. Later she would consider his words. But for now all she wanted was to get home so she could crawl back in bed for a short nap. Or maybe she'd take a nice cold shower. Anything to make her forget about Rylan Cooper and her snowballing need to get him naked.

She shoved the Jeep in gear and peeled out of the parking lot. "I have better things to worry about than my sister."

Beside her Rylan chuckled, clearly pleased that he'd gotten under her skin.

Aggravating ass.

Chapter Eleven

Rylan made no effort to break the brittle silence as Jaci drove them back to her house.

He knew he'd hit a raw nerve. It was no secret that the Hamiltons had always treated Jaci like crap. But holding on to her bitterness wasn't going to change the fact that her mother was a bitch. Or that her half siblings had been raised to be shallow, self-centered brats.

He wanted her to be proud of her accomplishments, not dwell on the family who were incapable of recognizing the true worth of a person.

At the moment, however, he didn't think she was in the mood to appreciate his efforts.

She pulled into her muddy driveway and shut off the engine. Before she could speak, Rylan was out of the Jeep and heading to the back to pull out her bags of fresh produce. Joining him, she grabbed her empty trays, and hustled behind him as he headed around the house to the back door.

"There's no need to come in," she said.

"I want to check the house."

She made a sound of impatience as she brushed past

him to climb the steps so she could unlock the door. Instantly the sound of barking echoed inside the house.

"There's a security system that you installed, plus Riff and Raff," she said, punching in the number on the electronic pad he'd placed next to the doorjamb.

He shrugged. "I still intend to check."

She released her breath on a hiss as he urged her to the side so he could enter first. Then, kicking off his shoes, he walked into the kitchen and placed the bags on the counter.

Riff and Raff greeted him with sharp barks, but he'd spent enough time with them yesterday to ensure they didn't see him as a threat or a tasty treat. After a few intrusive sniffs they galloped into the mudroom to dance around Jaci as if she'd been gone days instead of a few hours.

Leaving the kitchen, he made a circuit through the living room into Jaci's bedroom and the connecting bathroom that she'd converted into a master suite. After checking in the bathroom, he halted in the center of the bedroom.

Against his will, his gaze lingered on the large, four-poster bed with the hand-stitched quilt. A sharp, vivid image of Jaci stretched across the mattress, her lush curves shivering beneath the stroke of his hands, seared through his brain.

Christ. He wanted her.

He wanted to kiss every inch of her satin skin.

And feel her legs wrapped around his waist as he surged deep inside her.

And to wrap her in his arms as they slept together in a tangle of sweaty limbs.

With a low curse, he moved to take a quick peek at the upstairs loft that was used for storage, before heading back downstairs.

A part of him knew that only a heel would take advantage of a woman who was alone and vulnerable and scared.

But another part was fiercely determined not to make the same mistake he had years ago.

Back then Jaci had looked at him with stars in her eyes and he'd pushed her away. This time he intended to be holding her so close that she couldn't escape when those stars returned.

And they would return.

He would accept no less.

Not entirely sure what was happening to him, Rylan retraced his steps to the kitchen. Jaci was bustling from cabinet to cabinet, putting away her groceries. It was something she no doubt did every day, but he felt an odd pang in the region of his heart.

Home . . .

The word whispered through the back of his mind.

Easily sensing his intense interest, Jaci slowly turned, her expression unreadable.

"Satisfied?"

His lips twitched as he bent down to pat the heads of the dogs, who were butting their noses against him to gain his attention. He doubted she would be happy if he explained just how unsatisfied he was.

"Where did you get these beauties?" he asked.

"Andrew," she said, running her fingers through the short, damp strands of her hair. "He found a litter dumped in a ditch and brought them home. He asked if I wanted one, but when I went up I found I couldn't choose between these two."

His jaw tightened. He would bet money every unattached male in the area was finding excuses to call Jaci. And probably a few men who were supposed to be attached.

"So you took both?" he asked, keeping his tone light.

Her lips twitched. "It seemed reasonable when they

were just puppies. Now I realize I should have gotten smaller dogs or moved into a bigger house."

He gave each of them a pat before he straightened. "What are your plans for the day?"

She shrugged. "A short nap, a hot shower, and then I need to do some work in my shop before I start baking."

The memory of her bed returned with a vengeance. He stepped forward, his lips curling with satisfaction as her cheeks heated with awareness.

"I could help with the nap and the shower," he said, not halting until she was pressed against the edge of the counter.

"You're crowding me."

"I know." He bent his head, stroking his lips over her forehead and the soft skin of her temple before he traced the delicate shell of her ear. Her sweet scent instantly filled his senses. He drew in a slow, deep breath. "You smell like home."

Her hands lifted to lie against his chest. Not pushing him away, but not drawing him in closer.

"Home?"

"Warm, soft." He pressed a path of kisses down the stubborn line of her jaw. "Welcoming."

She made a sound of annoyance even as her body shivered with need.

"You make me sound like an old pair of slippers," she complained.

He nuzzled at the corner of her mouth, his arms wrapping around her waist. He wanted to yank her hard against him. To feel her pressed tight against his thickening arousal.

Hell, he wanted to devour her.

Instead he forced his hands to lightly skim up and down

her back. She might tremble at his touch, but she hadn't forgiven him for his lack of trust in the past.

The last thing he wanted was to drive her away.

"Flash and dazzle can be a fun distraction, but they quickly become tarnished," he assured her in husky tones.

"Really?"

"Yes, really."

"So boring is better?"

He slowly lifted his head, studying her with a brooding gaze.

"There's nothing boring about you, Jaci," he assured her. "In fact, you're the most dangerous woman I've ever known."

Her brows snapped together. "Very funny."

He swallowed a sigh. Of course she didn't believe him. He'd devoted a lot of energy to convincing her that he would never see her as anything but the girl next door.

"It's true," he insisted.

"What's so dangerous about me?"

He held her gaze, his expression somber. "You make a man think about putting down roots."

She stiffened, instantly wary. "Rylan."

Too smart to press, Rylan lowered his arms and stepped back. If nothing else, he at least knew that she was still physically attracted to him.

It was a start.

He brushed a light finger over her flushed cheek. "Make sure the dogs are in the house and the doors are locked before you take your nap."

"Yes, sir."

His gaze swept over her face, lingering on her lips. "Or I could stay."

Need darkened her eyes before she was pointing toward the back door.

"Go."

"I'll be back this afternoon."

She shook her head. "I have work to do."

He planted a soft, lingering kiss on her lips. "I'll be back."

Before she could decide if she wanted to wrap her arms around his neck or knee him in the 'nads, Rylan was heading into the mudroom. Pulling on his boots, he let himself out the back door.

Intending to head around the house to his truck, he was halted by the distant sound of a chain saw. It had to be Andrew Porter.

Angling toward the barn, Rylan followed a narrow trail down a sloping hill that Jaci's grandfather had used as pasture for his cattle. He reached the muddy field that was closest to the river and followed the buzz of the chain saw toward a large pile of logs. It looked as if Andrew had collected the debris that had been swept over the levee by the floodwaters and piled the rubbish together. No doubt he intended to burn it once the rain stopped.

For now, he was busy cutting up driftwood and placing it in a separate pile.

Rylan frowned, recalling the frames that Jaci had created from the wood Andrew brought to her. It was obvious the two of them were close.

The question was, how close?

Rylan squashed the fierce blast of anger at the mere thought the two might be dating. Right now all that mattered was getting information from the man that could help to protect Jaci.

Slogging through the field that was a muddy mess, Rylan studied the younger man. He'd been a couple years behind Rylan in school, and rarely involved in any extra activities. Not unusual for children of farmers. They were expected to be up at the crack of dawn to help with the animals and then to return home as soon as classes were out to help in the fields.

What he did remember about Andrew was that he was always quiet, and seemed to prefer melting into the background. It would be easy for him to move around the area without attracting attention.

Belatedly realizing he was no longer alone, Andrew turned off the saw and reached up to remove the headphones protecting his ears.

He was nearly as tall as Rylan, with the thick muscles of a man who did physical work. His face was long and ruddy from years in the sun. And his short, dark hair was covered by a worn seed hat. At the moment he was wearing a pair of heavy coveralls and rubber boots to protect him from the mud.

"Hey, man," Andrew said, stepping forward. "Long time no see."

Shaking hands, Rylan covertly studied the man's wide, welcoming smile and guileless brown eyes.

It was difficult to imagine him sneaking around, planting bloody lockets. Or worse, killing young women and dumping them in the river.

Still, Rylan wasn't about to let a man's jovial nature scratch him off his mental list of suspects. He'd been around law enforcement long enough to know that a face of an angel quite often hid the soul of a devil.

Rylan nodded toward the pile of debris. "Looks like you're keeping busy."

"You know how it is. A farmer's work is never done," Andrew said, his smile fading as he glanced toward the stagnant water that covered the bottom half of the field. "'Course, if the rain doesn't stop, there won't be any crops this year."

Rylan grimaced. Few people understood the stress of having their livelihood be at the mercy of the weather.

"A shame."

"Yep." With a shake of his head, he returned his attention to Rylan, his eyes narrowing. "Are you going to tell me what's up?"

"What makes you think something is up?" Rylan demanded, studying the man's jaw as it hardened.

"I was here yesterday when the cops arrived," he said. "I could see they were taking pictures, looking around. Then you came later and put up the cameras. I assume someone must have broken into Jaci's house."

Rylan folded his arms over his chest. "There was some trouble."

Andrew's face flushed with instant anger. "Is she okay? If she was hurt I'll—"

"She's fine," Rylan assured him, trying not to bristle at the man's belief he should be protecting Jaci. "She wasn't home when someone trespassed on her land."

Andrew studied him, clearly sensing there was a lot more going on than a trespasser.

"Did the intruders cause any damage?" His beefy hands clenched at his side. "I can get my toolbox and return later today to help fix it."

"There wasn't any damage."

Andrew's frown deepened. "What was taken?"

"Nothing."

"Then why was the sheriff here?"

Rylan hesitated. The young man's reaction seemed completely natural. He'd have to be a hell of an actor to maintain his air of confused anger.

"There was a locket left on her door," he at last admitted.

"Locket?" Andrew blinked. "Like one of them heart things?"

"Yes."

"Doesn't seem like a reason to call nine-one-one," Andrew said.

"We believe it was left by a stalker," Rylan said.

"Some weirdo is harassing Jaci?" The anger returned to Andrew's long face. He might not fully understand what was going on, but he knew how to deal with a jerk who harassed women. You kicked the shit out of them.

"Yep."

"Do you have any idea who it is?"

"Not yet." Rylan's words were clipped, his tone making it clear that it was only a matter of time until he tracked down the creep.

Andrew gave a shake of his head, glancing at the white farmhouse on top of the hill.

"I never did like the idea of her living out here by herself," he said.

"Neither do I, but she's determined to stay," Rylan said.

"Stubborn."

Rylan's lips twisted. Andrew was obviously a master of understatement. "No crap."

"How can I help?" Andrew demanded.

"What time did you get here yesterday?" he asked.

"Six thirty." Andrew paused, then gave a shake of his head. "You know, it was probably closer to seven," he said. "I stopped by Frank's after I heard about the body."

Rylan tucked the information in his brain, trying to determine a time line for when the stalker had placed the locket on Jaci's porch.

"Did you notice anyone around?"

Andrew shook his head. "No."

"What about the road?" Rylan pressed. "Did you notice any tracks?"

The younger man thought back, his brow furrowed. "I could see where Jaci pulled out of her driveway and headed south before she had to turn around and take the long way to town."

Rylan's lips twisted. For once the sloppy, loathsome mud might be of use.

"So whoever brought the locket did it after seven," he said, thinking out loud.

"Unless he walked," Andrew offered.

Well, hell. He glanced around. No one could have approached from the east. Not unless they had a boat. And it seemed unlikely they would have passed through his father's land. There was a clear view of the back fields from the house.

But it would have been easy for someone to come from the south. The thick brush that had been allowed to grow wild on the old Johnson place meant that a person could approach without being seen until they were close to Jaci's garage.

"Possible," he agreed. "What about later? Did you see anyone hanging around the house?"

Andrew grimaced. "When I get back here working I really don't notice anything that's going on."

Rylan couldn't argue. He'd been nearly on top of Andrew before the younger man realized he was approaching. Of course, Andrew's isolation in this area meant he could easily have walked up to Jaci's house without anyone being the wiser.

Something that Rylan intended to keep in mind even as he reached into his pocket to pull out his wallet. Andrew could be a valuable ally, as long as Rylan could double-check his claims.

"Thanks, Andrew," he said, handing the man his business card. "Here's my number. Give me a call if you happen to notice anything strange."

The man scowled. "Trust me, if anyone tries to bother Jaci, they'll be sorry."

With a nod, Rylan turned to retrace his path up the hill and around Jaci's house to his truck. Then, starting the engine, he flicked a button to blast the heater. Christ. He'd been in California for too long. The damp, chilled weather felt as if it was settling into his bones.

Or maybe he was just getting old, he wryly acknowledged, backing out of the drive and turning to head toward Jaci's mysterious neighbors.

It was bound to happen.

Bumping down the road, he nearly missed the old turnoff to the Johnson place. There were branches hanging low and a number of rusting barrels that were dumped along the edge of the road.

A deliberate attempt to keep the driveway hidden?

Turning between two barrels, Rylan allowed the truck to crawl forward, his gaze darting from side to side as he drove between the line of trees. A few minutes later, he was in the front yard, which had been allowed to become a nasty mess.

Rylan grimaced as he took stock of the abandoned cars that were rusting in the clumps of weeds, and the piles of scrap metal that he'd bet had been stolen from neighboring farms. The house itself was in dire need of a new coat of paint, with a small front porch that was blocked by a stack of bulging garbage bags. Two of the front windows were covered by slabs of plywood, and the brick chimney had fallen across the roof, which sagged beneath the weight.

Only the front door looked new. It was made of heavy steel and bolted into the frame. There was also a sign nailed to the porch with a warning that trespassers would be shot.

Nice. Clearly the current residents didn't encourage drop-in visitors.

He shifted his attention to scrubs and tangled bushes that hadn't been trimmed in years. The undergrowth ran along the edge of a deep culvert that Rylan had forgotten about that ran along the north side of the property.

It would be hard for anyone to cross from the house to Jaci's place. Not unless they used the road.

Hmm.

There was the sudden sound of angry barking and Rylan glanced toward the back of the house where a large dog was straining at his leash.

Time to go.

Not in the mood to press his luck, Rylan backed his way out of the yard and along the private road. He wasn't going to risk getting stuck in the mud in an effort to turn around.

Once he was back on the gravel road, he hesitated.

He needed to run by home. His father would no doubt have lunch waiting for him. But then again, he wanted to track down the sheriff and discuss what he'd learned from Griff.

In the end, his decision was made for him when he heard the crack of gunfire, quickly followed by the sound of shattering glass.

Ducking low, Rylan reached over the seat to grab the shotgun his father kept in the narrow storage space. Then, peeking into the side mirror, he checked to see if anyone was approaching.

From his angle the road looked empty, and blowing out a shaky breath, he pushed open the door and slid out of the truck. Keeping low, he moved to the tailgate, his gaze searching his surroundings for any sign of the shooter.

Nothing.

Whoever had shot at him had disappeared in the thick line of trees that framed the road.

Rylan cursed, moving to crawl back into the truck. He wasn't idiotic enough to crash through the woods in search of a trigger-happy enemy. Not without backup.

Turning in his seat, he studied the hole that had been blown into the center of the window. Just a few inches to the left and the blast would have hit him in the back of the head.

He shuddered, his gaze moving to the bits of glass that had sprayed across the leather seat. His eyes narrowed, his hand reaching out to gather the tiny balls sprinkled among the slivers of window.

Shit.

Chapter Twelve

Sheriff Mike O'Brien returned to his office with a tight ball of frustration lodged in his gut.

It'd been an impulsive decision to travel to Quincy and speak with Anne Dixon's sister. The older woman was fiercely concerned for Anne, reinforcing Payton's insistence that Anne was a creature of habit who would never, ever take off without telling people where she was going.

She'd also been a font of information. Finding relatives who were close to their missing loved one was always an asset to law enforcement.

It was those people who cut off all ties to friends and family who were the most difficult to track down.

The morning away from his office, however, meant that he was far behind on his routine duties. And it didn't help to discover that Sid hadn't returned from the short field trip Mike had sent him on.

Closing his door, he moved to settle in his chair and reached for the phone on his desk. Punching in the numbers, he waited for the call to be transferred to the appropriate department.

"Hey, Jenkins," he said when a male voice at last

answered. "Did you have time to look at the locket I sent you?" Mike grimaced as the man released a string of swear words that were remarkably inventive. Waiting until the forensic analyst was forced to halt and take a breath, Mike jumped in. "I know the DNA hasn't been processed, but can you give me a blood type?" There was another angry burst, but without the swear words. "Just let me know as soon as possible," Mike said, replacing the receiver with a click.

Yeesh. The lab rats could always be grumpy when he was trying to urge them to work faster, but Jenkins was downright pissy.

Taking off his hat, Mike was running his fingers through his hair when the intercom buzzed. Swiveling in his chair, he turned to look at the monitor that showed Rylan Cooper standing on the other side of the connecting door.

For a long minute Mike considered ignoring the unwelcomed visitor. Finally, he gave a shake of his head. If he didn't open the door, Carol would be calling to make sure everything was okay.

Pressing a button on his desk, Mike heard the lock click open, and Rylan stepped into the office.

"And now my day is perfect," Mike said, watching Rylan cross the floor to stand directly in front of the desk.

"I'm glad one of us is happy," Rylan growled.

Mike resisted the urge to rise to his feet. He didn't like the feeling that Rylan was looming over him, but he'd be damned if he revealed his unease.

This was his office, by God.

"I'm really not," he said. "What do you want?"

Rylan's jaw tightened. He looked like his mood was about as good as Mike's.

"Did you manage to get the locket examined?" he demanded.

Mike leaned back in his seat. Suddenly he understood why Jenkins had gone a little nuts on him.

"This is Heron, not Hollywood. Testing takes time," he said. "And even if I did have any information, I wouldn't share it with a civilian."

Rylan planted his fists on his hips. "I'm not exactly a civilian."

"Unless you carry a badge, you're a civilian."

"Fine." Rylan's lips stretched with a humorless smile. "I'd hoped that we could work together to protect Jaci, but I can call in my private associates."

"This is my investigation, Cooper," he warned.

"And we both know that I have the technology, not to mention the direct contacts that can fast-track any forensic evidence," Rylan said.

Mike's hands clenched with anger. He'd already done some snooping last night. Rylan and his partner, Griffin Archer, had created a company that had revolutionized hunting down cyber-criminals, and then continued on with programs that were used by federal agencies around the world. Hell, he'd been publicly praised by the director of the FBI.

Mike didn't need to be told that this man had the sort of connections and resources any lawman would envy.

"I may be a small-town hick, but I'm capable of doing my job without your fancy equipment or bigwig contacts," he snapped.

Rylan narrowed his gaze. "Why are you making this into a pissing match?"

Mike had a dozen different answers for that particular question, but he stuck with the only one that mattered.

"I don't want you screwing with my investigation," he

said. "When we catch whoever is responsible, I have to take my evidence to trial. Something that's not going to be possible if you screw with it."

Rylan drew in a slow, deep breath. No doubt silently counting to ten.

"Then I'm here to report a crime," he at last said.

Mike rolled his eyes. The day already felt too long. Having to deal with Rylan Cooper wasn't making it any shorter.

"Now what?"

"Someone took a shot at me."

Mike studied him, waiting for the punch line. "Are you serious?"

The light brown eyes flared with anger. "I don't joke about near-death experiences."

Mike leaned forward, planting his hands on the desk. This meeting just went from being an annoying waste of his time to attempted murder.

"Where?"

"I'd just driven out to the old Johnson place—"

"What were you doing out there?" Mike interrupted.

"Trying to figure out if someone could have walked from there to Jaci's without being seen by Andrew."

Oh. That actually made sense. He'd been too busy to sit down and work out the mechanics of how the stalker had placed the locket on Jaci's door.

"Could they?" he asked.

"It's possible, but doubtful," Rylan said. "You'd have to wade through the culvert that's been turned into a swampy mess with all the rain."

Mike gave a slow nod. It wasn't just the Mississippi that had been flooded by all the rain. Every tiny creek and tributary in the county was swollen with water.

"What happened?" he asked.

"I'd just pulled out of the drive and onto the road heading to my father's house when my back window was shattered."

"You're sure it was someone shooting at you?" Mike asked. He wasn't trying to be a dick. Well, not entirely. But it'd been years since Rylan had driven on gravel roads. It was easy to forget the dangers. "A rock could have flown up and busted it."

A muscle twitched in the man's jaw, but grimly swallowing his hot words, he reached into his pocket and pulled something out that was hidden in his hand. Then, leaning forward, he opened his fingers and allowed a half dozen tiny balls to bounce on Mike's desk.

"I'm sure," Rylan snapped.

Mike pressed his finger against one of the balls, easily recognizing it.

"Buckshot," he said, lifting his head to meet Rylan's icy glare. "Did you see who was shooting?"

"No, I was too busy ducking," Rylan retorted. "By the time I got out to look around the bastard had disappeared."

Mike frowned, trying not to jump to conclusions. The one thing he'd learned over the past few years was that his job as sheriff meant that he had to be the one to see the "big picture." He couldn't just assume he knew what had happened. He had to have the facts to back up his conclusion.

"It could have been a poacher," he said.

"It could also be someone who isn't happy that I'm around to protect Jaci."

Mike instantly bristled. The man talked about Jaci as if he had some right to claim her.

"Clarify your protection," he commanded.

Rylan studied him for a long moment before answering.

"I've installed a new security system," he said. "And this morning I went with her on her deliveries."

Mike forced himself to sit back in his seat. Right now nothing mattered but keeping Jaci safe. Even if it meant swallowing his instinctive male need to compete with Rylan Cooper.

"It's possible the stalker is trying to drive you away."

"I'd say they were more interested in putting me in an early grave."

"Or it could have been whoever rented the Johnson place," Mike continued. "You know as well as I do that people don't like trespassers in this area."

"True," Rylan surprisingly agreed. "They obviously have something to hide."

"Why do you say that?"

Rylan folded his arms over his chest, peering down the length of his nose.

"I have information from one of my contacts you claim you're not interested in."

"Christ, you're annoying," Mike snarled, shoving himself to his feet.

Rylan shrugged. "So I've been told."

Mike took a second to leash his temper. It was ridiculous to let the man get under his skin.

"What did you discover?" he asked.

"The house is being rented by a Vera Richardson," Rylan said.

"Vera Richardson." Mike repeated the name, a faint memory teasing at the edge of his mind. "Why is that name familiar?"

Rylan snorted. "Maybe you attended her funeral."

What the hell was he talking about? "She's dead?"

"Yep," Rylan drawled. "Three years ago."

Mike thought back to when Frank had made a passing

comment that he'd finally rented out his old place. At the time Mike hadn't paid much attention. But he did know it hadn't been three years ago.

"The house has only been rented for the past six months. Maybe less," he at last said. "It has to be a stolen identity."

"Or a miracle," Rylan said in dry tones.

Mike rolled his eyes. "I'll run out there and do some checking."

The sudden ring of the phone sliced through the air, and with a sound of impatience, Mike reached to grab the receiver, pressing it to his ear.

"O'Brien." He felt a chill inch down his spine as he listened to Jenkins's brief report. "You're sure?" he demanded before he could halt the words. "Okay, got it," he soothed the analyst. "Thanks for getting back so quickly."

He replaced the receiver, lifting his head to discover Rylan watching him with an unwavering gaze.

"Was that about Jaci?" the older man demanded.

Mike paused before releasing a slow sigh. As much as he wanted to toss Rylan from his office, the phone call had been a sharp reminder that this was bigger than him and his pride.

Right now he needed any help he could get.

And as Rylan Cooper was so quick to point out, he could provide resources that were way out of Mike's reach.

"A hunch," he at last admitted.

"And?"

Mike grimaced. "This isn't public information, but Anne Dixon is missing."

Rylan gave a sharp lift of his brows. "Are you sure? We ran into Payton and she said her housekeeper was on vacation."

"I've asked her not to talk about Anne until we know

what's happened," Mike said, relieved to learn that Payton was actually doing as he asked.

Surprise, surprise.

"Did you find her?" Rylan asked.

"No." Mike tapped his finger on the top of his desk, his mind absorbing what the latest information meant. Anne might be technically a missing persons case, but he was already preparing for the worst. "I spoke with her sister this morning, and while I was there I asked her Anne's blood type."

Rylan was smart enough to guess why he would be interested in her blood type.

"The locket?"

Mike nodded. "The blood type matched."

Rylan's nose flared, as if he was struggling to hold back his burst of emotion. No doubt he was already thinking of Jaci, and how this was going to impact her.

"Has the DNA been run?" he asked.

"No." Mike's lips tightened. "All I know is that the blood type is A-negative."

"Rare," Rylan said.

"Yep."

"So the blood on the locket belongs to the missing housekeeper." The words were a statement, not a question.

Mike shrugged. "I'm not prepared to leap to conclusions."

Rylan nodded. He'd worked in a sheriff's office before. He understood that Mike wasn't going to commit himself. Especially not to someone who wasn't on the payroll.

"What about the body in the field?" Rylan moved to the next logical question. "Do you have an ID?"

"No." Mike didn't bother to hide his impatience. "Like I said, this isn't Hollywood. Testing takes time."

Rylan held his gaze. "I can make a few calls and get the evidence fast-tracked."

Mike's muscles clenched, but he forced himself to give a sharp nod. "Then do it," he said, lowering himself back into his seat as he sent his companion a dark glance. "Now, I have work to do."

As if sensing Mike had reached the end of his patience, Rylan turned to stroll toward the door. Of course, he couldn't let Mike have the last word.

Pulling open the door, he glanced over his shoulder. "One more piece of information."

"What?" Mike snapped, understanding why someone had taken a potshot at this man.

He wanted to squeeze off a couple bullets himself.

Not to kill, but . . .

Rylan's lips twitched, clearly reading his annoyance. "You might ask Christopher Hamilton what he's been doing the past two years."

Mike frowned. Okay, he hadn't been expecting that. "He was in St. Louis," he said.

"Maybe," he said. "But if he was there, he wasn't attending college."

Stepping out of the room, Rylan shut the door behind him and Mike released a hissing breath as the throbbing behind his right eye amped up to a full-blown headache.

"Crap."

What had Christopher been doing for the past two years? And why had he been driving past Jaci's house yesterday? And when was the last time he'd seen their housekeeper?

Questions that clearly needed to be answered.

Unfortunately, he'd dealt with the powerful Hamilton clan before. As soon as they realized that he was trying to dig up information on the precious Christopher, they would lawyer up. Mike wouldn't have a chance of having a reasonable conversation that would easily clear Christopher of any suspicion.

Trying to decide how he could investigate without wading through the Hamilton lawyers, Mike's dark thoughts were interrupted when the door opened and his deputy stepped inside.

He frowned as the young man strolled forward, his black Windbreaker lightly coated with raindrops. "Where have you been?"

Sid tilted his head, as if confused by the question. "You wanted me to go to the airport, didn't you?"

Mike deliberately lifted his arm to glance at the watch strapped around his wrist. He'd called Sid before dawn this morning to ask him to wait in the airport parking lot to see if Blake Hamilton was one of the passengers.

"The plane took off hours ago," he said.

Sid shrugged. "I stayed for the second and third flights. Just in case he overslept."

Mike swallowed his angry words. Sid was a good deputy, but he'd been born and raised in Heron. Under normal circumstances he couldn't leave the office without stopping to chitchat with every person who crossed his path. With the dead body as the center of town gossip, it was going to be impossible for the younger man to complete a task without taking time to savor the limelight.

"I'm assuming Hamilton didn't make an appearance?" he asked.

"Nope," the deputy said. "They haven't seen him for two days. Of course, they said it wasn't that unusual. One of the pilots said Mr. Hamilton told him that he intended to do more work from home and only go to his office on days when he sees his clients. Do you want me to track him down?"

Mike considered before giving a shake of his head. He'd deal with the Hamiltons.

"No." He scribbled a name on a sticky note and held it out. "I want you to do a search on this name," he commanded.

Sid reached for the paper. "Vera Richardson?" he read out loud. "Who is she?"

"Supposedly she rented the old Johnson place. I want to know everything you can find out about her."

Sid shrugged, turning to leave the office. "No problem."

Chapter Thirteen

Leaving the sheriff's office, Rylan strolled around the corner of the courthouse. He'd left his dad's truck with the local auto body shop, who promised to have the window replaced by Monday. In the meantime, he was driving a decrepit Ford truck that was as solid as a tank and apparently built without suspension. Which meant even the smallest bump sent him bouncing off the seat and hitting his head on the roof.

He quickly realized it was wise to keep it on a paved road whenever possible.

Thankfully his father had an SUV that he preferred over his truck unless he was driving through the fields. The older man wouldn't be forced to rattle around in the loaner.

Heading for the monstrosity that was parked at the end of the block, his gaze was captured by the recently remodeled storefront across the street.

When he'd been a young boy the narrow brick building had been used by the local physician. Dr. Marsh had been an old-fashioned sort of doctor. He offered suckers that took the sting out of vaccine shots. He shared stern warnings of what happened to young boys when they jumped off roofs while he set broken arms. And unfortunately doled out Valium like candy, keeping a considerable number of upright Heron citizens in a glorious haze until he'd retired twenty years ago.

Now the brick facade had been whitewashed and large plate-glass windows installed, with gold lettering that read: NELSON GALLERY.

Unable to resist the opportunity to check out a man who had access to Jaci's property, he crossed the street and entered the gallery through the glass door.

Instantly he felt as if he'd been transported far away from Heron.

Gone was the dark paneling and low ceilings of the reception room. And the walls that had sectioned off the two exam rooms and farther back the doctor's private office had been torn down.

The inside had been completely gutted, giving a chic, industrial style that was more suited to a big city than a small farm town.

The space was long and narrow, with exposed brick walls and an open ceiling where the muted lighting hung from iron wires. The floor was a polished cement, and toward the back was a small reception desk.

The stark decor ensured that the focal point of the room was the enormous photos that were hung on the walls.

Rylan's nose wrinkled as his gaze skimmed over the pictures. Most of them had been shot in black-and-white, featuring bleak locations. An overgrown car lot. A barn with peeling paint. A wet city street with a homeless man curled in a corner.

Grim.

There was a stir of movement as a woman rose from the desk and moved to stand in front of him. She was young, not much more than twenty, with dark hair that was carefully smoothed to frame a pale, oval face. Her lips were painted a brilliant red and her dark eyes took a bold survey of Rylan.

She was at the vulnerable age where she craved male attention without fully understanding just how shallow it could be.

"Hi, I'm Lilly," she said, her voice pitched low, as if she was trying to sound sexy. "Can I help you?"

"Yeah." He glanced around the gallery. "I need to speak with Nelson."

"I'm sorry." She stepped forward, her tight, gray dress barely covering the necessary parts. "He's busy with a project."

Rylan flashed his most charming smile. "Tell him an old friend is in town. I'm sure he'll want to see me."

"Oh. Okay." A flustered blush touched her cheeks. "Wait here."

She hurried toward the back of the room, exiting through a small opening. Rylan absently ambled toward one of the pictures. It looked like a vast forest that had been frozen in time. Pure white with hints of shadows between the trunks.

His gaze moved to take in the rough wooden frame. Jaci's work? It seemed likely. Then his gaze lowered to see the discreet tag at the bottom of the photo.

Four thousand dollars.

Holy crap.

"Hello?" A male voice cut through the air and Rylan turned to watch the man approaching him with a frown.

Nelson Bradley looked like an artist. His blond, naturally curly hair was long enough to brush his shoulders. His face was lean, and his dark eyes were emphasized by a pair of round, wire-rimmed glasses. His smile was crooked and his teeth perfect. At the moment he was wearing a pair of faded jeans and a suit jacket.

His approach slowed as he realized just who was waiting for him.

"Rylan Cooper," he said.

Rylan smiled. "Nelson."

The younger man studied him with a gaze that seemed to peel away his outer skin. Like most talented photographers, he no doubt had a keen ability to see the truth beneath the surface.

The knowledge was more than a little unnerving.

"Lilly told me that an old friend had stopped by for a visit," Nelson drawled, a humorless smile playing around his lips. "You'll forgive my surprise. I didn't realize we'd ever been buddies."

Rylan shrugged. Nelson was two years behind him in school and had enjoyed shocking the community by embracing the whole goth fad. His hair had been spiked, his thin body covered in an ankle-length black coat, and his nails painted black.

"We were at least schoolmates," he pointed out.

"If you say so." Nelson shrugged, not particularly impressed. "Are you here to buy a print?"

"They are"—Rylan searched for a suitable word—"something," he at last landed on. "A little grim."

Nelson curled his upper lip. "If you want daisies and clowns painted on velvet you might try the convenience store near the highway."

Rylan kept his expression bland despite the fact he'd just been called a philistine. He wasn't an art expert and he never would be.

He was, however, skilled in getting people to talk.

"I remember you were always taking pictures when we were young," he said.

Nelson shrugged. "I was the photographer for the school paper."

"That's right." Rylan snapped his fingers, as if he'd just remembered something. "Jaci Patterson did something with the paper too. Didn't she?"

"Yeah. She was the editor." The overhead lights glinted off Nelson's glasses, making it impossible to see his eyes. "I wasn't in journalism class, but she talked me into helping out."

"She clearly could spot talent even at an early age," he said.

A portion of Nelson's tension eased. He liked having his ego stroked.

"Jaci has her own share of talent," the younger man said. "I tried to convince her to get her art degree when she left for college. Instead she went into advertising."

Rylan nodded toward the photo of frozen trees on the wall. "Where was this taken?"

Nelson stepped toward the photo, pride etched on his lean face.

"Siberia."

"Impressive," Rylan said. Now he knew Nelson's vulnerability. He liked to talk about his work. For some people it was their family. For others it was a hobby. Or sex. Or the past. Once you knew how to open them up, it was easier to steer them toward what he actually wanted to discuss. "I bet you didn't think when you were growing up in this small town that you would one day leave and travel the world."

Nelson snorted. "Actually I never doubted for a second that I would leave."

"Really?" Rylan covertly studied the man's profile. During high school Nelson had been a little weird, but

Rylan didn't remember him being treated badly by the other kids. "You were unhappy here?"

Nelson sent him a confused glance. "It wasn't a matter of being happy or unhappy. I was stifled," he explained. "The only way to pursue my goals was to leave. Just like you did."

"True," Rylan agreed, willing to promote a sense of brotherhood. "Although I can't claim your fame."

A sly expression settled on Nelson's pale face. "Don't be so modest. I've seen the magazine articles. Aren't you engaged to some starlet?"

Rylan's jaw clenched. Christ. Had his father gone around town shoving that stupid magazine in people's faces? Why not print it in the church bulletin?

"No starlet," he said, not adding the fact that his taste ran more to a pretty girl next door. Or woman next door.

Jaci was definitely no longer a girl.

Nelson turned away from the photo, his gaze once again searing over Rylan with a piercing intensity.

"Engaged or not, I can't imagine you intend to linger in town," he said. "Not when you could be in sunny California."

Hmm. Was the man making casual conversation? Or probing for a time line when Rylan would be leaving the area?

Rylan held his gaze. "Actually I intend to stick around for a while."

"Really?" A meaningless smile touched Nelson's lips. "That will please your dad."

"So he says." Rylan turned the conversation back in the direction he wanted. "I'm surprised you decided to return. With your reputation you could have opened a gallery in New York or LA."

He shrugged. "Most of my business is done over the

Internet. And when my mother became ill I needed to be closer to home."

"I didn't know your mother was sick," Rylan said, racking his brain for a memory of Patricia Bradley. All he could remember was a thin woman with fading red hair and an anxious air.

"She died of cancer last year," Nelson said.

Rylan grimaced. It'd been years since his own mother had died, but he still felt the ache of her loss.

"I'm sorry," he said with sincere regret.

"Thank you. We were very close."

"Do you intend to stay in Heron?" he pressed.

"I have to travel to take my pictures, but this will always be home." The sound of a ringing phone came from the reception desk, quickly followed by Lilly's low voice. Nelson's expression hardened, as if suddenly reminded that Rylan was interrupting his work. "If you're not here to buy, then what do you want?"

"Just catching up," Rylan said smoothly.

"Catching up on what?"

Before Rylan could come up with a legitimate excuse, the young receptionist was standing at Nelson's side.

"I'm sorry to interrupt, but Barry Wallace is on the line," she said.

Nelson nodded, sending Rylan a dismissive glance. "That's my West Coast agent. I have to take his call."

"Go ahead," Rylan urged, casually glancing toward the door. "I need to get back to help Dad with the evening chores."

Nelson offered a mocking smile. "If you change your mind about a print—"

"You'll be the first to know," Rylan drawled.

With a short nod, Nelson pivoted to walk across the room, rounding the reception desk and disappearing up a narrow flight of stairs that led to the upper floor. An office? Or maybe he'd converted the space into an apartment.

Either way, Rylan wasn't about to waste the unexpected opportunity.

Turning toward the photos on the wall, he aimlessly drifted toward the back of the gallery, well aware the young receptionist was following him.

He halted at a black-and-gray picture of a foggy London street when Lilly at last made her move.

"See anything you like?" she said in suggestive tones.

Rylan bit back his instinctive urge to tell her that she should be flirting with boys her own age. When did he become the grouchy old dude who worried more about a young woman's lack of common sense than seeing her naked?

"They're all very original," he said.

"Nelson is a genius," she breathed, hero-worship in her tone.

Were the two lovers? Rylan gave a small shake of his head. No. She wouldn't be blatantly flirting with him if she was involved with Nelson. Not when her job depended on his goodwill.

"How long have you worked for him?" he asked.

She shrugged. "Almost a year. I started right after I graduated from high school."

"A year." He acted impressed. "He must be a good boss."

"He's gone a lot, and when he's here he's usually working in his studio out back." Lilly's gaze flickered toward the opening at the back of the gallery. "As long as I don't intrude into his private studio he's pretty easy to get along with."

The fact that the artist didn't want anyone in his work space only intensified Rylan's determination to get a peek inside.

"Does his wife help with the gallery?" he asked.

"Oh, he's not married," Lilly said, leaning toward him, as if sharing some big secret. "I think every woman in town has tried to get him to the nearest church, but he's not interested."

"I'm assuming he prefers to play the field."

"Yeah." Lilly heaved a wistful sigh. "But no one local. He likes women from the city who are more sophisticated."

Realizing that Nelson was smart enough to keep his private life secreted from the local gossips, Rylan gave an absent nod. He needed to get to the back before Nelson returned to the gallery.

"I should be taking off," he said, acting as if he'd been struck with a sudden thought. "But before I go, is there a restroom I could use?"

With a tiny pout of disappointment, Lilly stepped away. "Down the hall." She waved a hand in an absent gesture. "First door on the left."

Keeping his pace to a casual stroll, Rylan followed her direction, finding himself in a dark hallway. On the left was the public bathroom, and to the right was a closed, unmarked door.

With a quick glance over his shoulder to make sure Lilly hadn't followed him, Rylan reached to grab the handle. Unlocked. Pushing open the door, he stepped into a large room that had been transformed into an art studio.

Edging forward, Rylan took in the large prints that were placed on easels, and the stack of frames in the corner. There was a long table across the cement floor that groaned beneath the weight of the expensive computer equipment.

There was no sign of a darkroom, although Nelson might have one at another location. Perhaps photographers no longer used them? Rylan shrugged, making a quick circle of the room.

Nothing looked out of place. He checked through the shelves and opened the two cabinets at the back. Then he moved to the computer, touching the mouse to get rid of the screen saver so he could see whatever it was Nelson had been working on before Rylan had interrupted.

A screen of tiny images popped up.

Ah, Nelson's latest pictures.

He leaned forward, not really interested when he caught sight of the floodwaters that were the primary focus of the photos.

The massive destruction was a perfect theme for the photographer's love of all things dark and grim.

Then Rylan's brows drew together as he realized that it wasn't the deluge of muddy water that the man had been capturing, but what was floating in it.

Shit. Rylan shuddered. It was misty enough to make it difficult to make out more than the long tangle of dark hair and shadowed form. But there was no mistaking it was the unknown woman from Johnson's field.

His gaze moved to the next photo. It was the skull that was stuck in the mud, the empty eye sockets staring toward the gray sky as if pleading for peace.

A chill inched down his spine, even as he said a curse and straightened.

The pictures might be gruesome, but they proved nothing more than Nelson was willing to profit from the darker side of human nature.

Time to leave.

With quick steps he retraced his way to the outer room, suddenly anxious to be out of the gallery.

Hovering near the reception desk, Lilly rushed to intercept him, pushing a sticky note into his hand.

"Here."

Rylan glanced down in confusion. "What's this?"

She brushed her fingers down his arm. "My number, in case you want a private showing."

Rylan stepped out of the gallery with a small shake of his head. He felt a sudden need to see Jaci. There was something fresh, and clean, and down-to-earth about her.

Exactly what he needed.

Crossing the street, he balled up the sticky note, intending to throw it away. Instead, he shoved it in his pocket.

There was a chance he might have more questions for Lilly.

He glanced up at the murky sky that shrouded the area in darkness as he circled the cabin, ensuring there were no tracks in the soggy yard.

The incessant rain might be a pain to most of his neighbors, but it proved to be a bonus for him. Not only did the gloom and shadows mean he could move around the countryside unnoticed, but he could easily see if anyone had been near his cabin.

And, if things had been normal, the soft ground would have been a blessing. Burying a body was far more difficult than most people could imagine.

In the movies they showed a man with a shovel who could dig a grave in less than five minutes. Idiots. It could take hours to get a body deep enough to keep it from being found by animals.

Doing two more sweeps, he at last approached the cabin from the side. His footprints wouldn't be noticed by anyone using the narrow path that wound through the thick cluster of trees. Plus, it took him directly toward the root cellar that had been built by the previous owner.

Pulling the key from his pocket, he knelt beside the wooden door that was built into the ground next to the foundation. Then, using the key in the heavy padlock, he gave a last look around before he was tugging it up far enough so that he could slip inside.

Making sure that the door was firmly closed behind him, he pocketed the key and made his way down the narrow stairs. Only when his feet were firmly planted on the packed earth, and he was wrapped in the cool, musky air, did he pull a flashlight from the backpack he was carrying and switch it on.

A bright beam of light sliced through the darkness, revealing that he was standing in something that looked remarkably like a hobbit house. The roof was slightly domed, with wooden shelves that lined the walls with dusty mason jars filled with beets and turnips and something he assumed were potatoes. Maybe parsnips.

He hadn't really taken much notice of them. Most of the time he kept the cramped space covered in sheets of plastic. Even when he wasn't planning to have a guest, he'd kept everything primed.

Organization. Preparation. Attention to detail.

The keys to success.

And all of them had served him well over the past hours.

He turned the flashlight to the center of the cramped space, revealing the woman lying in the middle of the floor.

At a distance, she looked as if she'd stretched out for a nap.

Her dark hair, which was streaked with silver, was pulled into a sensible bun. Her large-boned body was dressed in a velour jogging suit. And her round face had an expression of sweet contentment.

There was no sign of violence. Not unless you pulled aside the zipped top to reveal the bruises that marred the skin of her throat.

A rare pang of regret sliced through his heart.

Anne Dixon hadn't been like the others. She didn't use her sexuality as a weapon. She didn't enjoy teasing and tormenting men as if it was a game.

No. Anne had been like a mother. All warm and kind and smelling like oatmeal cookies.

But a sacrifice had been demanded.

Kneeling at the woman's side, he reached out to lightly touch her cold face, but he wasn't seeing Anne Dixon. No. He was remembering the pleasure that had surged through him like a tidal wave as he'd watched Jaci receive his gift.

Briefly he considered his next move.

A part of him wanted to end the game. Why not dispose of Anne and bring Jaci home where she belonged?

That was the goal, after all.

But another part of him wasn't ready to bring it all to an end.

There was still fun to be had.

And scores to be settled . . .

Chapter Fourteen

Jaci was removing the loaves of bread from the oven when her cell phone began to make a shrill, obnoxious sound.

Scowling at the horrible noise, she set down the bread and tossed aside the oven mitts. Then grabbing the phone she'd left on the counter, she stared down at the flashing screen.

It took a full minute for her tired brain to realize what was happening.

Then her heart slammed against her ribs. The alarms. Her glance instantly shifted to the two dogs who were curled on the floor by the stove, soaking up the heat.

Clearly they didn't sense an intruder.

Grabbing a knife off the kitchen table, she cautiously made her way through the house to the living room. She felt ridiculous, but it was the only weapon she had. At least until she could get ahold of the shotgun in her closet.

Her mouth was dry as she moved across the shadowed room. She'd been in the kitchen for hours. She hadn't bothered to turn on the lights anywhere else.

She crept past the window, her gaze naturally glancing through the open curtains. The breath she was holding was released on a hiss as she easily recognized the large tractor parked next to her garage.

How did she miss the sound of Andrew pulling out of the back field?

Obviously the short nap she'd taken didn't do a thing to clear the fog from her brain.

Returning to the kitchen, she set the knife on the table and grabbed her phone to switch off the alarm. Keeping it in her hand, she moved into the mudroom to pull on her boots and coat.

Then, whistling for her dogs, she headed out into the rain. There was no way she was leaving the two miscreants alone with the four loaves of bread and three pies she'd just baked for the local bank's staff appreciation dinner. The branch manager was coming by to pick them up later that evening.

Rounding the house, she headed straight toward the shop. The dogs charged ahead of her, dancing around Andrew as he turned to face her.

"Sorry," he said, giving Riff and Raff a pat on the head before straightening. "I didn't mean to disturb you."

She smiled. "No problem. I should have warned you that I had locks installed."

"I'm glad you did." He sent her a chiding glance. "About time you decided to take your safety serious."

Her lips twitched. Andrew had been nagging her forever to get some sort of alarm. She wondered what he would think if he knew the full extent of her new security system.

"Did you need something?"

"I have a few pieces of wood I thought you might want." He nodded his head toward the pile of thick sticks he'd stacked near the door of the shop.

"They're wonderful," she said, pulling the keys from her pocket to unlock the door. Reaching around the edge of the jamb, she flicked on the light. "I'll put them in the corner to dry."

Together they carried the branches into the shop, spreading them over a tarp she pulled from a shelf.

Once they were done, Andrew tugged off his heavy gloves while Jaci reached for a rag to wipe her muddy hands.

"I thought you might want some driftwood to make those garden signs," he said, referring to the small posts with the names of various vegetables painted on them. Andrew had taken them to several small stores when he'd traveled to Kansas City during Christmas. "Those sold like crazy."

Jaci wrinkled her nose. She'd made a fortune on the signs. After all, they were nothing more than reclaimed wood and a little paint, and they'd sold for twenty bucks apiece. But she didn't have the time to travel and peddle them around Kansas City.

"I don't know when I'll get over there," she said in regretful tones.

Andrew shrugged. "I'm going next week."

"To Kansas City?"

"Yep."

"Visiting Irene again?" Jaci asked.

Andrew's aunt had married a man with a farm near the suburbs of the large town. Andrew had stayed with them when he'd attended UMKC to get his degree in agriculture. He still spent time with them each year. The couple had never had any children and Andrew went over to take care of the tasks that his uncle could no longer do on his own.

"Yeah," he said. "Uncle Josh needs help patching up his roof."

She smiled. "You're a good man."

He blushed, shifting from foot to foot. "It's not completely unselfish."

Jaci arched her brows. "Why do you say that?"

His blush deepened. "I have a college friend I've been chatting with online," he admitted. "She recently moved back to Kansas City. We're hoping for a chance to get together."

"Why, Andrew Porter," she teased, before reaching out to lightly touch his arm. "I'm glad. I hope the two of you have a great time."

He studied her with a small smile. "And speaking of old friends, I spoke with Rylan this morning."

It was Jaci's turn to blush. Like she was still that fifteen-year-old girl with an unrequited love for her gorgeous neighbor.

She cleared her throat. "Did you?"

"Yep."

Jaci tried to act casual. "Anything interesting?"

He reached up to grab his seed hat, pulling it off to shake away the clinging raindrops.

"He told me you were being pestered," he said.

Jaci's lips tightened. After the humiliation she'd endured the last time the lockets had started to arrive, she'd hoped to keep her latest harassment from making the rounds of the town gossips.

"I'm glad he feels the need to share my private business with the whole neighborhood," she said.

"It wasn't the whole neighborhood, it was me." Andrew didn't bother to hide his concern. "He wants me to keep an eye out when I'm in the fields."

She stubbornly refused to be soothed. "It's not his place to ask you to do anything."

"He's worried about you." Andrew stepped forward,

tugging her rigid body in his arms. "Just like I'm worried about you."

She heaved a rueful sigh, laying her head against his broad chest. "I'm fine, Andrew," she told him. "I'm being careful."

He dropped a brotherly kiss on the top of her head. "I want you to know that I'll be working in the back fields for the next few days. If you need me I can be at the house in less than five minutes."

The knowledge was reassuring even as it was slightly terrifying. The last thing she wanted was for Andrew to be put in danger because she had some crazed stalker.

"Thank you," she said.

Without warning the sound of a male voice sliced through the air.

"Am I interrupting?"

Jaci jerked as if she'd been struck, wondering why her dogs hadn't warned her there was an intruder. But Andrew took his time lowering his arms and stepping back. Then slowly he turned toward the door where Rylan was standing.

Her heart gave a familiar flutter, even as Jaci realized that this man wasn't the same boy who'd left Heron. Not only had he physically changed, with broader shoulders and features that had been honed to a stark beauty. But there was a ruthless air of command that seemed to fill the shop with his sizzling power.

"Nope. I was about to head out," Andrew said, slapping his hat back on his head. "See you tomorrow, Jaci."

A silence filled the shop as Andrew crossed the room, nodding to Rylan as he stepped aside to let him through the doorway.

Jaci instinctively slammed her hands on her hips, her chin tilted to a defiant angle.

Prowling forward, Rylan lifted his brows at her aggressive posture.

"What's up?" he demanded. "I haven't said anything to earn that frown."

"You've been talking about me behind my back."

He blinked, as if caught off guard by her accusation, then his eyes narrowed as he realized what she was talking about.

"Andrew is quiet, he's not stupid," he said.

"I know that," she snapped.

Rylan moved until he was standing directly in front of her. "He saw the sheriff and the deputies looking around the house."

"So you asked him to keep an eye on me?"

"Yes." He paused, his expression still hard. "But that doesn't mean I fully trust him."

She blinked. "Andrew?"

"Until he's proven innocent, he remains on the suspect list."

Her mouth parted to remind him that she'd known Andrew since they were both in diapers, only to snap her lips shut. She didn't think Andrew would ever do anything to hurt her, but he was right.

She had to be careful.

"What are you doing here?" she instead demanded.

"I installed a few more cameras around the property," he said.

"More?" she asked, her gaze skimming over his thick jacket and down to the damp jeans that clung to his legs. His boots were thick with mud, indicating he'd been doing the work himself.

His lips stretched with a dangerous smile. "These are far more high-tech than those we put in yesterday. Anyone approaches your place and they'll be caught red-handed."

Jaci swallowed a sigh. It was obvious that Rylan was in his element.

"What am I supposed to do with them?"

"Nothing," he assured her. "I'll keep them monitored, and when this is over I'll have them removed."

She gave a slow nod. No point in arguing.

"Is that all?"

"No." A portion of his tension eased as he flashed his most charming smile. "I hoped to beg for my dinner."

She battled back an answering smile. "Aren't you eating with your dad?"

He shook his head. "The library board members are meeting to make plans for the yearly spaghetti dinner."

"I forgot the fund-raiser was coming up," she said. The town library depended on state grants and local donations. The spaghetti dinner was the biggest source of funding to keep the doors open three days a week. "Tell Elmer I'll donate two-dozen cupcakes and four loaves of garlic bread."

An indefinable emotion darkened his eyes. "Are you always so generous?"

She furrowed her brow. Elmer had told her that Rylan and his partner, Griff, had given away millions of dollars to charity. A few cupcakes and some bread didn't seem like much in comparison.

"I like to support the library," she said. She still remembered the day her grandmother had taken her to get her library card. The old building was long and narrow with warped floors and lights that flickered from a cavernous ceiling. But Jaci had felt as if she was walking into a secret paradise. Her heart had missed a beat at the sight of the endless rows of books that lined the walls, and the scent of aging leather that had laced the air. "It was my home away from home when I was young."

He chuckled, his gaze moving over her face. "I remember. I used to tease you for always having your nose stuck in a book."

"You weren't the only one. My friends used to warn me that carrying around books made me look like a dork." She grimaced, abruptly struck by an unwelcomed memory. "And once Christopher grabbed my favorite book and tossed it into the boys' bathroom. The jerk."

He reached to brush the damp strands of hair that clung to her forehead.

"*Pride and Prejudice*."

Her eyes widened in surprise.

"How did you know?" she demanded. As far as she knew, Rylan had never paid enough attention to her to know the name of the worn book she'd carried around like a security blanket. Then, she was struck by another memory. This one far more pleasant. "You," she breathed. "It was you."

"Me?"

"You left the new copy of *Pride and Prejudice* in my school locker."

Ancient anger clenched his jaw. "I would have beat the crap out of the little pissant, but he was younger than me and half my size. So instead I bought a new book."

She shook her head. At the time, the thoughtful gesture had meant more to her than she could ever express. Not just because she had a new copy of the book she loved. But the kindness had helped to ease the sting of her half brother's cruelty.

"Why?" she demanded.

"I knew how much it meant to you." His fingers lingered, tracing the line of her brow.

She felt a flutter in the pit of her stomach. A dangerous sensation.

"Why hide it in my locker?" she pressed. "Why not give it to me?"

He hesitated, as if searching for the right words. "I didn't want a fuss."

A fuss? What was that supposed to mean?

It was the hint of regret in his eyes that finally made her suck in a sharp breath.

"I get it," she said. "You didn't want me to think you actually cared about me."

His hand slid to cup her cheek. "Jaci, the truth is that I always cared about you," he said, his voice rough. "Just as I knew you were special in my life. I simply wasn't ready to accept what it might mean."

The flutter intensified, spreading through her body until she was shivering.

Aggravating ass. He'd known she loved *Pride and Prejudice*. And had eased her pain after Christopher had hurt her. And now he was doing everything possible to protect her. Including mucking through the mud to put up more cameras.

How the heck was she supposed to remember she didn't want anything to do with him?

"It's no wonder your partner made you the salesman of your company," she said dryly. "You have a golden tongue. I don't doubt that you could convince anyone to buy your products."

His fingers drifted down the side of her neck. "Can I convince you to share your dinner with me?"

With a roll of her eyes, she turned to head out of the shop. "Come on."

Mike deliberately waited until dinnertime to approach the old Johnson farmhouse.

Sid's background check on Vera Richardson had revealed what Rylan had already told him. The woman had died three years ago of lung cancer and had been buried in a small town forty minutes away. A deeper dig revealed that Vera had one son, Paul, who'd been caught up in a meth bust in Hannibal. The reason Vera's name had been familiar to Mike was that she'd actually turned in her son when she discovered he and his buddies were cooking drugs in her basement.

Paul had been released from jail six months ago. And Mike was willing to bet good money that the idiot had returned to his former profession.

Pulling the patrol SUV to a halt in the darkness of the trees, Mike glanced at the deputy sitting next to him.

"Is everyone in place?" he demanded.

"Yep." Sid nodded, his fingers fidgeting with the holster of his gun. The younger man had only been on a handful of busts. It was no wonder he was a little twitchy. "Hal and Bobby will keep a watch on the back."

There'd been no way in hell Mike would approach the house without backup.

"You warned them that there might be guns?"

"Yeah." Sid sent him a wry smile that was barely visible in the darkness. "'Course, around here there's always guns."

"Isn't that the truth," Mike said, shoving open the door and stepping out of the SUV.

Local townsfolk were notorious for having multiple

weapons in the house. The upside was that they very rarely felt the need to use them for more than hunting.

Sid joined him as they moved out of the trees and crossed the yard, which had turned into a disgusting bog.

Instantly there was the sound of barking.

"Dog," Sid said, his voice tense.

"Great." Mike worried more about a dog attacking him than getting shot. "Let's try to keep this friendly."

They were climbing the steps to the sagging porch when the newly installed door was yanked open and the light from inside spilled out.

The man standing in the doorway was average height, with a body that was so slender it looked gaunt beneath the filthy T-shirt and jeans. His hair was lanky and hung to his shoulders. His thin face was lined with wrinkles that made him look closer to sixty than to the thirty Mike knew him to be.

Because there was no mistake that this man matched his mug shot.

He was Paul Richardson.

"Whaddaya want?" Paul growled. A straggling patch of hair grew on his chin.

"I don't think friendly is going to be an option," Sid said, moving to stand at Mike's side.

"Nope." Keeping his motions slow, Mike pulled out his badge despite the fact he had on his uniform. Tweakers weren't famous for their intelligence. "Sheriff O'Brien. I have a few questions."

The man licked his lips, his eyes darting from side to side. He was higher than a freaking kite.

"I haven't done nothing wrong," he rasped.

"This will only take a few minutes." Mike tucked away his badge, glancing over Paul's shoulder to the shabby interior of the house. "Can I come in?"

"No, you damned well can't come in. Not without a warrant," the man snapped. "This is my property."

"Actually the property belongs to Frank Johnson," Mike corrected.

Paul hunched a thin shoulder. "I pay my rent and I know my rights."

There was the sound of movement toward the back of the house. Unfortunately, the man had hit the proverbial nail on the head. Mike couldn't force his way in.

"The rental agreement was made between Frank and a Vera Richardson," he said. "Is she here?"

The eyes darted faster. "Not now."

Mike smiled. "I can wait. What time will she be home?"

There was the sudden sound of shouting coming from the backyard.

"Sid, keep an eye on him," he commanded.

The deputy pulled out his gun, holding it at his side. A silent warning.

"Got it," he said.

With a last, warning glance toward Paul Richardson, Mike jumped off the porch and cautiously made his way around the corner. He wasn't going to stumble into a potential shootout.

Reaching the rear of the house, he found the back door wide open, with four miserable people lying face-first in the muddy yard. His two deputies were standing over them with their guns drawn.

"What's going on?" he demanded, his gaze turning to Hal.

The older man offered a rare smile. "These four yahoos took off through the back door. I told them to stop and they tried to get rid of their stash." He nodded his head toward a camouflage backpack that'd been tossed toward the nearby culvert.

Mike reached into his pocket to snap on a pair of latex gloves as he walked across the soggy ground. Using the tips of his fingers, he pulled the pack open just far enough to catch a glimpse of the tiny plastic baggies that had been stuffed inside.

Straightening, he turned toward the people lying on the ground. In the light from the back door he could make out that there were three women and one man. They all looked as thin and sickly pale as their host.

The man lifted his head, his body twitching as if it was impossible to lie still.

"He's lying," he shouted, as if he talked loud enough and fast enough, Mike would believe his accusations. "I've never seen that stuff. This is police brutality."

Bobby gave a sharp laugh, pointing toward the patrol vehicles. "It's on the dashboard cameras, you—"

"Put them in cuffs, and take them to the station," Mike interrupted. The sooner he had them locked down, the better. "Hal, you take Mr. Chatty and one of the women. Bobby you take the other two women in your vehicle. And when you get back to the station call animal control to come and pick up the dog. I don't want the poor creature left alone here."

Mike waited for the deputies to get the suspects off the ground and cuffed and wrestled to the separate SUVs. Then, moving up the back steps, he paused and keyed the mike on his walkie-talkie.

"Sid, I'm going through the back door," he warned. He tried to avoid spooking his deputies. They were great guys, but inexperienced.

Sid's voice crackled back, "Okay."

He pulled his gun before stepping directly into the

kitchen and calling out. "Sheriff's Department. Come out with your hands in the air."

He waited to the count of a hundred, then he moved forward. Instantly the hairs on his nape stood upright. There was a familiar, pungent stench of chemicals that permeated the house.

A stench that only came from the manufacturing of meth.

Trying his best to hold his breath, he moved from room to room, checking in closets and under beds to make sure there was no one hiding inside. Only when he was certain that they had all the bad guys, he moved to the living room, stepping over piles of pizza boxes and empty beer cans.

Christ. The house had once been the pride of the Johnson family. Every inch had been scrubbed clean and freshly painted every year. Now it was fit for nothing more than a bulldozer.

A shame.

Moving to the doorway, he slapped his cuffs on Paul Richardson.

"Call in the Drug Task Force," he told Sid, shoving his prisoner forward. "Don't let anyone go in there."

Sid took a hasty step backward, his nose curling with disgust. "Meth?"

"Yep. A full working lab."

Mike did his best to ignore Paul. The idiot shouted obscenities from the time he was placed in the back of the SUV until Mike had him in the interview room.

It wasn't until he'd read the man his Miranda rights and had the video set up to tape the session that he finally sat across the table and started his questions.

"Now." He leaned back in his seat, emphasizing his own comfort in his surroundings. He was top dog here. A silent intimidation that made Paul slump lower in his seat. "Who is Vera Richardson, and what's her connection to you?" he asked.

Paul stuck out his lower lip, looking like a petulant child. "I don't have to tell you nothing."

"True," Mike easily agreed. "You have the right to remain silent."

Paul licked his lips. Mike waited. In his experience, tweakers could never keep their lips shut.

The clock on the wall ticked. Less than two minutes later, Paul leaned forward, placing his hands on the table.

"If I answer your questions will you tell the judge that I cooperated?"

Mike gave a lift of his shoulder. "It depends on what you give me."

Tick, tock. Tick, tock.

"Vera was my mother," he abruptly burst out.

Mike studied him with an unwavering gaze. "Was?"

"She died a few years ago."

"How did her name end up on the lease?"

"I was fresh out of jail." Paul's eyes darted from side to side. Guilt? More likely he was trying to think how to admit the truth without confessing that he was in the wrong. Long-term drug use destroyed any morals the man might once have had. "I knew no one would rent me a place."

"So you used the name of your dead mother?"

"She owed me," he said. "It was because of her I was arrested in the first place."

Mike hid his grimace of disgust. "Why choose the Johnson farm?"

"I wanted someplace without a bunch of nosy neighbors."

"Yeah, hard to keep a meth lab secret when the neighbors are complaining about the stench," Mike drawled.

"I don't know what you're talking about." Paul's lips tightened, and Mike sensed he was going to clam up. He had to soothe the man's agitation. "I'm not interested in your kitchen experiments."

Paul frowned. "Then whaddaya want? I admitted I used my mom's name to rent the house. That's not a crime."

"As a matter of fact, it is, but I'm more concerned with the woman you buried in the back field."

Mike delivered the accusation in a smooth tone, watching as Paul's forehead furrowed with confusion.

"Is that some sort of code?"

"What happened?" Mike continued. "Did she overdose and you had to get rid of her? If that's what happened, then you need to tell me now. Disposing of a body is a lot different from first degree murder."

It took a long time for the words to penetrate Paul's drug-addled brain. Then, a dark red color stained his pockmarked face.

"No way," he snarled. "I'm not going to let you pin some murder on me. I've never hurt anyone in my life."

Mike gave a sad shake of his head. "It's going to be a little hard to believe when a dead woman was discovered less than a mile from your meth lab."

"Look, I don't know who offed her, but it has nothing to do with me." Genuine fear flared through the man's eyes. "I swear."

"Fine." Mike leaned forward, offering a way for the man to escape the electric chair. "Maybe it was one of your buddies. Things get out of hand at parties," he sympathized. "It could be that she didn't feel like playing and your friend had to rough her up."

"No." Paul slammed his fist against the table. "We might be trash to most people, and it's true we've all made our share of mistakes, but there's never been anything more than a couple of scuffles in my house."

Mike kept his expression unreadable, even as he instinctively doubted that this man had anything to do with the dead woman. Or the locket on Jaci's door.

The man was too stoned to be capable of feigning such sincere outrage.

"Define scuffles," he ordered.

"Some pushing and shoving." He gave a restless shrug. "Maybe a black eye."

Mike tried a new angle of attack. "If you're so nonviolent, then why did you take a potshot at Rylan Cooper earlier today?"

The man gave him a blank stare. "Who?"

"He was driving past your place and someone shot out his back windshield."

Paul threw himself back in his seat, his cuffs rattling as he glared at Mike with bloodshot eyes.

"This is bullshit," he snarled. "Do you plan to try and pin every crime in the county on me?"

Mike drummed the tips of his fingers on the table. "I have the buckshot to prove that someone on your property was the shooter."

"Well, it wasn't . . ." The man's words trailed away, as if a coherent thought had managed to form in the fog of his mind. "Wait. What time did it happen?"

Mike thought back to when Rylan had entered his office. "Around one in the afternoon."

"Ha." Paul sent him a smug smirk. "I wasn't home."

Mike rolled his eyes. "Of course you weren't."

"No, really," the man insisted. "I had a meeting with my parole officer in Hannibal at one. You can call and ask her."

Mike made a mental note to call the parole office. He

wasn't going to accept this man's claims. Not without double-checking.

"Who was in the house?"

"No one. My old lady had to drive me," he said. "When I left I had the place locked up tight."

Mike released a slow breath, disappointment curling through the pit of his stomach. He'd hoped that he could at least clear up Rylan's shooting.

"Have you noticed anything unusual?" he asked, more out of habit than any hope Paul might have some useful information.

"Whaddaya mean?"

"Anyone roaming around that shouldn't be there?"

"I don't pay much attention."

Of course he didn't. Mike's lips flattened as he shoved himself to his feet.

"Don't move," he commanded, locking Paul in the interview room.

He was done interrogating the man for now. If he had more questions later he knew where he could find him.

This drug bust was strike three for Paul Richardson.

He was going away for a long, long time.

Entering the reception area, he glanced toward Carol, who should have gone home hours ago.

"Is the head of the task force here yet?"

Carol shook her head. "No, but they called and said they were on their way. They should arrive in the next fifteen minutes."

"Would you tell them to keep me posted if they find any weapons during the search of the house?"

"Yep." Carol pointed toward the door. "Now go home and get some dinner."

Chapter Fifteen

Jaci sipped her wine as she watched Rylan polish off the last of his dinner.

It felt surreal.

She'd spent a good chunk of her youth fantasizing about having Rylan Cooper sitting at this table with her. Of course, back then her imagination rarely got past the idea of holding hands under the table, and sneaking kisses when her grandparents weren't looking.

Now . . .

Now her mind was capable of conjuring all sorts of vivid images that included a naked Rylan, the kitchen table, and a bowl of homemade whipped cream that was waiting for her in the fridge.

Heat swirled through her, an ache deep inside making her shift uneasily on her seat.

Seemingly unaware of the chaos he was creating inside her, Rylan pushed aside his empty plate and regarded her with a warm gaze.

"Delicious," he said. "I haven't had homemade potpie in years."

"It's not very fancy," she said, hoping he would assume the blush staining her cheeks was caused by his compliment and not the fact she wanted to rip off his clothes.

He gave a lift of his shoulder, his gaze sweeping down her body, which was casually covered by a gray sweatshirt and yoga pants that she'd changed into after coming back from her workshop.

"I don't like fancy," he said.

She rolled her eyes, remembering the blond beauty standing beside him in the magazine picture. She'd been the very definition of stylish glamour.

"Right."

"It's true." With a smooth motion, Rylan was on his feet. "Go make yourself comfortable. I'll take care of the dishes."

Jaci lifted her brows as Rylan stacked the plates and headed toward the sink.

"You?"

"I'm not completely helpless," he assured her.

Pushing herself out of her chair, Jaci moved to lean against the counter next to the sink.

"Do you have a housekeeper in California?"

His lips twitched as he squirted a dollop of soap into the deep farm sink and filled it with water.

"Will it make you think less of me if I say yes?" he demanded.

"Does what I think of you matter?" she asked as he efficiently washed the plates and put the pie pan in the water to soak.

He grabbed a dish towel, wiping his hands before turning to face her with an oddly somber expression.

"More than I ever imagined possible."

There was a fierce intensity in his gaze that sent a tiny flare of panic through her.

"I should—"

"Kiss me," he interrupted, stepping closer until she could feel the hard brush of his body.

She tilted back her head to meet his brooding gaze, her mouth going dry.

"That's not what I was going to say."

"Are you sure?" he said, bending his head to brush his mouth over her brow.

She jerked. Had she been struck by lightning? It felt like it.

"Pretty sure."

"Hmm." The searing lips moved over her temple and over her cheek. "That's what you should say," he assured her.

"According to you?"

"Yep."

An exhilarating fervor heated her blood, igniting sparks of lust. Her hands lifted to grasp his shoulders.

"Arrogant," she said.

He laughed. "We've established that on several occasions."

She swallowed a low groan, a shiver racing through her. God, he smelled good. Soap and warm male skin.

She wanted to bury her face against his chest and just breathe him in.

"And no doubt will on several more," she said.

"No doubt." He pressed a soft kiss on her lips before tracing the line of her jaw with the tip of his tongue.

Her fingers dug into his shoulders. She felt like she'd been caught in a current and was being swept away by an unstoppable force.

The sheer ferocity of the sensations was frightening.

"I told myself I wasn't going to do this."

"We aren't doing anything," he said, whispering in her ear. Like the serpent in the Garden of Eden. "Just two friends sharing dinner and a glass of wine."

Was he kidding? She was on fire. Her entire body was clenched with a need that he'd stirred to life the minute she'd seen him walking across her yard.

And the danger that had thrown them together had only amped up her sizzling hunger.

"It feels like more than dinner," she told him.

He nuzzled a tender spot just below her ear. "Consider it dessert."

Jaci released a burst of laughter. His words were just so corny she couldn't help herself.

"Does that line ever work?"

Lifting his head, his golden eyes sparkled with amusement. "It was a first try. Is it working?"

"I haven't decided," she lied, her heart melting. Was there anything sexier than a man who could laugh at himself?

He returned his attention to seducing her with the brush of his lips down the curve of her neck. His hands spread over her hips, tugging her against the hard thrust of his arousal.

"Will you let me know when you've reached your conclusion?"

She tilted back her head to give him better access. "Maybe."

He nipped the skin at the base of her throat. "Tough crowd."

"That's what I'm worried about," she said before she could halt the revealing words.

He stilled, his lips brushing against her skin as he spoke. "What?"

It was too late to stop now. "Being part of a crowd," she admitted, cringing at the knowledge that she sounded as if she was expecting far more from this man than just a night or two of great sex.

He sucked in a sharp breath, his hands tightening on her hips. "There's no one but you, Jaci," he said, his voice harsh with a shocking sincerity. "Just you."

She licked her lips. "I—" Whatever she was about to say was forgotten as she felt something buzz against her lower stomach. It took a minute for her to figure out what was going on. "You're vibrating," she said.

"Damn straight, I am." He nuzzled a path of kisses back up her neck, his hand slipping beneath her sweatshirt so he could cup her breast. "You make me shiver all over."

Jaci was doing her own share of shivering. "Your phone," she managed to say. "It's vibrating."

He said a curse, his thumb stroking over the hard tip of her nipple. Pure bliss jolted through her.

"Ignore it."

She wanted to. Her body was aroused to the point of near pain. But even as she arched closer to his enticing warmth, she felt another buzz.

"It might be important."

He groaned, rubbing his hardness against her. "Nothing is more important than this moment."

Buzz, buzz, buzz.

"Rylan," she said.

"Christ." Stepping back, he yanked the phone from his pocket and pressed it against his ear. "What?" he barked. His brows snapped together. "Now?" He listened, his frown deepening. "Fine. Give me directions."

A minute later he was sliding the phone back into his pocket and studying her with open regret.

He was leaving.

She could see it etched on his beautiful male face.

Disappointment washed through her.

"Your partner?" she asked, briskly stepping back as if her entire body wasn't consumed with need.

"No." He grimaced. "O'Brien. He said he's received some evidence he wants to talk to me about."

Her heart missed a beat. Good news or bad? Rylan's expression was impossible to read.

"What kind of evidence?" she demanded.

"That's what I'm about to find out." He brushed a light kiss over her mouth before he was moving toward the mudroom. "Lock your door and keep the monsters inside with you."

She rolled her eyes as he pointed toward the dogs, who were sound asleep beneath the table.

"Yes, sir."

He halted in the doorway. "One more thing."

"What's that?"

He flashed a wicked smile. "This is just a temporary postponement. Don't forget where we left off."

She released a shaky breath, her palms damp.

As if she could ever forget.

Rylan wasn't happy.

It wasn't just the fact that he'd finally had Jaci in his arms. Or that he'd intended to spend the evening slowly and methodically chipping away her refusal to trust him.

It was the fact that he was leaving her all alone in her isolated house with a crazed killer on the loose.

Pulling into the long, tree-lined drive, he studied the small house that was built on the edge of town. Hidden from the road by a high hedge, and surrounded by empty fields, it was painted white with fading blue shutters.

He climbed onto the postage stamp–sized porch, not surprised when the door was pulled open before he could knock.

Mike had sounded edgy on the phone. And not in a good way. It didn't take a psychic to know something had spooked him.

Entering the narrow hall, he allowed Mike to lead him directly into the small kitchen at the front of the house.

"Isn't this the old Hillman place?" he demanded, glancing around as Mike halted in the center of the chipped linoleum floor.

There was an attached dining room that was currently being used as a study, with a desk piled with file folders and a bookcase stuffed with binders and law books.

No surprise that he was a man who brought his work home.

They might not be BFFs, but he didn't doubt for a second Mike O'Brien was a dedicated lawman.

Turning his gaze back to Mike, he took in the man's jeans and sweatshirt. The lawman had been home long enough to change out of his uniform.

"Yeah," he said. "I bought it a couple years ago. I intended to do some remodeling, but—"

Rylan gave a short laugh. "A sheriff never has spare time."

"Nope." He offered a tight smile. "Beer?"

"Sure," Rylan agreed. He'd only had a few sips of wine with his meal.

"Have a seat."

Rylan pulled out a chair, watching Mike as he grabbed the beers out of the fridge and took a seat across the table.

"Is there a reason you wanted to meet here instead of the courthouse?" he asked.

Mike pushed one of the beers across the table before twisting the top off his bottle and taking a long drink.

"I got some information I'm not ready to officially share," Mike told him. "Besides, I didn't want to be interrupted."

"Tell me."

"I had a message from the medical examiner's office."

"They identified the body?"

"The skull."

Rylan lifted his brows. That wasn't what he'd been expecting.

"That was quick."

"Her dental records were already in the system."

Ah. That always cut down the time it took to identify a victim.

"Who was it?"

Mike took another drink. "Angel Harper."

"I know that name," Rylan said. There was something teasing at the edge of his mind. A recollection of when he worked part-time at the sheriff's office. At last he released his breath on a low hiss. "The runaway."

"Yep."

Rylan shook his head, trying to piece through his memories. It'd been almost a dozen years ago. And, he hadn't personally known the young girl who'd been in the area for a few months before she disappeared. But he had seen her around town on occasion. She'd been pretty, with long, red hair and green eyes, although she'd plastered her pale face with too much makeup. And she'd worn clothing that looked like it'd been through a woodchipper. Ripped jeans, a shirt that was torn to show her belly, and gloves with no fingers.

"I was afraid something bad had happened to her," he said.

Mike leaned his elbows on the table, his face shadowed with weariness.

"I barely knew the girl at school, and she went missing before I started working for the department," he said. "What can you tell me about it?"

Now he understood why Mike had called him over. Rylan sipped his beer, trying to dredge up any information that might help.

"Angel was fifteen when she ran away from her aunt's house," he said.

Mike slowly nodded. "Her aunt was Teresa Graham, right?"

"Yeah. Angel was sent there by her mother, who was living in Kansas City. From what Teresa told us, it seemed that Angel had been in trouble with drugs and skipping school."

Two habits that followed her to Heron, Rylan recalled. They'd caught her a dozen times at parties with alcohol, and twice they'd received tips that she was sharing ecstasy with her fellow classmates, but they'd never caught her with the drugs.

Mike absently wiped the beads of sweat off his beer bottle. "What happened when she disappeared?"

"It was one of her teachers who contacted the sheriff's office to say that Angel hadn't been in school for almost two weeks," he said.

"Did you talk to the aunt?" Mike asked.

"Yeah." Rylan shuddered. "The sheriff called her in and she said Angel had taken off. She assumed the girl returned to her mother in Kansas City."

Mike looked predictably confused. "She didn't call her sister to check?"

"I was there when she was talking to the old sheriff."

Rylan had stood in the corner, growingly disgusted with the thin, bitter old woman who'd been vitriolic in her condemnation of being hauled to a police station over something so inconsequential as the disappearance of her niece. "My sense was that she was too happy to be rid of her niece to care. The last thing she wanted was us to find Angel and drag her back."

Mike narrowed his gaze. "Was the aunt happy enough to get rid of her to do something that would ensure she disappeared?"

Rylan wrinkled his nose. During the interview with Teresa he'd been unnerved by the woman's shrill aggression. He remembered thinking he wouldn't blame poor Angel for running away, swiftly followed by a dark concern that maybe Angel hadn't left Heron.

At least not alive.

"The sheriff didn't think so, but he did at least list Angel as a missing person," Rylan said. "To be honest, he was as relieved as Teresa to have the girl out of his jurisdiction."

"He considered her a troublemaker?"

Rylan shrugged. "She liked to party."

"What about you?" Mike abruptly demanded.

"Me?"

"What was your impression of Teresa Graham?"

"From what little I knew about her, I didn't like her. Not just because she obviously didn't give a crap about her niece, but I had friends who had her as a babysitter over the years. They told me horror stories."

"What sort of horror stories?"

Rylan gave a lift of his shoulder. "About being locked in barns and hit with a switch. I even heard that she put kids in an old well."

Mike gave a sudden grunt. "That's right. I remember

those rumors. It was pretty bad." He shook his head. "No authorities tried to shut her down?"

"Who listened to kids back then?" Rylan demanded.

"True." A grim emotion briefly clenched Mike's features and Rylan felt a pang of sympathy.

Everyone in town knew that Mike's dad used to beat the shit out of him, but no one actually stepped in to help him.

"There's more," Rylan said, pulling the other man out of his dark place. "When Teresa was in the office I could smell alcohol on her breath."

Mike polished off his beer before turning in his seat to toss the bottle in a trash can next to the fridge. Then he turned back to Rylan, the ghost from his past once again buried.

"Do you think she might have done something to Angel?" he asked Rylan.

Rylan took time to think through his answer. It would be easy to leap to the conclusion that the older woman was responsible. She was a pathetic excuse of a human being who'd clearly tormented young children.

But right now he couldn't let his opinion of the woman cloud his memory. They had to figure out the truth.

What'd happened to Angel Harper?

"I think she would be capable of making the young girl's life a misery. Or even kicking her out of her house. But murder . . ." He let his words trail away with a shake of his head.

Chapter Sixteen

Rylan met Mike's searching gaze. "You don't think she could have killed her?" the lawman pressed.

"She might accidentally have hurt her and disposed of the body," Rylan conceded. "But cold-blooded murder?" He gave another shake of his head. "No."

Mike tapped his finger on the table, his eyes distant as he tried to imagine how a young girl's skull ended up in a muddy field over a decade later.

Rylan waited, allowing the sheriff to speak.

"What about suicide?" the lawman asked.

Rylan considered the question before giving a lift of his hands. "I suppose she could have thrown herself in the river, but there was no note left behind."

Mike shoved his hands through his hair. "So accident, suicide, or murder. All three are possible."

Rylan's gut twisted. They were both trying to cling to logic. It was vital to keep an open mind when working a case. But inside, they both knew it was murder.

The fact that there was a body of a young woman floating in the same field made it almost a certainty.

"You don't have a cause of death?" Rylan asked.

"Not yet." Mike grimaced. "And with just a skull it's doubtful we'll get many answers."

Rylan held the man's gaze. "I have a few calls I can make."

Mike's lips tightened before he gave a shrug. "Go ahead. Right now I'm willing to take any help I can get."

"I—" Rylan's words were cut short as a horrifying thought seared through his brain. "Shit."

Mike's eyes darted around, as if he was looking for a potential threat.

"What is it?"

"Do you have the date that Angel disappeared?" Rylan demanded, his voice tense.

"I can bring up the official missing person report." Rising to his feet, Mike moved into his makeshift office and grabbed his laptop off the desk. Then, returning to the kitchen, he sat down and fired it up. "Why?"

"A hunch."

Thankfully, Mike didn't feel the need to be a jerk. Instead he logged into his account and pulled up the file on Angel Harper.

"Here." He read from the screen. "November eleventh."

An ugly stab of regret sliced through Rylan's heart. "Halloween."

Mike lifted his gaze, staring at Rylan in confusion. "What about Halloween?"

Rylan planted his hands on the table and shoved himself to his feet. A toxic combination of regret, fear, and fury blasted through him.

The memory of a young, vulnerable Jaci standing in the old sheriff's office, her face pale and her fingers clutched around the gold necklace, seared through his mind.

God. There'd been a killer stalking her and he'd patted her on her head and sent her on her away. He'd not only put her life in danger, but he'd allowed a potential serial killer to continue his murderous game.

If something happened to her, he'd have no one to blame but himself.

"Cooper." Mike interrupted his dark thoughts. "What's going on?"

"That's when Jaci found the first locket on her porch," he said, turning to face the lawman.

"You're sure?"

"Yeah." Rylan clenched his hands, bleakly battling to contain his guilt. "I tried to convince her that it was some sort of Halloween hoax that was meant to scare her. I told her to throw it away and forget about it." A shudder shook through his body. "God."

Mike's jaw hardened, but he understood that now wasn't the time to vent his frustration at the knowledge Rylan had allowed a killer to slip through his fingers.

"Did Jaci have any connections to Teresa Graham?" he instead demanded.

Rylan considered the question. He knew for a fact that Jaci's grandparents never used a babysitter. After the tragic loss of their son, they'd been determined to spend every possible minute with their only grandchild. At least until she went off to college. And the Patterson family wasn't related to the Grahams.

"I don't think so."

Mike glanced back down at the computer screen where he'd pulled up the missing person report for Angel Harper.

"I know Teresa was widowed when she was young," he finally said. "Did she have a man she was seeing?"

Rylan gave a sharp shake of his head. "Not that I know of," he told his companion. "In fact, I had a distinct impression that she didn't like men very much. She told the sheriff several times that she blamed the local boys for all of Angel's troubles, and that she probably ran away because she was being pestered by unwanted attention."

Mike arched a brow. "Did Teresa say if Angel was dating anyone in particular?"

"She was dating a lot of boys," Rylan dryly admitted, his muscles clenching as he suddenly recalled something the aunt had told them. "But the night before she disappeared, she'd been at a party with Christopher Hamilton."

Mike cursed. "Why am I not surprised?"

He was asleep in his bed when the memories returned.

He twitched and moaned, struggling to squash them. He didn't want to endure the horror. Not when he'd just rediscovered his beautiful muse.

But perhaps it was because of Jaci that he was suddenly forced to relive his most painful humiliation. She was his greatest joy, after all. And everything came with a cost.

Releasing a resigned sigh, he conceded defeat, allowing himself to be sucked into the past.

It was dark. Terrifyingly dark, with the stench of his own feces filling the air. He'd shit his pants when the hands had hit him in the middle of his back and pushed him into the abandoned well. It hadn't just been his fear of the shadows. Or the terrifying eight-foot drop. Or even the knowledge that he didn't have the strength to climb out of the pit.

It'd been the mocking laughter of the girl he'd been so anxious to impress.

Angel . . .

He'd thought she might actually be a creature from the heavens when he'd first seen her. The long, fiery hair. The eyes that'd promised a sensual pleasure he'd longed to experience.

The soft, soft skin that his fingers itched to explore.

Angel had been the one who'd invited him to the house after they'd been talking during detention. In a rare moment of weakness, he'd revealed that he'd once been placed in the care of Teresa Graham. And how terrifying it'd been for him to be left in the abandoned well for hours at a time. Angel told him she understood. That she'd also been tortured by her nasty, embittered aunt. And that she wanted to play a trick on the woman they both hated.

He'd naively believed her.

But instead of finding a way to punish Teresa Graham, Angel had instead lured him toward the well at the back of the house. She'd smiled and flirted, and arched her back so her big tits had pressed against her shirt.

Like a Pied Piper for horny boys.

He'd eagerly rushed to stand at her side. And then she'd shoved him over the edge.

Twisting and turning on his mattress, he forced away the shame he'd endured. Far better to remember the night he'd followed the treacherous bitch through the woods.

He'd seen her at the party, and even watched as she'd slipped away with Christopher Hamilton to have sex in the bushes. Whore. As if the rich boy was ever going to give her more than a quickie in the mud.

Following behind her, he waited until she was walking home along the high bluff beside the river before he'd struck.

He'd tackled her from behind, wrapping his fingers around her neck as he'd squeezed the life from her.

Over the years, he'd read about serial killers. He'd always known he had the capacity to murder another person. Hell, he'd spent countless hours fantasizing about doing the deed.

But unlike the twisted perverts who took joy in watching the life leach from the body of their victim, he'd pressed Angel's face into the mud where it belonged. He had no desire to soil himself by raping her, or even masturbating, while she screamed for help.

This was retribution.

She was a filthy pig that deserved to be punished. So that's what he did. It was only when he was digging a hole in the levee to hide the body that he'd caught sight of her golden locket.

A slut like Angel didn't deserve the pretty necklace. Even if it was a cheap imitation.

But he did know of one girl who did.

A sweet, kind girl who never treated boys like dirt. And certainly never thought she was better than everyone else.

Driven by an impulse he didn't fully comprehend, he'd yanked the necklace from around Angel's neck. He stared at the dull gold in the moonlight. It wasn't enough. He needed something . . . personal. A piece of Angel.

How better to prove his triumph over her?

Pulling out his knife, he'd tried to cut a lock of hair that was wrapped in a ribbon near her temple. His hands had slipped and the blade had sliced through the tender skin of her scalp, allowing blood to flow freely down the side of her face. It'd coated her hair and ribbon with a ruby-red color that had made his heart leap.

Yes. It was perfect.

Wrapping the bloody lock of hair and ribbon in the locket, he'd left Angel to rot in the mud, and headed down the levee. Once he reached Jaci Patterson's house, he'd snuck to the front porch and placed the locket on the swing. Then he'd hidden in a spot across the road and waited.

He didn't know how much time had passed, but eventually Jaci had returned home. The early afternoon sunlight had allowed him to see the confusion on her pretty face as she'd discovered his gift, swiftly followed by horror as her fingers had been stained red from the blood of his sacrifice.

It'd been glorious.

The arousal that'd been absent while he'd strangled Angel had hit with the force of a tsunami. He'd gripped his hard-on, stroking as Jaci had stumbled backward, her gaze darting around as she sensed that he was watching from the shadows.

Then, her scream had sliced through the air and he'd released his seed in a flood of pure bliss.

That had been the beginning.

And now the end was coming.

But first he needed one last sacrifice.

And a very special locket.

Chapter Seventeen

Jaci fell asleep on the couch.

It wasn't that she was waiting for Rylan to return. Certainly that's what she told herself. It was just that she hadn't slept well the night before.

But when she'd heard the soft knock on the front door, she hadn't hesitated to let Rylan in. She hadn't even protested when he'd urged her into the bedroom so they could crawl into the double bed and fall into a deep sleep.

Feeling oddly refreshed when her alarm went off well before dawn, she'd cracked open her eyes and studied the face that was only inches from hers.

In the shadows she could make out the strong lines of his features, and his tousled hair. His jaw had a night's growth of whiskers, and his upper torso was bare. She wanted nothing more than to snuggle against his broad chest and forget her troubles.

Unfortunately, she had people who depended on her.

They especially depended on her pastries.

Slipping out of the bed, she took a quick shower and pulled on a pair of heavy leggings and a comfy sweater. Then, heading into the kitchen, she plunged into her morning routine.

Pretending that she wasn't keenly aware of the gorgeous male who was sleeping in her bed, she baked her muffins and a batch of lemon tarts. She was placing them in her heated trays when Rylan strolled into the kitchen.

Her heart missed a beat as he moved across the floor, bending his head to place a soft kiss on her lips. His hair was damp, revealing that he'd taken a shower, the scent of her soap clinging to his skin.

She shivered as the image of sharing a shower with this man burned through her mind. Their naked bodies pressed together as the warm water glided over them.

With a shake of her head, she stepped back. Who knew she had such a vivid imagination?

A faint smile touched his lips, almost as if he could read her mind. *God forbid.*

"I'll carry the trays if you get the door," he said.

She didn't bother to argue. Instead she opened the door for the dogs—she'd let them out when she first crawled out of bed—and pulled on her boots. The rain had stopped sometime during the night, but it was still muddy.

After she waited for Rylan to step into his boots, they headed out the door and around to the Jeep.

Rylan put the trays in the back while Jaci started the engine and buckled herself in. She waited for Rylan to take the seat next to her before she put the Jeep in gear and slowly started down her drive.

She crept forward at a snail's pace, doing her best to avoid the deep ruts caused by Andrew's tractor.

"Are you going to tell me why Mike called you last night?" She asked the question that had been plaguing her since he'd so abruptly left.

He took his time answering.

"It's not been made public yet, but the skull was identified," he finally said.

She sucked in a sharp breath, her stomach churning. "Was it someone local?"

"Angel Harper."

Jaci's fingers tightened on the steering wheel as the Jeep splashed through a deep puddle. Once the rains ended she was going to have to have the driveway graded and a new layer of gravel put down.

"I don't think she's from Heron. . . ." Her words trailed away as a faint memory niggled in the back of her mind. "Wait. Was she the girl who ran away?"

"That was the theory," Rylan said.

"Oh my God. The skull belonged to Angel?" she said, trying to wrap her brain around the thought.

She hadn't known Angel well, but she remembered her as a vivid, brash girl who'd loved creating disturbances and attracting attention.

It seemed impossible to think of her bright light snuffed out.

"Yes," Rylan said in a grim tone.

Jaci pulled out of the driveway and onto the road that would lead to the highway. She instinctively turned to take the long way around.

She wasn't ready to drive past the Johnson field. Especially now that they could put a name to the skull. It was horrifying to think Angel had been buried just a couple of miles from her backyard.

"Did she fall in the river and drown?" she demanded.

"There's no cause of death yet."

She grimaced, once again struck by the sheer "wrongness" of Angel being reduced to a bleak skull stuck in the mud.

"How awful," she breathed.

"What did you know about her?"

"Not much," she said, trying to remember if she'd ever

actually talked to the girl. She couldn't think of sharing a conversation. "She was younger than me. And I don't think she went to school here for very long."

"Did she have any enemies?"

Hmm. It was impossible to go through high school without at least some drama. And she seemed to recall that Angel had gotten into a fistfight with another girl shortly after she'd moved to town. But the two had made up and seemed to be BFFs after the skirmish.

"Not that I know of." She leaned forward, peering at the sky, which was lightening to a deep lavender as dawn approached. Could it be that they would actually have a day without rain? "She seemed popular," she continued, her lips twisting. "Especially with the boys."

"Were there any rumors when she disappeared?"

She rolled her eyes at the ridiculous question. "There are always rumors."

"What did they say?"

She shrugged. "Most people assumed she was pregnant and took off to have her baby in Kansas City."

"Did they say who the father of the baby might be?"

She glanced toward her companion. "Christopher."

His jaw tightened, but he didn't look shocked. Which meant he'd already known that Angel and Christopher had been an item during school.

His lips parted, then without warning his hand was slamming against the dashboard, his face draining of color.

"Stop."

Instinctively, Jaci slammed on the brakes, her eyes following his gaze to a dark lump in the middle of the lane. In the glare of the headlights, it looked like a log that'd been washed onto the road. But Rylan's shocked reaction warned her that it wasn't anything so harmless.

"What is it?" she demanded.

He opened his door. "Stay here," he commanded.

"No way." Leaving the engine running, she climbed out of the Jeep and joined him.

"Jaci—"

"I'm as much a part of this as you are," she insisted.

He hesitated, clearly torn between locking her in the Jeep and the need to keep her close.

"Stay on the side of the road." He at last conceded defeat. "We don't want to destroy any evidence."

Jaci nodded, her throat dry as they stepped onto the grassy edge and moved forward. It felt surreal. Like they were in a dream as they hiked through the wet grass, bathed in the lavender morning as they approached the log that wasn't a log.

They were still several feet away when she could make out the distinct outline of a body. A female body.

Nausea rolled through Jaci's stomach. The woman looked like she was peacefully sleeping. Which only made the whole thing more creepy.

"You think she's dead?" she breathed.

He reached to lightly touch her arm, bringing her to a halt. Then, he shoved his cell phone in her hand.

"I'm going to feel for a pulse," he said.

He didn't have to tell her to stay where she was. Suddenly she didn't want to approach the woman. She didn't want to see death up close and personal.

Rylan moved forward, choosing the straightest path to avoid disturbing any tire tracks or footprints. He paused as he stood over the body, carefully inspecting the area around her before he was kneeling down and placing his fingers lightly against her throat.

He glanced toward her, giving a small shake of his head. "Call nine-one-one."

Swiftly she dialed and told the operator where to send

the sheriff as well as an ambulance, although she logically knew it was too late for a medical miracle.

Rylan straightened and the first rays of dawn fell over the body, illuminating the woman's round face.

"Oh my God," Jaci rasped, disbelief jolting through her. For whatever reason she'd assumed that the woman would be a stranger. "That's my mother's housekeeper."

Rylan straightened, his face wiped of emotion. "Anne Dixon?"

She nodded. Hadn't Payton told them the woman was on vacation? Surely that meant she was out of town.

So why would she be out on this remote road at such an early hour? It didn't make any sense.

"What happened?" Jaci asked as Rylan retraced his steps and reached for his phone. "Was she hit by a car?"

"I don't know." His gaze darted toward the thick line of trees on the other side of the road, his expression stark.

Jaci frowned. Rylan didn't seem freaked out to see her mother's housekeeper in the road. Or even confused. He seemed resigned.

Had he known something that she didn't know?

"You don't think it was a car, do you?"

His gaze slowly turned in her direction, taking in the tight line of her jaw.

"No," he reluctantly admitted.

"What's going on, Rylan?"

He grimaced. "O'Brien mentioned that your sister had reported Anne was missing."

"But she told us the housekeeper was on vacation."

"I presume they were hoping to avoid any gossip in case the woman turned up."

She folded her arms over her chest. "But you didn't think you should tell me there was a woman missing?"

He hesitated. "There was no use worrying you before

we were certain Anne's disappearance had any connection to you."

Jaci felt a burst of frustration. "I'm not a child, Rylan. And the fact that you believe I should be treated like one is making me nuts."

He released a harsh sigh before glancing over his shoulder at his father's farmhouse, directly behind them.

"I'm sorry, Jaci." His hand lifted as her lips parted to continue her chastisement. "I promise you can yell at me later. But for now would you take the Jeep and go warn my dad that the police are about to descend?"

Her brows snapped together. "I—"

"Please, Jaci," he urged in rough tones. "I don't want him to worry."

Dammit. She didn't want Elmer worrying either. And more importantly, she didn't want him stepping out on his porch to see a woman lying dead in the road.

"Okay." She sent Rylan a warning glare. "But you have to promise me that you won't try to hide things from me because you think it might upset me." She wasn't going to back down. Not from this. "The not knowing is worse."

Raw regret darkened his eyes as he reached to lightly touch her cheek.

"I won't keep anything from you."

"You promise?" she insisted.

"I promise."

Rylan stood to the side of the road, watching as the officials went about the business of death.

The ambulance had left shortly after it arrived, but the sheriff and his deputies remained, except for the younger lawman who'd helped the coroner load the body so it could be driven to Columbia for an autopsy.

The sun rose, splashing the road with a golden glow

that did nothing to erase the horror. Still, the light made it easier for the lawmen to carefully photograph the area, as well as search for any evidence that might have been left behind.

Not that Rylan was hopeful.

Whoever was responsible for stalking Jaci, and no doubt killing Anne Dixon, was careful.

Worse, he was clever.

A combination that made him more dangerous than Rylan could ever have imagined.

Leaving the deputies to continue processing the scene, as well as keeping away the crowd of people that was beginning to form behind the barriers, the sheriff strolled to join Rylan.

"Can you tell what happened to her?" Rylan asked as Mike pulled off his cap to scrub his fingers through his hair.

"There're no obvious signs of trauma besides the cut on her temple, and the bruises around her neck," the lawman said, fitting the cap back on his head. "My guess is that she was strangled."

Rylan nodded. That's what he'd suspected.

"Damn shame," he said.

Mike glared at the spot in the road where Anne had been dumped, as if personally offended. Then, with an effort, he gave a shake of his head and turned to study Rylan with seething frustration.

"Tell me exactly what happened."

Rylan shrugged off the man's sharp tone. They were all on edge.

"I was driving with Jaci—"

"Start at when you left your house this morning," Mike interrupted.

Rylan held his gaze. "I stayed with Jaci."

"You stayed the night?"

"I did."

Mike scowled, but he was smart enough not to try and poke his nose where it didn't belong.

"What time did you get up?"

"Around five." He'd awoken with the anticipation of seducing the woman who'd fallen asleep in his arms, only to find she was gone. "But Jaci was already up baking. I don't know what time she got up."

"Did either of you notice anyone in the area?"

"No. But I need to check the video."

Mike frowned in confusion. "What video?"

"I installed a security system that covers Jaci's farm."

Mike glanced down the road, mentally judging the distance from Jaci's home.

"All of it?" he asked.

"Yep."

"Shit." Mike shifted his attention to Rylan. "Are you telling me that we might actually be able to put a face to the killer?"

That had been Rylan's first thought. But as he'd stood at the edge of the road and studied the crime scene, he'd come to an unsettling realization.

"Doubtful," he said.

"Why?"

Rylan half turned to point at the large oak trees that framed his father's house. They'd started off as mere saplings that had been given to him when he was still in grade school by a teacher to celebrate Earth Day. His dad had wanted to toss them in the trash. Elmer had rightly claimed that they had hundreds of trees on their property and the last thing he wanted to do was mow around two more. But his mother smiled, kissing her husband on the cheek before taking Rylan into the yard with a shovel so they could plant the trees together.

It was a memory Rylan cherished.

The sort of soul-deep memory he'd never been able to achieve in California.

Roots.

The word whispered through his mind, before he was impatiently brushing it aside. There were more important things to concentrate on.

"I also put two cameras on those two trees to monitor anyone driving toward Jaci's house from the highway," he explained.

"Great." Mike gave a lift of his hands. "That should double our chance of catching the bastard."

"Nope." Rylan took several steps down the road, halting at the shallow ditch that marked the edge of his father's property. He'd been careful to align the cameras so they covered his dad's place as well as public property without intruding into the neighbor's land. "Someone knew exactly where the line of sight ended. Which means they've been watching me closely enough to know that Jaci's place has been wired."

Mike's jaw hardened, unwilling to give up hope. "It could be coincidence."

"I'll check," he promised his companion. "But I don't believe in coincidence. Not when the body was placed in the road less than three feet from where he would have been captured on video."

Mike's breath was released like a balloon that had just been punctured.

"He's taunting us," the lawman said, his face hard with fury.

"That would be my guess," Rylan agreed. From the second he'd realized that the placement of Anne in the road hadn't been random, but instead a calculated choice, he'd tried to determine why. The only thing that made sense was that it was a flagrant insult. Whether it was directed toward Rylan or the cops was impossible to say. "Which is a change in his MO."

Mike gave a slow nod, carefully thinking things through. At last he grimaced.

"I hate to do this, but let's take some shots in the dark." Mike glanced toward the deputies who still scurried around the crime scene, keeping back the onlookers as the coroner's black vehicle slowly headed down the road. "Eleven years ago, someone killed Angel and buried her near the river," Mike said, his tone pitched to ensure it wouldn't carry. "And for whatever reason he left the locket with Angel's hair and blood on Jaci's front porch. Why?"

Rylan hadn't trained to be a profiler, but understood basic psychology.

A man went to the trouble of giving a piece of jewelry to a woman for one reason.

"A gift," he said. "The killing made him feel powerful and he was trying to impress Jaci with what he'd accomplished. He clearly is obsessed with her."

Mike's jaw clenched. They both knew that the killer's obsession wouldn't remain satisfied with leaving gory trophies. Eventually the mystery stalker would decide he wanted a more personal connection to Jaci.

Mike clenched his hands, clearly trying to contain his emotions.

"Do you remember when Jaci got the second locket?"

Rylan stilled, dredging up his ancient memories. The first locket had arrived around Halloween, and it didn't seem as if it'd been long before another one had shown up. Had it been Christmas? No. It was after that—he distinctly recalled he'd been taking down the decorations when she came racing into the office.

He'd been hoping to get done early so he could go

sledding with his buddies. That was his excuse for telling Jaci that he didn't have time to listen to her fears.

He'd all but patted her on the head and told her to run along.

God. He'd been an ass.

"It was January."

Mike considered. "Around the new year?"

"Yeah."

"Was there anyone reported as missing during that time?"

Rylan arched a brow. O'Brien was slow and methodical, but he wasn't stupid. He'd immediately honed in on the pertinent question.

"Not in this area." He grimaced. "I'd kept an ear open. Not because of Jaci, but because I was still worried about Angel."

Mike watched as the coroner's car disappeared down the road with his deputy, Sid, in the front seat.

"He must have hunted somewhere else."

Rylan agreed. Heron and the surrounding towns were too small for women to go missing without being noticed. There would have been panic years ago if the killer had remained local.

"That makes the most sense." Rylan allowed his gaze to drift over the rolling fields and the narrow road that was normally deserted. It was easy to move through such a rural neighborhood without attracting notice. Especially if the killer was familiar with the area. "And he probably brought them back here to bury them."

Mike easily followed his train of thought. "That would explain the female body that'd been found the same time as the skull."

Rylan took a minute to think through the mind of a psychopath. The man would hunt the females. Probably

Chicago or St. Louis. Someplace where a missing woman wouldn't hit the radar.

Then he'd return home to where he felt safe.

"The levee would make a perfect place to stash his kills."

"Until the floods came and washed them away." Mike grimaced. For years to come the sheriff would no doubt have nightmares about seeing the body floating in the muddy river. He gave a sharp shake of his head. "How many lockets did Jaci get?"

"She officially reported four of them." Rylan frowned, scouring his memory. "Maybe five."

Mike's square face paled. "When she returned to Heron she told me she'd been harassed in the past. I think she was worried it was going to start again now that she was back. When nothing happened I dismissed it as some stupid high school prank." He shook his head. "To be honest, I assumed it was that jerk of a half brother who was responsible."

Rylan blew out a sigh. "We all failed her."

They shared a guilty gaze before Mike squared his shoulders.

"Did anyone receive the lockets after Jaci left for college?"

"No one."

"What does that mean?" Mike's brows drew together. "Did the killer leave the area?"

It was a question that nagged at Rylan. "It's a possibility." He shoved his fingers through his hair, anxious to return to his father's house and ensure that Jaci was okay. "Or he stayed and found a new obsession somewhere else."

"In either case, he's turned his attention back to Jaci," Mike said, as if Rylan needed the reminder.

He was acutely aware of the danger that stalked her.

"And upped his game," he added.

"No crap." Mike's fingers unconsciously grasped the grip of his gun. The man had been unnerved by the appearance of a dead woman and skull in his county. But Anne's death had happened on his watch. He was clearly taking it personally. "He not only chose a local woman, but he took one who was sure to be noticed."

Rylan nodded toward the deputies, who had finished their most pressing duties and were now chatting with the small crowd.

"And left her where it's a warning to me." Rylan's stomach clenched. "He considers Jaci his possession."

Mike muttered a curse. "She needs to leave until we find this sicko."

Rylan gave a short laugh. He wanted nothing more than to put Jaci on a plane and take her to his condo in California. There was no place that would be safer. Well, maybe the Pentagon. But he didn't even bother plotting how quickly he could get her packed and to the airport.

He knew Jaci well enough to suspect she'd partially chosen to go to college at Mizzou with the hope of ending the harassment. And that if she left again, she would feel as if she'd allowed herself to be run out of her home.

Besides, if she left, the killer might simply disappear into the shadows.

Which not only meant that countless women would be in danger, but that Jaci could never return.

That was unacceptable.

He shook his head. "She won't go."

"Fine." Mike glanced toward the nearby farmhouse. "I'll stay with her."

Rylan snorted. "Not a chance in hell. I'll stay with her."

Mike pointed a finger in Rylan's face. "I'm holding you responsible for her safety."

"Nothing's happening to Jaci as long as I'm alive," Rylan swore.

Mike sighed as the clouds rolled in, the threat of rain once again hanging heavy in the air.

"I need to notify Anne's sister." He sent his chatting deputies a resigned gaze. "Before the gossip reaches her."

Rylan nodded, half turning toward his father's house. He was finding it increasingly difficult to think of anything beyond getting to Jaci.

"I'll look through the security tapes. We might get lucky."

"If not, you might try to make a list," Mike suggested, reaching into his pocket to pull out the keys to his nearby patrol truck. "Who knows that you installed the cameras?"

Good question. Rylan took time to consider his answer. "Andrew Porter, for one." He tried to recall seeing anyone passing by when he was working. He couldn't remember anyone. "Potentially the people who rented the Johnson place."

Mike gave a sharp laugh. "Trust me. They haven't been noticing anything."

Rylan arched a brow. How could the man be certain the neighbors weren't spying on Jaci?

"You talked to them?"

"I did better than that. I raided the house." The sheriff shrugged at Rylan's surprise. "Meth."

"Christ." He made a sound of disgust. It wasn't bad enough that there was a serial killer on the loose? Now there was a meth lab only a mile from Jaci's front door? Maybe he should reconsider the idea of hauling her onto the nearest plane. "That would explain why they shot at me."

Mike shook his head. "It wasn't them."

"You're sure?"

"Unless they were smart enough to dump the shotgun. Which is doubtful. The drug task force did a thorough search of the property. They didn't find any guns."

An icy tingle inched down Rylan's spine. If it hadn't been a warning shot from the tweakers, then there truly was someone out there who wanted to kill him.

"So someone was lurking along the road waiting for me to pass."

Mike nodded. "Probably the same person who watched you put in the cameras."

Rylan's gaze jerked toward the heavy line of trees on the opposite side of the road. Had it been yesterday morning when he'd thought he'd seen someone creeping through the early morning shadows?

Damn. He should have insisted that Jaci stop so he could check it out.

His jaw tightened, his hands clenching at his sides. How many opportunities to expose the killer had he let slip through his fingers?

"Whatever game he's playing, he's not going to quit now," Rylan warned.

"He'll quit once I have his sorry ass in jail." The sheriff offered a tight smile before he was walking toward his truck.

Rylan's gaze remained locked on the trees, his thoughts dark as the skies opened up and the drenching rain returned with a vengeance.

He'd been wrong. So wrong.

For years he'd assumed the lockets were the key to his pleasure.

His routine had never altered.

He chose his sacrifice.

Usually a woman like Angel. Not in looks. Physical features didn't matter. The only important thing was that they were women who had clearly been created to purge his anger. They were a vessel to accept the evil that lived in all of them.

Once he was cleansed, the sacrifice was placed in his cellar so he could harvest what he needed to create the gift for a woman who was worthy of his adoration. Then he would wait until darkness to dispose of the body. He took extreme measures to ensure that he didn't attract unwanted attention.

But now . . . the flood had busted through his rigid routine with the same devastating force that it'd busted through the levee. The old rules had been washed away.

Watching from the shadows, he'd seen the Jeep approaching, briefly disappointed. He'd intended to use Anne's body to taunt Rylan Cooper. The bastard had no right to intrude into his game. No right to treat Jaci as if she belonged to him.

But then Jaci had stepped out of her vehicle and the sight of her face had been glorious.

He'd orgasmed on the spot.

Each change to his game only intensified the pleasure.

Moving deeper into the shadows, he disappeared as Jaci jumped into her vehicle and drove away.

He might not have wanted to alter the rules of his game, but the changes had amped up his excitement.

What came next was going to be epic.

Chapter Eighteen

Most people assumed that the worst part of being a sheriff was dealing with angry drunks or the mothers who screeched at him when he arrested their precious child.

The truth, as far as Mike O'Brien was concerned, was that the worst part of his job was notifying the next of kin.

It wasn't something he had to do that often, thank God. But it was always awful when it happened. And it was even worse when he had to tell someone that their loved one had been deliberately killed.

Death came to them all. Old age, disease, or accident. It was a fact of life.

But murder was unacceptable.

Finally leaving Anne's sister quietly sobbing in Quincy, he traveled back across the swollen river and straight to the Hamilton estate.

He felt tense, edgy. As if his skin was too tight for his body.

There was a killer out there. Hunting women and tormenting Jaci. Hell, he'd even taken a shot at Rylan Cooper.

And he was going to strike again. Soon.

Mike could feel it in his bones.

Driving up the winding road that led to the huge house

on the hill, Mike was forced to halt at the gate. Pressing the button on the intercom, he waited for the barrier to swing open. Then, continuing up the driveway, he pulled his truck to a halt in the circle drive. Stepping out of his vehicle, he hesitated in front of the wide terrace.

The rain was in a momentary lull but the clouds remained low and sullen, making it look as if it was dusk rather than midday.

Mike allowed his gaze to scan the house before he was moving toward the garage and then the gardens.

Had Anne walked away from this estate and simply disappeared? Had she been strolling in the gardens and been snatched by some mysterious intruder?

Or had she seen something she wasn't supposed to see and never made it out of the nearby house alive?

Questions that he intended to have answered before this day was over.

Retracing his steps, he'd reached the terrace when the front door was opened to reveal Loreen Hamilton. The older woman was dressed in a dark, tailored pantsuit that emphasized the slender lines of her body and the pale ivory of her skin. Her red hair was styled and her makeup perfect.

He had a sudden memory of his own mother, who'd died two years ago. She'd never had fancy pantsuits or had time to go to the hairdresser. Certainly she didn't wear makeup unless it was to cover a bruise left by her jackass of a husband.

By the time she was fifty she'd looked at least twenty years older, and tired by a life that had been a constant struggle.

He squashed the faint spurt of envy at the thought that Loreen had spent her life pampered by money, while his own mother had never had a dime.

There was a petulant look of discontent on Loreen's face that assured him wealth didn't equal happiness.

Forcing his feet forward, Mike removed his hat and offered a small dip of his head.

"Mrs. Hamilton," he murmured.

Her lips thinned. "If you're here to collect for the orphan fund, I already sent a check."

"Thank you for your generosity, but that's not why I'm here." He glanced over her shoulder. "Can I come in?"

Loreen stepped forward, as if she could physically prevent him from entering.

"Now is not a good time."

He narrowed his gaze. "You need to make it a good time."

A brittle anger tightened her delicate features. "I don't care for your tone, Sheriff."

His lips twisted. Loreen Hamilton was accustomed to giving orders. In truth, she was a bully who used her power and position to get her way.

There was the sound of shoes clicking against marble. Then Payton appeared to stand beside her mother.

Mike clenched his teeth.

Unlike her mother, Payton didn't need the fancy clothes and coats of makeup to be stunning. Even with her hair pulled into a ponytail and her face scrubbed clean, she was strikingly beautiful.

And what was she wearing? It looked like some sort of workout outfit. Stretchy pants and a tight top that made his mouth go dry.

Flicking a guarded glance toward Mike, the younger woman reached out to touch her mother's arm.

"Mother, let me deal with this."

Mike cleared his throat. "Actually, I need to speak with the entire family."

Loreen sent him a sharp glare. "Why?"

"Mother, please." Payton pasted a faux smile on her lips as she tugged the reluctant Loreen away from the door. "Come in, Sheriff."

He stepped over the threshold, ignoring the older woman's pointed glance at his boots. A woman was dead. Loreen Hamilton could deal with a little mud on her floors.

Perhaps sensing he wasn't leaving until he'd had his say, the woman turned to stiffly usher him across the foyer and into a room with a fancy desk and matching chairs with spindly legs. There was a wall filled with framed pictures of Loreen being honored by various charities for her generous donations. And one of her in her glory days being crowned as queen of some beauty pageant.

"There's no need to use the formal salon. We can speak in here," Loreen told him.

Mike didn't miss the barb. He was being told he wasn't worthy of a visit to the formal salon. Still, he allowed the insult to roll off his shoulders as he wandered across the tiled floor to study the large framed prints stacked on a table next to the window.

He flipped through the dozen black-and-white photos. They looked as if they'd been taken during the mammoth snowstorm that had fallen in late December. The pristine layer of snow added a stark beauty to the pictures. As did the golden-haired woman featured in different locations around the grounds.

There was one of Payton in a white fur coat on the front terrace. Another of her turned away as she walked up the long driveway. And several of her in a provocative red dress, posed in the garden.

He frowned, oddly disturbed by the photos. On one level they were simply beautiful pictures of a beautiful woman in a beautiful setting.

On another level there was a strange intensity to each shot. As if the photographer was stripping Payton bare and leaving her exposed to the world.

"What are these?" he asked.

Loreen moved to stand next to the desk, her elegant movements clearly rehearsed.

"I hired Nelson Bradley to do a series of photographs of our estate." An expression of pride touched Loreen's pale face. "The house is going to be a feature story in *Midwest Décor*."

Mike curled his lips. That explained why the photos were so disturbing. Nelson enjoyed seeking out the most dark and bleak settings.

Still, these were more haunting than creepy.

He lifted his head. "This isn't his usual style."

"No." It was Loreen who answered, still preening at the thought of her upcoming fifteen minutes of fame. "These are quite magnificent."

His gaze shifted to Payton, who was tensely standing next to the door.

"You look cold in the garden shots."

She managed a small smile. "I was freezing. Nelson had me posing for hours."

"Why not take pictures inside?"

"He said artificial light destroys the truth of his subject." Payton gave a small shrug. "Whatever that means."

"He's an artist." Loreen sent them both a glare, her limited patience at an end. "Now can we get to the point of your visit?"

Mike folded his arms over his chest, his legs spread as he turned his attention to the older woman.

"I'm sorry to be the one to bring bad news, but Anne Dixon was found dead this morning."

He heard Payton's pained gasp, but his gaze remained

locked on Loreen's expression. Was that relief that rippled over her face?

"Anne?" The older woman took a moment to gather her thoughts. Clearly she'd been worried he'd come there for another reason. But what? "I don't understand," she continued. "What happened? A heart attack?"

"We haven't determined cause of death," he smoothly answered.

She frowned, as if surprised by his words. "What else could it be?"

Payton stepped forward, her eyes filled with tears she was trying to blink back.

"Where was she?"

He held up his hand. "I have a few questions."

Loreen's earlier tension returned. "What sort of questions?"

He hooked his thumbs in his belt buckle. He'd found that acting like just another good ol' boy helped encourage people to talk to him.

"Just trying to determine a time line for Anne's movements, ma'am."

Predictably, Loreen wasn't impressed. Instead her eyes narrowed. "I don't understand."

"Is Mr. Hamilton here?"

"No. Of course not." She waved an impatient hand. "He's at his office in St. Louis. He will take the commuter flight home this afternoon."

Did she really believe her husband was in St. Louis? Or was she covering for him?

Now wasn't the time to press.

"What about Christopher?" he asked.

Loreen jerked. Almost as if she'd been slapped. "I'm calling our lawyer."

He met her aggressive glare with a bland smile. He'd hoped the family would cooperate, but it didn't matter.

He was getting answers. The easy way. Or the hard way.

"That's fine, Mrs. Hamilton. While you're calling your lawyer, would you also call your husband and son? They need to return home as soon as possible."

With a scathing glare, Loreen crossed the room, her heels clicking an angry tattoo against the floor.

"I warned you he was trouble," she said to her daughter as she disappeared through the door.

Mike arched his brows. "I'm trouble?"

Payton heaved a sigh, dismissing her mother with a shake of her head. "Please tell me what happened to Anne."

Mike tried not to notice the tears gathered in her eyes, or the wounded air of grief that shrouded her. It wasn't his duty to tug Payton in his arms and offer her comfort.

It'd never been his duty, despite his wild fantasies.

And besides, right now everyone was a suspect in the death of Anne Dixon. Especially anyone with the last name of Hamilton.

He nodded his head toward the chairs set beside the bookshelf

"Sit down, Payton."

She shook her head. "Please, just tell me what happened to Anne."

He swallowed a sigh. The one thing he'd learned when he was dating Payton was that she was as stubborn as a mule.

"As I said, we don't have a cause of death."

"How did you find her?"

There was no easy way to say it. "She was dumped on the gravel road that runs in front of Elmer Cooper's farm."

Payton wrapped her arms around her slender waist, her face ashen in the muted light.

"Dumped? What does that mean?"

"Someone drove her to that particular spot and laid her dead body across the road."

She hissed, shock darkening her eyes. Mike watched as she apparently struggled to absorb the fact that the woman who'd been a part of her life since the day she was born was not only dead, but that she'd been found in the middle of a gravel road.

"You're sure someone took her there?"

Mike was caught off guard by the question. "What are you asking?"

She licked her lips. Not nerves. At least he didn't think so. More of a reaction to her intense emotions.

"I've heard about how people having strokes can sometimes wander off. Maybe she stumbled into the road and was hit by a car."

He shook his head. He didn't intend to give out details. The more information he could keep secret about Anne's murder, the better. But Payton would have information about the housekeeper that would be vital to discovering who was responsible for her death.

"She's been dead at least twelve hours. I would guess even longer."

"So it wasn't an accident?" She pressed her fingers to her lips, the tears trickling down her cheeks. "Oh God, her sister."

Mike held up his hand. "I've already been to see her."

"She must be devastated."

He grimaced. "It's never easy."

Payton gave a shaky nod, her body visibly trembling. Once again Mike was forced to battle back his instinctive urge to pull her into his arms.

"I need to invite her to the house. I would like to help

with the funeral arrangements. And of course, she'll want to get Anne's things—"

"Not yet," he interrupted. "I don't want anyone in or out of Anne's room. Not until I tell you it's okay."

Her lips parted to protest his sharp command, only to snap shut at his grim expression.

With an effort, she wiped her cheeks and squared her shoulders. "What do you want from me?" she asked.

"I need to speak with your family about Anne."

"Why?"

He chose his words with care. "I need to know what they remember of the past weeks. If Anne said anything unusual. Or if she had any visitors."

She studied him for a long minute. "That's all?"

He shrugged. "I want to see the security video from the morning Anne disappeared."

She wrinkled her brow. "I think I can get it for you."

He hid his smile of satisfaction. He wanted his hands on the video before the damned lawyer arrived demanding warrants.

"Now?"

She gave a brisk nod, looking relieved to have something to do to distract her from her grief.

Leading him out of the room, she headed toward the back of the house. They walked without speaking, the silence emphasizing the emptiness of the grand house. Did Payton ever feel as if she was lost among the acres of marble and gilt?

He shook away the ridiculous thought as she halted at a small table that was set beside a pair of double wooden doors. Lifting a large crystal vase, she grabbed the key that had been hidden beneath it.

Mike watched as she turned to unlock one of the doors. Did Blake Hamilton leave the key there to be used by his family? Or had Payton discovered the hiding place by accident?

He was betting on the latter.

Pushing open the door, Payton headed across the Oriental rug toward the heavy armoire that was set near the massive desk. Mike slowly wandered in behind her, his lips pursing in a silent whistle.

Now, this was an office of a man who liked to think he was important.

Cherrywood furnishings that looked hand-carved. A twelve-foot ceiling with one of those fancy medallion things in the center. Towering bookshelves stuffed with leather-bound books. And charcoal etchings that were hung on the walls.

All expensive.

All designed to impress.

He gave a mental shrug. He preferred his own grubby office. At least there he could kick back in his seat and put his feet on the desk without caring about scuff marks.

Payton pulled open the armoire doors to reveal a flat-screen monitor that was attached to a DVR.

"This is the surveillance equipment." She stepped aside, waving her hands in a vague motion. "I've never used it, so I'm not entirely sure how it works."

"May I?" he asked, deliberately waiting for her to answer.

"Of course."

It wasn't a direct yes, but it was good enough for a prosecutor to say he had full consent to search the tapes.

Moving forward, he hit the button to turn on the monitor. Instantly the screen flickered, and four boxes with separate camera angles appeared.

The main gate. The front door. The garage. And the back terrace.

So. Daddy hadn't been entirely honest with Payton

about the number of security cameras. Why? Protection? Or the desire to know where the family was so he could slip away unnoticed?

Leaning forward, he pressed the play button on the DVR. The monitor went black. And stayed black.

He pressed rewind. Then fast-forward. Nothing.

"Shit."

Payton pressed close to his side, her light, feminine scent a perilous distraction.

"Is something wrong?"

Mike straightened, his thoughts sifting through the various possibilities. "It's been erased."

Payton looked confused. "You're sure?"

"I'm sure." He turned to circle the room, pausing at the French doors that led onto a small, private balcony. It would be easy to move in and out of the house without being noticed from this room.

"You know, it could be programmed to erase the previous day's recording," Payton said. "It's not like we have any reason to save them unless we were robbed or something."

Mike resumed his slow inspection, moving to the desk that was scrupulously organized, with a small stack of files on one corner and a laptop in the center. There was a silver-framed picture of Payton and Christopher when they were young. None of his wife. Interesting.

"This system would simply loop back to the beginning and start recording over the older video. It wouldn't erase it completely," he explained. "It was either turned off so it didn't record." He paused, glancing toward Payton, who remained beside the armoire. "Or someone deliberately destroyed evidence by wiping it clean."

"Why would anyone do that?"

"The most obvious explanation is that they had something they wanted to hide."

She studied him with an incredulous expression. "You can't possibly think someone in this house could be responsible for hurting Anne?"

He held her gaze. "She lived here. And you all knew her better than anyone."

Her features tightened with anger. "Yes, we did. She was a part of our family. We loved her."

He snorted, his attention returning to the desk. "You might have loved her, Payton. But I find it impossible to believe everyone in this household felt the same way."

There was a telling pause. Not even Payton believed the rest of her family felt anything toward their devoted servant.

Loreen, because she thought about nothing beyond her perfect image. Christopher, because he was a self-centered prick. And Blake Hamilton, because his world revolved around dollar signs.

"No one in this house would have hurt Anne," she stubbornly insisted.

Mike moved toward a small glass case next to the desk. Inside were a dozen coins in various sizes nestled in a velvet lining. He assumed they must be rare, and no doubt worth a lot of money. Still, it seemed a weird thing to collect. If his father had left him a trust fund instead of a mountain of debt, he would have a storehouse filled with bars of gold, not tiny coins stuck beneath a glass case.

He moved toward the bookshelves. "Have you had any unusual visitors?"

"What do you mean unusual?" Her voice was sharp, angry.

He turned back to face Payton, belatedly realizing that he couldn't afford to stir her animosity. Right now she was willing to talk to him. If she clammed up, he'd be forced to get his answers through a gaggle of lawyers.

That's the last thing he wanted.

"Someone you didn't expect?" he asked, softening his tone. "Someone who didn't usually come by the house?"

A portion of her tension eased as she tried to think of any likely candidates.

"Not that I can think of." She shook her head. "Mother had to cancel her garden club because of the rain, and Father has been too busy to entertain."

"What about deliveries?"

"We have deliveries almost every day."

Mike moved back to the French doors. From his angle he couldn't see the front drive.

"Do they have codes to get through the gate or do you have to buzz them in?"

"We don't give the codes to anyone." There was absolute certainty in her voice. "Not after Christopher handed them out to a bunch of his buddies and they had a drunken orgy in the pool."

Mike rolled his eyes. He had a vague memory of the event. It was when he'd first started working at the sheriff's office. The old sheriff had been called to the property to haul off a dozen underage kids, but Loreen Hamilton had refused to allow her precious son to be taken with the rest of them. She claimed the kids had broken in and that Christopher was in his room sleeping the whole time.

"Where is your brother?"

"I'm not sure." She offered a tight smile, trying to mask her concern for Christopher. It was a familiar habit. As long as he'd known Payton, she'd been fretting over her sibling. "I haven't seen him since yesterday morning."

Mike didn't press for a location. Instead he concentrated on who had been in and out of the Hamilton house over the past weeks.

"Has he had any visitors since he came home?"

"No." She absently closed the doors and leaned against the edge of the armoire. "I don't think he kept in contact with his old friends."

"What about his college buddies?" Mike asked. "Have any of them been hanging around?"

"There hasn't been anyone."

"Don't say another word, Payton." Loreen's shrill voice cut through the air as she stepped into the office, her expression hard with warning as she turned toward Mike. "Our lawyer is on his way."

Any hope of getting information that could help track down Anne's killer was squashed.

Lawyers were the kiss of death to an active investigation.

With an effort he managed a polite smile. "And what about Mr. Hamilton and Christopher?"

"I left messages on their phones." Loreen sniffed, moving to stand at rigid attention next to Payton. "I'm sure they'll be here as quickly as they can."

Mike moved to take a seat behind the desk, silently assuring the older woman he wasn't leaving until he had his answers. He smiled as she stiffened in outrage.

"Let's hope so."

Chapter Nineteen

Jaci moved through the morning in a fog of shock.

What kind of sick person could kill poor Anne Dixon and then dump her like trash in the road? It just didn't seem real.

More like a horrible dream that wouldn't end.

At Rylan's urging Elmer had packed a bag and climbed into his vehicle, to spend some time with Rylan's aunt in a small town fifty miles away. Then, after collecting a few of his own belongings, he'd led Jaci to her Jeep so she could make her deliveries despite the fact she was several hours late.

He'd even insisted they stop for lunch before returning to her house.

Now she busied herself in the kitchen. Usually a few hours of cooking could soothe her raw nerves. Today, however, she barely noticed as she dusted a board with flour and pulled out the culture she used for her sourdough bread. It was a mixture of flour and water that had been started by her grandmother fifty years before. It was a perfect combination of wild yeast and bacteria that gave her bread its distinctive taste.

Efficiently kneading the dough, she covered it with a

damp cloth to rise as Rylan strolled into the kitchen, Riff and Raff on his heels.

She watched as he slid his cell phone into the front pocket of his jeans.

"Your partner?" she asked as she used her apron to wipe the flour from her hands.

He shook his head. "I already spoke to Griff. That was a contact in the governor's office. I'm having them light a fire under the medical examiner to make sure Anne's autopsy is a priority, as well as the Jane Doe who was found in the floodwaters."

Jaci willed herself not to flinch. Rylan might logically understand her need to know whatever evidence he discovered, but his natural urge to protect her was a powerful force. Any hint she was recoiling from the truth and he would eagerly use it as an excuse to lock her out of the information loop.

"Do you think the woman was from this area?" she asked.

He shook his head. "Not really, but I'm hoping we can make a connection between her and Angel Harper. Something that will tie them to the killer."

Two women dead. No, wait. Three women.

"Anne was murdered, wasn't she?" Her stomach clenched at the memory of the woman lying in the muddy road. "Just like those other two women."

"I think it's possible."

Jaci shuddered. She hadn't known Anne well, but she was certain her mother wouldn't have hired a woman who liked to go to wild parties, or hang out in bars.

"Why her?"

"That I can't explain." Rylan moved to lean his hip against the counter. In the soft glow of the kitchen light his pale hair shimmered like silk, emphasizing the fascinating hints of gold in his eyes. "On the surface she doesn't seem to have anything in common with the other women. At least not with Angel. She was twice her age. She had a steady job. She seemed to come from a loving family."

Jaci absently tugged off her apron and tossed it on the table. "I know. It doesn't make any sense."

He considered for a long time. "Was Anne any relation to Teresa Graham?"

"I don't think so." Jaci had known Teresa Graham well enough to recognize her when her grandmother took her to church, but she couldn't remember ever having an actual conversation with the woman. "If I remember right, Teresa wasn't from this area. She moved here with her husband when he retired from the military. I think he died only a couple years later and she had to start babysitting to make ends meet."

He nodded. "Did she ever babysit you?"

"No." She wrinkled her nose. "My grandmother didn't like her."

Rylan looked surprised. Amy Patterson had been a woman with a warm and generous heart. It was rare for her not to try and see the best in people.

"Did she say why?"

"She never said anything to me, but I overheard her telling Grandpa that Ms. Graham was too fond of the bottle." Jaci's lips twisted. "She also said that she was a danger to the children who were placed in her care. I think she wanted to do something, but she wasn't sure who she should talk to about her fears."

He nodded. "I heard the same rumors. Do you know any of the kids she did babysit?"

She gave a lift of her hands. In the small area there had been no day-care centers. Which meant parents had to use family, teenagers, or Teresa Graham.

"Most of my friends." She tried to think of her classmates who'd actually complained about the older woman. "Sid was a regular. And I know Andrew went a few times before he refused to go back. He never told me why. And I remember Nelson getting in trouble for posting her picture online and claiming she was one of the FBI's Most Wanted." Her lips twitched. "Of course, he did that to our principal and the preacher who told him that he was going to hell if he didn't sit still in church."

"What about Payton or Christopher?"

Jaci lifted her brows. Was he kidding? Her pampered siblings would never, ever have been left with anyone who didn't warrant the Hamilton stamp of approval.

"They would have stayed with Anne most of the time." She rolled her eyes. "Except during the summer when Mother took them to Europe to give them polish."

His lips twitched. Could he sense her opinion of her siblings' "polish"? Then his grim expression returned.

"What do you know about the housekeeper?"

"Not much." She didn't have to tell Rylan that her mother had invited her manicurist to her home more often than she'd invited her oldest daughter. "I think she lived in Quincy until she started to work for my mother." Jaci racked her memory for the few times that she'd seen Anne around town. "I don't think I ever saw her with Teresa Graham."

Rylan lifted a hand to shove his fingers through his hair. "There's nothing that links them together except . . ."

She studied him in confusion as his words trailed away. "Except what?" Realization hit her like a sledgehammer. There was one thing that linked them. "Oh my God." She pressed her fingers to her lips. "The lockets."

He paused, then gave a slow nod. "Yes."

Jaci stepped back, flopping on the edge of a nearby

chair. The lockets had always been the same. Small, cheap, fake gold, and holding a lock of hair with a bloody ribbon.

Blood and hair that came from the victims.

She rubbed her fingers against her jeans, horror surging through her.

Being afraid that the lockets were linked to something terrible was considerably different from personally knowing the woman who'd been murdered. Now her vision narrowed and her heart slammed painfully against her ribs.

"The one I found must have had Anne's blood on it," she choked out. "God." The room tilted on its axis. "I'm going to be sick."

There was a blur of movement, then she felt the heat of Rylan's hand on her nape. With a gentle insistence he pushed her head down, not stopping until her nose was touching her knee.

"Breathe." He squatted down in front of her, pressing his cheek against hers. "I've got you, Jaci."

She struggled to suck in a deep breath, clinging to the feel of his fingers at her nape and the rough brush of whiskers against her jaw. He was solid. Real. The only thing tangible as the world spun around her.

She released a small sob. "This is so hideous."

"We're going to find who is doing this and put an end to it," he growled into her ear. "I swear."

She lifted her head, studying the smoldering determination that burned in his eyes.

"What if we don't? What if he kills again?"

"Jaci."

Whatever he was going to say was cut short as Riff and Raff suddenly bolted from the mudroom to charge through the kitchen and into the living room.

Jaci stiffened, her fingers digging into Rylan's shoulders. "Someone's here."

He slowly straightened, nodding toward her cell phone on the table. “Check your security camera.”

Her hands shook as she grabbed her phone and touched the app that was connected to her new system. Instantly she had a view of the front yard. She frowned, not recognizing the old black truck that had pulled behind her Jeep.

It wasn’t until an older man with silver hair and a lined face headed toward the door that she realized who it was.

“It’s Jarrod Walker.”

Rylan’s eyes narrowed with suspicion. “Do you know why he’d be here?”

She watched as Jarrod climbed onto the porch. He was wearing a pair of taupe coveralls and rubber boots. Reaching the door, he hesitated, almost as if he wasn’t sure he wanted to be there.

“I suppose he must be wanting to talk about mowing my yard this summer.”

“Come with me.” Rylan reached for her hand, tugging her out of her chair and into the living room. Then arranging her next to the end of the sofa, he went to the coat closet and pulled out the shotgun. He returned to her side, placing the loaded gun in her hand. “Don’t hesitate to shoot if you feel threatened,” he commanded.

“Don’t worry.” She was spooked enough not to argue. Not that there was a chance in hell that she could hit the broad side of a barn. Not when her hands were shaking.

But it should make someone think twice about attacking her.

Moving toward the door, Rylan cracked it an inch. “Hello, Jarrod. Can I help you?”

Jaci could hear the older man’s rasping sigh of relief. “Thank God, you’re here.”

Rylan pulled the door open another inch, his back rigid with tension.

"You're looking for me?"

"Yeah." There was an awkward pause before Jarrod was clearing his throat. "I've listened to your dad talking about you since you moved to California, and he said that you were some sort of supercop."

Jaci swallowed a nervous laugh as Rylan heaved a loud sigh.

"My father." Rylan shook his head. "He has a lot to answer for."

"I need your help," Jarrod said.

"We can speak on the porch."

Rylan started forward. At the same time Jaci carefully set the shotgun in a corner before she moved across the room and tugged the door wide enough that she could smile at her visitor.

"Come in, Jarrod." She ignored Rylan's fierce glare, pushing open the screen door and motioning her visitor inside.

She'd known Jarrod Walker her entire life, and while she understood they had to be careful, the older man had been in and out of this house on dozens of occasions since her return to Heron. He could have hurt her any time with no one being wiser. Besides, he could hardly overpower the both of them.

She led him to the sofa and urged him to take a seat. "Can I get you something to drink?" she asked.

He shook his head, his gaze turning to Rylan, who'd moved to stand protectively at her side.

"Thanks, but what I need is some advice."

"What sort of advice?" Rylan asked.

The man paused, glancing toward the door as if debating

whether or not he wanted to bolt. Then, with an obvious effort, he turned his gaze back to Rylan.

"Anne Dixon."

Rylan stiffened, his hands clenching at his sides. "Do you know something about her death?"

The older man flinched at Rylan's sharp tone, shrinking into the cushions.

"No." He gave a violent shake of his head. "Not that."

Reaching out, Jaci grabbed Rylan's forearm, giving it a warning squeeze. Jarrod was afraid. She didn't know why, but she did sense that it wasn't going to take much to make him decide he didn't want to talk to them.

Moving slowly enough she wouldn't startle her guest, she settled on the sofa beside him.

"Why don't you start at the beginning?"

Jarrod nodded, then he swiveled so he could face her, ignoring Rylan, who was nearly vibrating with impatience.

"I think you know that I lost my wife about five years ago."

"Yes." She offered a genuine smile of sympathy. Jarrod's wife had been the art teacher at the local school and one of Jaci's greatest inspirations. It was because of the older woman that Jaci had first discovered her love for crafts. "Clara was a wonderful woman. We've all mourned her loss."

"My life was empty without her." His dark eyes filled with tears. Jaci remained silent as she waited for him to regain command of his composure. At last he gave a small sniff. "Then I started working for your mom."

"You have my sympathies," she said in dry tones. It was no secret that their relationship was more or less nonexistent.

A faint smile curved his lips. "She can be challenging."

"A nice way to say 'a pain in the neck.'"

"Sometimes." His tension didn't disappear, but she

sensed it was easing. "But I like working outside, so I've been happy there."

"I'm glad." She paused. How could she turn the conversation in the direction she wanted without alarming him? "Is that how you met Anne?"

His hands twisted together, but he gave a small nod. "Yes. She had a habit of walking in the gardens in the morning. Eventually we started chatting for a few minutes. Nothing more than the usual talk about the weather and what flowers happened to be in bloom. Still, I looked forward to seeing her every day."

"It's perfectly understandable." She smiled. "You must have been lonely."

He breathed out a heavy sigh. "That's it exactly. We were both single and too old to want to be out in the dating world."

She leaned forward, covering his calloused hand with her own. "It's nice you found someone you could feel comfortable with."

"Yes, well, I liked Anne. Very much. She might not have had a lot of education, but she read a lot, and before she took the job with your mother she'd traveled overseas with her sister. She was more than just a housekeeper." His chin tilted, as if daring her to speak badly of the woman. "And I wanted us to see each other away from work."

"She didn't agree?" Rylan asked.

Jarrod's gaze never wavered from Jaci. She suspected the older man was intimidated by the younger man. Understandable. Rylan was like a force of nature that threatened to flatten anything in his path.

"Anne was afraid of what your mother might think," he told her. "She'd been saving money so she could retire in two years. She didn't want to risk getting fired."

Jaci frowned. "I know my mother can be selfish, but

surely she doesn't forbid her staff from having a personal life?"

He flushed. He was trained in the old school that warned an employee never spoke poorly of their boss.

"Begging your pardon, but Mrs. Hamilton could be unpredictable. What was okay one day might get you sacked the next."

"True." Her jaw clenched. Loreen was the Queen of Volatility. One second she could be cooing over her children's charming playfulness and the next she was condemning them as undisciplined brats.

Rylan made a sound of impatience. He clearly wasn't happy at her meandering way of gaining information.

"So Anne refused to go out with you?" he demanded.

Jaci sent Rylan a warning frown before returning her attention to Jarrod. She offered the older man an encouraging smile.

"What did Anne say?"

Jarrod hunched his shoulder. "She wanted to keep our relationship a secret. At least until she managed to retire."

Jaci gave a slow nod. His story seemed believable. No older woman would want to risk being fired when she was just a couple years away from retirement. Still, Jaci couldn't help but wonder if Jarrod was telling her the full story.

Clearly Rylan was just as skeptical. "Bullshit," he growled.

Chapter Twenty

Rylan was acutely aware of Jaci's disapproving glare. She'd just managed to soothe Jarrod Walker into confessing his relationship with Anne Dixon and now she no doubt feared Rylan was about to terrify the poor man into full retreat.

But while Rylan appreciated her delicacy, the time for pussyfooting around had come to an end.

This man had been in a relationship with Anne. Which meant that he was either the killer, or he was their best hope of learning who the killer might be.

Folding his arms over his chest, he studied the older man's lined face. He'd known Jarrod Walker most of his life. The handyman had worked at the local foundry until it'd closed. Then he'd made a living by mowing yards and taking on small construction projects. At least until he'd started to work for the Hamiltons.

As far as Rylan knew, the man had never been in trouble.

But until he was certain Jarrod wasn't a danger to Jaci, he had no intention of lowering his guard.

"It's true. I didn't like keeping our relationship a secret, but if that was the only way I could be with her, then I didn't have any choice but to accept her wishes."

Rylan studied the defensive jut of Jarrod's chin. "Where did you meet?"

Jarrod shrugged. "She would enter the gardens for her morning walk and then circle back to slip through the side gate," he said. "I would be waiting for her in the woods."

Rylan tried to visualize Anne darting out a small gate, and then slipping through the woods all alone.

He hadn't spent much time at the Hamilton house, but he knew the surrounding area was secluded. Anne had no doubt been hidden from the house as well as the nearby driveway. A perfect opportunity for her to be snatched.

His mind turned to envisioning how it could have happened.

Had a killer been lurking in the shadows, waiting for her? Or had he simply been in the right place at the right time and seized the opportunity?

Or . . . had the killer been the man who was seated on Jaci's sofa, staring at him with frightened eyes?

"How often did you meet?" he demanded.

Jarrod hesitated before answering. "Most days. We spent half an hour or so walking along the trails that crisscross through the trees just outside the estate." He cleared his throat. "Or if it was cold we'd meet in the old caretaker's place." Rylan's lips twitched. The older man was embarrassed to admit he'd taken the housekeeper into the abandoned house for sex. Jarrod turned his head toward Jaci. "I know it wasn't entirely proper to sneak away during work hours, but we always made up the time later."

"We understand." Jaci patted his hand. "How long had you been together?"

He thought for a moment. "Almost a year."

Rylan's brows snapped together. He'd assumed that this

was a recent development. The fact that Jarrod and Anne had been lovers for almost a year changed their association from a casual tryst to a relationship.

And when you were in a relationship, you did things a hell of a lot different than if you were hooking up for a quickie in the caretaker's house.

"Why didn't you come forward when Anne was missing?"

Jarrod paled, his guilt etched on his face. "At first I thought she was avoiding me. Then when I realized no one could find her, I went to Sid."

Deputy Sid was Jarrod's youngest brother's son.

"Why not Sheriff O'Brien?" Jaci asked.

"I was still trying to keep our relationship a secret. I didn't want Anne to lose her job." Jarrod looked distressed, a film of sweat coating his forehead. "I never dreamed she was in danger. I just don't understand."

Rylan might have had sympathy toward the older man if his decision to keep Anne's disappearance a secret hadn't put every woman in the area in danger.

"What did Sid tell you?" he asked.

Jarrod's gaze lowered to where Jaci's slender fingers covered his work-worn hand.

"Sid said there was a good chance something bad happened to her." Jarrod hesitated, clearly reluctant to confess the truth. "He was worried I might be implicated."

Rylan narrowed his gaze. He'd known that the Walkers were a tight-knit clan. They would always put family first.

But Sid was also a lawman. He should have hauled his uncle to the police station as soon as the man had come to him with his concerns about Anne.

"Did he warn you to keep quiet about your relationship with Anne?" Rylan demanded.

Jarrod kept his head lowered, his shoulders pulled up to his ears.

"Not in so many words," the older man said. "He just pointed out that I might be a suspect. So I kept my mouth shut."

Rylan wondered what O'Brien was going to think about having a deputy on his staff who withheld vital information in an investigation.

It probably wasn't going to be good.

He waited for Jarrod to continue. When the man remained silent, he asked the obvious question.

"So why are you talking now?"

Jarrod lifted his head, his expression hardening with determination. "When I heard she'd been found dead I knew I had to do something."

Rylan felt a burst of frustration. There was an old saying about better late than never.

But it didn't feel better.

"So you came to me?"

Jarrod gave an eager nod. "Your father said you knew all about the latest tech stuff. And that you had friends who went all the way to the White House."

Christ. He was going to sit his father down when this was all over and have a serious talk. He'd clearly convinced people in town that Rylan was some sort of James Bond on steroids.

He gave a lift of his hands. "What do you think I can do?"

"You and your people can figure out who killed Anne." Jarrod leaned forward, his eyes filled with desperate hope. "Then I won't be arrested."

"You're not going to be arrested," Rylan told him.

"How can you be so sure? I'm the most obvious suspect." With a sudden burst of nerves, Jarrod surged to his feet, his face flushing with fear. "I should go."

"Wait, Jarrod." Rylan moved to block the older man's path to the door. "I can help."

The older man's breath was coming in a short, staccato rhythm. He was on the verge of a full-blown panic attack.

"You can?"

"Yes." Careful not to spook the man, Rylan reached to grab his shoulders, firmly pushing him toward the sofa. "Why don't you sit back down?"

Jaci smoothly rose to her feet. "I'll make some coffee," she offered, heading toward the kitchen.

Smart woman. She must have sensed that Jarrod would speak more freely about his intimate connection with Anne if she was out of the room.

Waiting until she had disappeared into the kitchen, he returned his attention to Jarrod.

"Tell me what you know about Anne. Had she been worried about anything?"

Jarrod thought for a moment. "She did mention there'd been tension in the house since Christopher returned from college."

Rylan arched his brows. Had the family known that Christopher wasn't attending college? Or had they discovered the truth after he'd returned home? Rylan suspected that would cause a little friction with Papa Hamilton.

"Did she know why?"

Jarrod shook his head. "No, but I heard them arguing in the garage the morning Anne disappeared."

"Could you hear what they were saying?"

Jarrod's brow furrowed as he tried to recall the argument. "The only thing I heard was something about an alley and hope."

Rylan blinked. "Alley and hope?"

"That's all I heard," Jarrod said, watching in confusion

as Rylan pulled his phone out of his pocket and wrote a quick text to Griff. "What are you doing?"

Rylan allowed a wry smile to touch his lips. "Sending the words to one of my special contacts."

"Ah." Jarrod once again looked hopeful. As if expecting Rylan to conjure some mystery official who could solve everything.

"Did Anne speak about anything else out of the ordinary?" Rylan returned to his questioning.

"Nope."

"No enemies?" Rylan pressed. "No one threatening her?"

The man gave an emphatic shake of his head. "I swear she didn't seem troubled at all."

Rylan processed his words. If Jarrod was telling the truth, then Anne didn't have an enemy who might have wanted her dead. And she hadn't been worried about a stalker.

That meant her death had come without warning.

And that she hadn't given Jarrod any clue who might be responsible for killing her.

Dammit.

"Were you supposed to meet her the morning she disappeared?" he asked. The man had to know something that could help them.

"Yeah. I was headed in that direction when I noticed all the cars at the café. I decided to stop in and see what was going on. They were talking about the body found." He gave a sad shake of his head. "I should never have done it."

"Done what?"

"Stayed so long," he said. "I was sitting there drinking coffee and listening to the gossip. It made me late to my meeting with Anne." Disgust was thick in his voice.

Rylan was beginning to understand the man's reluctance to go to the sheriff. It wasn't just a fear of being branded a killer. But an overwhelming sense of shame that he might be responsible for her death.

After all, if he hadn't been late to the meeting, Anne might still be alive.

Any suspicion that this man was somehow involved in the killings was swiftly fading.

"Anne wasn't there when you arrived?" he asked.

"No. I waited around, but when she didn't show I just thought she was mad because I was late." He twisted his hands together. "She was a woman who liked things to be in an orderly way. I always caught the edge of her tongue if I was late."

Rylan squatted down until he was face-to-face with Jarrod. The man was battling through a toxic combination of grief and guilt. Two emotions that typically clouded a person's mind.

And right now, Rylan needed him thinking clearly.

"This is important, Jarrod." He held the man's teary gaze. "I want you to tell me everything you can remember after you left the café."

Jarrod gave a slow nod, his shoulders squaring. Perhaps he was belatedly realizing that he might hold the key to finding who killed Anne.

"Okay." He took a deep breath, taking a moment to shuffle through his memories. "I drove to our meeting place. I didn't stop anywhere after I left the café."

"Where do you park?"

"If I'm working I just slip through the gate ahead of Anne," he said. "On the days I'm not at work I leave my truck at the lumberyard. I'm there enough that no one would think it was weird to see it parked there."

Rylan felt a stab of surprise. Clearly the man had given some thought to keeping his affair secret.

"Then you walk to the caretaker's house?"

"It's not really a house," Jarrod said, wrinkling his nose. "More of a large storage shed the previous gardener converted into a place to sleep and keep his things."

"Can you see it from the road?"

"No." He sounded certain. "The place is surrounded by trees. Unless you knew it was there you could easily walk right past it. That's one of the reasons we met there."

Rylan drummed his fingers on the side of his thigh. If the place was that concealed, then it made it unlikely the stalker simply caught sight of Anne and took advantage of the situation.

"Does the land belong to the Hamiltons?"

"I think so." Jarrod shrugged. "But they never use it."

Rylan turned the conversation back to the day Anne disappeared.

"So you parked your truck and walked to the shed."

Jarrod nodded. "It was raining, so I assumed that's where Anne would be waiting for me."

"Did you see anyone?"

"No." His denial came without hesitation. "I'm always careful to keep out of sight of the main house."

"You didn't hear any voices? Or a car taking off?"

"Nothing," Jarrod insisted.

Rylan silently reminded himself that the older man would have been distracted by the morning gossip of a dead woman being found in Frank Johnson's field, as well as the knowledge he was late.

It was possible he might have missed someone leaving the area.

"And there was no indication of a struggle inside the shed?" he asked.

"No. I would have been concerned right away if I'd seen something."

Rylan forced himself to pause. His questions were getting him nowhere.

Which meant he wasn't asking them the right way.

A good interviewer understood that everyone looked at the world a different way. A mother would look around the room and instinctively search for any exits a child could slip through, any sharp items that might be lying around, and any choking hazards. A cop would instinctively check for weapons, or places where a perp could be hiding.

He needed to think like a gardener.

"Was there any water or mud on the floor of the shed?" he at last demanded. "Something that would have indicated that Anne had been there and left?"

Jarrod's head started to shake in denial, then he stiffened. Clearly he'd remembered something.

"Oh Lord, she couldn't have been there."

"Why do you say that?"

Jarrod rubbed his hands on his coveralls, eager to find a way to help.

"As I said, she was always very orderly. If she'd been there she would have wiped her shoes on the rug she'd put inside the door," he said. "It was dry."

"You're sure?"

"Yep." An emphatic nod. "I remember noticing that the rug had been recently washed when I was taking off my boots. At the time I was thinking that she was going to give me a good talking-to for making a mess."

Rylan's earlier supposition that the woman could have been easily taken from the woods returned.

"Who knew that you were meeting Anne in the mornings?" he asked.

Jarrod looked confused by the question. "No one. I told you. Anne wanted to keep it a secret."

Rylan wasn't convinced. In a town as small as Heron there was no such thing as secrets.

"What about Sid?"

Jarrod gave a stubborn shake of his head. "I never said a word to him. Not until she didn't show up the next morning and I knew something must have happened to her. That's when Sid told me that Miss Hamilton had reported her as missing."

Rylan didn't press. The man was clearly convinced that no one knew about their affair.

"You said Anne would slip out through a side gate?" he instead asked. "Where was it?"

"Just behind the garage."

"Could someone have seen her from the house?"

Jarrod took time to consider, no doubt trying to visualize the various angles.

"I suppose they could have." He shrugged. "But Mr. Hamilton always leaves before Anne took her walk and none of the others ever crawled out of bed until nine."

Rylan shook his head. Jarrod was either unbelievably naive, or dangerously cunning.

In either case, he couldn't delay the inevitable any longer.

"We need to give this information to the sheriff."

Jarrod surged to his feet, sweat dripping from his brow. "I can't."

"He's not going to arrest you," Rylan assured the older man. "But I'm sure he'll have some questions."

Jarrod's calloused hands clenched and unclenched. "How can you be so sure he won't think I'm guilty?"

"Just tell him the truth."

Jarrod snorted. "Yeah well, I've seen plenty of shows where a guilty man is sent to death row."

Rylan reached out to lay a hand on the man's shoulder. "I swear that I'll use every top official I know to keep you from being framed for a crime you didn't commit. Okay?"

The man gave a grudging nod. "Okay."

Rylan stepped back, silently hoping he hadn't just promised more than he could deliver.

Chapter Twenty-One

Mike calmly pocketed his phone. A simple task that wasn't simple at all.

Not when he was overwhelmed with the desire to throw it across the room. Maybe even stomp it beneath his heel. At the moment, however, he was acutely aware of the three sets of gazes that were watching him with blatant curiosity.

The lawyer, dressed in his thousand-dollar suit, who was standing near the window. Loreen Hamilton, who was perched on a leather wing chair. And Payton, who'd halted her nervous pacing when he'd gotten the call from Rylan.

They'd all sat in tense silence for the past two hours, waiting for the missing Blake and Christopher Hamilton.

Now, Mike stiffly rose to his feet and offered a meaningless nod toward Loreen.

"I need to go."

A chilled smile touched the woman's lips. "Finally."

"Oh, I'm not done," he warned, holding her gaze as he headed toward the door. "I intend to speak with your husband and son. We can do it here, or we can do it at my office. It's up to them."

The officious lawyer instantly took command of the conversation.

"The Hamiltons intend to be as cooperative as possible, Sheriff O'Brien. They are as anxious as you are to discover what happened to poor Ms. Dixon."

Mike snorted. The Hamiltons were going to be a pain in the ass from start to finish. It was their greatest talent.

"The clock is ticking," he warned. "They can willingly set up a meeting here or I'll get warrants to make them come to my office."

Loreen's lips parted, but before she could speak the lawyer had moved to place a warning hand on her shoulder. At the same time, Payton walked to stand at Mike's side.

"I'll show you out."

Loreen scowled. "Payton."

The younger woman waved away her mother's protest. "I'll only be a minute."

The lawyer pinched his lips, his hard gaze flicking from Payton to Mike.

"She's my client, Sheriff. I won't have her questioned without me present."

Mike muttered a curse beneath his breath and headed out the door. He hated lawyers.

Payton hurried to keep up with his brisk pace. "Has something happened? Did you find out how Anne died?"

He shot her a jaundiced glare. He'd reached the end of his limited patience with the Hamilton clan.

"Your lawyer made it clear that we're not to talk about the case."

She sent him a confused frown. "Why are you treating me like the enemy?"

They reached the large foyer, and Mike halted to turn and face his companion.

"Because Anne disappeared from this house and now she's dead."

She flinched as if he'd physically struck her. "Oh God." A shaky hand lifted to press against her throat. "It's so awful."

Mike grimaced. He was in a foul mood. And the recent phone call from Rylan had made it even fouler. Was that a word? Whatever. He wanted to punch something.

But it wasn't fair to take it out on Payton.

"I'm sorry," he said. "That was insensitive."

Payton blinked back tears, her beauty luminous in the sudden beam of sunshine that peeked through the windows.

"I loved her." The words were choked with emotion. "I truly did."

"I know." He reached to open the door. He needed to get out of the house. Not only because he had pressing business awaiting him at the office, but because he wanted to be away from the oppressive atmosphere. How the hell did Payton live in this place? It was choking him. "I have to go."

"You'll be back?"

There was an edge of near panic in her voice that had him turning back to study her pale face.

"Yeah, I'll be back."

She sucked in a slow, deep breath. "Please let me know if you find out anything about Anne."

His lips twisted. They both knew he wasn't going to tell her anything until the investigation was over.

Still, he allowed his gaze to brush over her perfect face. "Be careful, Payton. Until we know what's going on, anyone could be in danger."

Without warning, she stepped forward and brushed her mouth over his in a lingering kiss.

"*You* be careful."

Her lips were warm. Soft. A sensual delight. Lust blasted through him, but the second his hands lifted to grab the aggravating female, she was turning to disappear back down the hallway.

Shit.

It was always the same.

She teased him with the promise of paradise, only to snatch it away.

He stomped out of the house and down the stairs of the terrace. What he needed was a vacation. A hot beach with plenty of sunshine. And bikini-clad women who didn't make him want things that were constantly out of his reach.

Once in the driveway, Mike forced himself to halt and turn toward the garage that was set at the side of the house. Rylan had told him that Jarrod Walker had confessed to meeting with Anne Dixon in the nearby woods. And that she'd used a gate behind the garage to slip away for her lovers' trysts.

From where he was standing he couldn't see the gate. And since Loreen had already called in her high-priced lawyer, there was no way he was going to be allowed to search the property without a warrant.

That didn't mean he couldn't take a minute to mentally note that anyone on the second floor of the house could easily see over the top of the garage.

Anne Dixon's affair might not have been as secret as she assumed.

Returning to Heron at breakneck speed, Mike called to leave a message with Sid to meet him at the office. Then, finding Jarrod waiting for him in the interview room, he focused on grilling the older man on his relationship with Anne Dixon.

After an hour, he sent Jarrod home, warning him not to leave the area.

He truly didn't believe that Jarrod was responsible. But he would be a fool not to keep him on the suspect list. Who else had better opportunity to kill Anne?

Needing a few minutes to clear his head, Mike headed into his office and flopped onto his chair. He closed his eyes, trying to sort through the information that Jarrod had given him. He was desperate to find anything that would lead him in the direction of the killer.

But instead his treacherous thoughts returned to Payton's worried expression, and the feel of her mouth pressed against his lips. Even now the taste of her lingered.

It wasn't until the door was pushed open and Sid stepped into the office that he was able to banish the aggravating woman from his mind.

"You wanted to see me?" the deputy asked.

"Sit down."

Sid rocked from side to side. His nervous habit was more pronounced than usual.

"I—"

Mike stabbed a finger toward the seat across from his desk. "Sit. Down."

"Shit. You spoke to my uncle." Sid moved to settle on the wooden chair, his shoulders slumped. "I thought I saw his truck pulling out of the lot."

Mike leaned his elbows on the desk, glaring at the man whom he trusted for the past four years.

"Can you give me one reason why I shouldn't fire your ass right now?"

Sid grimaced. "I'm sorry."

"Sorry? You deliberately withheld a witness in an ongoing investigation."

Sid's expression became defensive. "I know my uncle. He couldn't possibly have hurt Anne Dixon."

"That would have been my first assumption as well. But the fact that you made an effort to cover up his relationship with her makes him look guilty."

His lips parted, as if he intended to excuse his decision. Then, seeing Mike's clenched jaw, he heaved a rueful sigh.

"I wasn't thinking."

Mike bit back his angry response. What was done was done. He couldn't change his deputy's poor decisions; he could only hope that he could find some silver lining.

"Did you go to the shed where your uncle was supposed to meet Anne?" he asked.

Sid hesitated, then gave a slow nod. "Yeah. I wanted to check and see if Anne had left a note that Jarrod missed. Or if there were any signs of an intruder."

"What did you see?"

"There was a narrow bed and some gardening equipment stacked in a corner."

"Nothing suspicious?"

Sid shook his head. "Nope. No note, no trash thrown in the can. No sign that Anne had been there." He shrugged. "And I couldn't see any footprints except my uncle's coming from the bottom of the hill."

Mike templed his fingers beneath his chin. "Anne didn't reach the shed?"

"Not that I could see, but I didn't go there until the day after Anne disappeared, so it's possible the rains could have washed away any potential evidence."

It seemed doubtful that the rains would wash away Anne's footprints, but leave Jarrod's.

"Did you notice anything?"

"I walked up to the gate that opens into the Hamilton estate."

"And?"

"It'd been left open."

Mike tensed. The fact the gate was open could mean

that Anne had gone out and had been instantly attacked. Or someone had come into the estate and forgotten to close the gate.

Or, that someone at the house had attacked Anne and carried her out the gate to hide her in the woods until they could drive her to a remote location and dump her body.

"Anything else?"

"No." Sid nervously shifted in his seat. "What's going to happen to me?"

Mike took a long time to consider his answer. When he'd first learned that his own deputy had been tampering with a murder investigation, he'd been determined to fire him on the spot. How could he ever trust him again?

Now, he'd calmed down. Okay, maybe he wasn't calm. But he'd at least leashed his anger enough to know that now wasn't the time to consider such drastic measures.

"Starting immediately, you're going to take your vacation days."

Sid swallowed hard. "Then what?"

"I'll decide after this investigation is over." Mike planted his palms flat on the desk as he leaned forward. "Until then, I don't want to see you anywhere near this office. Got it?"

"Yeah. I got it."

Sid rose to his feet. As he turned toward the door, Mike thought he caught a glimpse of something in his deputy's eyes.

Embarrassment. Anger. Maybe frustration.

He shook his head, rolling his tense shoulders. A problem for another day, he decided as Sid left the office at the same time that Carol walked in.

The middle-aged woman gave a lift of her brows as Sid swept past her without speaking.

"Trouble?" she asked, closing the door to ensure their conversation wouldn't be overheard.

Carol's discretion was only one of her many skills, but the one that Mike depended on the most. She was one of the few people he knew he could use as a sounding board when he was ready to smash a few heads together.

"Remind me why I ever wanted to be sheriff," he said.

She pretended to consider. "Hm. I got nothing."

"Thanks."

"You do look handsome in that uniform."

His lips twisted. "I'm glad someone thinks so."

Carol tilted her head to the side, not missing the sharp edge in his voice.

"You know, Jaci Patterson is a nice, pretty, young woman."

Mike arched a brow. Carol had been hinting that he needed a good, solid woman in his life for years. Ever since he'd broken up with Payton.

The older woman never bothered to hide her dislike for the Hamiltons.

"She is," he agreed.

"The sort of woman a smart man snatches up before some poacher comes along and steals her."

Ah. So Carol had heard that Rylan Cooper was staking his claim on Jaci.

"Very subtle," he said.

She heaved a long-suffering sigh. "You're a good man, Mike O'Brien, but like all men you can be distracted by shiny baubles."

He held up his hand. "Don't blame me. I did my best to convince Jaci that I'm the man she needs, but she slotted me into the friend role. We both know there's no coming back from that." He shrugged. "Besides, I don't think she ever got over her feelings for Cooper."

Carol clicked her tongue. "I thought that girl had more sense."

Mike smiled. He appreciated the woman's loyalty, but he couldn't let her blame Jaci.

"No," he said. "I'll admit that I like Jaci, and I hoped we could make something of our relationship. But if I'm being honest, there were never going to be fireworks."

She gave a sharp laugh. "Listen to the advice of a woman who's been married three times. Fireworks aren't all they're cracked up to be." She wagged her finger at him. "What you need is to find someone who's in it for the long haul."

The image of Payton seared through his mind. It was doubtful that she would be in it for the long haul. At least not with him. But he didn't doubt that there would be plenty of fireworks.

"I'll keep that in mind." He reached up to massage the tense muscles of his neck. Yet another problem he'd deal with later. "Did you need something?"

Resisting the urge to continue her chastisement on his love life—or rather, his lack of a love life—Carol nodded.

"The medical examiner's office called while you were out."

Mike stilled, instantly back in cop mode. "Did they leave a message?"

"The blood on the locket that was found at Jaci's house was the same type as Anne Dixon," she said, confirming what the tech had already told him. "The DNA hasn't come back yet."

Mike nodded. He didn't need the DNA. He was already convinced the bastard had killed Anne and used her blood and hair to create his creepy locket.

"Anything else?"

"The preliminary cause of death was strangulation, but

there was a wound on the back of her head that was consistent with blunt force trauma." Carol was forced to halt and clear her throat. She'd worked in the sheriff's office for years, but none of them were accustomed to talking about their neighbors in terms of strangulation and blunt force trauma. "They also said that she'd been dead at least forty-eight hours, although they don't have a precise time of death yet."

He drummed his fingers on the top of his desk. "When did they call?"

She glanced at the watch strapped around her wrist. "Two hours ago."

Which meant they must have started the autopsy on Anne almost as soon as she'd arrived at the facility.

"That was quick," he said.

"They mentioned the fact that the governor had contacted them. They were told this case is a priority," Carol said, giving a lift of her hands. "I'm assuming it was my charming personality that encouraged him to make the call."

Mike knew exactly who was responsible. "I'm guessing Cooper must have cashed in a few favors."

"Ah." She pretended disappointment.

He grabbed a pencil and scribbled the information on a piece of paper. It wasn't that he was going to forget, but seeing things written down sometimes helped to clarify his thoughts. "No word on the Jane Doe?"

"Not yet."

"Was that all?"

"They emphasized that this was all preliminary," she said. "They'll send the official report when it's done."

He nodded, leaning back in his seat as weariness crashed over him. When was the last time he ate? It seemed like it'd been days ago.

"At least we got something," he said.

Carol frowned, her hands on her hips. "You should go home. You look exhausted."

Habit had him glancing toward the clock on the wall. It was the old-fashioned kind with an ivory face and black hands that jerked from one minute to the next.

"Crap." He shook his head as he realized it was nearly six o'clock. No wonder he was starving. "I didn't know it was that late." He was struck by a sudden thought. "Why are you still here?"

"I'm getting ready to leave," she said. "I stayed late because I took some time off this morning to get a pedicure."

He rose to his feet, a smile on his face. There was only one reason Carol got a pedicure.

"Big plans for the night?"

"I'm taking Larry to the bowling alley in Quincy." She winked at him. "You know I can't date a man until I know how he handles a ball."

Mike gave a wry shake of his head. He wondered if poor Larry knew he was being sized up as Husband Number Four.

"Have a good time."

She made a shooing motion with her hands. "Go home."

"Aye, aye," he said as he watched her walk out of the office.

Chapter Twenty-Two

After a delicious dinner of grilled steak and salad that Rylan had insisted on cooking, Jaci had retreated to the bathroom for a steamy bubble bath.

She told herself she wasn't hiding from Rylan.

She just wanted some time alone to soothe her raw nerves. Something that wasn't possible when Rylan was hovering over her, his instincts to protect on full alert.

But it wasn't his vigilant attitude that occupied her mind as she was soaking in the soapy water. No. Her thoughts were entirely consumed with the way Rylan's gaze had lingered on her as they ate dinner at her small kitchen table. And how he'd pressed the hard line of his leg against hers as they'd sat on the sofa.

Every lingering touch was like being struck by lightning. Her skin tingled and her stomach fluttered with dangerous excitement.

At last she'd fled, hoping to regain command of her out-of-control hormones.

Unfortunately, it hadn't been as easy as she'd hoped.

She'd been unable to close her eyes without having her thoughts hijacked by images of Rylan joining her in the bathtub, his hard, naked body moving against her as the steam wrapped around them.

Finally, she'd conceded defeat. A hot bath wasn't going to ease the awareness that was sizzling through her.

Wrapping a towel around her still-damp body, she entered her bedroom. She'd already made sure the spare room was aired and the sheets changed for Rylan. Hopefully he was already tucked in for the night.

She was barely through the doorway when she realized her mistake. Rylan wasn't tucked in his bed. Instead, he'd spent the past half hour preparing for the perfect seduction.

Her startled gaze skimmed around the shadowed bedroom, which was lit by a dozen candles that flickered on her dresser and the two nightstands. Next to the double bed was a bottle of wine that he'd bought when they were in town earlier, and two fluted crystal glasses.

She blinked, barely managing to absorb the transformation of her boring room when she found warm arms wrapping around her as Rylan pressed her against the wall.

Raw excitement blasted through her at the feel of his hard body pressing against her. He'd changed out of his clothes and was wearing a loose pair of sweatpants that left his chest bare.

Her fingers twitched, longing to explore the chiseled hardness of his muscles and the dusting of golden hair that arrowed down the flat plane of his stomach.

He'd always been lean, but as he'd matured he'd gained a toned bulk. It was no wonder the women in California had been lining up to spend time with him.

Her mouth went dry, her heart racing.

It'd been a long time since she'd been this attracted to a man. Then she swallowed a sudden urge to laugh. Hell, who was she fooling? She'd never been this sexually attracted to another man.

It'd always been Rylan.

Always.

Pressing against her, Rylan allowed his fingers to trace the line of her shoulders, his eyes shimmering like pure gold in the candlelight.

"Did you enjoy your bath?"

His voice was low and already husky with desire. She shivered, her skin tingling beneath his light touch.

"It was relaxing."

His lips twisted in a knowing smile. Did he sense that she'd spent her time trying to squash her vicious hunger?

"Good." His head dipped down, his lips skimming over her cheek before they nuzzled the corner of her mouth. At the same time his fingers moved to trace the top of her towel, lingering on the upper swell of her breasts. The heat of his touch seared against her skin, making her nipples harden with anticipation. "I intend to relax you even more."

She sucked in a sharp breath, her toes curling against the hard floor.

"This doesn't feel relaxing."

He kissed her. Hard. His tongue pressed against her lips, demanding entry. Desire drenched the air, sucking her under like a whirlpool.

"Give me time," he assured her, catching her lower lip between his teeth. He pressed his hips forward, letting her feel the hard thrust of his erection. "I've just started."

Her stomach clenched, a damp need pulsing between her legs.

"There's more?" she asked.

"Much, much more."

With one skillful tug, he had the towel loosened, allowing it to fall from her body to pool at her feet. Jaci stiffened, feeling intensely vulnerable as his gaze ran a heated inspection over her naked body.

She was a woman. Which meant she'd spent far too much of her life looking in the mirror, searching for every imperfection. She was acutely aware that her breasts were full, but not perky like she'd seen in magazines. And her stomach wasn't flat. Instead it had a soft swell that spread even further at her hips. And her legs were sturdy, not slender like Payton's.

Rylan, however, didn't look disappointed as he studied every quivering inch of her. Instead, his eyes darkened to molten gold, and heat stained his cheeks with color.

"Christ," he breathed. "You're so beautiful."

She blushed. "I'm not."

He halted her protest with a fierce kiss. "Don't ever say that again."

She trembled, her hands lifting to smooth over the solid strength of his chest. He felt good. His skin was hot to the touch, and silky smooth beneath the rasp of hair.

Unlike her, he looked like he'd been sculpted by the hands of an artist.

"It's the truth," she said.

"Then you're not seeing what I'm seeing." Pressing his forehead against hers, he allowed his hands to brush through the damp strands of her hair. "I love everything about you," he insisted. "I love your hair. It makes me think of a wood sprite."

Her heart missed a beat. Did he truly think she was beautiful?

She sternly chided herself for her silly vanity.

A man would say anything when he was trying to lure a woman into bed.

"A wood sprite?" she instead teased.

His fingers moved to brush over her brow, his expression oddly somber.

"And I love your eyes," he continued as if she hadn't

spoken. "They can be the blue of a summer sky, or the mysterious silver of moonlight, depending on your mood."

"Very poetic."

His hands traced the curve of her throat before heading lower to cup the softness of her rounded flesh.

"And I love your breasts." His voice had dropped to a low growl. Sexual pleasure poured through her, arching her spine and making her nails dig into his hard flesh. "I've been fantasizing about your breasts for longer than I want to admit. I knew they'd be round and firm and your nipples would be rosy with invitation. Do they taste as good as they look?"

She glanced down, eagerness pulsing through her at the sight of his fingers molding her mounds, the darkness of his fingers in stark contrast to her pale skin.

Her nipples were tightly budded, offering a silent invitation as he lowered his head to close his lips around one tip.

Grabbing his shoulders, she moaned as he used his teeth and tongue to torment her tender flesh. A primitive need beat deep inside her, coaxing her to rub against the thick length of his erection.

For years she'd fantasized about this moment. But nothing could prepare her for the sheer male sensuality that cloaked around her.

A hot, erotic hunger cascaded through her, clenching her muscles.

"Delicious," he said, turning his attention to her other breast. His tongue rasped against her nipple, his hands sliding down the curve of her waist to grasp her hips. "But I'm not done."

Jaci's head tilted back against the wall, her mind fuzzy with a sensual haze. She was finding it increasingly difficult to concentrate on his words.

She was far more focused on the thunderbolts of pleasure that were making her knees weak.

"You're not?" she managed to rasp.

"Not even close." His lips stroked between her breasts, heading downward. "I love your skin." He kissed a small freckle on her upper stomach, then moved to another freckle just above her belly button. "Silky smooth with tiny speckles that lead precisely where I want to go."

A choked laugh was wrenched from her throat as he lowered himself to his knees, his lips continuing to press against her stomach.

"You're saying my freckles are some sort of GPS?" she asked.

"Shh." He tilted back his head to send her a chiding glance. "I'm not done."

"Bossy."

"And arrogant," he added, his attention returning to his delectable seduction.

"Yes." She bit her lower lip as he used the tip of his tongue to explore the swell of her hip, his hands moving to grasp the fullness of her backside.

"I love your butt." He squeezed her flesh, using his shoulder to urge her legs farther apart. "It fits perfectly in my hands."

"Rylan." His name fell from her lips as he nibbled a path to her inner thigh.

She'd gone from arousal to painful, aching need in the blink of an eye. It'd been so long. Too long.

Now she was drowning in desire.

Perhaps sensing her fierce hunger, he moved his attention to where she needed him the most.

"I've got you, Jaci," he assured her, stroking his tongue through her damp heat.

There was no hesitation. No tentative tasting.

He licked her with a strong, steady rhythm that sent her spiraling toward an explosive orgasm with a speed that was shocking.

Her fingers tangled in his hair, her eyes squeezed shut as sweet bliss pulsed through her, tiny bursts of aftershocks continuing to quake through her body.

Yow. It'd all happened so fast, she barely knew what hit her.

Clearly realizing that she was beyond words, Rylan surged upright, sweeping her off her feet. Cradling her against his chest, he moved to the nearby bed.

"I intended to have a glass of wine and dazzle you with my charm," he said, leaning down to place her in the middle of the mattress.

A slow, lazy smile curved her lips as he straightened and quickly yanked off his sweats. Her gaze moved down to the heavy jut of his arousal. Any doubt of whether or not he truly wanted her was erased.

He couldn't fake that.

"What happened?" she asked.

"I saw you in that towel and I lost all control," Rylan said, crawling onto the bed. He paused to slide on a condom that he'd left next to the bed, then he wrapped her tightly in his arms.

She studied his beautiful face, her arms looping around his neck.

"You were overcome with lust?"

"It's more than lust, Jaci. Never doubt that," he said, his expression determined as he rolled her onto her back.

She instinctively spread her legs, allowing his lower body to settle between them. Holding her gaze, he shifted until the tip of his erection was at the entrance to her body, then with one smooth thrust he was buried deep inside her.

She gasped, her back arching at the erotic penetration.

"Consider me dazzled," she assured him.

"Not yet." He pulled back before he was pumping into her with enough force to rattle the headboard. "But you will be," he promised, capturing her lips in a kiss of blatant possession.

She was.

He'd intended to play with Rylan Cooper. The bastard thought he could sweep back into town and claim Jaci. He needed to be taught a lesson.

Which was why he'd left Anne's body in that precise location. It was a place that would ensure that Cooper understood he'd been outmaneuvered.

And the sight of his reaction had been sweet.

Almost as sweet as Jaci's terror.

He'd replayed the tape over and over, zooming in to watch the color fade from her face and her hand lift to press against her lips. He could almost taste her fear. It was glorious.

It was only after he'd satisfied himself that he'd returned his attention to Rylan. He'd chuckled at the man's rigid frustration as he'd stood at the side of the road.

Rylan was smart enough to sense that the body was a warning. And that Jaci would soon be taken away from him. He'd always thought he was so special. The captain of the football team. The deputy with his crisp uniform who was too stupid to realize there was a killer beneath his nose. The filthy rich entrepreneur with his half-dressed bimbos and habit of swooping into town like some golden god.

Ah, yes. It was sweet to watch him floundering with no hope of figuring out who was taunting him.

But then the sheriff and his men had made their appearance and he'd realized that his enjoyment had come with a cost.

His talents were no longer being shrouded in shadows. Which meant he was going to have to be even more clever than usual.

He'd spent several hours worrying about the way he could finish his game. That's when he'd glanced out his window and realized that despite his love for meticulous detail, there was beauty in sheer blind luck.

Luck, or fate, or destiny had offered him precisely what he needed.

Chapter Twenty-Three

With Jaci safely wrapped in his arms, Rylan allowed himself to fall into a deep, dreamless sleep just after midnight. As much as he wanted to devote the entire night to exploring her lush sensuality, they were both exhausted. The past days had taken a toll, not only emotionally, but physically.

Not to mention the three sweaty bouts of amazing, mind-blowing sex.

His peaceful slumber, however, was rudely interrupted by the piercing shrill of Jaci's alarm. He muttered a curse, and briefly wondered what sort of sadist decided it would be a good idea to have an obnoxious *beep, beep, beep* to wake a person up.

Reaching across the slumbering Jaci, he slammed his hand on the top of the clock. He didn't know if he shut off the alarm or broke the damned thing, but at least it went silent.

Thank God.

Beside him, Jaci lifted her arms over her head in a slow stretch. Then her lashes lifted to reveal eyes that were astonishingly alert, considering that it was still the middle of the night.

Leaning on his elbow, he stared down at her with a brooding gaze.

"You said we could sleep in this morning," he reminded her.

An unexpected blush stained her cheeks. Was she remembering that he'd been buried deep inside her, both of them shuddering from their explosive climax, when she'd assured him that she wasn't going to be climbing out of bed at some ungodly hour?

"We did," she said, glancing toward the clock, which was now flipped on its side.

He scowled. "This isn't sleeping late."

"Stop bellyaching." She turned back, clicking her tongue in chastisement. "California has obviously made you soft."

Hmm. He didn't feel soft. In fact, the longer he was awake, the harder he was becoming. It no doubt had something to do with the warm, naked body pressed against him. As well as Jaci's warm, enticing scent that was teasing at his nose.

"It's not bellyaching to want to stay in bed with you," he said, his gaze moving over her sleep-flushed face before lowering to the tender swell of her breasts that peeked above the sheet. His mouth watered for another taste. "Besides, the sun isn't even up."

"I have stuff to do."

His hand moved to grasp the sheet, slowly tugging it down to reveal her naked beauty. Last night he'd been captivated by the sight of her sumptuous curves. The lush breasts, the narrow span of her waist, and the elegant line of her legs. But he'd expected to be sated. Well, maybe not sated, but at least for his lust to have eased to a manageable level after they'd had sex.

That was what always happened.

He wanted a woman. He seduced her. And then the thrill was gone.

But the intense reaction of his body assured him that his desire for Jaci wasn't going to be dulled by a night in her bed. It probably wouldn't be dulled by a few years in her bed.

This attraction wasn't a fleeting, physical awareness.

It came from his very soul.

His breath caught at the sight of her glorious beauty, revealed by the muted glow of the night-light.

"Does the stuff you have to do include this?" he asked as he lowered his head to brush his lips along the curve of her shoulder even as his hand cupped the full softness of her breast. "Or this?" he demanded. His lips traced the satin skin at the base of her throat, his thumb lightly circling the tip of her nipple.

She wiggled against him, her blush spreading as she became increasingly aroused.

"Rylan," she breathed.

"Maybe this?"

He captured her lips in a kiss that sizzled with heat. With a tiny sigh Jaci wrapped her arms around his neck, her legs parting as he rolled on top of her.

Almost three hours passed before they managed to climb out of the shower and get dressed for the day. Not that it'd been Rylan's idea to pull on his jeans and sweat-shirt. He'd voted on returning to bed.

Jaci, however, had insisted that she had to spend the morning in the shop, finishing up the crafts she intended to sell during the St. Patrick potluck dinner at the local school.

He bit back the urge to tell her he could easily buy all the crafts so they could concentrate on enjoying a leisurely day together. Jaci had done an amazing job of generating a career that not only paid the bills, but obviously fulfilled her creative talents. He would never undermine her pride in what she'd accomplished.

He did insist, however, on making breakfast. She spent enough time in the kitchen. He could scramble eggs and fry bacon. Plus, he'd located her stash of blueberry muffins in an old-fashioned tin container.

Perfect.

Once the dishes were done, Jaci grabbed her jacket and whistled for her dogs. She was clearly determined to get on with her day.

Rylan heaved a rueful sigh. It was ironic. He was usually the one looking for an excuse to bolt after a night of sex. No doubt he deserved to be the one clinging too tightly.

With a grimace, he trailed behind Jaci as she headed out of the house and directly toward the garage. The sun was making a rare appearance, splashing splotches of warmth over the muddy ground as they crossed the driveway.

Distantly he could hear the sound of a chain saw, revealing that Andrew was already hard at work. Closer, Rylan heard the chirp of a sparrow.

But he wasn't paying much attention to his surroundings. His thoughts were still distracted by the memory of the hot, soapy shower he'd shared with Jaci, which explained why he was caught off guard when Jaci came to a sharp halt in front of him.

"Rylan," she breathed, her eyes wide with horror.

On instant alert, Rylan focused his attention on the nearby garage. He didn't see anything at first. The door was closed and all the windows were tightly shut. Then a soft breeze whispered through the air and the glint of cheap gold captured his gaze.

A locket dangling from the doorknob.

It looked like the others. A plain oval on a gold chain. And inside, he didn't doubt, would be strands of hair wrapped in a bloody ribbon.

"Shit."

Grasping Jaci's arm, he swiftly tugged her back to the house, his gaze darting around. Suddenly it felt as if they were sitting ducks. A shooter could be hidden anywhere, just waiting to take them out. Calling for the dogs, he hustled them all inside and firmly shut and locked the door.

"Call the sheriff," he commanded. Jaci was in shock. He wanted to give her something to concentrate on beside her fear.

With a shaky nod she walked toward the landline phone and called the office. When there was no answer, she called O'Brien's cell phone, asking him to come to the house.

Rylan double-checked the doors and windows to make sure they were locked before he grabbed Jaci's laptop and set it on the kitchen table.

He'd downloaded the security tape from the night before when Jaci moved to stand beside him.

"What are you doing?" she asked.

"Checking the video," he said, hitting the fast-forward button on the keyboard.

Silence filled the kitchen as they watched the computer screen. There was nothing but the occasional raccoon, and a curious deer that wandered through the front yard. At last there was a hint of movement from the road. Rylan slowed the video to normal speed to watch the shadowy form that crept up the driveway.

"There." He halted the video, zooming in on the intruder as he placed the locket on the garage door. "Do you recognize him?"

They both bent down, studying the image. The camera was equipped with night vision, but the intruder was wearing a hoodie that kept his face hidden and plain jeans that could have belonged to anyone. He was even wearing a pair of rubber boots that every man in the county owned.

"No," Jaci admitted, her voice tight with frustration. "He never looks at the camera."

Rylan forced himself to suck in a slow, deep breath. They might not be able to see his face, but there were other clues that could help reveal the perp.

Laying his palms flat on the table, he did a logical inventory of the image.

It was definitely a man. That was obvious in the way he moved and the width of his shoulders beneath the hoodie. He was of average height. If Rylan was to make a guess, he would say the guy was shorter than himself, and he seemed to move like a man in his prime.

Of course, Rylan would be an idiot to scratch anyone off his mental list of suspects on a vague estimate.

It took a minute for him to actually realize the most obvious clue.

"You're right," he said. "He very deliberately doesn't look at the camera. Which means he knew it was there."

Jaci shivered, wrapping her arms around her waist. "What time was it?"

Rylan peered at the time stamp at the bottom of the screen. "Three a.m."

At that hour they'd both been sound asleep, unaware the killer was creeping around the property.

It was no wonder Jaci was shivering. The knowledge the man had been so close to them was creepy as hell.

Rylan, on the other hand, needed to punch something. Really, really hard.

"Why didn't he leave it on the front door like the last time?" she asked.

Rylan frowned. It was strange. It was as easy to walk to the front door as to the garage. And if the killer was hoping for maximum impact from the necklace, it would have made more sense to put it where he'd placed the others.

Could it be a copycat?

It was the sound of nails clicking against the linoleum floor that finally rattled the obvious explanation out of his sluggish brain.

"If he approached the house the dogs would have barked."

"Oh." She paused, her eyes widening with sudden distress. "If he avoided the camera and the dogs, then it has to be someone I know."

He grimaced. "That was always the most likely possibility."

"God." She buried her face in her hands, releasing a choked sob. "That makes it so much worse."

Rylan turned to wrap her in his arms, resting his cheek against the top of her head.

"Jaci, we're going to find him and stop him. That much I swear."

She leaned against him, for once accepting the comfort he was so desperate to offer.

"I want this nightmare over. It's just . . ." Her words trailed away as she stiffened, pulling out of his arms with an expression of horror on her pale face. "Rylan, if there's another locket that means there's another woman who's been killed. Maybe someone we know."

He held up a slender hand. As much as he wanted to pull her back into his arms, he needed to put the brakes on her gruesome speculations.

Whipping herself into hysteria was only going to hurt her.

"We don't know anything yet," he said in clipped tones. "And it's dangerous to try and speculate. All we can do is deal with the facts we have."

Her eyes flashed with fury, as if she was offended by his lack of concern for some unknown victim. Then, perhaps realizing he was trying to help her maintain control of her composure, she gave a sad shake of her head.

"Why is this happening?"

He lifted his hand, brushing his fingers down the length of her jaw. A ghost of a caress.

"We're going to figure this out."

He waited for her to give a jerky nod of her head before he returned his attention to the image frozen on the screen. If there was anything else to learn from the man, he wasn't seeing it.

Tapping the keyboard, he put the video into motion. Instantly the man was moving, leaving the locket on the door and turning away from the garage. For long minutes he simply stared toward the house, his gaze on the window to Jaci's bedroom.

Fury blasted through Rylan. The bastard had stood there and imagined Jaci in her bed. No doubt he'd even fantasized about joining her.

Very soon Rylan intended to make sure the creep's only view was a six-by-eight-foot prison cell.

Struggling to concentrate, he zoomed the camera out as the man abruptly turned to jog up the driveway. Within seconds, he disappeared from view. Rylan ignored Jaci's sound of frustration as he clicked out of her security program, concentrating on pulling up the remote feed from the cameras he'd placed along the road. Then rewinding the video to shortly before three a.m., he let it run.

"That must be him," Jaci said as headlights briefly cut through the darkness before they were shut off as they neared the house from the south.

Rylan tensed, expecting the approaching vehicle to stop before it came into full view. It's what the guy had done when he'd dumped Anne's body, although he'd been coming from the opposite direction. Instead, the vehicle continued on, not pulling to a halt until it was half hidden behind a large oak tree.

Rylan did his best to focus, but the vehicle was dark and barely visible behind the tree trunk. At last he zoomed in on the hood ornament glittering in the moonlight.

Jaci's breath caught. "I know that car," she said in a strangled voice.

Rylan nodded. He didn't need the fancy hood ornament to recognize the elegant lines of a Jaguar.

"Christopher."

"Yes." Jaci stepped back, her hand pressed against her throat as she tried to process what they were seeing. "I can't believe it."

He turned to study her tense profile. "Why not?"

She licked her lips, as if she was considering how to answer.

"We've never been as close as most brothers and sisters, but I know he's never been violent," she at last said. "He couldn't possibly be a serial killer."

Rylan couldn't deny a similar sense of disbelief. Christopher Hamilton was a spoiled little prick who'd spent his life doing exactly what he wanted with zero concern for the consequences.

But a killer?

He gave a sharp shake of his head. What was he doing? There was nothing more dangerous than assuming you could recognize a serial killer.

Trained professionals who'd studied the behavior of psychopaths knew that they could be anyone. The local mailman, or Sunday school teacher, or the son of the richest man in town.

Some were charming. Some were antisocial. Some were family men who'd kept their lust for violence hidden from their wives and kids for years.

They could quite literally be the person standing next to you and there would be no warning.

Rylan had to avoid the urge to allow his emotions to cloud his logic.

With an effort, he considered whether Christopher was a viable candidate for the stalker. Or if he'd somehow learned of the lockets and was taking the opportunity to torture his half sister.

At last Rylan had to concede that the evidence pointed in Christopher's direction.

"The time line would fit," he said.

Her brow furrowed. "The time line?"

"He was around the area when you first started receiving the lockets."

She wrinkled her nose. "Including a hundred other men."

"And they didn't start again until he returned to town," he continued, as if she hadn't spoken.

Jaci stilled. They both knew the fact that the lockets had started again at virtually the same time Christopher returned to town was highly suspicious.

"I suppose," she grudgingly conceded.

"And he's the one person we know who had a connection to Anne Dixon and Angel Harper," Rylan said.

It was Christopher's intimate knowledge of both victims that made Rylan seriously consider him as a suspect.

Who else in the area had the same access to both Angel and Anne?

Jaci looked confused. "I thought my brother liked Angel."

Rylan snorted. Christopher had "liked" a lot of girls. In fact, Rylan had heard rumors that he wasn't above renting out hookers from St. Louis when he had his infamous pool parties.

"He liked to party with her," he said, refusing to go into detail about what the partying might entail. "But if the rumors were true and she really was pregnant, that would change everything. Papa Hamilton wouldn't be happy to learn that his first grandchild was going to be born to an underage girl with a juvie record and a mother who was a known drug user."

She grimaced. "My mother would have had a fit."

That had to be the understatement of the year.

"Christopher would no doubt have done anything to avoid having Angel and a baby hanging like a noose around his neck," he said.

She took a few minutes to try and absorb the implication of his words. At last she gave a slow shake of her head.

"I can see Christopher panicking and deciding to get rid of Angel. He's a coward at heart," she said. "But why would he continue to kill?"

He shrugged. He didn't miss the edge in her voice. It was bad enough for her to know that there was some crazed lunatic who'd been stalking her for years. But to actually consider the thought that it might be her own half brother . . . It had to be profoundly disturbing.

"Some men develop a taste for it," he said. "The thrill of the hunt. The feeling of power when he steals the life from his victim. It can be sexual or just a need for control."

She flinched, no doubt thinking of poor Anne. The

middle-aged woman wouldn't have stood a chance against the killer.

"But why the lockets?" she asked, another shiver shaking her body.

His gaze moved toward the window that offered a view of the garage. Even now he could see the necklace glittering in the pale sunlight. An icy chill inched down his spine.

The lockets were the key. But he didn't have a damned clue what they meant. Or why Jaci was the only one to receive them.

"He's clearly obsessed with you."

She paused, her eyes narrowing as she studied his rigid body.

"There's something bothering you," she said.

He gave a short, humorless laugh. "Everything about this damned situation is bothering me."

"No, it's something else." She tilted her head to the side. "You don't sound convinced that Christopher is responsible."

"I think Christopher is the best suspect we have, but . . ." He released a deep sigh. "It's ridiculous, but none of this fits the pattern."

"What pattern?"

He drummed his fingers on the table, his thoughts jumbled. "Whoever this man is, he's managed to remain under the radar for years. Beyond the lockets that he left for you, he went to extreme measures to make sure no one realized that he was killing women and burying them in the levee."

"You're saying he didn't want to get caught."

"Exactly." Rylan nodded, his hand lifting to rub against the whiskers he hadn't had the chance to shave from his jaw. "Now he's started leaving bodies openly in the road, and he drove a car that's unmistakable and left it in view of the camera."

"Maybe he thought the tree would hide the car from view," she suggested.

He shrugged. His own guess was that whoever was responsible for the killing was swiftly spiraling out of control.

Whether it was Christopher or another maniac, the clock was ticking.

"It's possible."

He heard the sound of an approaching car. Motioning for her to remain in the kitchen, he swiftly moved through the house to peek through the front window. A swift glance revealed the squad truck pulling to a halt at the edge of the road. Rylan returned to the kitchen, his heart squeezing at the sight of Jaci's tense expression.

The past few days had taken their toll on the normally resilient woman. She looked brittle enough to shatter into a million pieces.

"O'Brien is here."

She stretched her lips into a tight smile. "I know. You want me to stay in here."

He moved until he could bend down and brush a soft kiss across her lips.

"Actually, I need you to do something."

"What's that?"

"Pack a bag."

Her brows drew together. "Rylan."

He pressed his fingers against her lips, halting her predictable protest.

"Once your brother is arrested I intend to take you to the beach for a few weeks of R and R," he said.

She remained rigid, as if she intended to argue. Then with a tiny sigh, she gave a slow nod of her head.

"It sounds like heaven."

Chapter Twenty-Four

Mike left his deputies at Jaci's to finish up processing the scene. At the moment he was far more concerned with tracking down Christopher Hamilton.

He shook his head as he pulled to a halt in front of the elegant mansion. He'd never liked the younger man. In fact, if Jaci had called to say she'd caught her half brother sneaking into her garage to steal from her, Mike wouldn't have batted an eye. It was exactly what he would have expected.

But a serial killer?

Of course, would it have been any easier if it'd been someone else from Heron?

Nope.

None of this made any sense.

Taking a minute to clear his thoughts, Mike swung out of his truck and headed up the front steps. As expected, the door was wrenched open before he could finish crossing the terrace.

He'd been buzzed through the front gate. Which meant they already knew the sheriff was coming.

It wasn't Payton, however, waiting for him. Or even her

mother. This time it was the great man himself, Blake Hamilton.

A tall man, Blake had once been the local cock of the walk. He was filthy rich, he had the biggest house in the county, and the women fluttered around him like he was some sort of god. He'd enjoyed his life as a swinging bachelor until he'd decided he wanted the pretty Loreen as his wife. He hadn't, however, wanted her newborn child.

Jerk.

Years later he was still handsome, although his dark hair was now silver and his lean face was lined with wrinkles. As Mike got closer he was surprised to discover that the older man looked like he'd aged twenty years since the last time Mike had seen him.

Did he know his son was a sick bastard?

Blake was wearing a dress shirt with pressed slacks, but his jaw was unshaven and he'd forgotten to put on his shoes.

Mike halted in front of the man, removing his ball cap. "Mr. Hamilton."

"Sheriff." The older man gave a stiff nod of his head. "I called your office this morning, but no one answered."

Mike felt a small stab of surprise. Carol was rarely late, even when she had to work weekends. The date must have gone better than expected.

Dang. He'd run out of ideas for wedding gifts for the woman. He'd already given her a toaster, a blender, and a microwave.

What else was left?

Giving a mental shrug, he met Blake's pale blue gaze. "Where's Christopher?" he demanded.

Blake's lips thinned. "I'm not going to have you speaking with him without our lawyer present."

"Fine." Mike shrugged. "Then call your lawyer and get Christopher."

Blake's jaw tightened. He was a man used to having people bending over backward to please him. He didn't like the fact he couldn't tell Mike to go screw himself.

"He's not home," he said.

Mike's stomach clenched. Had Christopher realized he'd been caught on camera and decided to make a run for it? With the Hamiltons' limitless bank account, he could be across the world before Mike could even get an arrest warrant.

"Where is he?"

Blake stiffened at Mike's sharp tone. "That's none of your business."

Mike's patience snapped. He'd left the office the evening before intending to have an early night, only to be called by his neighbor when her husband came home drunk and tried to take a swing at her. He'd hauled the idiot to jail and spent hours trying to comfort the wife before he could finally fall into his bed at dawn.

Now he was running on caffeine, adrenaline, and fumes. Not the best combination.

"Do you think this is a game, Hamilton?" Mike clenched his hands, resisting the urge to grab his gun. He wasn't a cowboy, and he didn't need a weapon to intimidate a man twice his age. "A woman is dead and your son is a suspect."

Blake made a sound of shock. "Suspect? In the death of Anne?"

"Yes."

"You can't be serious."

"I never joke about death."

Blake took a minute to gather his composure. He looked genuinely astonished that his son was being connected to the housekeeper's death.

"I know local law enforcement has always held a grudge against my son, but this is beyond outrageous." His gaze lowered to the star patch sewn onto Mike's uniform. "Maybe it's time we get a new sheriff."

Mike resisted the urge to roll his eyes. Blake sounded just like the whining meth dealer, always blaming the sheriff's office for his own troubles.

"And you always rush to protect him whether he's innocent or guilty," he countered, not in the mood to be diplomatic.

If this man wanted to put his money behind another candidate for sheriff, then more power to him. There were plenty of jobs. Most of them paid better, with a lot fewer headaches.

"He's my son," Blake said, his expression defensive.

Mike might have coughed up a little sympathy for Blake if he didn't suspect the older man's concern was for the Hamilton name, not for Christopher. Blake might not be as cold-blooded as his wife, but he was equally obsessed with avoiding any tarnish on the family dynasty.

"This time you're not going to be able to protect him," Mike told him.

Color streaked along Blake's cheekbones. "Christopher didn't have anything to do with Anne's death. It's absurd you would imagine anyone in this family could be responsible."

Mike hesitated before deciding to take a gamble. Logically he accepted that it was best to hold back as much information as possible. That way he kept a suspect guessing exactly what he did or didn't know.

But he'd already accepted that he had to keep the Hamilton clan off-balance. Otherwise he was going to end up dealing with one slick lawyer after another.

"Then why did you erase the security tapes?"

Blake stiffened, his eyes widening with shock before his face was wiped of all expression.

"I don't know what you're talking about."

"Of course you don't." Mike stepped into the older man's personal space. "Listen, Hamilton, you can tamper with evidence in your own home, but you can't erase the evidence of Christopher from Jaci's video."

Blake took an instinctive step backward. "What the hell are you talking about?"

Quick to take advantage, Mike moved forward, entering the foyer. He cast a covert glance around, looking for any sign of Christopher lurking in the shadows.

Nothing.

"Your son was captured on tape," he informed the older man.

Blake shook his head, his brow furrowed. "Where?"

"I just told you. Jaci's house."

"Why would Christopher go to his sister's house?" The man sounded genuinely baffled. "They have never been close."

Anger seared through Mike. Once again Jaci had been terrorized. And worse, the locket meant there was a woman who was missing, maybe even dead.

"To leave one of his sick gifts."

"Gift?" Blake looked even more confused. "What gift?"

"Ask your son," Mike snapped. "And while you're at it ask him where he put the body of the woman he just killed to create that twisted gift."

An awful silence filled the foyer and Blake's face paled to a sick shade of ash.

"There's another dead woman?" he rasped.

"If she isn't dead yet, she soon will be," Mike said. He knew he was being harsh, but how else was he going to convince the stubborn man that he couldn't protect his son? "Tell me where to find Christopher."

"This is madness." Blake rubbed a weary hand over his face, then his head jerked around as the sound of footsteps could be heard coming down the nearby staircase. "We can talk in my office," he said, abruptly pivoting and heading down the hallway.

Mike followed without protest. They both halted as Blake pulled his keys from his pocket to unlock the door and push it open. Mike briefly wondered if the older man realized Payton had already figured out where he hid the spare key.

Then his thoughts returned to his reason for being at the house as they stepped into the large office and Blake firmly shut the door. He couldn't afford to waste time. Not when there might be a woman in danger.

"Hiding Christopher from me isn't doing him any favors," he warned. "He needs to come with me and make a statement."

The older man paced across the floor, his hands clenching and unclenching as he tried to maintain his composure.

"Why are you trying to pin these murders on my son?" he at last demanded.

Mike swallowed a curse of frustration. He wanted to grab Blake Hamilton by the shoulders and shake him until he told him where Christopher was hiding. Thankfully, he'd been at his job long enough to know that nothing was ever simple. Especially when it came to dealing with people.

It was always one step forward, and two steps backward.

"Why did you erase the security tape?" he asked.

Blake stopped his pacing and slowly turned to face him. His arrogant bluster was gone, replaced by a stark concern.

"It had nothing to do with Anne," he said. "Her death is

tragic, but when I erased the tapes I had no idea that she was dead."

"What did you think happened to her?"

Blake shrugged. "I assumed she'd hooked up with some man on the Internet and taken off."

Mike frowned. From everything he'd learned about Anne Dixon she seemed like the last sort of woman who would do random hookups. Especially with some stranger she met on the Internet.

"Why would you think that?"

"She'd seemed different over the past few months. Distracted." He gave a lift of his hands. "I thought she must be in love."

Mike snorted. He hoped the man was more observant when it came to his business transactions than dealing with people. He didn't have a clue about human nature.

"You still haven't told me why you erased the tapes," he said, his tone warning he wasn't going to ask again.

"After we realized Anne was gone, I knew someone would decide to look at the recording," he at last said, his voice hard with resentment.

Blake Hamilton wasn't a gracious loser.

"You have something to hide?"

The older man hesitated, his gaze flicking toward the closed door.

"Maybe I should wait for my lawyer."

"Christ, if you're having an affair, I don't give a crap," Mike snapped, trying to keep him distracted. The longer he could avoid the appearance of the lawyer, the better.

It worked. Blake looked outraged by the accusation. "I'm not having an affair."

"I know you haven't been traveling to St. Louis." Mike played his ace in the hole.

Blake was near the breaking point. He couldn't let up now.

"How?" the older man breathed, then he held up a hand, his eyes darkening with defeat. "It doesn't matter now."

"Tell me what you're hiding," Mike pressed.

Blake released a harsh sigh. "If you're determined to haul Christopher in for questioning I suppose you'll eventually find out."

Mike folded his arms over his chest. "I intend to know everything about that boy, down to the color of his boxers, before I'm done."

Blake sent him a frustrated glare before he was moving toward the desk and pulling out a dark bottle and a glass. Then, pouring himself a healthy shot of the expensive whiskey, he tossed it down his throat.

Seemed a little early in the day to start drinking, but Mike understood the necessity. It wasn't easy for a man like Blake Hamilton to swallow his pride.

"You're right." The older man set the empty glass on the top of his desk. "I've always done everything in my power to protect my son. Even when I knew he was in the wrong. I told myself that he was young and I couldn't let his immature decisions ruin his future."

Mike's lips twisted. His own father was eager to lay any blame at Mike's feet. It was a perfect excuse to vent his perpetual anger at a life he'd wasted with booze and pills.

"It didn't occur to you that constantly making his troubles disappear only encouraged his bad behavior?"

"It's easy to judge when you don't have children," Blake snapped.

Mike silently cursed his impetuous words.

"You're right," he soothed, offering an encouraging smile. "Go on."

Blake shifted to lean against the edge of the desk, his

gaze moving toward the French doors that offered a view of the side terrace. For once the sun was shining, the golden glow emphasizing the elegant beauty of the manicured yard and nearby woods.

"Christopher had some trouble around the area," Blake slowly admitted. "But it wasn't until the year after he graduated from high school that I realized his occasional partying had turned into an actual drug addiction."

"What was he using?"

"Pills, at first. Stuff he could get out of our medicine cabinet."

Mike grimaced. It was an all-too familiar story in the area. Parents didn't realize their old prescriptions left lying around could be the spark that ignited their kids' descent into hell.

"And then?" he asked.

"Anything he could get his hands on. Heroin. Meth." Blake's face twisted with disgust. "I found him with a needle in his arm and gave him an ultimatum. He would go to rehab or I was throwing him out of the house."

Mike had known Christopher was dabbling with trouble. Underage drinking, petty theft, and once stealing the mayor's car and driving it into the Mississippi River. But he hadn't realized the extent of his drug use.

"Did he go?"

"For a couple of weeks." Blake lifted a hand to massage the muscles of his nape. It was obvious his concern for Christopher was a burden that had taken its toll. Had Loreen been equally stressed? Or had Blake hidden his son's troubles even from his wife and daughter? "Then he came back and promised he was done with the drugs."

"I'm guessing he wasn't?"

"No. I wanted to believe him, so I turned a blind eye to the clues. It made it easier that he was spending time with my sister in Chicago," the older man said. "I would go months without seeing him."

Christopher had been in Chicago? Mike made a mental note to check on missing women and cross-check them with the precise dates the younger man had been in the Windy City.

"Was he working?" he asked.

"He helped my sister set up her computer and escorted her to her various social functions," Blake explained.

Mike's lips twisted. Is that what young, rich men did for a living?

"What does this have to do with what's going on now?"

Blake hesitated, his jaw clenched so tight it was a wonder his teeth didn't shatter. His reluctance to reveal the truth was a tangible force in the air and for a minute Mike feared he might clam up. Then Blake reached for the bottle of whiskey, pouring himself another shot.

"Two years ago he was with my sister at a charity auction and he was caught stealing an emerald ring that had been donated by a close friend of my sister."

Mike's brows arched. He didn't know Christopher had a record.

"He was arrested?"

"No." Blake shrugged. "The charity preferred to deal with the matter discreetly. I was called instead of the authorities."

Ah. That explained why the younger man's name hadn't popped up in the system. And it was proof of what he'd always suspected.

With enough money you could get away with anything.

Maybe even murder.

"Yeah, it's not very good press for the charity to have its patrons stealing the merchandise," Mike said in dry tones.

Blake thankfully ignored his taunting words. "I went to

Chicago and took Christopher to the nearest rehab facility, Hope Valley. He was warned that if he left I would insist the charity press charges of theft. He spent the past two years there. First he detoxed from the drugs, then he was put in a private apartment where he could take online college classes while still meeting regularly with his rehab counselor."

Mike made another mental note. This one to talk to the supervisor of the facility and make sure that Christopher had been a patient there. He wasn't going to take anything Blake Hamilton said at face value. He'd already proven he was willing to do anything to protect his son.

"And you told everyone that he was attending Washington University?"

Blake flinched at the sharp question. "I wanted him to be able to return home without carrying a lot of baggage," he said. "So I told people that he was at college."

Mike resisted the urge to ask if Payton knew her brother had been in rehab. What did it matter?

Except it did. He didn't like the thought she'd been deliberately lying to him.

He gave a shake of his head. "So you got him clean and brought him back home," he said.

"Yeah." Lifting the glass, Blake once again swallowed the shot in one gulp. He shuddered, setting aside the empty glass. "For a few days everything seemed to be going well. He was talking about joining me at the office. Then I noticed he was disappearing from the house without telling anyone where he was going."

"You assumed it was drugs?"

"Of course," Blake said with absolute confidence.

Mike wasn't nearly so sure. He might find it hard to wrap his head around the thought of Christopher as a cunning serial killer, but he had to agree with Rylan that the time lines fit. And now he was discovering that during the time Jaci hadn't been receiving the lockets, her half brother had been in and out of rehab facilities away from Heron. It was likely he chose his victims from Chicago and brought them back to this area to bury them.

"It could have been something worse," Mike said.

Blake stiffened, his face flushing with anger. "Christopher has never hurt anyone."

Mike shrugged. There was no point in asking if Christopher had ever been cruel to animals. Loreen wouldn't allow pets into her house.

"You don't know what he might do when he's high," he instead said.

"I know that he hasn't been killing women," Blake snapped. "I've been following him for the past week."

His words caught Mike off guard. "You've been following him?"

"Yes." Blake tilted his chin to a belligerent angle. "Instead of going to work in the mornings, I would park at the bottom of the drive and wait. If Christopher took off I would follow him wherever he went."

Mike studied him in disbelief. This man had spent his days shadowing his grown son?

"Did he know you were behind him?"

"Of course." Blake's sharp laugh echoed through the cavernous room. "It was making him crazy, but I think he assumed I'd eventually give up."

"Where did he go?"

"Usually he went to places in Quincy." His eyes narrowed. "A couple of times he went to the old Johnson place. You should do your job and get rid of the people who are living there."

Mike felt a sudden pang of sadness. He didn't have to like Blake Hamilton or his son to feel pity for the fact that their lives had been ruined by drugs. It didn't matter if they were rich or poor, it was a terrible thing.

Still, he couldn't let his pity distract him from the fact that Christopher was still his best suspect.

"None of this proves that Christopher didn't kill Anne. Or that he wasn't at Jaci's last night," he said.

"Yes," Blake said, his expression bleak. "It does."

"How?"

"I took Christopher to a new rehab center in St. Louis."

Mike stared at him with blatant suspicion. He wouldn't put it past the man to try and throw him off the trail so he could give his son time to escape.

"When?"

"Yesterday afternoon."

Well, shit. Mike scowled. "What's the name of the facility?"

"Gateway to Sobriety." Blake grimaced. "They promised that they have specialized care that could actually help Christopher." He shook his head, his expression resigned. "I've heard the same promises before. I'll believe it when I see it."

Mike planted his hands on his hips, tapping his fingers against his gun. Not in a threat. Just a habit.

"He could have left," he pointed out.

Blake shook his head. "I would have been alerted if he tried to leave. I made sure of that." He shrugged. "You can check with them if you want."

"I will," Mike warned, although he found it hard to believe that Blake would look so confident if he was lying. It would be an easy matter to get a warrant to determine the time Christopher had been checked into the facility and if he'd left. "Did you leave his car in St. Louis?"

"His car?" Blake sent him a confused frown. "You mean the Jaguar?"

"Yeah."

Blake shook his head. "He ran it into a ditch yesterday morning trying to get away from me. That was the last straw, as far as I was concerned."

Mike studied him, searching for some sign he was lying. If Christopher wasn't driving his car, then who was?

"Where's the car now?"

Blake gave a lift of his shoulder. "I called Lowe's to bring the wrecker and pick it up. As far as I know it's at their shop."

Mike swallowed a curse. Someone had deliberately played them.

Was it a game? Did the killer enjoy proving that he was smarter than the authorities?

Or was it something more convoluted?

Something he wasn't able to see?

He was busy trying to determine how easy it would be to take the car from the local auto shop when he felt a familiar buzzing from his pocket.

With a scowl, he yanked out his phone and pressed it to his ear.

"O'Brien." His frown deepened as he listened to the annoyed voice of his deputy telling him that Carol was now three hours late for work. "As far as I know she should be there. Did you call her?" he asked, grimacing as Hal reminded him that he wasn't stupid. Of course he'd called. Several times. "She had a big date last night. She might have overslept," Mike said, a tingle of worry snaking down his spine. "I'll swing by her house on my way back to the office."

He slid the phone back in his pocket. He had more questions for Blake, but the phone call had unnerved him.

Carol might have had a hot date, but that'd never made her late before. And if she had a hangover, she would have called to tell him she wasn't feeling well. She'd never, ever simply not shown up for work.

Something was wrong. He could suddenly feel it in his bones.

"I'm not done with you or Christopher," he warned. "Make damn sure he doesn't try to leave the state."

"He's not going anywhere." Blake abruptly stepped toward the French doors as Mike turned to leave. "I'd prefer that you go out this way," he said. "I don't want my wife to be further upset."

Mike shrugged. It was hard to imagine that anything could upset the cold-as-ice Loreen Hamilton, but whatever.

He was stepping onto the terrace when he glanced over his shoulder at the older man.

"Where's Payton?"

Blake slowly blinked, as if it took him a minute to recall that he had a daughter, let alone what her current location might be.

"I'm not sure," he said with a shrug. "I think she might spend her weekends at the food pantry. Or maybe she's giving out clothes to the poor. One of those things where she works like a dog, but doesn't make a penny for her efforts."

Mike made a sound of disgust. "Maybe you should spend more time appreciating the child who isn't in constant need of attention."

Chapter Twenty-Five

Jaci couldn't sit still when she was nervous.

So, leaving Rylan to study the security footage over and over, she grabbed her cleaning supplies and polished the house from top to bottom.

She'd just finished scrubbing the kitchen floor when Rylan strolled into the room, shoving his cell phone into the front pocket of his jeans.

A pang of regret twisted her heart. Just a couple hours ago Rylan had been warm and naked lying next to her. His golden hair had been mussed from her fingers and his eyes dark with hunger.

She wished they could go back to that time. She would have insisted they stay in bed.

It wouldn't have solved her problems. But it would have been a lot more fun than worrying about what was going to happen when her mother discovered her son was a psychotic killer.

A shudder raced through her as she straightened and studied Rylan's grim expression.

"That was O'Brien," he said as she sent him a quizzical glance.

Dread lodged in the pit of her stomach. Had he arrested Christopher?

"What does he want?"

"He asked us to meet him at his office. He wants to go through the video from last night."

She frowned. Mike had spent over an hour watching the security tape earlier in the day. It seemed impossible to believe he'd missed anything.

"Again?"

"Yep."

Jaci narrowed her gaze. He'd been edgy since they'd found the locket. Now he was nearly vibrating with tension.

"Did he say why?" she asked.

His hands clenched at his sides. "He claimed the figure we caught on camera isn't your brother."

Jaci jerked in surprise. She'd spent the past hours trying to reconcile herself to the thought that her half brother was not only a cold-blooded killer, but that he'd harbored some sick obsession with her.

"I don't understand." She gave a slow shake of her head. "How does he know it wasn't Christopher?"

"Your stepfather had him committed to a rehab facility in St. Louis."

"Rehab? You mean for drugs?"

Rylan nodded. "Yeah. And it's not the first time he's been committed."

She leaned against the edge of the counter. It was a lot easier to see her brother as a drug addict than a serial killer. He'd been partying since he was in junior high. In fact, he'd gotten thrown out of school for hiding beer in his locker when he was just fourteen.

"When?" she asked.

"Yesterday."

Which proved he couldn't have been sneaking up her drive to leave behind the bloody locket.

"But that had to be his car," she said. "Who else in town can afford a Jaguar?"

"Your stepfather told the sheriff that it was at the auto shop in town." A muscle twitched in his cheek. "Anyone could have stolen it."

Jaci tapped her fingers against the side of her leg, trying to imagine the killer stealing a car so he could deliver his gruesome necklace. Why choose a vehicle that would be so easily noticed? Then, she abruptly remembered Rylan's confusion about the killer parking so close to the house.

He'd wanted them to catch the car on camera.

"Someone deliberately tried to pin the crimes on Christopher."

"It seems so."

Jaci rubbed her aching temples. The killer had been so cautious until now. He hadn't left the smallest clue. Now he was stealing expensive sports cars and making sure he was seen on security cameras?

It didn't make sense.

"But why?" she demanded.

"Another way to taunt me." Rylan's voice was edged with a lethal fury. "He likes to prove how smart he is."

She understood his anger. If her half brother wasn't the serial killer, then he was still out there. Waiting to strike again.

"I didn't want it to be Christopher," she said. "I might not get along with my family, but I would never wish for them to go through something like that." She was fairly sure that the humiliation of a trial, let alone the potential death sentence for her only son, would have sent Loreen

Hamilton over the edge. "Still . . ." Her words trailed away as a shudder raced through her.

Rylan moved across the kitchen, pulling her into his arms. "You want this to be over."

"Yes."

He pressed his lips to the top of her head. "No one could blame you, Jaci."

She heaved a rueful sigh. "Then why do I feel guilty?"

"Because you're a kind, gentle woman who cares about others. Even when they don't deserve it."

He made her sound like a saint. A very boring saint.

"I'm not always kind," she protested. "Or gentle."

He chuckled, easily picking up on her annoyance. "True." He lifted his head to reveal a wicked smile playing around his lips. "I have scratch marks on my back that prove you have violent tendencies when properly motivated."

Heat flooded her cheeks. She had a vivid memory of making those scratch marks. And an equally vivid fantasy of making more of them.

But not until they'd taken the security tapes to Mike. If there was the slightest possibility the tapes could help track down the killer, they couldn't afford to waste any time.

"We should go," she said.

His arms tightened around her. "I don't like you leaving the house."

"I can't stay locked in here forever."

"Why not?" He lowered his head to brush his lips over her brow. "We could order our food and have it delivered. I could work from my computer, and you could have your customers drive out here to pick up their usual orders." He pressed a lingering kiss on her lips. "A perfect solution."

It did sound perfect.

And completely unrealistic.

"I'd give you twenty-four hours before you were pacing

the floor," she said. Rylan had a restless energy that would be stifled by being stuck in the house. "Besides, Mike is waiting for us."

He traced the curve of her lower lip with the tip of his tongue. "Let him wait."

It was a temptation. What woman in her right mind wouldn't prefer to lock the doors and spend the next few weeks in the arms of Rylan?

Unfortunately, it wasn't just her life that was in danger.

"The sooner we find the killer, the sooner we can go to the beach," she reminded her companion.

He arched a brow. "Blackmail?"

She shrugged. "Incentive."

Rylan heaved a sigh. "Let's get this over with."

Mike had been prepared for the worst when he'd gone to Carol's tiny house. As much as he told himself not to leap to conclusions, he couldn't help but consider the fact that his administrative assistant had failed to show up for work the morning after Jaci had received a locket.

It could be a thousand other reasons.

Well, maybe not a thousand, but certain three or four.

Larry could have turned out to be Mr. Right and they were on their way to Vegas. There could have been a family emergency and she forgot to call him. She could have told one of the deputies that she was sick, and they hadn't passed along the message.

But he was already preparing to discover she was simply gone.

Vanished into thin air like Anne Dixon. And Angel Harper.

Arriving at her house, he'd found the front door unlocked

and had done a quick search. She wasn't there. And her bed hadn't been slept in. His fear had only deepened.

While he was checking with the local hospital to make sure she hadn't been in an accident, he'd called in his deputies. Even Sid. He wanted all hands on deck to start searching the area for Carol.

He was watching the last two squad cars squeal out of the lot to head toward their search area when the Jeep pulled in. With an effort, he forced himself to wait for Rylan and Jaci to jump out of the vehicle and walk toward him.

He wanted to be out on the hunt. Carol was like family to him. The thought of staying in his office while everyone else was searching for her was making his gut twist into painful knots.

It was only the knowledge that they didn't have any clue where she might be hidden that kept him from leaping in his truck. What was the point in dashing around like a madman?

It made far more sense to devote his energies to discovering who was responsible for taking her.

That was the only way they were going to be able to bring her home safely. *God willing, let it be safely.*

Rylan stopped next to him, a laptop in his hands. "What's going on?"

"Let's go inside," he said, aware that several locals had already noticed the unusual activity around the courthouse and were gathering on the corner to watch him with curious gazes.

Rylan glanced toward the small crowd. "Good idea."

The three of them entered Mike's office and he firmly closed the door behind them.

"Carol is missing," he told them, instantly regretting his blunt confession when Jaci swayed in shock.

"Oh my God," she breathed, leaning against Rylan as

the man wrapped his arm protectively around her shoulders. "Do you think she was taken by the killer?"

Mike moved to lean against the edge of the desk. He was tired, frustrated, and acutely afraid for his friend. It all combined to make it difficult to think clearly.

"I'm trying not to jump to conclusions," he told Jaci.

She visibly shivered. "We should be looking for her."

"I have everyone I could call in trying to find her."

"How long has she been missing?" Rylan demanded.

"She didn't show up for her shift this morning," Mike said, glancing toward the wall clock. One o'clock. Damn. The day was slipping away. "She should have been here by eight."

Rylan's expression was grim. "I'm assuming you checked her house."

Mike glared in his direction. "You assume right."

"When was the last time her family saw her?"

"She lives alone. She doesn't have any children and her mother is in the local nursing home. She's suffered from Alzheimer's for years."

Rylan easily realized what the lack of relatives would mean. "So no one would notice if she was taken?"

"Exactly." Mike grimaced. "She went to Quincy with her current boyfriend last night. I called him as soon as I realized she was missing. He says he brought her home around midnight."

"Do you believe him?" Rylan asked.

Mike had grilled Larry until the man had broken down in tears. It wasn't that he'd suspected the man as Jaci's stalker. A quick background check had revealed that he'd been living in Tennessee until two years ago. But he knew it would be a mistake to simply assume that Carol's disappearance was connected to the serial killer.

After all, bad things happened to women all the time. And usually it could be blamed on the man in their lives.

He had to eliminate the most obvious person first.

"He claims he has a credit card receipt from a quickie mart in West Quincy," Mike said. "He stopped on his way home to buy a pack of cigarettes. I sent Hal to check the video, but for now I'm going to assume he's telling the truth."

Rylan moved to set the laptop he was holding on the desk. Almost as if sensing that Mike needed a minute to regain the leash on his temper.

The truth was that Mike was furious with himself.

He'd known there was a killer in the area, but he hadn't insisted that Carol stay with him until the danger had passed. Hell, he hadn't even considered the fact that she might be a target.

Now she was gone and he had no one to blame but himself.

He sucked in a deep, steadying breath. The only way to help her was to keep his shit together and concentrate on figuring out who the hell was responsible.

"Was there any sign of struggle at her house?" Rylan asked as he moved back to stand next to Jaci.

"No, but when I got there the front door was unlocked and the lights in the kitchen were on."

Jaci bit her bottom lip. "Can you use her cell phone to track her?"

Mike shook his head. That'd been his first thought. Until he'd caught sight of the bag carelessly tossed on the table.

"I found her phone and her purse in the kitchen."

"It sounds like someone was waiting when she got home," Rylan said.

"Yeah." Mike had done a sweep of her small yard, finding a set of footprints that went from the side of the house to the front porch. "It would have been easy to stay hidden in the bushes and follow her through the door. Or even for him to have popped the lock and waited inside."

Jaci made a sound of distress. Her face was pale, her body rigid as she anxiously clenched and unclenched her hands.

"What can we do?"

Understanding her need to help, Mike moved to take a seat at his desk, flipping open the laptop.

"I want to look at the video. There has to be a clue to who is responsible."

"Let me," Rylan said, crossing to stand at Mike's side. He reached down to tap on the keyboard, bringing up the video.

"If it wasn't Christopher at my house last night, how did someone get his car?" Jaci asked.

Mike leaned toward the computer screen. The man was average height. Average weight. Wearing average clothing.

Average, average, average. It could be anyone, dammit.

"Someone obviously stole it from Lowe's lot. It was parked near the back alley," he answered in distracted tones. "It would have been easy to take it for a few hours and return it without anyone knowing."

"Was it hot-wired?" Rylan demanded. "That's not as easy as they make it look on TV. Someone would have to know what he was doing."

Mike gave a short, humorless laugh. "The keys were left under the front seat."

Rylan muttered a low curse. "Of course they were."

"It's a small town," Mike said.

It was the neighborly sense of trust that made it so easy for a serial killer to move unseen through the town. There were no security cameras. People left their keys in their cars and their doors unlocked. And they didn't hesitate to walk alone at night.

And while a part of Mike was frustrated by the thought that they were all more or less sitting ducks, a greater part of him was saddened by the thought that their innocence was going to be stripped away.

Even if they caught the bastard who was terrorizing Jaci, things in Heron would never be the same.

Rewinding the video to watch it again, Mike was interrupted when Jaci made a strangled sound, her head turned toward the window.

"Oh my God," she breathed. "It's Carol."

"What?" Mike jumped to his feet, heading toward his private door to wrench it open.

It wasn't until he caught sight of the woman stumbling across the nearby park that he finally accepted the she truly was alive.

God. He'd tried desperately to hold on to hope, but he'd known deep in his heart that the likelihood of her being alive was almost nonexistent.

The killer had slaughtered at least three other women, and probably many, many more.

Plus, Jaci had received another bloody locket.

Why offer his gruesome tribute if he hadn't killed his victim?

Unless Carol had managed to escape.

Shaking off his weird sense of disbelief, Mike forced his heavy feet to move forward. He met Carol as she reached the edge of the parking lot, wrapping his arm around her waist and leading her directly into his office.

The crowd was still gathered at the corner. The sooner he got her away from prying eyes, the better.

Rylan was waiting as Mike led Carol over the threshold, firmly closing the door behind them. At the same time, Jaci was moving his chair away from the desk and swiveling it so Mike could ease his companion onto the worn leather cushion.

He crouched directly in front of the shivering woman, his worried gaze skimming over her.

Her white slacks were grubby, as if she'd been rolling in dust, and a couple of cobwebs were clinging to her cherry-red sweater. Her face was the shade of paste and a trickle of blood ran from her temple down her cheek. Her lower face was red and chapped, as if she'd been rubbing it against something rough.

Or as if she'd just ripped off duct tape.

His gaze skimmed down to her throat where dark bruises that looked like fingerprints stained her pale skin.

A combination of relief, anger, and unease churned through Mike as he reached to brush away a cobweb.

"We should get you to the hospital," he said.

Carol shuddered, her expression dazed. "I'm fine."

"I prefer a doctor tell me that," he informed her.

A fleeting smile touched her lips. "I promise I'll go get myself checked out later. First I want to make my report."

He scowled. "Stubborn."

"I was born and bred in Missouri," Carol said, a bit of color returning to her cheeks. "Stubborn is what we do."

"Here." Jaci suddenly appeared at Carol's side with a glass of water.

The older woman grabbed the glass and drank deeply. Using her momentary distraction, Mike nodded toward Rylan. He knew Carol well enough to accept that she wasn't leaving until she'd told him what had happened to her. But he wasn't going to let her stubbornness put her health at risk.

Plus, she needed to be thoroughly examined for any evidence. If she'd been in close contact with the killer, then there was a chance he might have left behind a DNA sample that would allow them to track down the bastard. Or at least put him away once they had him in custody.

Meeting his gaze, Rylan instantly understood what he wanted. Crossing to the far side of the office, Rylan pulled out his cell phone to call for an ambulance.

Mike returned his attention to Carol, who started to cough from gulping the water so fast.

"Breathe," he commanded in soft tones as Jaci took the empty glass from the older woman's hand and stepped back, allowing Carol a sense of privacy. He waited for her to stop coughing before urging her to speak. "Now tell me what happened," he said.

Her hands twisted together in her lap, tiny shivers still shaking her body. But with a courage he fiercely admired, she squared her shoulders and met his steady gaze.

"I went out last night with Larry." She forced the words out, her voice husky. From lingering fear, or had her throat been damaged? "It was going well enough, but I started thinking back to our conversation about fireworks."

"Fireworks?" Rylan questioned as he put away his phone and regarded Mike with a lift of his brows.

Mike ignored the interruption, giving Carol's fingers another squeeze.

"And?"

"And I decided we weren't going to be more than friends, so I asked him to bring me home."

"Was he angry?" Mike demanded.

Carol looked confused. Then she gave a sharp shake of her head as she realized he was asking if Larry had been responsible for hurting her.

"No. Nothing like that. He was a perfect gentleman." She winced, as if the movement of her head was painful. "It's a shame I couldn't feel more for him."

Mike's lips twisted. Yeah. It was a shame that a person

couldn't choose whom to love with their head and not their heart.

"Larry took you home?" he asked as Carol became lost in silent regret.

"Yeah." She glanced toward Jaci, who hurried to refill the glass. Tugging her hand out of Mike's grasp, she accepted the water and took another deep drink. "I waited for him to drive away and I went inside," she at last continued.

Mike visualized Carol waving good-bye to her date and then walking up the steps to her front porch.

"Did you notice anything before you went inside?" he asked.

"Nothing." Carol shuddered. "But I wasn't paying much attention."

"No car parked in the street that you didn't recognize?" Mike pressed. "Was the porch light on or off?"

The older woman's brow furrowed. "I don't remember seeing any car. I think I would have noticed that." She paused. "And I'm pretty sure the porch light was off."

Mike gave an encouraging nod. "What happened next?"

"I went inside."

"Was the door locked?" Mike asked.

Carol paused, clearly trying to organize her scattered thoughts.

"Oh," she finally breathed. "Now that I think about it, I didn't have to use my key." She hunched her shoulders. "I didn't really notice since it's not that unusual for me to forget to turn the latch when I'm in a hurry."

"Someone was waiting inside?"

The older woman made a muffled sound of fear before she was grimly tilting her chin, refusing to give in to the panic that no doubt threatened to consume her.

"Yes." Carol licked her lips. "I went into the kitchen to get a bottle of water. I was almost to the fridge when I felt a pair of hands around my neck." A shudder shook through her body and the empty glass fell to the floor. Her fingers lifted to touch the splotches of color on her throat. "I tried to scream but he just kept squeezing. I thought I was going to die."

Jaci hurried across the room to grab Mike's Windbreaker that he'd hung on a hook on the back of the door. Then, returning to Carol, she wrapped it around her shoulders. The office felt smothering hot to Mike, but Carol was in shock.

"It's okay," Jaci said softly. "You're safe now."

"Thank God," Carol rasped. "Thank God, thank God."

Mike resisted the impulse to tug her out of the chair and into his arms. Right now, Carol didn't need him to be a friend. She needed him to be a sheriff who could capture the bastard who'd attacked her in her own home.

"Can you tell me what happened after you felt him grab you by the neck?" he asked.

"No." She shook her head, this time making sure she didn't rattle her sore brains. "I passed out."

"Do you know how long you were unconscious?" he asked.

"Not for very long," she said. "It was still dark when I woke up."

Mike gave a slow nod. Was it possible that she'd woken up before the killer expected? He might have left the locket and then planned to return and finish off Carol at his leisure. Serial killers liked to take their time with victims, didn't they?

Or maybe he was interrupted.

"Where were you?" he abruptly asked.

Surprisingly Carol hesitated, biting her lower lip. "You're not going to like this."

Mike frowned. "Tell me."

"I was in the small shed behind your house."

It took a full minute for Mike to absorb what she was telling him.

While he'd been sleeping, and then during the hours he'd wasted trying to locate Christopher, his friend had been locked in the old shed just a hundred yards from his back door?

The wooden structure had been there when Mike had moved in, but the roof leaked and the boards were rotting around the edge of the floor. He'd been intending to have it torn down, but he never could seem to find the time.

Now he surged upright, a blast of fury shaking his tightly coiled body.

"That bastard," he hissed.

He felt Rylan moving to stand next to him, as if the other man understood that he was on the point of doing something idiotic. Like running out the door and arresting everyone he could round up. If he locked up everyone in town, he was bound to catch the serial killer. Right?

Easily sensing his distress, Carol pasted on a stiff smile.

"You should have seen me. I was tied up like a Christmas goose and I had a piece of duct tape over my mouth. It was something more than one of my ex-husbands always wanted to do."

Her attempt to tease Mike out of his grim mood fell flat. He felt sick to his stomach.

He'd originally thought Carol's disappearance had been somehow related to Jaci. The killer clearly had a weird fascination with her. Or it could have been that Carol simply had been a target of convenience. He could have known she lived alone and that he could take her without attracting notice.

Now he realized that she'd been taken because of him.

The killer was telling him that he wasn't afraid of the law. And in particular, the sheriff.

It was a direct insult.

Mike struggled to regain control of his emotions as Rylan smoothly took command.

"How did you get away?"

Carol absently rubbed her wrists, which were sore and raw.

"It took me hours, but I finally managed to wriggle my hands enough to loosen the ropes."

Rylan nodded. "Then you walked here?"

"Yeah, I wasn't thinking very clearly." She glanced toward Mike. "I knew you would be frantic. I had to get here and tell you that I was okay."

"I was frantic," Mike assured her, squashing his anger as he once again squatted down in front of her.

This woman had escaped a lunatic and then walked across town to make sure he wouldn't be worried about her. He needed to concentrate on her needs, not allow himself to be consumed with anger.

"What can you tell us about him?" he asked.

"Nothing. I'm sorry." She heaved a frustrated sigh. "Believe me, I spent the past few hours trying to recall anything that might help, but there's nothing."

"You didn't see him?" Mike asked.

"No." Her features tightened as she forced herself to think back to the moment she'd been attacked. "He came from behind. I could see a fuzzy reflection in the kitchen window, but he had on a mask and a heavy hoodie."

Mike turned his head to share a glance with Rylan. They were both leaping to similar conclusions. The guy on the video leaving the locket at Jaci's garage had been wearing a hoodie. It had to be the same person.

"Was he wearing gloves?" Rylan asked.

Carol paused before giving a small nod. "Yes. I remember feeling the leather against my skin."

Mike frowned. He could hear the distant sound of sirens. Which meant he had only a couple of minutes to get any clues that might lead him to the stalker.

"Do you know how tall he was?" he asked.

"A few inches taller than me," Carol said. "I could feel his chin pressing the back of my head."

He smiled. Carol was proving to be almost as efficient in her role as witness as she was as an assistant.

"Less than six foot?"

She gave a slow nod. "I think so. But he was strong. I thought he was going to snap my neck in two."

His smile faded as he lifted a hand to lightly touch her temple where blood stained her skin. He couldn't see any visible wound.

"Did he hit you?" he demanded, his fingers pushing aside her tangled hair.

"No. I don't know how I got the cut. It's not very deep," Carol assured him.

Mike's spine stiffened as he caught sight of the clump of hair that had been cut off at the root, and the shallow wound that looked like it could have come from a razor.

He exchanged another glance with Rylan. This had to be the spot where the stalker had gotten the hair and blood to put in the locket.

Of course, he hadn't had the latest locket tested for DNA, but it didn't take a genius to guess that it was going to match this woman.

The sound of sirens became deafening as the ambulance pulled into the lot.

"Your ride is here," he murmured, about to rise and open the door.

Carol reached up to grab his hand, her expression troubled. "I don't understand."

He grimaced. He hated like hell that she'd gotten caught up in this mess. She certainly didn't deserve to be terrorized just because she happened to work in the sheriff's office.

"None of this makes any sense," he told her.

Her grip tightened. "No . . . I mean, I don't understand why he didn't kill me."

Mike slowly shoved himself upright, gazing down at her pale face.

"Did he say anything to you?"

"Just one thing," she whispered, her eyes darkening with a lingering fear. "A pawn for a queen."

Chapter Twenty-Six

Jaci couldn't shake the sensation that she was trapped in a nightmare as she watched Carol being loaded into the ambulance.

Mike had been right. None of this made any sense.

Why would anyone hurt Anne or Carol? And why would that person create some sick necklace with their hair and blood and leave it on Jaci's garage?

She paced from one end of the floor to the other, her stomach tied in tight knots as Rylan and Mike returned to the office.

"A pawn for a queen?" she questioned, latching on to the last words Carol had said. They'd been nagging at her. "What does that mean?"

"I don't know, but he's toying with us," Rylan growled, glancing toward Mike. "That's the only reason he left Carol alive and stashed in your shed."

The sheriff nodded, his anger a tangible force in the air. He was clearly shaken by the knowledge that Carol had not only been kidnapped, but that she'd been left on his property.

He turned his head to stab Jaci with a fierce frown. "Jaci, you have to get out of town."

"I agree," Rylan said without hesitation.

She halted her pacing, glaring at the two men. "And go where?"

Rylan stepped toward her. "To my condo."

She shook her head. Running away might be a temporary solution, but it did nothing to solve her true problem.

Only catching the person responsible for killing Anne would bring an end to the nightmare.

"How do you know this killer wouldn't follow?" she demanded. "Or go into hiding until I come back again?"

Rylan's lips parted, but before he could speak there was a pounding on the office door.

Mike stomped across the floor. "Now what?"

Jaci glanced out the window, instantly recognizing the silver-haired man dressed in an expensive cashmere sweater and charcoal slacks.

"It's my stepfather," she said, her gaze turning toward Rylan in confusion. "Why would he be here?"

Mike opened the door and was nearly plowed over as the older man stormed into the office.

"Blake, please come in," Mike growled, slamming shut the door behind the man.

Belatedly realizing that the sheriff wasn't alone, the older man came to an abrupt halt, his face smoothing as he offered a strained smile. Blake Hamilton was nothing if not polite.

"Hello, Jaci," he said, his gaze turning toward the man who'd moved to stand at her side. "And Rylan. I heard you were in town."

Jaci suppressed her grimace.

Blake had never been an evil stepfather. On the few occasions that Jaci had visited his big house on the hill, he'd treated her with a cool civility. But Jaci had been painfully aware that he'd forced her mother to choose between being a mother to her baby daughter or becoming his wife.

That wasn't something a girl could forget.

Or forgive.

"Can I help you?" Mike demanded as he studied the older man with blatant impatience.

The man grimaced, nervously twisting his diamond wedding band.

"Payton didn't come home for lunch."

Any other day, Jaci would have mocked her stepfather for overreacting. A grown woman didn't have to tell her parents if she decided she didn't want to go home for lunch.

But today they all stiffened, a thick tension filling the office.

"Were you expecting her?" Mike asked.

"Yes." Blake's face was drawn as he struggled to contain his concern. "I tried to call, but she didn't answer."

The tension ramped up. Mike moved to grab his spare Windbreaker from a small coat closet.

"Do you know the last place she was supposed to be?" he asked the older man.

"The food bank at the back of the Baptist church," Blake said.

Mike slid on his jacket. "Did you go there?"

Blake nodded. "Yes. Her car is in the parking lot, but no one inside has seen her." He gave a helpless glance toward Jaci before returning his attention to Mike. "It's like she just vanished."

"Shit." Mike clutched the back of a nearby chair, almost as if he was overcome with emotion. Then, with a visible effort, he was taking control of the situation. He pointed a finger at Blake. "I want you to start calling everyone she knows and ask them if they've heard from her. I'll get my deputies working on a search of the town."

Jaci moved toward Mike, dread lodged in the pit of her stomach.

She might not like Payton, but they were family. And she knew if something happened to the younger woman, her mother would be devastated.

"What can I do?" she asked.

Mike glanced in her direction. "Go to California."

Jaci was shaking her head before he stopped speaking. "No way. I'm not leaving while Payton is missing."

Mike held her gaze. "The search will be much easier if I don't have to worry about you."

"Concentrate on your search," Rylan said, moving to place his arms around Jaci's shoulders. "I'm taking Jaci to the airport."

She sent him an impatient frown. "I can't go today."

His expression was grim. Ruthless.

"We're going as soon as we pack a bag," he said, his voice warning he wasn't in the mood to debate the issue.

Not that she was intimidated. But before she could argue, Blake was surprisingly sending her a pleading glance.

"Jaci, if you're in danger, please go." He had to stop and clear his throat. "It's what Payton would want."

She had a brief, uncharitable thought that her spoiled sister would prefer that Jaci stay and be upset, even if it put her in danger, before she was shoving it away.

Now wasn't the time for family drama.

And if it would help ease Mike's stress so he could concentrate on tracking down the killer, what choice did she have?

"It seems I'm outnumbered." She held Mike's worried gaze. "You'll let me know as soon as you find Payton?"

"Of course," he said before giving a wave of his hand. "Go."

Rylan didn't give her the opportunity to protest as he grabbed her upper arm and practically dragged her out of the office.

Jaci stumbled behind him, her independent spirit currently willing to take a backseat to logic. Whoever was stalking her had altered his tactics, blatantly targeting local women. She wasn't an expert in psychology, but she knew that any change in patterns usually meant the killer was spinning out of control.

Lost in her thoughts, Jaci was unprepared for the sight of the slender man who abruptly rushed around her Jeep.

"Jaci." Nelson Bradley reached out his hand, only to have it sharply knocked aside as Rylan moved to stand between them.

"Back off," Rylan growled.

"Rylan," she protested, moving to stand at his side. She offered her friend a small smile. "Hello, Nelson."

"I saw the ambulance and then noticed your vehicle in the lot," he said, ignoring Rylan, who continued to glare at him. "I was worried something had happened to you."

With a grimace she glanced toward the corner where she could see several locals gaping at them in open curiosity. Birdie was there, along with Andrew, and Sid's uncle, Jarrod Walker.

She turned back to meet Nelson's dark gaze. "I'm fine."

"Good." Nelson flashed his most charming smile. "Are you going to be home today? I need to pick up my photos. I'm opening a new show in Kansas City next week."

Her lips parted to answer, only to have Rylan speak before she could say a word.

"Jaci's going to be out of town."

Nelson blinked, looking confused. Since Jaci's return to Heron she rarely left the farm.

"For how long?" he asked.

Jaci grimaced. "I'm not sure."

"But what about my photos?"

She considered the possibility of telling Rylan they had to postpone their trip, only to dismiss it. She had a feeling Rylan would toss her over his shoulder and carry her to California if necessary.

"I'll leave the door to the garage unlocked," she suggested. She didn't worry about anyone bothering her crafts. Right now, they were the least of her concern. "After you get your photos you can lock it on your way out."

"I'll drop by later today." Another charming smile. "Enjoy your trip."

Nelson turned away, and Jaci's attention was captured by Andrew, who waved at her from the sidewalk. She took a step toward him, but once again Rylan was hauling her to the Jeep.

Heaving a sigh, she yanked open the passenger door and climbed in.

"Do you have to be so rude?" she demanded as Rylan settled behind the steering wheel and turned the key.

"I don't trust anyone today," he told her, his gaze flicking from side to side before he was pulling out of the lot. Was he expecting someone to leap from the sidewalk and try to stop them?

Jaci gave a shake of her head. She felt jumpy. As if there were ants crawling beneath her skin.

"Both Nelson and Andrew are harmless," she said, as much to reassure herself as to convince the man sitting rigidly beside her.

"You don't know that," he said, turning off the main

street and onto the highway. "Andrew has had ready access to your property."

She rolled her eyes. "And Nelson?" she prompted, wondering what he had against the photographer.

"He has pictures of the dead body that was floating in the field." He shook his head in disgust. "That's just sick."

Jaci grimaced. She had to admit that Nelson's art was too dark for her taste. But he clearly had an audience that appreciated his work.

Leaning back in her seat, she tried not to dwell on the thought of Payton being kidnapped by some lunatic.

Okay, she could be a bitch. And there'd been times when Jaci had wanted to pull out every strand of her perfect golden hair. But if she truly allowed herself to consider the thought her sister might be fighting for her life at this very moment—a shudder raced through her.

She was going to fall apart.

Instead she forced herself to concentrate on what she needed to do.

"I have to call my customers and tell them I'll be gone for a few days," she said, ticking off her to-do list out loud.

"Or a few weeks," Rylan said.

She ignored his suggestion. She had to cling to the belief that Mike was going to find Payton and arrest the killer within a matter of hours. Not weeks.

"And I need to see if Andrew will come and fetch Riff and Raff."

"There's no need," Rylan told her, slowing the Jeep as he glanced in the rearview mirror. Was he checking to see if they were being followed? "I'm sure my father will be happy to take them in."

She sent him a frown. "You can't dump two massive dogs on your father without asking him."

"He loves those dogs," Rylan said without hesitation,

his gaze still locked on the rearview mirror as he turned onto the gravel road that led to her farm. "And they'll offer him protection while we're gone."

Jaci glanced over her shoulder. Seeing no one behind them, she returned her attention to Rylan.

"I thought he was staying with your aunt."

Rylan snorted. "They can't be beneath the same roof without driving each other nuts." His hands tightened on the steering wheel as they splashed through the narrow ditch where the road had been washed away. "He sent me a text saying he'll be home for dinner. The monsters will be good company for him."

She heaved a resigned sigh, accepting the inevitable. She would be leaving Riff and Raff with Elmer. Not only would it be easier than expecting Andrew to come and pick up the animals, but they were already comfortable with the older man.

"You're very efficient," she said in dry tones.

His gaze cut in her direction. "Is that another word for bossy?"

"Yes."

He shrugged. "I'm a problem solver. It's what I do."

She didn't argue. Rylan had been a natural-born leader from an early age. It didn't surprise her at all that he'd gone into business for himself. Or that the business was a roaring success.

Still, she didn't intend to puff up his already outrageous ego. So she followed her grandmother's advice and kept her lips sealed shut. The older woman had been a big believer in the power of silence.

Rylan pulled the Jeep into her drive, grimacing as he glanced out the windshield, which was being peppered with tiny raindrops. The clouds had returned, ensuring their drive to the airport was going to be a wet one.

Jaci shrugged. Soon enough they would be in sunny California. A few more hours of drizzle weren't going to matter.

Hopping out of the vehicle, Jaci dug in her purse for her keys and headed directly for the garage.

Rylan was swiftly behind her. "Where are you going?"

She sent him a small frown. "I need to unlock the garage for Nelson."

His jaw tightened, his golden hair shimmering as it became coated with the fine mist falling from the clouds.

"I have a better idea," he said in gruff tones. "Let's get the pictures and pile them beside the road. That way he doesn't have an excuse to come to the house."

She sent him a shocked glance. "Those pictures are worth thousands and thousands of dollars."

He shrugged. "They're creepy."

Hiding her smile at his lack of artistic appreciation, Jaci used the key to turn the lock and pushed open the door. Before she could step inside, Rylan was brushing past her, his gaze making a quick sweep of the shadowed space before he was allowing her to enter.

Not entirely annoyed that he was close by to offer protection, Jaci crossed toward the long table where she'd lined up the photographs after putting them in their frames.

She gently touched the edge of the closest photo, ensuring the enamel she'd brushed on the frames wasn't still tacky. It'd been days since she'd coated them, but with the damp weather it could take forever to dry.

Once assured they were ready to go, she moved to grab a tarp from the corner and headed back toward the door.

"I'll stack them on the floor," she said. "It will make them easier for him to load into his car."

Rylan's lips tightened as he grudgingly grabbed the two

largest photos and carried them across the room and laid them on the tarp.

"I don't like him coming in here."

"We're going to be gone," she pointed out, grabbing two of the photos and moving to add them to the pile. Then she pointed toward the corner of the room. "Besides, he'll be on camera the whole time."

"I still don't like it," he said.

She rolled her eyes, continuing to move the photos next to the door. It took less than ten minutes, and dusting her hands on her jeans, she sent a lingering glance around her workroom.

A part of her was excited at the thought of joining Rylan in his condo. She was sick and tired of the rain, and a few days on a sunny beach was just what she needed. Not to mention hot, sultry nights spent in Rylan's arms.

What woman wouldn't be thrilled?

But another part of her was already homesick. This place was a part of her soul.

It sounded melodramatic, but that's how she felt.

As if sensing her growing reluctance to leave, Rylan urged her out the door.

"No more procrastinating," he said, reaching up to brush her damp bangs off her forehead. "Pack your bag so we can get the hell out of here."

She blew out a sigh of resignation. "Fine."

She was turning to head toward the nearby house when there was a sharp *pop*. The sound echoed in the thick air, sending a covey of quail flapping from the bush at the edge of the garage.

Jaci jumped in shock, glancing toward the tree line across the road.

Had the land been rented out to hunters?

Clearly she needed to have Mike come out and have a

word with them. There was no way they should be shooting this close to the road.

It wasn't until she heard a low groan that she belatedly turned just in time to see Rylan tumble to the ground.

Stark horror blasted through her as she dropped to her knees and gently turned Rylan onto his back. Thick blood covered his face, revealing he'd been hit by the bullet.

"Rylan," she choked out, her fingers pushing back his hair. She couldn't see the wound, but with so much blood it had to be bad. Really, really bad. Her heart halted, her breath lodged in her throat, and she tried to think.

She needed help. An ambulance. Paramedics who could stop the bleeding. Yes. That was it.

Still on her knees, she scrambled for her purse, which she'd dropped. Turning it upside down, she shook out the contents, snatching at the phone before it could hit the muddy ground. Then dialing 9-1-1, she waited for the operator to answer.

An eternity seemed to pass.

"Nine-one-one, what is your emergency?"

"This is Jaci Patterson—" Jaci's words abruptly cut off as the phone slipped from her nerveless fingers. Her gaze was trained on the man who appeared from behind the house, a rifle pointed directly at her head. "Oh my God," she breathed.

She truly had been flustered. Her first thought should have been that they were being attacked by the serial killer. It was the most logical conclusion. Instead she'd randomly assumed it'd been a careless hunter.

Now she watched in horror as the man moved toward her, the rifle held with an efficient ease that warned he could kill her before she could blink.

It was the same man from the video. Or at least he was wearing the same hoodie with a mask pulled over his face.

This was the madman who had been stalking her for years.

Now she was about to discover what sick fantasies he'd been waiting to unleash.

The moment wasn't perfect.

He'd hoped he would find her alone. That way he could slowly pull off his mask and watch as her terrified horror was replaced by profound relief.

But his hand had been forced.

Which meant he'd had to alter his plan on the fly. Never a good thing.

Moving cautiously forward, he glanced toward the man lying motionless on the ground. Pleasure filled his heart. He'd wanted to pound the bastard to a bloody pulp. Maybe even gut him with his hunting knife. But he wasn't stupid. Rylan Cooper might have turned his back on law enforcement, but he still kept himself in good physical shape.

No doubt he liked to impress the women when he was strolling along the beach.

Arrogant bastard.

Whatever the reason, he wasn't going to risk being injured. Not when he was so close to gaining his prize.

One bullet through Rylan's head would solve all his problems. Even if it didn't give him the satisfaction he'd been craving.

Holding the gun steady, he moved across the soppy ground, ignoring the drizzling rain as he savored Jaci's terror. Soon she would lose her fear, but for now . . .

His cock hardened, the tang of terror in the air as sweet as any aphrodisiac.

Maybe he would leave his mask on until after he'd had her a time or two. He liked the thought of her tied to the ground, her screams filling the air as he exploded deep inside her.

After that he could be gentle. She would surely understand. Every man had needs. And it wasn't like she hadn't been satisfying the man who was currently lying in the mud, his life draining out of him.

She owed him.

His erection pressed painfully against the zipper of his jeans as he reached into the pocket of his sweatshirt and grabbed the syringe he'd prepared earlier in the day.

Then, stepping over Rylan's body, he reached down to run a gloved hand over Jaci's upturned face, anticipation licking through him like flames.

"Mine," he whispered. Then with one swift movement he stabbed the needle into the side of her neck.

She made a muffled sound of pain, jerking away from him as she tried to crab walk backward.

He let her go, enjoying her futile struggles.

Now that Rylan was dead, he had all the time in the world.

Chapter Twenty-Seven

Mike was vibrating with nervous energy as he finished his futile search of the parking lot behind the Baptist church. He'd already been inside to speak with Pastor Dave, who was in charge of the food bank. He said he'd arrived at ten a.m. and that he was certain he was the first car in the lot. Then he'd spoken to Carla Williams, who'd arrived at ten thirty. She was certain that Payton's car had been in the lot, and had been surprised when she'd gone inside and discovered Payton wasn't there.

The killer had had a thirty-minute window to grab her. Plenty of time. Especially when the entire Sheriff's Department was busy searching for the missing Carol.

Mike cursed, knowing he'd been played. Again.

The bastard had deliberately kidnapped Carol and tied her up, knowing that Mike and his deputies would be so occupied with the search for his assistant they wouldn't notice if he snatched Payton from a parking lot in broad daylight.

The question now was, why Payton?

Did it have something to do with Jaci? Or was it just another way for the killer to prove he was smarter than the rest of them?

Mike was standing beside Payton's car when Blake walked out of the back of the church. The older man had been calling every acquaintance he could think of who might know where Payton could be. Mike knew it was a waste of time. Payton might be spoiled and self-absorbed, but she would never deliberately worry her parents. Not when Christopher had just been taken to rehab.

If she'd decided not to come home for lunch, she would have called.

"None of her friends have heard from her." The older man halted next to Mike, his expression grim. "I don't understand who would want to hurt her."

"I'm working on that." Mike glanced toward the nearby alley. It would have been a simple matter for someone to have parked behind the Dumpster and waited for Payton to arrive. Of course, that would mean that whoever was responsible knew Payton well enough to realize she would be working at the food bank that morning.

A thought that made his gut twist with fury.

"Oh." Blake's eyes suddenly widened with hope. "Her phone. We can use it to track her."

Mike shook his head. "Her phone was in her purse. I found it under the car."

The older man slumped, as if someone had just let the air out of him. Mike sympathized. He'd felt his own share of anguish when he'd spotted the expensive purse on the muddy ground.

"Someone took her," Blake breathed, his gaze locked on his daughter's car.

"Yes."

"The same person who killed Anne."

The words were a statement, not a question.

"That's my fear," Mike agreed.

Blake looked momentarily lost, as if he was incapable

of processing the thought of Payton in the hands of a killer. Then he gave a sharp shake of his head, the droplets of rain flying from his gray hair.

"I can call the governor."

Mike lifted his brows. "What could he do?"

Blake gave a frustrated wave of his hand. "He can send in the National Guard to search for Payton."

Mike shrugged. He wanted to tell the older man that the National Guard had already been sent out by the governor to help flood victims up and down the river. Blake Hamilton would naturally assume that everyone should drop what they were doing when he called.

"You can call anyonc you want," he told the older man. "What we need is a damned clue."

Almost on cue, Mike felt his phone vibrate in his pocket. Pulling it out, he pressed it to his ear.

"O'Brien."

Less than a minute later he was ending the call and shoving the phone back into his pocket.

"Damn," he growled, struggling to ignore the sensation he was drowning beneath the tidal wave of disasters.

He couldn't let himself become overwhelmed. That was exactly what the killer wanted.

"What's going on?" Blake demanded.

Mike sent his companion an impatient glance. "A call just came in to nine-one-one from Jaci Patterson."

"Jaci?" Blake's brows snapped together. "What happened?"

"They don't know." Mike headed across the parking lot. "She called and said her name, but the phone went dead."

Blake hurried to walk at his side. "Where are you going?"

They walked between the church and the hair salon that was next door.

"I need to head out to Jaci's place to see what happened."

Without warning, Blake reached out to grab Mike's arm, jerking him around to meet the older man's fierce glare.

"What about Payton?"

Mike pulled his arm out of Blake's grip, hanging on to his temper by a thread.

The older man was worried about his daughter. Mike got it. He truly did.

"I have every deputy I can call in looking for her," he said.

Blake's square face flushed with anger. "That's not good enough."

"What do you want me to do?"

"Find her. Find her before . . ." Blake's words broke off as he blinked back his tears.

Mike grimaced. He didn't like Blake. He thought the older man was a braggart who was more concerned with the Hamilton name than his family. But at this moment, he looked like any other father who was desperate to find his missing daughter.

"I think this is all tied to Jaci. If I can figure out who's been stalking her, I can find Payton."

"If something happens to her I can promise you that I'll hold you personally responsible," the older man snapped.

Mike heaved a sigh, his fleeting goodwill toward his companion vanishing.

"Go home, Blake," he commanded. "And call me if you hear from Payton."

Without giving Blake the opportunity to issue more threats, Mike jogged across the empty street to climb into his patrol truck. Firing up the engine, he flipped on his lights and siren and tore out of town at full speed. He usually preferred to travel without attracting unwanted attention. There was rarely any traffic to deal with and he didn't want half the town trailing behind him to see what was going on.

Today, however, there was no need for subtlety.

His tires threatened to hydroplane as he reached the highway. The pavement was slick from the persistent drizzle that continued to fall from the low clouds, but he kept his foot pressed on the gas pedal. He sustained his reckless pace even when he turned onto the gravel road leading to Jaci's house. His truck bounced and splashed through puddles, occasionally spinning out as he hit the boggy spots.

Coming around a curve, he caught sight of the ambulance that was pulled into Jaci's drive. He halted at the edge of the road and hopped out. His boots squished in the mud as he angled across the front yard, the rain trickling down the back of his neck.

He barely noticed. His concentration was consumed by the sight of Rylan Cooper seated on the edge of a portable gurney, his face covered in blood.

Shit. Mike had been hoping he would arrive and discover that this man had managed to overpower whoever was threatening Jaci and that they could quickly learn where Payton had been taken. Instead it looked like Rylan had come out the loser in the battle. And worse, Jaci was noticeably absent.

Fear for both women thundered through him as he stepped around the back of the ambulance, but he still found his lips twitching at the sight of Rylan, who was battling away the three EMTs who were busy trying to determine the extent of his wounds.

"What's going on?" Mike demanded.

A large man dressed in a uniform grimly used a swab to wipe the blood from Rylan's face.

"We're trying to treat our patient, but he refuses to cooperate."

Rylan whacked at the man's hand, only to mutter a curse when the paramedic refused to be pushed away.

"I'm fine," he said between clenched teeth.

Mike glanced toward the silent house, still hoping that Jaci would appear in the doorway. When it became obvious that wasn't going to happen, he returned his attention to Rylan, his heart clenching at the red stains that marred his clothing.

"You have blood all over you," he said. "Is it all yours?"

Rylan met his worried gaze with a grimace. "I think so."

Mike arched a brow. "That's a lot of blood."

Rylan made another futile swat at the man, who continued to wipe away the blood to reveal the deep gash that marred his temple and disappeared into his hairline.

"It's just a flesh wound," Rylan said.

The paramedic glared down at his ornery patient. "It needs to be properly cleaned."

Mike moved to stand beside the gurney, his hands clenching at the knowledge that the bullet had missed by less than a fraction of an inch. The slightest turn of Rylan's head and his brains would have been splattered across the yard.

Christ. It was no wonder Rylan was refusing to consent to treatment. A miracle had saved his life. He was no doubt anxious not to waste one single second he'd been given.

"Is that all?" Mike asked the paramedic.

The man shrugged. "He'll probably need stitches."

Rylan yanked his head back, his expression tight with frustration.

"Put a bandage on it."

The paramedic frowned. "But—"

"Will he bleed to death without stitches?" Mike asked.

The paramedic paused before giving a small shrug. "Doubtful."

"Then put a bandage on it and give him whatever waiver he needs to sign," Mike said.

They didn't have time for a prolonged argument that Rylan was going to win anyway. The man was stubborn as a mule. And the sooner he was patched up, the sooner he could get the information he needed to begin the search for the missing women.

With a silent efficiency, the paramedic took care of his business, cleaning the wound, which continued to leak blood, and finally placing a large bandage over it. Rylan absently signed the form that said he was refusing to be taken to the hospital, and hopped off the gurney. Five minutes later they were at last alone.

Mike turned toward Rylan. The man's face was pale and dotted with flecks of blood that hadn't been wiped off. His legs were spread wide, as if he was having trouble keeping his balance.

Clearly he should be in the hospital, but for now Mike was willing to pretend he didn't notice the man was near collapse.

Too much was hanging in the balance.

"What happened?" Mike asked in clipped tones.

Rylan squared his shoulders, calling on his rapidly draining strength.

"We were stepping out of the garage when a bullet grazed my head."

Mike walked toward the door of the garage, turning so he could glance around the yard, trying to imagine where he would hide if he was a gunman.

"Did you see the shooter?" he asked.

"No. I was turning toward Jaci when I heard the sound of the shot. The next thing I knew it felt like a sledgehammer had hit the side of my head and I was falling to the ground."

Mike nodded. It was no doubt that turn had saved his life.

"What about Jaci?"

Rylan pointed toward a spot a few feet from where Mike was standing.

"She was about there when I went down."

Mike squatted down. There was a small puddle of blood where Rylan's body had been lying. It was quickly being washed away by the rain. His attention turned toward the place where Rylan had indicated that Jaci was standing.

He couldn't see any blood. Instead, a glint of metal caught his eye. He brushed aside a clump of grass, finding Jaci's phone. Grabbing it, he rose to his feet and met Rylan's burning gaze.

The man was close to the edge.

"Have you done a search?" Mike asked, as much to keep Rylan busy, as in any hope they could find Jaci.

"Not yet." Rylan lifted a hand to touch the bandage on the side of his head. "I woke up with those damned paramedics trying to load me in the ambulance."

Mike glanced toward the road, before his attention returned to the garage.

"Where did the shot come from?"

Rylan took a minute to consider. "The back of the house," he at last said, already moving along the edge of the drive.

Mike hurried to catch up, half expecting the stubborn fool to collapse.

Rylan halted at the back corner of the house, his gaze locked on the ground.

"Footprints," he said.

Mike nodded, easily making out the outline of heavy boots. He glanced toward the nearby garage. It wasn't the best place to take a shot, but whoever had been waiting here had no doubt been expecting them to go from the vehicle directly into the house. Or maybe the shooter had been in a hurry.

Considering the various possibilities, Mike was struck by a sudden realization.

"Footprints, but no tire prints," he said, moving to inspect the backyard for any sign of ruts. "Where was his car?"

Rylan narrowed his gaze. "He must have parked it down the road and walked here."

Mike agreed. "I'll go check," he said.

"Wait." Rylan reached up to grab his arm. "I need to get my gun."

Mike parted his lips to protest, only to snap them shut as he nodded toward the back door. He needed to get Rylan inside. This was the easiest way.

Together they climbed the steps and Rylan punched a series of numbers on the electronic pad, unlocking the door. Then, moving through the mudroom, they entered the kitchen and headed into the living room. That's where Mike informed his companion that he wasn't going to be a part of the search.

Not just because he was near collapse, but because Mike couldn't have him interfering in an official investigation.

"You need to stay here."

Rylan whirled around, his face tight with fury. "Bullshit."

"This is police business."

"I don't give a shit," Rylan growled. "If you think I'm staying here while Jaci is in the hands of some maniac you're out of your mind."

"I wasn't asking," Mike informed him, pointing a finger in his face. "Stay here or I'll shoot you myself."

Rylan glared at him, no doubt considering if he had the energy to beat the crap out of him. Mike didn't stay around to find out.

With a last, warning glance, he headed toward the nearby front door. Yanking it open, he was out of the house and crossing the porch.

Behind him he heard the sound of Rylan's curses, then a loud bang as if the frustrated man had slammed his fist into the wall. There was an even louder crash as something fell.

Mike shook his head. He understood Rylan's fury. He'd be doing some punching himself if he was told to stay home. But it wasn't like he could let him join in the hunt. He intended to do everything by the book.

When he got ahold of the killer, the bastard wasn't going to get off death row because of a technicality.

He'd reached the steps when the screen door was slammed open.

"O'Brien," Rylan called out.

Mike considered ignoring the man. He had two missing women in the hands of a madman. He didn't have the time or interest in having a pissing match with Rylan Cooper.

Unfortunately, he sensed that Rylan wasn't going to give up until he'd had his say.

"What now?" he asked as he turned to discover Rylan's eyes glowing with a fierce determination.

"I know who has Jaci."

Jaci was lost in darkness when she felt the fingers grip her shoulders, giving her a sharp shake.

"Jaci," a female voice said next to her ear. "Wake up."

Jaci didn't want to wake up. Not when she could already feel the painful pounding behind her right eye, and taste the blood from where she'd bit her tongue.

"Stop shaking me," she rasped. "My head hurts."

"Too bad. You don't have time for a headache," the female informed her with a blunt lack of sympathy.

Jaci heaved a resigned sigh, forcing open her heavy lids.

For a horrifying second she thought she'd gone blind. There was nothing but darkness.

Then, forcing herself not to panic, she sucked in a deep breath and truly concentrated on her surroundings.

She was in a dark room. Really dark. With just a small sliver of light coming from above her. She could smell dust, and old wood. It was musty, like a basement. And she wasn't alone.

She blinked, concentrating on the woman who was leaning over her.

"Payton," she said, catching the faintest glimmer of her sister's blond hair. With an effort, she pushed herself to a sitting position. "Where are we?"

"I don't know," Payton said, staying close to Jaci. As if seeking her protection against the dark. "I think it's some sort of cellar."

Jaci raised a shaky hand to her aching head. Slowly she was remembering what'd happened.

The trip to Heron where they'd discovered Carol was okay, but that Payton was missing. And then returning to her house and Rylan being shot . . .

She instantly squashed the memory of Rylan lying on the ground, his face unnervingly pale as the blood dripped from his forehead. She had to believe he was okay. Otherwise she wouldn't be able to function.

Clearing the lump from her throat, she concentrated on her sister. At least she knew Payton was alive.

For now.

"How long have you been here?"

"I'm not sure. A few hours maybe," Payton said, her voice not entirely steady. "The last thing I remember I was getting out of my car at the food bank."

"What time?"

"Ten." There was a rustle of clothes and Payton shrugged. "Maybe ten fifteen."

"Were you drugged?"

"I think so. Someone grabbed me from behind and I felt a pain at the side of my neck," her sister said. "I woke up in here."

Jaci shuddered at the vivid memory of the needle sliding into her neck. Rough hands had grabbed her as her knees started to buckle. Then there had been a voice whispering in her ear.

What had he said?

Mine.

Another shiver shook through her. "You don't know who it was?" she demanded.

"I don't have any idea." There was a faint pause before Payton was asking the question that had no doubt been plaguing her since she'd been kidnapped. "What's going on?"

Jaci didn't have an answer. At least not one that was going to ease Payton's fears.

With a low groan, she forced herself to her feet. Her head spun, and her knees trembled, but she managed to stay upright. She was counting that as progress.

"We need to get out of here."

"What do you think I've been trying to do?" Payton rose to stand beside her. "There're no windows and the only door out of here won't budge."

Jaci ignored her sister's petulant tone. "Maybe if we work together we can get it open."

Holding out her hands, Jaci inched her way forward. Within a few seconds she reached a narrow set of wooden steps that led up to the door. That was why the light seemed to be coming from the ceiling.

Still moving slowly, Jaci climbed up the stairs to grab the door handle. No big surprise that it wouldn't turn.

Payton remained at the base of the stairs, her pale face illuminated by the faint glow.

"You know what's going on, don't you?"

Jaci shoved her shoulder against the door. The movement jarred her aching head, but she refused to acknowledge the pain.

They had to get out of there.

"Not really."

"Dammit," Payton snapped. "This is your fault."

Jaci halted her shoving, glancing down at her sister in disbelief. Was she kidding?

"What's my fault?" she demanded. "That some psychopath has been terrorizing me since I was sixteen? That he's been killing women and sending me gruesome necklaces with their blood and hair?" All the frustration that had been bubbling through her for days—maybe years—came to a violent head. "Or let's just say what you truly mean." Her voice was shrill, her body shaking with emotion. "It's my fault I was ever born."

"If you hadn't been born, then I wouldn't be trapped in this awful place."

It was difficult to see, but Jaci was certain that Payton's lower lip was stuck out. Just like when she was a child.

Jaci returned to slamming her shoulder into the door. Even facing death, some things never changed.

"I have never understood why you resent me so much," she said, grunting as pain jarred through her body. "I've never done anything to you."

"Sweet Jaci who everyone loves," Payton mocked in low tones.

"Everyone but my own family," Jaci countered.

Payton's harsh laugh echoed eerily through the cellar. "Trust me, you weren't missing out on anything. The Hamiltons don't do affection."

Jaci paused, glancing over her shoulder at Payton's pale face. "If that's true, then I'm sorry for you," she said with utter sincerity. Jaci's grandparents had showered her with affection. And now she had Rylan. Maybe Payton had a right to be jealous of her. "Everyone should be loved."

Payton grimaced. "The last thing I need is your pity."

"Fine." Jaci's momentary sympathy was swiftly squashed. "Then I don't give a crap if you were loved or not."

The younger woman hunched her shoulders. "Are we going to try and get out of here or what?"

Chapter Twenty-Eight

Jaci rolled her eyes. So much for a moment of sisterly camaraderie.

She turned back toward the door, determined to get out. Unless she'd already died and gone to hell, she silently acknowledged. There were few things worse than spending eternity locked in a dark cellar with Payton.

On the point of slamming her shoulder against the wooden panels, Jaci froze when she caught the unmistakable crunch of boots against gravel.

Someone was coming.

Turning around, Jaci scrambled down the stairs, pushing Payton backward as she stood in the way.

"What's going on?" her sister demanded.

"I hear someone," Jaci said, keeping her voice low.

"Oh God." Payton released a low cry of fear. "It has to be the kidnapper. What's he going to do to us?"

Jaci couldn't allow herself to think about what was in the mind of her stalker. Instead she wrenched off her light coat and handed it to her sister.

"Here."

"What are you doing?"

"Put the coat on and lie on the ground," Jaci commanded.

Payton took a step backward, shaking her head. "Why?"

"I want him to think I'm still unconscious," Jaci whispered. "I'll hide next to the stairs and attack him from behind."

Payton paused, considering the hasty plan. "You won't leave me here, will you?" she at last rasped, her voice trembling.

Jaci grimaced. As tempting as it was to run off and leave her aggravating sister behind, she knew she could never live with the guilt.

"No, I won't leave you," she promised.

Moving as quickly as possible in the darkness, Jaci edged her way along the side of the stairs, trusting that Payton would remember to pull up the hood of the jacket to make sure her blond hair was covered.

Then, crouching down, she blinked against the splay of light that spilled over the stairs as the door was opened.

Terror thundered through her. This was the man who'd haunted her life for years. The man who'd brutally killed at least three women. Probably many, many more. A man who was obsessed with her to the point of madness.

She clenched and unclenched her hands, worried she might freeze at the critical moment.

Then she caught sight of heavy boots on the stairs. They were muddy. No doubt from standing at the back of her house as he prepared to shoot Rylan in the head.

Her fear crystallized to a pure, ruthless fury.

No more. She was done with the games.

It ended today.

Sucking in a deep breath, she waited as she heard the boots hit one step and then the next, coming ever deeper into the cellar. She caught sight of his jeans and the gray hoodie. And the dark mask that hid his identity.

Still, she knew it was the same man as on the video.

As she'd hoped, he was focused on the motionless form lying in the center of the dirt floor. He crept forward, his breath a loud rasp in the musty air.

He halted next to Payton, his hand reaching down as if he intended to push back the hood.

This was it.

Refusing to give herself time to consider the cost of failure, Jaci launched herself forward. Three long strides and she was leaping on the man's back.

The stalker grunted in shock, pitching forward to slam into the line of shelves. Mason jars tumbled to the ground, shattering beneath his feet.

His brief moment of confusion, however, didn't last nearly long enough.

Even as she was trying to dig her fingers through the knit mask to scratch at his eyes, he was ruthlessly shaking her off his back. With a frustrated growl, she clung to the mask, yanking it off the man as she went flying backward.

She hit the shelves, briefly stunned. *Damn.* She gave a shake of her head.

She had only seconds to recover before . . .

Her fuzzy thought came to an abrupt end as the man moved to bend over her, his blond hair and lean face visible in the muted light.

"Nelson," she breathed, too shocked to notice the fist that was zooming directly toward her chin. Not until it connected with enough force to make the world explode in a shimmer of dazzling agony.

Rylan grimly stepped aside as the sheriff crossed the front porch and entered the house.

"You're wasting my time, Cooper," the man growled.

Rylan pretended that his wound wasn't burning like

someone was pouring hot lava into it, and that his legs didn't feel like wet noodles. He could deal with his injuries later.

Nothing was going to keep him from finding Jaci. And he'd just had his first stroke of luck.

It'd been a complete accident. Predictable. He'd struggled for days to figure out who could possibly be responsible for terrorizing Jaci, and it'd taken him losing his temper and pounding his fist into the wall to finally give him their first clue.

"Look at the photo," he said, using his toe to push at the heavy frame.

The picture had tumbled to the ground when he'd hit the wall, and it'd been when Rylan had turned it over to make sure he hadn't destroyed the stupid thing that he'd caught sight of the answer they'd been seeking.

Mike sent him an impatient glare. "What about it?" he snapped. "I've seen it a dozen times."

"Have you truly studied it?"

"I'm not in the mood to be jerked around," Mike snapped.

Rylan pointed his finger toward the photo. "Look."

Muttering his opinion of pigheaded, arrogant jackasses who should be in bed, Mike bent over the black-and-white image of a ghost town. For a second he said nothing.

At last he released his breath on an impatient sigh. "So what . . ." His words trailed away as he abruptly dropped to his knees, his fingers reaching toward the abandoned grain store at the end of the desolate dirt road. The door was leaning at an odd angle, as if it was blowing in the wind, and from the handle was hanging a small necklace.

"Oh hell," Mike breathed. "A locket."

"Exactly like the one left on Jaci's door," Rylan said.

Mike slowly lifted himself upright, his expression troubled.

"It's impossible to know if it's the same," he pointed out. "The image is too fuzzy."

Rylan released a hiss of frustration. He knew exactly what he was seeing.

Nelson had always lurked around Jaci. Even in high school.

At the time, Rylan had dismissed the younger man as a weakling who'd latched on to Jaci's kind heart. But clearly it'd been more. Much more.

And when he'd started his killing, Nelson had chosen Jaci to receive his macabre gifts. And when Nelson had left town to do his photography, he'd continued to create the lockets, only they'd been put in his photos, not on Jaci's door.

Rylan didn't know why the creep had returned to his original obsession with Jaci. Maybe it was the fact his burial grounds had been uncovered by the floods. Or maybe something had happened in his life that had caused him to start spiraling out of control.

Whatever the reason, that bastard had Jaci.

Rylan would tear the community apart looking for her.

"It can't be a coincidence," he said.

Mike scowled. "How do you know? We don't have the luxury of chasing false leads."

Rylan resisted the urge to shake some sense into the sheriff. He might be confident that Nelson was guilty, but Mike had a point. The picture was so fuzzy that the necklace on the doorknob was little more than a shadowed blur.

He had to find a way to convince the lawman so he would call in the cavalry.

It took a long minute. His brain was sluggish from his wound. Or it could be the blood loss.

Eventually, he thankfully realized he had an entire stack of proof waiting for them.

"We can figure out if it's a fluke," he said, quickly turning to head out the door.

"Where are you going?" Mike's heavy footsteps stomped behind him. "Dammit, Cooper."

Rylan continued across the porch and down the stairs. The rain was taking a momentary break as he splashed through the puddles, crossing the driveway while Mike growled low curses behind him.

His head throbbed with every step he took, but Rylan didn't slow as he yanked open the door to the garage and pointed toward the pile of photos.

"I'm betting that each of these photos has a locket," he said, leaning toward the wall to switch on the lights.

Mike squatted down, grabbing the top photo while Rylan picked up the next in line. It didn't take long for Mike to suck in a startled breath.

"There," Rylan rasped, pointing toward the locket that was placed on top of a rusting barrel of toxic waste.

Rylan's lips flattened as he tilted his photo of a crumbling building that looked like an old insane asylum from a horror show. Now that he knew what he was looking for, it was easy to see the locket draped over the front gate.

"And here," he said.

"Son of a bitch," Mike breathed, dropping the photo and wiping his hands on his uniform.

Rylan didn't blame him. He'd sensed there was something wrong with the pictures. But he didn't know just how wrong.

He tossed the photo against the wall, taking pleasure as the frame busted, ripping through the canvas.

"The answer was beneath our noses the whole time."

Mike released a short, humorless laugh. "No wonder

he assumes he's so much smarter than the rest of us." He nodded toward the pile of photos. "How did we miss this?"

"He's clever," Rylan grudgingly admitted.

"Not anymore." Mike allowed his hand to stroke the butt of his handgun. "We've got him."

Rylan gave a slow shake of his head. His initial burst of joy had been replaced by the stark realization that knowing who had kidnapped Jaci didn't solve their most pressing problem.

"Not yet, we don't," he said.

Mike glared at him, his expression hard with annoyance. As if he suspected that Rylan was being deliberately contrary.

"What are you talking about?" he growled. "It's Nelson. We have proof. . . ." Abruptly realizing what was bothering Rylan, the lawman grimaced. "We don't know where the hell he is."

"Where does he live?"

Mike furrowed his brows. "He renovated a space above his shop in town."

That was what Rylan feared. There was no way he used his public gallery. A serial killer needed privacy to work.

"Does he still own his mother's old place?" he demanded.

Mike gave a nod. "Yeah, but he had the house demolished just a few weeks after she died. I assumed he intended to build a new home, but right now it's just an empty lot."

Damn. Rylan tried to think of any other relatives that might have left Nelson property. He came up blank. As far as he knew, Nelson's mother had never shared the truth of who had gotten her pregnant, and his grandparents had moved to Phoenix when Nelson was still in high school.

"Does he own any land?" he asked.

"Not that I know of." Mike pulled out his phone. "Right now our only hope is that he has Payton and Jaci at his gallery."

Rylan gave a sharp shake of his head. "It's too risky. Heron isn't big, but there's usually someone around. His back door is visible from Birdie's place. If they saw him carrying women in and out of the building they would have said something."

Mike frowned. "Heron is fairly deserted at night."

"But none of the women we know were taken at night," Rylan reminded him.

"I'm getting a search warrant," the sheriff stubbornly insisted. "I agree it's a long shot that he would use such a public place, but we have to start somewhere."

Rylan pulled out his own phone, thankful to discover that it'd survived the time he spent facedown in the mud.

"Go for it," he told his companion.

Mike sent him a suspicious glance. "What are you doing?"

"Calling Griff," he said. "My partner will be able to discover if Nelson has property in the area that he's kept secret." His lips twisted in a humorless smile. "And he doesn't need a warrant."

Jaci slowly regained consciousness.

Once again her head throbbed. But this time the pesky ache was completely overwhelmed by the agonizing pain that shot up her jaw. Crap. It felt like he'd fractured a bone.

Cautiously opening her eyes, she realized that they were no longer in the cellar. She was lying on a couch, and while the room was shadowed with heavy curtains, she could see that it was ruthlessly clean.

For a crazed moment she thought that she must have

been found. This place wasn't exactly homey, but it didn't seem like the lair of an evil killer. Confused, her gaze skimmed over the few pieces of furniture.

Had she got it wrong?

Had Nelson been there to help her?

And where was Payton?

There was the sound of a door opening, and she turned her head to watch as Nelson stepped through a door and closed it tightly behind him.

Instantly any hope that the nightmare had ended was crushed.

Nelson had changed. He was wearing a clean pair of jeans that were artfully split at the knees, and a linen jacket over his blue tee. His hair was combed and he had on a pair of round, wire-rimmed glasses.

It should have been reassuring. He looked exactly like the Nelson she'd always known and loved.

But there was a strange expression on his familiar face that clenched her heart with an icy fear.

Moving across the floor, Nelson knelt beside the couch, reaching out his hand to lightly touch her jaw.

"Forgive me, Jaci," he said, genuine regret in his voice as she jerked beneath his light caress. "I'd hoped we could enjoy each other before you discovered my identity. When you ruined my fantasy I'm afraid I lost my temper. I hope you aren't hurt."

She barely heard his words. She was too consumed with the memories of growing up with Nelson Bradley.

Playing together during recess. Working together on the school newspaper. Going to the movies because they hadn't been invited to one of Payton's pool parties. Struggling to do the math homework they both hated.

He could have killed her a thousand different times. A thousand different ways.

"This whole time." She blinked, as if she could somehow see beneath the charming smile and boyish good looks to the monster below. "It's been you?"

His eyes glowed with a sudden light. As if they were sharing some wonderful secret.

"Are you surprised?"

She shuddered. "I can't believe it."

His fingers drifted over her cheek. They were soft, but she wasn't stupid enough to underestimate his strength.

Those same fingers had wrapped around Anne's neck and squeezed the life from her body.

They could do the same to her.

"I've been very clever, haven't I?" he crooned, bragging as if he was a child. "Of course, people have always discounted me. Even my dear, happily departed mother. She told me I'd never amount to anything. That I was a loser just like my father. As if I could ever be a worthless nobody drifting from town to town." His lip curled into a sneer. "But I showed her that I was born to greatness."

Her mouth felt dry as her heart lodged in her throat. His touch was making her flesh crawl, but she didn't know what would happen if she slapped his hand away.

Besides, she understood the importance of keeping her captor talking.

The longer he was boasting about his cleverness, the longer she had to figure out a way to escape.

"I don't understand." With an effort she met his feverish gaze. "I thought we were friends."

He looked momentarily confused. "We are. Of course, we are. You've been my only true friend." His fingers grabbed her aching jaw. "Do you remember when your brother stole my camera and threatened to smash it if I didn't pay him a ransom? You whacked him on the back of his head with your book."

Jaci winced. She'd forgotten that she'd used her favorite copy of *Pride and Prejudice* to punish her brother for being such a jerk. The same book that Christopher had destroyed, and that Rylan had secretly replaced.

It was all strangely tangled together.

"If we're friends then why would you torment me with the lockets?" she demanded.

"They were a gift to prove I was worthy of your respect."

Jaci searched the face she knew so well. Did he truly believe that giving her pieces of the women he'd murdered would earn her respect?

She shivered, feeling a sharp pang of guilt. As if she was somehow responsible. After all, if Nelson hadn't been obsessed with her, maybe he wouldn't have started killing.

A part of her mind wanted to close down. To simply stop functioning so she didn't have to deal with the horror. Then she sternly squashed the ridiculous swell of remorse.

None of this was her fault. Nelson was clearly unbalanced. And if it hadn't been her, then he would have found someone else to fulfill his sick fantasies.

Right now she had to concentrate on surviving.

And to do that, she had to keep Nelson talking.

"You killed Angel," she said.

Nelson's expression brightened, as if delighted by her interest in his gruesome deeds.

"Yes. She was my first."

"Why Angel?"

"It wasn't planned. I barely knew her." His smile abruptly faded, his pleasure replaced with fierce hatred in the blink of an eye. "Not until we both had to stay after school for detention one day and we started talking."

"Talking about what?"

"Her aunt," he said.

"Teresa Graham?"

His hand tightened on her jaw until a sound of distress was wrenched from her throat. Easing his grip, he allowed his fingers to skim down her neck.

"The devil woman," he growled.

Jaci blinked back her tears of pain, barely daring to breathe as his thumb pressed against her thundering pulse just below her jaw.

Was he already considering his desire to strangle her like the other women? Or did he have other plans?

"She was your babysitter, wasn't she?"

"Babysitter?" His harsh laugh grated against her raw nerves. "She was a demented demon who made my life hell."

"What did she do to you?"

His fingers stroked up and down her throat, sending shock waves of panic through Jaci. Her gaze briefly darted toward the door. If she shoved him backward could she make it across the room before he could catch her?

No. It was too much of a risk. She'd have to wait until he left the room.

"She beat me. She starved me. She humiliated me," Nelson revealed in harsh tones, thankfully unaware of her inner thoughts. "But her greatest sin was tossing me in an abandoned well. She would leave me there for hours. Sometimes the entire day."

Jaci frowned. She'd known that the older woman hadn't been the best babysitter, but she'd never imagined that she had been torturing the helpless children in her care.

"Did your mother know Teresa was hurting you?" she asked.

Nelson's lips twisted. "I told her over and over, but she claimed that she had no choice after my louse of a father had walked away. She said she couldn't take care of me without help. Her nerves were too delicate." He made a sound of disgust. "Of course, the truth was that she was stoned out of her mind on Valium and didn't want to deal with an overactive boy bouncing around the house."

Pity twisted Jaci's heart. Not that she would ever, ever justify what Nelson had done. Nothing could excuse killing innocent women. But his future might have been much different if he'd been raised with love and kindness.

She sent up a quick prayer to her grandparents. She'd taken their constant affection for granted while she was growing up. Now she realized just how lucky she was.

"That's awful," she breathed with absolute sincerity. "I'm sorry you had to endure that hideous woman."

He shrugged. "It made me stronger."

It hadn't made him stronger. It had shattered him. At least his mind.

"I don't understand what Angel had to do with you being tormented by her aunt." She prompted him to continue his story. The last thing she wanted was for him to decide it was time to finish his plans for her. "She wasn't around back then."

"Angel was complaining about the devil woman and I made the mistake of telling her about being trapped in the well," he admitted.

Jaci grimaced. "I didn't know Angel very well, but I'm sure she didn't have much sympathy."

His thumb pressed against her throat. Not choking her, but close. Terrifyingly close.

"She pretended that she did," he rasped. "She even offered to help me get my revenge on her aunt."

"Revenge?"

"I wanted the bitch to suffer," he said. "I wanted her to be locked in the darkness with the fear that she was never getting out again."

"What happened?"

"It was a trick." He shook his head, his eyes darkening as he became lost in his memories. "Angel lured me to her aunt's house and pushed me into the well. Then she laughed at me."

Jaci shook her head. She wasn't surprised by Angel's cruelty. She'd been one of those people who seemed to enjoy other people's misery.

"Oh, Nelson," she said. "Angel was as bad as her aunt."

"True." His lips twisted. "But she taught me my true destiny."

An unexpected pang of regret pierced her terror at the thought of Nelson being trapped in the dark well, his innocence being crushed along with his sanity. She didn't want him to be evil.

She wanted him to be the friend she'd known and trusted.

"No," she breathed. "Your art is your destiny."

He scowled, as if annoyed by her words. "My art allows me to reveal the truth of death in its naked form," he said. "My true art is ridding the world of the vermin."

She swallowed her urge to protest. It was dangerous to allow herself to think of Nelson as the boy from her past. Whatever had broken inside him had stolen away the Nelson she'd known. In his place was a lethal killer who could snap her neck without hesitation.

She scooted back on the cushion, as if she simply wanted to make herself more comfortable. What she wanted was a little distance from the man who was making her skin crawl.

"But why the lockets?"

"After killing Angel, I took her necklace," he explained. There was no regret in his voice for ending the life of a young, vulnerable girl. Instead there was a hint of wonderment.

"I decided I wanted to keep a memento. It was my triumph over evil."

"Then how did it end up at my house?"

"Because I couldn't keep my glory to myself." Sensing her retreat as she pressed her head against the back cushion, Nelson leaned forward, his hot breath brushing over her cheek like a tangible threat. "I had to share it with the only woman who was worthy."

Her heart stuttered, her breathing ragged. "But you had to know that it was terrifying me. If you cared about me, why would you do that?"

He chuckled, an unnerving desire tightening his features. "I suppose I should be honest. At least with you. I like fear." He closed the small space between them, abruptly biting her bottom lip. Hard enough to draw blood, and Jaci released a low cry of pain. Nelson lifted his head, revealing his satisfaction at her blatant terror. "I find it . . . exciting."

She lifted a hand to press it against his chest, her head arching back.

"Nelson."

"You're shivering." He clicked his tongue, even as his gaze lingered on the drop of blood that slid from her lip down her chin. "I'm not going to hurt you. Not again."

She didn't believe him. She could sense his mounting arousal. The sight of her blood was stirring his inner demon. Soon a small drop wasn't going to be enough.

"Why did the lockets stop?" she asked in a desperate attempt to stall for more time.

"You left me." His fingers tightened around her throat. A deliberate punishment as he recalled the fact that she'd fled Heron, leaving him behind. "I tried to use my photos to ease my need. Other times I tried to find a new partner to share in my game, but they were always a pale imitation of you."

She sucked in a sharp breath. No. She didn't care if she pissed him off. She wasn't going to let him claim she was a willing part of his sick delusion.

"I'm not your partner," she breathed. "And this isn't a game."

Anger clenched his jaw before he was making a visible effort to leash his temper.

"Perhaps you're right," he said, his fingers skimming up and down her throat. A caress? A threat? Probably both. "You're my muse. I knew as soon as I witnessed your reaction to my sacrifices that I'd been wasting my time with the others. It's you." The fingers tightened until Jaci struggled to breathe. "Only you."

Chapter Twenty-Nine

Jaci remained frozen beneath his threatening touch. Like a rabbit cornered by a hungry dog, hoping if she didn't move she wouldn't be devoured.

The world was spinning in slow motion, her brain trying to process too many things at once. Which was why she almost missed the muffled sound coming from across the room.

With a blink, she cautiously turned her head toward the closed door.

"What's that?" she demanded.

"Ah." His grip on her neck eased. "My final gift for you."

She grimaced. Which meant it wasn't a savior.

A chill trickled down her spine. *Oh Lord.* She had a sudden, hideous suspicion what was behind the door.

She had to find some way to distract Nelson long enough to escape.

Easier said than done.

For now, all she could do was keep him talking.

"I thought your gift was always a locket."

His fingers once again stroked up and down her throat,

his gaze drifting down to the thrust of her breasts, visible beneath her damp shirt.

"That had been my initial plan," he admitted. "Until I watched you with Anne's body."

Horror shuddered through her. He'd been spying on her? For how long?

"Poor Anne." She gave a shake of her head. "How could you hurt her?"

He caught her off guard by heaving a regretful sigh. "Yes, that was a pity. But I was in a hurry."

A pity? She thought of the older woman who'd spent her life being at Loreen Hamilton's beck and call. And just when she was on the cusp of claiming her freedom, she'd been brutally murdered by a cold-blooded psychopath.

"You killed Anne because you were in a hurry?"

His brows snapped together as he sensed the disdain she couldn't entirely hide.

"I needed to create my gift for you and I knew Anne would be walking through the woods on her way to meet her clandestine lover," he snapped.

She sent him a startled frown. She'd thought the romance was a secret.

"How did you know about Jarrod Walker?"

He shrugged. "Your mother somehow convinced a local yokel magazine to include the Hamilton estate in a photo spread," he said. "Naturally she assumed I would be delighted to spend an entire week snapping pictures of the lovely Payton posed around the place."

Of course her mother would demand a world-renowned photographer drop everything for the privilege of taking pictures of her home.

"Why did you do it?" she asked.

Another shrug. "She offered me a fortune."

"And you saw Anne?"

"Yes. I was setting up a shoot in the garden when I saw her slip through a side gate. I was curious so I followed her." His lips twitched. "I'll admit I was surprised to discover she was doing the nasty with Old Man Walker." His hand moved along her aching jaw before he used the tip of his finger to trace her lips. "After a week at the house I realized that it was an ongoing affair. Every morning, like clockwork, Anne would enter the garden and then sneak off to enjoy a quickie in the shed."

His touch made her stomach cramp with revulsion. "Who was the woman in the field?"

"Just some worthless whore I found in Kansas City," he told hcr. "Nobody."

His tone wasn't angry. Or regretful. It was empty.

As if the poor woman truly had been nobody. Just a piece of trash he'd killed and tossed into a shallow grave.

Jaci was distracted by a muffled noise. She bit her lower lip, trying to pretend she hadn't heard it.

Nelson wasn't fooled. Shoving himself to his feet, he reached down to grab her hand.

"It's time you saw my gift to you."

His grip crushed her fingers together as he steadily tugged her off the couch. She staggered as her head spun in a circle. For a minute she thought she was going to fall face-first, but with an effort she managed to regain her balance.

Indifferent to her shaky knees and the pain shooting through her head, Nelson hauled her across the polished wood floor.

Then, with a dramatic flourish, he shoved the door open.

Jaci blinked at the muted light that filled the small bedroom. Her gaze instinctively moved toward the window that offered a view of the thick woods that surrounded the cabin. Then her gaze dropped to the heavy curtains that were piled on the floor.

Clearly the noise she'd heard was someone jerking the drapes off their rod, which was now hanging from the wall at a drunken angle.

No, not someone.

Payton.

Her heart twisted, her stomach heaving with nausea as she reluctantly allowed her gaze to move to the woman who was huddled against the wall, watching them with terrified eyes.

Her half sister had been stripped naked, except for the golden locket that was hung around her neck. Her arms and legs were bound by rope. And there a piece of duct tape across her mouth to prevent her from screaming.

Her face was pale and stained with tears, her terror a palpable force in the small space.

"Payton," she breathed.

Nelson chuckled, rubbing his hands together in anticipation. "I knew you would be pleased."

She sent him a confused glance. "Pleased? Why would I want you to hurt my sister?"

"She's been nothing but a bitch to you," he said. "Remember when we were in grade school and she would tell the teacher that you pushed her down or stole her stupid doll?"

Cautiously Jaci inched her way toward her sister, careful not to give Nelson any reason to think she was trying to escape.

Her jaw still throbbed from the last time he felt the need to punish her.

"We were just kids," she said, keeping her head turned to watch Nelson even as she moved until she was standing next to her sister.

Instantly Payton wiggled to press herself against Jaci's leg, clearly seeking the comfort of having her close.

Nelson's attention moved to Payton, his expression twisting with a blatant loathing.

"Even later, she did everything possible to make your life a misery. Don't pretend she didn't," he growled. "She stole your boyfriends, she spread rumors, and even tried to buy your friends."

Everything he said was true. Payton had been a first-class bitch. She'd seduced her boyfriends. She'd lied. She'd manipulated.

But now that they were faced with death, Jaci realized just how meaningless the squabbling had been.

"It's in the past, Nelson. It no longer matters."

She lowered herself to her knees, placing her hand on Payton's arm. She gave her sister a light pat, as if she was just trying to comfort her. At the same time, she angled her body to hide her other hand as she reached to run her hands over the rope around Payton's ankle, searching for the knot. Then, with a sharp tug, she had it loosened.

She'd been raised on a farm. Her grandfather had served in the navy.

There was no knot she couldn't unravel.

Unaware of what she'd accomplished, Nelson glared at her in frustration.

"Of course it matters," he snapped. "The past molds us into the people we were destined to be. You and I were treated like shit by our mothers and yet we managed to survive." He puffed out his chest, a smug smile curving his lips. "Actually, we did more than survive. We're like finely tempered steel." His smile disappeared with unnerving speed as he pointed a finger toward the cringing Payton. "And then there are those who are selfish bullies. They take joy in trying to undermine those who are better than they are."

Jaci shifted, pretending to turn so she could fully face Nelson. She kept her hand behind her back, gesturing for Payton to move so she could reach the rope that was tied around her wrists.

"She's my only sister," she said, releasing a silent breath of relief as Payton gave a low moan and slumped to lean her head against her shoulder.

The movement pressed Payton's hands against Jaci's lower back. A perfect location for her fingers to find the knot between Payton's wrists.

"You don't need family," Nelson was assuring her. "They're nothing but anchors that weigh you down." His gaze skimmed over her body, a dark, dark hunger glowing in the depths of his eyes. "Together we can soar."

"Is that what you want for us?"

"It's what I've always wanted." He took a step toward her, his hands twitching at his side. Was he imagining that he was touching her? "You belong to me."

"Then let Payton go," she pleaded, fumbling to grab one end of the rope without looking over her shoulder.

Nelson stiffened, annoyance etched on his handsome face. "No. She's my gift to you."

"I don't need a gift."

"I want to do this for you," he insisted, his voice thickening with remembered pleasure. "You can't imagine the power of watching someone die," he told her. "The fear in their eyes. The pleas for salvation. The final resignation as they accept they have been judged and found unworthy." A visible shudder raced through his body. "It's glorious."

Jaci's mouth went dry. It wasn't just the description of choking someone to death. Although that was horrible enough. It was the whisper of joy in his voice. And the unmistakable arousal that pressed against his jeans.

God. He truly was insane.

"Not for me." She sent him a pleading glance. She knew it was futile to hope he had a conscience, but she had to keep him occupied. Anything so he wouldn't notice her frantic attempts to tug the knot free. "I could never forgive myself if something happened to my sister. I've had too much loss."

He hunched his shoulders, suddenly looking like a peevish child. What had he expected? That Jaci would swoon with anticipation at the thought of watching him kill her sister?

"Don't ruin this," he warned her.

There was a prickle in the air that raised goose bumps on her skin. She'd pressed too far. Nelson was on the verge of snapping.

"I'm sorry." She gave a final tug on the knot, swallowing a groan of relief when she felt it at last give way. She brought her hands in front of her, lifting them in a gesture of apology. "If you'll let Payton go we can discuss our future."

The tension eased from his body, but there was a wariness that remained in his eyes.

"Come here."

"Okay."

She slowly rose to her feet, trusting that her sister had the intelligence to curl her body in a way that would hide the fact that her ropes were loosened.

Jaci's feet felt like they were encased in cement as she forced them to take one step after another, crossing the short distance to stand directly in front of the maniac.

Nelson studied her with a brooding gaze. "You accept that we were meant to be together?"

"Yes. Of course."

"And what about Rylan Cooper?"

She flinched. She hadn't expected the question. "What about him?"

"I know he was your lover."

She lowered her lashes to hide the sudden flood of tears. She fiercely clung to the belief that he was alive, but that didn't ease her pain at the knowledge he might be critically injured.

"He's dead," she forced herself to say.

Nelson was reaching some critical point in his madness. It was obvious in his violent mood changes, and the twitching that had moved from his fingers to encompass his entire body.

Somehow she had to convince him that she was willing to go along with his plans.

"But you loved him?" he demanded.

She hesitated. "I cared about him," she said, knowing he would never believe her if she said she felt nothing for Rylan.

"And yet you're prepared to be with me?"

"If that's what you want."

"Hmm." Without warning he reached to grab the short strands of her hair, yanking her head back so he could skim his gaze over her face. "I begin to doubt your sincerity, my love."

She licked her dry lips. "Let Payton go and we'll discuss our future."

"She dies, Jaci. It has to be done," he rasped, his voice vibrating with impatience. "Then we'll leave this place and start our new lives together."

He was increasingly anxious to kill Payton. As if he was being driven by something deep inside him.

And nothing was going to stop him.

Grasping the last of her shriveling courage, Jaci glanced over her shoulder.

"Go, Payton," she yelled. "Run."

With a speed that had to be fueled by sheer adrenaline, Payton was scrambling off the floor and charging toward the open door. At the same time Nelson cursed, lurching to follow behind Payton's retreating form.

Jaci impulsively jumped in front of him, tangling their legs together. They went down in a snarled heap, with Jaci on the bottom and Nelson landing on top of her with enough force to blast the air from her lungs.

Glancing up, she met Nelson's furious gaze. In that second she knew if Payton didn't find help and send them to the cabin in the next few minutes, she was going to die.

Rylan had always been a thrill seeker. He'd jumped off the top of his father's silo at the age of ten. He'd started dirt bike racing at the age of fourteen. And he'd been an avid surfer since he'd moved to California.

But as he paced from one end of Jaci's living room to another, he silently swore he would never again seek out danger.

All he wanted was a long, peaceful life with Jaci. No drama. No surprises. Just one boring day after another.

Continuing his pacing, he watched as the sheriff stood by the front window, his phone pressed to his ear. Rylan didn't have to ask if he'd found out where Nelson was hiding. The man's face said it all.

Still, he couldn't help but ask the question hovering on his lips as Mike shoved his phone in his pocket and turned to face Rylan.

"Well?"

"Nothing at his gallery or in his apartment." Mike

grimaced. "I have the clerk at the courthouse searching through the public deeds."

Rylan stared at his phone, ignoring the dark wave of dread that threatened to drown him. He couldn't be distracted with panic. He needed Griff to call with the information that he was so desperate for.

He had to focus his concentration on finding Jaci.

"We don't have time for—" His words were cut short as he felt the phone he was holding in his hand abruptly begin to vibrate. He pressed the screen, holding it next to his ear. "Griff. Give me good news."

He listened to his best friend, his spine stiffening in disbelief as Griff revealed what he'd discovered.

God. Damn.

Ending the connection, Rylan slid his phone into the pocket of his jeans and moved to the end table where he'd left his handgun. Making sure it was loaded and that the safety was off, he headed toward the front door.

Mike was swiftly at his side. "Did you get an address?"

"Yeah." Rylan charged forward, prepared to bulldoze his way past Mike's solid body if he dared to try and stop him again.

The truth was, he'd pick the man up and toss him aside if necessary.

Mike struggled to keep pace as they left the house and crossed the boggy yard.

"Give it to me."

"Go to hell, O'Brien," Rylan growled, angling straight toward the road that ran in front of the house. "I'm not going to hand over information that my partner uncovered and then be told that I have to sit here with my thumb up my ass."

Clearly having assumed that Rylan would head toward his nearby truck, Mike was scrambling to catch up as

Rylan leaped across the ditch that was filled with stagnant water. The rain had thankfully stopped, but it would take weeks for the earth to dry out.

"This is an official investigation," the sheriff snapped.

"Yeah, well, it was my unofficial investigating that got an address."

Rylan's gaze scanned the trees that lined the opposite side of the road. There. He could see a small opening. Either a game trail or a pathway.

He jogged toward it.

"I understand why Nelson shot you," Mike growled from behind, reaching out to grab Rylan's arm to yank him to a halt. "Dammit, Cooper. Wait."

Rylan resisted the urge to shove the man away. The urgency to reach Jaci was a violent force that pulsed through him. Still, he had enough sense to know that having backup would double his chances of rescuing her.

"Partners?" he demanded.

Mike clenched his teeth. The man no doubt was weighing the legal complications of allowing a civilian to be involved in the takedown of Nelson against the danger of allowing a serial killer to escape.

"I'll allow you to come with me as long as you understand that I'm the sheriff, which means I'm the one in charge." He at last gave in to the inevitable.

Rylan shrugged. He didn't give a shit about his ego. Not when Jaci's life hung in the balance.

"Whatever makes you happy."

"Tell me where he is," Mike ordered.

Rylan pointed across the road. "There."

Mike scowled. "Don't screw with me, Cooper."

Rylan made a sound of impatience. "Nelson set up a corporation to purchase that land." His waved his hand toward the trees. "He has two hundred acres and a cabin."

"Shit." Mike snatched his hat off his head and slapped it against his leg. "We've had a dozen different farms around here being sold to outsiders who rent out the land to hunters. I never thought to check out who was behind the investment."

Rylan grimaced. He sympathized with the sheriff's frustration. He was working through his own share of blame.

He'd known the bastard had to be keeping a close watch on Jaci. How else could Nelson have found out about the security cameras he'd installed? Hell, Rylan had even noticed shadows moving in the trees.

He should have listened to his instincts.

Maybe then Jaci would be home where she belonged and not in the hands of a madman.

"We both should have taken better care of Jaci," he admitted, turning to head up the trail, his gun in his hand.

He'd gone only a few feet when Mike was once again reaching out to grab his arm.

"Look."

It took a second for Rylan to spot the trail camera that was strapped to the tree. Mike reached out to grab the device, unstrapping it from the trunk. He turned it over to reveal the insides had been removed and replaced with high-tech equipment. This wasn't designed to snap pictures of passing wildlife. Instead it was a camera designed to send wireless video of Jaci's house.

Rylan cursed, pointing to the footprints. Nelson had not only been watching Jaci on video, but he'd been standing in the precise spot. God only knew what he'd been doing.

Mike easily followed his dark thoughts.

"He probably stood right here while we loaded Anne's body into the hearse," he rasped.

Rylan shook his head. Later they could beat themselves up for having missed the clues. Right now they needed to find the cabin.

"There's a trail through here," he said, already moving around the tree.

Mike hurried to jump in front of him as they followed the narrow path up the hill.

"Let me go first."

"Fine." Rylan clenched his teeth. "But if you don't shoot the bastard I will."

Chapter Thirty

Jaci was frozen in pure terror.

Nelson's body continued to press heavily against her, grinding her spine against the hard floor. His hand moved to wrap around her throat.

But it was his eyes that made her heart screech to a petrified halt.

They were flat. Empty of all emotion.

"I suppose I shouldn't be surprised," he at last said, his voice soft. Lethal. "Women always prove to be a disappointment."

She swallowed the lump in her throat. Would Payton have enough sense to go to the nearest house and use the phone to call the sheriff?

Or would she simply find someplace to hide, leaving Jaci to face Nelson on her own?

"I'm not going to disappoint you, Nelson." She tried to force her still lips to curve into a smile. "We're friends, aren't we?"

His thumb pressed against the frantic pulse at the base of her neck.

"I'd hoped we were." His gaze lowered to the neckline

of her shirt, which had been tugged down to reveal the upper curve of her breasts. "And so much more."

Jaci struggled not to shudder as she felt the hard thrust of his arousal against her thigh.

Oh God. Was he planning to rape her?

"I'm not like you." She lifted her hands, smoothing them over his chest. "As much as I hate Payton, I can't bear the thought of violence."

"Violence?" His lips twisted with annoyance. "Is it violent to shake the chaff from the wheat? How can the beauty in the world be exposed if I don't get rid of the trash?"

She studied his lean face. Did he truly believe that he was doing the world a service? Or were these just words he used to excuse his evil?

Not that it mattered.

He killed without regret. He'd squash her like a bug if he decided she was unworthy of his respect.

"Tell me about your plans," she desperately urged.

His hand swept downward, grabbing her breast in a rough grip.

"I wanted us to go away together," he said, squeezing her flesh with enough pressure to make her wince. "To travel the world."

She hid her grimace. "That sounds perfect."

Anger flared through his eyes, his fingers deliberately digging into the softness of her breast. He wanted her to feel pain.

"Yes, it did."

"Did?"

He glared down at her. "I can't trust you, my love."

Pretending to enjoy his disgusting touch, she ran her hands over his shoulders.

"Yes. Yes, you can," she assured him. Inwardly she was wondering how long Payton had been gone. It felt like a lifetime, but it probably had been mere minutes. "Tell me where we're going to travel first. Paris? I've always wanted to go there."

He shook his head, heaving a sad sigh. "I put you on a pedestal, my love. My own private muse."

"I'm sorry," she breathed. "I'm just a woman."

"Yes." Again his emotions did a quicksilver change. He pushed himself up until he was straddling her thighs. Grabbing his glasses, he tossed them aside. His hair was tangled and his face flushed with desire. "Just a woman. Maybe it's better this way." His hands traced down the curve of her waist, gripping the bottom of her shirt. "I can purge you from my system."

Panic detonated inside her as he tried to yank her shirt up her body. No. She couldn't lie there and let him rape her.

She had to fight.

Pounding her fists against his chest, she tried to wriggle from between his knees.

"Nelson, you promised you wouldn't hurt me," she gasped.

Excitement glowed in his eyes. Her struggles were only ramping up his lust.

"A little pain with the pleasure is a good thing." He ripped off her shirt, his gaze latching onto her lacy bra. "Let me teach you."

She continued to slam her fists against his chest, arching up in a desperate effort to get her knee in a position to hit him at his most vulnerable spot.

"No, please."

He ignored her entreaty. Or perhaps he was just too far gone in his madness to hear her.

His hands cupped her breasts, his breath rasping between his parted lips.

"I wanted to take my time. I've dreamed of this moment

for so long." His expression twisted with a flare of fury. "But eventually that bitch will reach town and tell them we're here."

"Please, Nelson." Her heels skidded against the slick floor as she continued to try and escape. "There's still time for us to get away."

"It's too late. Too late."

His head lowered and Jaci thought he intended to kiss her. She sharply turned her head to the side, feeling his lips brush the skin of her upper breast. Then, without warning, his teeth sank into her flesh.

Jaci screamed.

Charging up the hill at a speed that made his legs burn, Rylan nearly ran into the back of Mike as he came to a sharp halt.

"What the hell?" he snapped in frustration.

"I hear someone," Mike whispered.

Together they moved off the path, silently hiding in the shadows as the sound of footsteps crashing through the undergrowth echoed through the air. Whoever was coming was making no attempt to sneak around.

Lifting his gun, Rylan pointed it in the direction of the noise, his finger on the trigger.

He was ready to shoot at the first sight of Nelson Bradley.

Then he caught the shimmer of blond hair just seconds before Payton burst out of the trees and onto the pathway.

The young woman was stark naked and clearly terrified as she ran for her life.

Rylan heard Mike suck in a shattered breath before he was rushing forward to wrap the woman in his arms.

"Payton," the sheriff choked out, awkwardly shrugging

out of his Windbreaker to wrap it around her shivering body.

"Oh God, oh God, oh God," she repeated over and over, her teeth chattering.

Rylan cautiously moved out of the shadows, his gun still raised as he remained on full alert. For all they knew this could be a clever trap.

"Shh," Mike was saying, his hands smoothing back Payton's tangled hair. "You're safe."

"It's Nelson," she babbled, tears streaking down her face. "He's crazy."

"We know," Mike said.

She struggled to speak through her sobs. "He has Jaci."

Rylan sharply glanced in her direction. "Is she hurt?"

"Not yet." She abruptly buried her face against Mike's chest, her words barely audible. "She sacrificed herself to save me. And I left her there."

Rylan bit back a curse. It wasn't Payton's fault that Jaci had more courage than sense. But when he got his hands on the stubborn female, he fully intended to . . .

Well, he wasn't sure what he intended to do beyond kissing her silly. But he wanted her to understand she wasn't allowed to take any more risks with her life.

Not ever.

"It's okay, Payton," Mike said, his voice surprisingly tender. "We're going to get her."

Rylan wasn't nearly so concerned with the young woman's distress. She'd abandoned Jaci to save herself. Now she could damned well do whatever necessary to help rescue her sister.

"Is Nelson armed?"

His sharp tone had the desired effect, and with a last sniff Payton lifted her head and wiped away her tears.

"I didn't see a gun."

Rylan nodded. "Where is he holding Jaci?"

Payton squared her shoulders, pointing up the pathway. "He has her in the bedroom of a cabin at the top of the hill."

"What side of the cabin?" Rylan demanded. "North? East?"

She grimaced, waving her hand toward the right side of the trees. "This side."

Rylan exchanged a glance with Mike.

"North," Rylan said.

Mike grabbed Payton's shoulders and gave her a gentle push down the pathway.

"I want you to go down to the road and wait for my deputies," he told her. "They'll need directions to the cabin."

Surprisingly Payton hesitated, her expression troubled as she glanced over her shoulder at Rylan.

"You'll save her?"

He didn't hesitate. "Yes."

With a nod she hurried down the pathway, not seeming to notice her bare feet slipping on the mud.

Crossing the pathway, Rylan entered the trees where Payton had appeared. She'd been in a frantic flight to escape her captor. Which meant she'd taken the most direct route from the cabin.

"Rylan, wait," Mike growled.

"Screw that." Rylan shoved aside branches and kicked aside small stones that blocked his path.

Within a few minutes he at last reached the edge of the clearing.

He paused to study the small structure that looked like any other hunter's cabin in the area. It was no wonder that no one had bothered to give it a second glance.

Determining the best way to enter, his body jerked with terror as he heard a scream pierce the air.

"Jaci."

He was lurching forward when Mike grabbed his arm and grimly pulled him to a halt.

"Rylan. We can't go charging in there like cowboys," the sheriff snapped. "Take a breath and think."

Rylan jerked away from the man's grasp, but he forced himself to pause and consider his words.

Mike was right.

Payton might not have seen a weapon, but that didn't mean Nelson didn't have one. If they barreled into the cabin without checking it out first, they might very well put Jaci at more risk.

Again he studied the cabin. "You go in the front," he at last said. "I'll go through the back window."

Mike gave a grudging nod. "Don't go in before me. Got it?"

"Yeah. I got it."

Staying in the shadows of the trees, Rylan circled to the north side of the cabin. Distantly he was aware of Mike crossing directly to the front door, but he never allowed his gaze to waver from the nearest window. Crouching low, he darted forward, reaching the back of the cabin with a speed that would have made his old football coach proud.

Pressing his back against the rough logs, he cautiously peered through the window, deeply relieved that there was nothing blocking his view.

Not that his relief stayed for long.

Glancing around the seemingly empty bedroom, he at last caught sight of Nelson, who was kneeling in the middle of the floor. A closer glance revealed that Jaci was trapped beneath him, her hands desperately beating against the man's chest.

Instinctively he raised his gun, but before he could pull the trigger, the sound of Mike's voice echoed through the house.

"Sheriff," he bellowed. "Come out with your hands in the air."

Nelson leaned down to grab Jaci by the throat, tugging her to her feet as he used her as a human shield.

Rylan pushed at the window, not at all surprised to find that it was tightly locked. Dammit. He had to find a way to get in. Glancing over his shoulder, his gaze landed on a pile of firewood.

Perfect.

Relief flooded through Jaci at the sound of Mike's voice. Thank God. She'd been found. But even as she parted her lips to call out, Nelson grabbed her by the neck, dragging her to her feet.

She made a harsh sound of agony as he crushed her throat, pressing his chest against her back as he whispered directly in her ear.

"I loved you, Jaci," he hissed. "Truly loved you."

"You're sick," she struggled to choke out.

His fingers tightened, and dark spots began to dance in front of her eyes. He was blocking her air. If she didn't get free, she was going to pass out.

Or die.

"No," he said in grating tones. "I've been blessed with the ability to see beneath the surface. Sometimes I use my camera to reveal the truth. And sometimes my hands. I thought you could share that with me." He gave her a violent shake. "You worthless bitch."

Her knees went weak, her ears ringing as Mike stepped into the room with his gun pointed toward Nelson.

"It's over, Nelson," the sheriff warned, spreading his legs as he prepared to fire his weapon. "Remove your hands from her or I'll shoot."

She could feel Nelson's rigid muscles as he realized the game was over. He had nowhere to run. Nowhere to hide.

Then she could feel the tension ease out of his body. Almost as if he'd accepted his destiny.

"Ah. Fate has changed yet again," he whispered into her ear. "I'd lost faith in you. I feared I would have to sacrifice you and find a new muse. But now I understand. We were meant to be together for all eternity."

Jaci's eyes widened with horror as his fingers dug into her throat with lethal force.

Oh hell.

He'd realized he couldn't escape and now he was determined that they would die together.

And the worst part was that she couldn't do anything to warn Mike what he was intending.

Lifting her hands, she dug her nails into Nelson's arm, but his fingers tightened as he lifted her off her feet.

Her vision narrowed, as if she was looking through a tunnel. At the same time, she heard a loud crash, as if glass was breaking. Had Mike turned over a lamp?

She frantically tried to focus her fuzzy vision as Nelson jerked around, his sharp motion putting a few inches of space between them.

In that second there was another loud noise. This one was the crack of a gunshot.

Nelson grunted, his fingers jerking until they abruptly loosened and Jaci felt herself falling.

She hit the floor face-first, gasping for air like a fish out of water. There was the sound of footsteps, and she thought she saw Mike race past her.

Was he handcuffing Nelson? Or was her onetime friend dead?

God, she hoped he was dead.

The world continued to spin dizzily around her. A part of her told her that she needed to get up. Or at least cover her half-naked torso. But a larger part wanted to lie on the hard floor and simply appreciate the sweet air filling her lungs.

At last she heard another set of footsteps hurrying across the bedroom, then a large form was crouching beside her.

It was too much of an effort to turn her head to see who it was. She assumed it had to be one of Mike's deputies.

Then gentle arms wrapped around her, and she found herself being scooped off the floor and cradled in a warm lap.

Squinting her eyes, she tried to focus on the lean, decidedly male face that hovered just inches away.

"Rylan," she at last breathed, pure joy jolting through her. "You're alive."

He tilted his head down to press his lips tenderly against her mouth.

"You're never getting rid of me, Jaci Patterson."

Chapter Thirty-One

The next two days were a whirl of activity.

After spending the night in the hospital along with Rylan, who'd finally agreed to have his wound stitched up, Jaci had been taken to the sheriff's office to give her official statement.

Nelson was well and truly dead.

A relief. And yet, his death ensured that there would always be questions.

Had there been something wrong with his brain, or had it been Teresa Graham's harsh punishment that destroyed his sanity? Maybe it was Angel's childish cruelty that had been the snapping point.

And how many women had he killed?

Six? A dozen? Two dozen?

She'd returned to her grandparents' home along with Rylan, simply content to be alive and with the man she loved.

Rylan, however, was determined to get her to his condo in California.

He claimed that he needed to check on his business. And that he wanted her on the beach, where she could relax without being bothered with the endless visitors who'd been stopping by to offer their condolences for her near-death experience.

Deep inside, however, Jaci suspected that he knew she was still having nightmares. She only had to close her eyes to once again feel Nelson's fingers tightening around her neck. Rylan no doubt hoped a change of scenery would help ease the trauma.

She appreciated his concern. And actually, she was pleased with the thought of spending some time in the warm sunlight.

But a part of her was reluctant to leave her home.

It didn't matter that Riff and Raff were already happily settled at Elmer's house. Or that her customers were urging her to take some time for herself.

With a shake of her head, she left her bedroom to find Rylan pacing the floor with mounting impatience.

She paused, drinking in the sight of his male beauty.

Would there ever come a day when she didn't feel a zap of excitement whenever her gaze caught sight of his lean face and golden eyes? She hoped not.

As if sensing her approach, he abruptly turned, a smile curving his lips as his gaze skimmed down her new yellow sweater and the jeans that hugged her curves.

"Are you packed?"

She nodded. "Yes," she said, her voice still hoarse from the damage Nelson had managed to inflict.

Rylan crossed to loop his arms around her waist, studying her upturned face with a searching gaze.

"You could sound more enthusiastic," he told her.

She wrinkled her nose. "I am."

"We'll be back. I just want you to myself for a week or two. And I need to get my things organized so I can have them shipped back here."

Suddenly she realized why she was so reluctant.

Deep inside she was afraid he would return to his fancy condo and his gorgeous California girlfriends and recall why he'd left Heron—and her—behind.

"You're sure you want to move here?" she cautiously asked.

His brows arched, as if he was surprised by her question. "Of course. We'll have to spend time in California, and I'll have to do some traveling, but this is my home."

The absolute assurance in his voice eased her inner fears.

"Our home," she softly corrected.

A slow smile curved his lips. "Our home."

His head lowered and Jaci parted her lips, anticipating his kiss. But before their mouths could touch, there was a loud knock on the door.

Rylan cursed, leaning his forehead against hers. "This is why I want to get you on a plane."

With a chuckle she went on her tiptoes to plant a kiss on his stubborn jaw, then before he could protest, she slipped out of his arms and moved across the room. Ignoring the lingering tingle of fear, she pulled open the door. She had high hopes there would come a day when the terror that Nelson had inflicted on her would fade completely.

She smiled as she caught sight of the man who'd helped to save her life.

"Hello, Mike." She stepped back, motioning him forward. "Come in."

Dressed in his uniform, Mike took off his ball cap as he stepped over the threshold. Since Nelson had been shot in the cabin the sheriff's office had been working nonstop to try and uncover his dark secrets. It was a grim task that was leaving its mark on her friend.

Mike managed a weary smile. "How are you feeling?"

"Better," she assured him, not surprised when Rylan moved to place a possessive arm around her shoulder.

The two men might have worked together to rescue her, but there remained an unspoken competition for top alpha.

She rolled her eyes. *Men.*

"Good," Mike said, pausing before he heaved a sigh. "The gossip will soon be flying through town, so I wanted to come and tell you what we found firsthand. Otherwise it will be so garbled you won't know what's true and what's exaggeration."

She pressed tight against Rylan, already prepared for the worst.

"You found more bodies?"

Mike nodded. Thcy'd been digging up and down the levee now that the floodwaters had receded.

"Two more were buried next to the Johnson farm. And one more was found at the edge of the river south of Hannibal."

Even prepared, Jaci flinched at the sheer horror of what they'd discovered. How could one man destroy so many innocent lives?

"Have any been identified?" Rylan asked, dropping a light kiss on the top of her head.

"The body we found before we knew Nelson was the killer belonged to Katie Ernst. She worked as a bartender in Kansas City." Mike's lips twisted with frustration. "It will take a few more days to identify the rest of them."

Jaci made a sound of distress. "Will we ever know how many he killed?"

Mike gave a shake of his head. "Probably not."

"It seems unbelievable that none of us knew what was going on," she said.

Even days later she struggled to accept that the man she'd counted as a friend had been a monster.

Rylan tightened his arm around her shoulder, surrounding her with the promise of safety.

"A serial killer's greatest talent is his ability to hide his madness beneath a pretense of sanity," he said.

"I suppose," she said, accepting she would never fully understand Nelson or the demons he'd hidden beneath his charming smile.

A sad silence settled in the room as each of them tried to come to terms with Nelson and the scars he'd left behind. Then there was another knock on the door.

"Oh hell," Rylan breathed. "I'm never going to get you out of here."

With a rueful shake of her head, she moved to pull open the door, her eyes widening at the sight of the two elegant women who were standing with obvious discomfort on her porch.

They were both wearing designer dresses with ridiculous high-heel shoes. The rains might have ended, but the mud remained.

"Hello, Mother," Jaci said in her hoarse voice, her gaze turning toward her sister. "Payton."

She stepped back and the two women entered her small living room. Instantly the air was laced with icy disapproval and the hint of expensive perfume. A familiar combination.

"Jaci." Loreen gave a stiff nod of her head, completely ignoring the two men who were standing mere feet away. "I heard you were leaving town."

"Just for a few days," Jaci said.

"Or weeks," Rylan intruded.

Jaci's lips twitched, although she kept her gaze trained on her mother.

"Did you need something?" she asked.

Loreen's expression unexpectedly softened, her lips trembling with an inner emotion.

"I wanted to tell you that I'm very relieved that you've fully recovered," she at last forced herself to say.

Jaci blinked in shock. "Thank you."

"And I wanted to express my gratitude for what you did for Payton," her mother plowed on, glancing toward the woman standing at her side. "She told me you saved her life."

Jaci shrugged. "We worked together."

Her mother's gaze snapped toward Mike, her expression once again layered in frost.

"It shouldn't have been necessary," she said. "Our law enforcement should have locked Nelson away years ago." She gave a delicate shudder. "To think that I invited him to my home. It gives me nightmares."

Jaci swallowed a sigh. This was the Loreen Hamilton they all knew.

"Mother," Payton chided in low tones.

"Yes, well." Loreen gave a sniff, her hand lifting to toy with the strand of pearls around her neck as her attention returned to Jaci. "I just wanted you to know that I was very concerned and that I'm glad you are no longer in danger."

Reeling from the fact that her mother had driven all the way out to the farm, and actually revealed that she possessed feelings for her oldest daughter, Jaci was completely unprepared for Payton to abruptly rush forward to give her a hug.

"Thank you," she whispered softly. Then, pulling back, she interlocked her arm with Loreen's and steered the older woman toward the door. "We should go," she said.

The two women stepped back onto the porch, but before the door closed, Payton glanced over her shoulder, sending the sheriff a lingering glance.

On cue, Mike was rushing to follow behind them. "I need to get back to the office," he said, offering Jaci a distracted smile. "Enjoy your time on the beach."

Jaci watched as her guests drove away, the feeling of unreality remaining as she heard Rylan moving behind her.

"The world truly has gone mad," she admitted, her thoughts dwelling on that last glance between her sister and the sheriff. "Do you think there is something going on between Mike and Payton?"

"What I think is that I don't care," Rylan told her, abruptly sweeping her off her feet.

She gave a startled laugh. "Rylan, what are you doing?"

He leaned down to grab the purse she'd left on the table next to the door.

"Clearly the only way I'm getting you out of here is to carry you out," he told her.

"But my suitcase."

"We'll buy whatever you need in California."

He glared down at her, as if waiting for her to argue. Instead, she lifted her arms to wrap them around his neck, happiness flooding her heart.

"I've waited a lot of years for you to finally sweep me off my feet, Rylan Cooper."

"Hold on, darling." He carried her out the door. "This is just the beginning."

Please turn the page for an exciting sneak peek of Alexandra Ivy's next romantic suspense thriller

WHAT ARE YOU AFRAID OF?

coming soon wherever print and eBooks are sold!

Prologue

A voice in the back of Jeannie Smith's mind whispered that she should be resigned to her ugly fate.

She'd always known that she was going to come to a bad end. Everyone had said so. Her mother said it just before the older woman had run off with her latest lover. Her grandparents said it when they'd kicked her out of their house when she was just sixteen. And even her pimp said it when he'd caught sight of the infected track marks on her inner arms.

A bad end was what happened to girls like her.

And it wasn't like she hadn't had any warning. Since she'd started working as a whore she'd been beaten, robbed, and dumped in the gutter. It'd only gotten worse when she'd left the streets of Kansas City to become a lot lizard.

Trolling the truck stops and rest areas along the interstate was considered the lowest of the lowest, even for whores. Which meant that it was only for the most desperate women.

But even after all the beatings and rough sex she'd been forced to endure, nothing had taught her the true meaning of horror until the john who'd picked her tonight.

Which was weird, really.

He was so handsome.

Dark skin, glossy black hair and rich brown eyes.

The sort of dude who could have any woman he wanted.

Of course, that might explain why she hadn't instantly been wary when he'd urged her into the long trailer attached to his semi truck. Not even when she realized it was equipped with a freezer. It was better than doing the john against the wall of the diner. Or on the hard gravel of the lot.

But as she climbed into the back of the trailer, she caught sight of the other men already waiting for her. Shit, she was in trouble.

She jerked her arm, struggling to free herself from her companion's grip.

"Hey, there was nothing said about this being a party," she protested.

One of the men stepped forward, his face wrapped in shadows.

"It took you long enough," he snapped. "There's a half dozen whores out there. What were you doing?"

The john holding her arm flinched. Clearly the other dude was in charge.

"You said she had to be a blonde. This was the first one I could find."

The man in charge snorted. "Well, while you were dilly-dallying the rest of us nearly froze off our balls."

There was a grumble of agreement from the shadows at the back of the trailer. Jeannie hissed in fear. How many were there? Four? Five? Maybe even more?

"You cleaned up from the last one?" the man holding her rasped, clearly attempting to hide his nerves behind an air of bluster.

"Of course," the other stranger drawled. "Our previous

guest is hidden with the others. Now it's time for some more fun."

The numbing sense of resignation was abruptly replaced with a savage need to fight back.

Maybe her destiny had been decided on the dismal day she'd been born. Maybe her fate was to die in a bad way.

But by God, she'd spent twenty years fighting to survive.

She wasn't going down easily.

She struggled against the bastards as they strapped her down and ripped off her clothes. And even when they took turns raping her.

She struggled until her original john was standing over her bruised and bloody body, a crowbar in his hand.

There was a brief hesitation as he gazed down at her. Almost as if the man wasn't certain he was prepared to commit the ultimate sin. Then, with the shadowed man whispering in his ear, he at last lifted the crowbar, swinging it with desperate power. There was an odd whistling sound as the metal cut through the icy air. Jeannie was strangely mesmerized by the sheer horror of what was happening. At least until she felt a blast of pain as it connected with the side of her face.

Then she felt nothing.

A bad end . . .

Chapter One

December 20th, Rocky Mountains

The large overnight envelope was waiting for Carmen Jacobs on the porch.

She grimaced as she glanced through the frosty window of the front door. Her first instinct was to ignore the unwelcomed reminder of the outside world.

She'd rented the isolated cabin in the Rocky Mountains precisely to forget the demands of her high-profile career. Or at least, that's what she'd told her literary agent. And in part, it was true. She'd spent the past twelve months flying from city to city to sign copies of her blockbuster book, *THE HEART OF A PREDATOR*. Her hectic schedule had also included TV and radio interviews as well as speaking engagements. She'd even spent a month in California, teaching a creative writing class.

Soon it would all start again when the paperback version of the book was released.

She deserved a break.

But the deeper need to retreat to this cabin in the dead of winter was to avoid the yearly madness that was a mandatory part of the Christmas season. She wasn't a Grinch.

Okay, maybe she was a little bit of a Grinch. But it wasn't her fault. She was a woman without a family. And, if she was honest, without any close friends.

Usually it didn't bother her to be alone. In fact, she preferred to concentrate on her career without being encumbered by people who would be a constant distraction.

At this time of year, however, she couldn't help but feel the lack of intimate companionships. Maybe it was the sappy commercials. Or the sight of giggling children who darted through the stores. Or the distant memories of when she hadn't been alone.

Whatever the reason, she always felt the urge to retreat from the world during this time of year. And despite the fact she'd just celebrated her twenty-sixth birthday, she had the necessary funds to grant her wish.

Sipping her morning cup of hot chocolate, she watched as the snow lazily drifted from the clouds, coating the porch in a pristine layer of white.

In a few more minutes the envelope would be hidden.

Problem solved.

She took another sip. And then another. The snow continued to float in the air. Silent. Hypnotic.

A swirling cloud of peace.

She tried to force herself to turn away. Her plans for the day included a long, hot bath. A leisurely lunch. Some prime-time romance in the form of a paperback novel. And later, a bottle of wine in front of the fire.

Nowhere in her schedule was a mysterious envelope.

Unfortunately, Carmen had one deeply imbedded character flaw.

Curiosity.

It was the reason she'd snooped on her eighth-grade teacher after catching sight of the woman disappearing into a storage shed with the principal. That little adventure had gotten her kicked out of school. Probably because she'd posted the pictures she'd taken on the classroom bulletin board.

Three years later that same curiosity had urged her to sneak into her grandparents' attic to try and peek inside the small safe that had once belonged to her parents. She hadn't managed to open it, but she'd been caught in the act. Her grandfather had grounded her for a month and her grandmother had cried. The tears had hurt more than being forced to miss the spring formal.

On the brighter side, her curiosity had inspired her to become a journalist. And later to interview five of the most prolific serial killers to ever terrorize North America. The book she'd written after the nerve-wrenching meetings had become a number one bestseller and launched her into the world of fleeting fame.

Like disco balls and Crocs.

With a grimace she set her half-empty mug on a nearby table. She wasn't going to be able to relax until she knew what was in the envelope.

She might as well get it over with.

Wrapping the belt of her heavy robe tighter, she reluctantly pulled open the door. An instant blast of frigid air slammed into her with shocking force. Crap. The cabin had looked so picturesque in the brochure. The pine trees. The snow. The majestic mountains.

She hadn't really considered just how freaking cold it would be.

Now she scurried forward, her fuzzy slippers sliding over the icy surface. She bent down, snatching the envelope off the edge of the porch. Next year she was going to a sandy beach with lots of sun and fun.

Straightening, she paused to glance around, ensuring there was no one lurking in the small clearing. Then, with a small shiver, she darted back through the door and closed it behind her.

She brushed off the few flakes that clung to her robe before she grabbed her mug of hot chocolate and returned to the kitchen. Since she'd arrived ten days ago, the cozy room had become her favorite spot in the cabin. The wood-planked floors. The open-beamed ceiling. The worn table that was set near a window that overlooked the frozen back garden. There was even an open fireplace where she'd toasted marshmallows last night.

Now she moved to pour out the old cocoa in the sink and rinsed out her mug. She wasn't an obsessive neat-freak, but she preferred to keep her surroundings organized. A psychiatrist would no doubt tell her it had something to do with her need to control some small aspect of her life. She preferred to think that she was just tidy.

Taking a seat at the table, she wavered one last time. She should toss the envelope into the fire she'd stoked to life while she was brewing her morning cup of cocoa. Snap, crackle, pop and all her troubles would be gone. Instead, she gave a rueful shake of her head and turned it over to stare at the front.

Her name was neatly typed, along with the address of the cabin. Then her gaze shifted to the return address, not surprised to find the name of her PR firm. There were fewer than ten people who knew where she was staying.

She ripped open the envelope, only to discover another envelope inside. It was a plain manila one, with her name scrawled across the front.

She scowled.

Usually this would be a desperate plea for help from some unknown person.

Since the release of her book, she'd been besieged with requests for her to investigate the murder of some relative.

Or pleading with her to use her contacts to get their beloved son out of prison, despite the fact he'd bludgeoned his girlfriend to death or shot a neighbor in the head. On occasion some enterprising soul managed to discover where she was staying and shoved the information under the door of her hotel, but usually the requests ended up on the desk of her agent, or even her editor, who sent them on to the PR firm.

The same firm she'd given strict orders to hold all correspondence until after the first of the year.

Which meant that they knew better than to pester her with unwanted mail unless they were hoping to be fired. Something she doubted so long as her book remained on the bestseller lists.

So why were they sending her an overnight package?

A Christmas present? An appearance on the *Today Show* they'd been desperate to book for her?

There was only one way to find out.

Running her finger beneath the sealed flap, she pulled out the sheet of paper. Her gaze impatiently skimmed over the handwritten note.

Holiday Greetings, dearest Carmen. The new year approaches and I offer a challenge. You can be the predator or the prey.

She scrunched her nose. Well, that was cryptic. Her gaze lowered to the signature at the bottom.

The Trucker.

From one beat of her heart to the next, her annoyance was replaced by a bone-deep shock. With a gasp she was on her feet, knocking over the chair as she took a sharp step backward.

Crap.

The Trucker.

Details from her investigation fired randomly through her stunned brain.

Neal Scott. A forty-two-year-old truck driver from Kansas City who'd hunted whores and runaways along I-70 from Denver to Topeka. He'd killed at least twenty-seven women with a crowbar and dumped them along the highway. After his arrest in 1991 he'd admitted that he'd kept the bodies in the freezer of his semi truck until he found a new victim.

She pressed a hand to her racing heart, forcing herself to inch back toward the table. The envelope had been too heavy to contain only one thin sheet of paper.

Reaching out her hand, she grabbed the corner of the envelope and slowly tipped it upside down. There was a strange rustling sound and Carmen tensed. She didn't know what she was expecting, but it wasn't the stack of Polaroids that fell out of the envelope and splayed across the table.

Her breath rasped loudly in the silence as she reluctantly leaned forward. She'd seen the pictures before. They'd been found on Neal Scott when he'd been pulled over by a highway patrol. They had helped to prove Scott was the mysterious serial killer the press had dubbed the Trucker. As if the dead hooker in his trailer hadn't been enough.

Carmen pressed her lips together and reached for the pictures. She'd used copies of them in her book, which meant she was intimately familiar with the gruesome images.

On the point of shoving them back into the envelope, she stilled, her gaze locked on the shattered face of the young blond woman.

The picture was grainy, and there was blood covering the woman's brow from the brutal wound on her temple, but the rest of the features were visible.

Her face was thin, almost gaunt, with faint scars. There were newer sores on her chin. Probably from meth. And her long hair was tangled, as if she hadn't combed it in a long time.

She looked forty, but she was probably closer to twenty.

A woman who'd lived hard, and died even harder.

Carmen's hands shook as she shuffled to the next picture. Another blonde. Her face was a little more square and had been tanned to the texture of leather. But she shared the same painful thinness. And the same bloody wound on the side of her head.

There were three more pictures. All of them of young women who'd been brutally murdered.

They looked exactly like the Polaroids that'd been found on Neal Scott when he was captured. But not one of these had been used as evidence in the trial.

What the hell did that mean?

Had Scott been hiding the pictures? But where? And why send them to her?

Carmen dropped the Polaroids, wiping her fingers on her robe as if she'd been contaminated.

She had to do something. That much she knew. Unfortunately, her brain was churning without spitting out any answers. Like it was stuck in neutral.

Her gaze darted from side to side, at last landing on the large envelope that was still wet from the snow. Yes. This had started it all. The destruction of her fairy-tale vacation.

And she knew precisely who to blame for that destruction.

Cautiously backing away, she kept her gaze locked on

the table. As if the pile of Polaroids were a rattlesnake that might decide to strike. At the same time, she stuck out her arm, blindly searching for the cell phone she'd left on the kitchen counter.

She knocked off an empty plate and tipped over a vase of flowers. Minor casualties. Then her fingers at last clenched around her phone.

Lifting it to a position where she could glance at the screen while still maintaining a close watch on the Polaroids, she hit the third button in her speed dial.

There was the sound of buzzing as the connection was made, then a pre-recorded voice floated through the air, warning Carmen that the offices were closed until after the New Year and that she was to leave a message so they could get back to her as soon as possible.

Oh, and then a bubbly wish for her to have a happy holiday season.

Perfect.

She ended the connection and scrolled through her contacts to find the personal number of her PR person. Lucy Cordova was ten years older than Carmen, with the sleek beauty of a supermodel and the soul of a great white shark.

It was no accident she was the top in her field. She ate her competitors and spit them out.

"Pick up, pick up, pick up," Carmen muttered as the phone buzzed and then went straight to voice mail. "Dammit."

She hit redial. Same result. She hit it again.

On the point of trying a fourth time, her phone buzzed with an incoming call.

Lucy.

Thank God.

"Okay, Carmen," a voice croaked. Obviously Lucy had decided to sleep in this morning. "What's the emergency?"

Carmen was forced to clear the lump from her voice before she could speak.

"The package that landed on my doorstep this morning."

"What package?" Lucy demanded, then there was the rustle of covers as if the woman was crawling out of bed. "Oh, wait. I remember sending an envelope to you."

Carmen licked her lips. Why were they so dry?

"Where did you get it from?" she demanded.

"It came by messenger three days ago," Lucy told her.

"From where?"

"It was from the office of the public defenders who'd handled the Scott case," Lucy explained, her voice echoing as if she'd put the phone on speaker.

No doubt the woman was pouring her morning coffee. She was a caffeine fiend who was never without her insulated cup in her hand.

"Was there a letter with it?" Carmen asked.

There was a slurping sound, then a soft breath of relief. Lucy had just had her fix.

A second later she spoke, her voice stronger as the caffeine kicked in.

"No, there was no letter. Just a handwritten note that said they'd been forwarded all of Neal Scott's possessions after his execution and that they were just now sorting through the box."

Scott had been executed three months ago. "Why would they send it to your office?" Carmen demanded.

"The note said that they'd found the envelope and tried to deliver it to your condo. When there was no one home, they sent it to our office."

Carmen's gaze moved toward the nearby window. The snow continued to fall at a leisurely pace. As if it couldn't decide if it intended to pick up speed or just call it quits for the day.

I should be drinking my coffee and enjoying the winter wonderland, she thought. Instead her peace had been shattered by visions of death.

Not the sort of Christmas anyone wanted.

"And you decided to send it here?" she demanded.

"I thought it might contain some new information from the killer," Lucy told her. "You know, something you could add to the paperback version that would spice up sales."

Carmen made a choked sound of distress. Having the Polaroids in her home—actually touching them—somehow made them far more disturbing than the black-and-white copies she'd used in her books.

These were more personal. Almost intimate.

"The deaths of those young women is a tragedy, not a spice," she snapped.

There was an awkward silence before Lucy cleared her throat. "You know what I mean."

Carmen forced a strained laugh. She didn't know why she was angry with Lucy. The older woman had merely forwarded the envelope. She hadn't known what was inside.

"Yeah, I guess I do," she said.

"What's going on, Carmen?" Lucy abruptly asked.

Carmen's gaze returned to the table, her stomach clenching.

"There were pictures inside the envelope."

"What kind of pictures?"

"Polaroids of dead women. Five of them."

"Christ, I'm sorry, Carmen," Lucy breathed. "I assume they were from the trial?"

Carmen shook her head despite the fact that Lucy couldn't see her.

"No. I've never seen these before."

"Wait." The word sounded like it was wrenched from Lucy. She wasn't a lady who was often shocked. "Are you saying there are pictures of dead women that haven't been released to the public?"

Carmen shuddered. She was three feet away from the table, but she felt as if the unknown women were staring at her. Pleading for something she couldn't give them.

Justice.

"I'm saying I've never seen them. And you know the research I did," Carmen said. "I think it's possible that I'm the only one besides Scott to know they exist."

There was a sudden clatter through the phone, as if Lucy had dropped her coffee cup.

"God almighty, this is fantastic!" the woman said, not bothering to hide her burst of glee. "Do you know what will happen to your book sales if you can add in pictures from new victims?" There was a pause, and Carmen imagined she could hear the calculator in Lucy's mind clicking away, adding up each new sale. "Hell, you could write a whole new book."

Carmen grimaced. She would be a hypocrite to act shocked by Lucy's response. The reason Carmen had hired her was because the woman was a ruthless master at taking advantage of any situation.

Even a situation that included dead women.

"These need to go to the authorities," she said in firm tones.

"Fine, but first we need to make copies," Lucy insisted. "It could be months or years before the cops will give back the originals."

"Let's worry about figuring out who these poor women are before we start cashing in, okay?" she said dryly.

As if sensing that Carmen wasn't in the mood to discuss business, Lucy did her best to squash her excitement.

"What do you want from me?"

Carmen took a minute. She was still rattled and it was

unnervingly difficult to think. Like her brain cells were wading through syrup.

"I want you to call the lawyers and find out everything you can about the envelope," she eventually demanded.

Might as well start at the beginning.

"You got it," Lucy said, the crisp determination easing a portion of Carmen's unease. "I'll get back to you."

Carmen hung up the phone and forced herself to turn and head to the back of the cabin. She felt in dire need of a hot shower. It couldn't erase the images from her mind, but it might wash away the feeling that she'd been contaminated.

Entering the small bathroom, she dropped her robe and stepped beneath the spray of water. She shivered as she waited for the hot water to kick in, not for the first time wondering if she'd made a mistake in writing *THE HEART OF A PREDATOR*.

It wasn't like she'd started off her journalism career with the dream of spending her days in dank prisons interviewing monsters. And they were monsters—each of the five men she'd profiled had killed at least ten women, and most of them much more than that. But when her college professor had warned her that the articles she was writing for the school paper were too mundane to earn her any notice by any reputable newspaper or magazine, she'd forced herself to examine what she could offer that was different from every other wannabe journalist.

What truly made her unique?

The answer was simple.

Murder.

She was intimately acquainted with death. And the sort of man who could kill an innocent woman without mercy.

She'd reached out to Neal Scott, not believing for a minute that he'd respond to her request for an interview.

He'd been on death row for seventeen years and had never once spoken about his crimes. But her letter had been answered by Scott's lawyers within the week.

"Yes, Mr. Scott would be pleased to meet with Ms. Jacobs at a time of your convenience."

And that had been the start of her twisted journey through the minds of serial killers. A trail she thought would be over once the paperback book was released.

With a grimace she stepped out of the shower and dried off. Then, heading into the bedroom across the hall, she slipped on a pair of jeans and a heavy cable-knit sweater. Her blond hair was already curling around her face, making her look about twelve. She clicked her tongue as she pulled her hair into a tight ponytail.

Her grandmother might have thought that it was cute that Carmen looked like a perpetual child, but it was a pain in the patootie.

She'd just tugged on a pair of warm socks and returned to the kitchen when her phone rang.

Carmen hit the speaker button. "What did you find out?"

Lucy's voice floated through the air. "Nothing."

Her tension returned. Dammit. Had the older woman just pretended she was going to help in an effort to get Carmen to use the pictures in her book?

"Lucy, I'm not in the mood for games," Carmen snapped.

"I wasn't trying to annoy you, Carmen," Lucy said. "I meant the word literally."

There was no missing the edge in Lucy's voice.

This wasn't about making money. The woman was truly worried.

"Explain," Carmen said, dropping into a kitchen chair and rubbing her aching head.

Lucy cleared her throat. "I called the law office that

represented Neal Scott only to be told that they didn't have a clue what I was talking about."

Carmen frowned. "They don't remember sending the package?"

"They don't remember, because they never sent it," Lucy clarified. "In fact, they had direct orders from Neal Scott that all his possessions were to be destroyed after he was executed. He didn't want some prison guard selling his toothbrush on eBay after he died."

Carmen's gaze moved to the pictures that were still spread across the kitchen table.

There was no reason for the law firm to lie. At least none that made sense.

"You're sure the package wasn't from a different law firm?" Carmen asked.

"I'm sure. I even double-checked with the receptionist who keeps a log of packages we receive. Each one is labeled with who the package is for, and what company it's from."

Carmen felt an odd sense of dread lodge in the pit of her stomach.

"What was the name of the messenger company?"

"Dullus Express," Lucy said without hesitation. No doubt she'd anticipated Carmen's question.

"Do you have their number?"

"I already tried to contact them."

"Tried?"

Lucy released an aggravated sigh. "The telephone number that was left on the sign-in sheet actually belongs to a Chinese restaurant," she admitted. "And when I googled the name of the company I couldn't find it listed anywhere."

"So who sent the envelope?"

"I don't have any idea."

Carmen shivered. "Shit."

"Yeah," Lucy agreed. "Shit."

Carmen disconnected the phone. Right now she needed to think. Something that would be impossible when she had Lucy chattering in her ear.

Wrapping her arms around her waist, she glanced at the envelope before shifting her gaze toward the note.

Was it possible that the Polaroids had been taken by Neal Scott and never found by the cops? But who could have uncovered them? And why go to the trouble to make her believe that they were from the serial killer, including a note signed *The Trucker*?

Was this some sick joke? Her book had made her the target of all kinds of whackos. Could one of them have staged the pictures to attract her attention?

It was a plausible theory. There were all sorts of crackpots in the world.

But as much as she wanted to dismiss the Polaroids as a prank, there was something deep inside her that warned this was no joke.

She paced the floor, a terrible fear beginning to form.

If they hadn't been taken by Scott, and they weren't a prank, there was only one explanation for them.

A copycat killer.

She paced the floor, the horrifying suspicion churning through her mind. Was it possible? Was there some maniac out there who'd decided to follow in the footsteps of Neal Scott?

Was he even now bashing in some innocent girl's head?

Halting near the table, she reached to touch the picture that was lying on top, her dread hardening to determination.

There was nothing she could do to save them. Not if they were already dead.

But maybe, just maybe, she could give them justice.